The Memsahib

The Memsahib

Berkely Mather

Charles Scribner's Sons

NEW YORK

1 3 5 7 9 11 13 15 17 19 H/C 20 18 16 14 12 10 8 6 4 2

Printed in the United States of America
Library of Congress Catalog Card Number 77-78115
ISBN 0-684-15186-3

Summer 1938

The girl watched the dancing specks in the shaft of sunlight that came through the triangular tear in the blind and struck the wall beneath the pitch-pine dressing table. When it slid down another oblique inch and touched the skirting-board it would be time to make the first tentative move towards getting up – that was if her uncle was clear of the bathroom. He wasn't yet, because through the thin dividing wall she could hear his tuneless singing above the gurgle and clunk of the defective plumbing. She stretched, catlike, and her feet overreached the bottom edge of the sheet and rasped against the scratchy blanket, and she reacted like a snail touching salt and coiled into a foetal curve, knees under chin, eyes tightly shut, head beneath the bedclothes, in a last desperate effort to hold back the inexorable daily intrusion of dreary reality into her own private world. Down below she could hear her mother moving about in the kitchen. That was one of the major curses of this horrible house, she thought bitterly – this almost total lack of privacy. True, with the doors closed they weren't actually intervisible, but every move the others made plucked on her tautened nerves like a plectrum – and once inside there wasn't a single room in which one could lock oneself.

Her mother was calling from the bottom of the stairs now, grating, querulous, with the arid echo of forty-five empty and unrewarded years in her voice. 'Nearly eight o'clock already, and not a move out of you. You'd look funny, my lady, if one morning I slept in and left you to it. Now come *on* or you'll miss your train again.'

The girl raised her head from the clothes and called back, 'All *right*. I'm coming, aren't I?' recognizing in her own voice

7

an identical note of shrill plaint. 'Christ! I'm getting just like her,' she muttered to herself. 'I sound like her. Soon I'll look like her – and smell like her – of Sunlight soap and stale cooking fat and dust. And I'm getting *old*. Oh, God! Twenty-two next birthday.'

She swung her feet out of bed and groped with curled toes for her slippers, then she stood up and glanced down at her slim, straight young figure, smoothing the crumpled 'art' silk of her nightgown with both palms so that it moulded itself over breast and hips. She looked across the narrow space between bed and dressing table, grimacing as she saw herself in the mirror – touseled hair escaping from under the head-scarf she had bought last summer in Herne Bay, her face greasy from the cold cream she rubbed and patted into it assiduously each night. She tore off the scarf and shook her head violently, then scrubbed at her face, and in this impatient action achieved the daily transformation that in itself was a minor miracle – because she was really beautiful.

'I don't look so bad,' she assured herself afresh. 'No, not so bad at all. I'm prettier than any of those rich biddies who come into the shop – *and* younger. And I've got a new frock, and I'm going out tonight and –'

There was a thump on the door and a hearty, beery voice bellowed, 'Wakey! Wakey! Rise and shine! Show a leg, lovie! The bog's empty and the sun's burning your bleeding eyes out.'

'Oh, piss – go *away*!' she blazed furiously, and her uncle answered in waggish reproof, 'Naughty! Naughty! Somebody's got the reveille hump, eh?' and she heard him chuckle phlegmishly as he padded along the landing in his socks.

'Let me get away from here,' she whispered desperately. 'Please – *please* let me get away. A little flat – even just one room – anywhere that isn't South London. *Anywhere.*'

She crossed to the window and jerked up the blind, letting in the brilliant morning sunshine to strike an answering gleam from the little brass goddess, Lakshmi, on the window-sill, that the silly old devil had brought her from India.

'Goddess of – what was it he said? – khush kismet – good

luck. Rub her tummy and it'll come true, he told me. Like
hell – but if you *can* do something to get me out of this dump
I'll change my bloody religion. That's a promise.'

She stroked the protuberant belly gently with her fingertip,
smiled wistfully, then shrugged hopelessly, and went through
to the bathroom.

Part One

Chapter One

His sister bumped the bedroom door open with her knee and brought his morning tea in. 'You'll catch your death of cold standing at the open window in your pyjamas like that,' she said. 'Fancy getting up when you don't have to.'

George grunted monosyllabic thanks and continued to stare through the lace curtains up the gritty length of Effra Road. Dorothy put the tray on the bedside table and came and stood behind him.

'What's so interesting?' she asked, peering past him. 'Blasted road gets more desolate every day. They say they're going to dig up the tram lines and get these new trolley bus things. At least it ought to be quieter then.'

'Why the devil don't you sell this place and move somewhere decent?' he asked impatiently, and she shrugged.

'You know the answer to that. You'd never shift Ma.'

'It's not Ma's house.'

'It's her *home* – '

'I'm talking about the actual property. It's yours and mine, jointly. As far as I'm concerned you can have the bloody lot – ' He broke off and bent closer to the window. 'Ah, there she is. Right on the dot.' He scowled. 'If those swine working in the next-door garden whistle after her again, I'll – '

'What?'

'Well – somebody ought to speak to them,' he mumbled.

'Try it,' she scoffed. 'That's if you don't mind getting an earful in return. You're in Brixton now, my lad – not Calcutta. Anyhow, *she* doesn't mind a few whistles. Come on away from there. You ought to be ashamed of yourself. Old enough to be her father – '

'I've just turned forty,' he said sullenly.

13

'And she's just turned twenty.'

'She's more than that.'

'You can't tell *me* her age, laddie. I had her in Standard 4, and a right little madam she was. All bum and bust even at the age of twelve. Come on, drink your tea before it gets cold. I've got to get off to school. Ma said do you want a kipper as well as bacon and eggs?'

'No, thank you,' he said with icy dignity, then added venomously, 'Soor ka bachas! They *did* whistle.'

'She'd have been disappointed if they hadn't. Come on, George – drink your tea.'

'Oh, take the damned tea away. I don't want it,' he said pettishly.

'Stop behaving like an overgrown schoolboy,' she told him. 'If you've really got it as bad as all that you'd only have to take her to a tea-dance at the Locarno and the back row of the cinema afterwards.' She picked up the tray and went out and he continued to watch the girl in the street below until her foreshortened figure was lost behind the soot-grimed laurel hedge of the next house but one, then he became conscious of three grinning faces looking up at him from the adjoining garden where they were erecting an illuminated showcase for the photographer who rented the ground floor of the next-door house. He stepped back hastily, tense with futile rage, shivering and mouthing incoherent filth in English and kitchen Hindi. He caught sight of himself in the spotted wardrobe mirror, and his anger left him momentarily, to be replaced by a wave of self-pity. Lanky and stooping, with thinning gingerish hair and as blind as a bat without his thick-lensed glasses. What chance had he ever had of meeting women on equal terms? Day-boy at Dulwich, with Ma and Dorothy, ten years his senior, watching his every move up to the age of eighteen, when most of his contemporaries were going out to the trenches. He couldn't go because of his bloody eyes, but that hadn't stopped bitches giving him white feathers. Four years in Head Office in Mincing Lane – bowler hat and umbrella, when all the rest were in uniform – then out to Calcutta. He'd pictured himself in a sun helmet, lean and bronzed, shooting tigers round the tea gardens of Assam, but in the eighteen years he had served the Hollins-Bland Tea Company he had found himself no further afield than the offices in Clive Street and the Bachelors' Mess in Tollygunj. Women? White women? God, they were scarcer than hens' teeth – and as attractive. Wives of members of his firm, and other firms, for the most part. Daughters were sent Home to school when they were kids, and if they had any sense they never went back to India. Anglo-Indians? Very pretty some of them, but HB was an old and very conservative firm, and you'd have been fired if you'd been seen consorting with them, let alone marrying one. They underpaid you and sweated your guts out, but you were still expected to carry the white man's burden, in public anyhow. That left only the Indians, which meant the brothels because no woman of caste could ever meet a white man socially. Yes, he'd tried the joy-houses once or twice when pot-valiant, learning each time that whisky, while heightening the desire, dulled the performance, and he'd always been so deathly frightened of VD. Some of the old-timers up-country used to establish native women in discreet bungalows outside cantonment limits, so he'd heard, but that was in another age, certainly not in 1938.

This was his third Home leave – six months every six years, plus the three weeks each way by P & O that they allowed – and each had been exactly the same. Back to this ghastly house, where his long-dead father had brought Ma on their marriage in 1880. A month at Eastbourne, with Dorothy joining them for a fortnight during the school holidays. See a few shows in the West End, usually with his spinster sister – the Old Boys' match up the road at Dulwich – a couple of visits to the local Lodge – 'Hearty greetings, Worshipful Master, from Lodge Clive of India, Calcutta' – the Overseas Dinner the Firm gave each year at one of the City Guilds and to which any of its scattered flock who happened to be on leave from India, Ceylon or Nyasaland were invited. Well, this would be the last time. He couldn't face another leave. He'd take a few weeks' holiday locally when it became due, and accumulate the balance until he retired. Fifty-five was the age with HB. Ma, seventy-five now, would be dead by then surely, and Dorothy would be drawing her pension. She could have the house, which his father had left to them rather than Ma, in order to save the latter some income tax on her annuity. It ought to be worth five or six thousand now, freehold. It must have been the last single-family house in the whole length of Effra Road, all the others being cut up into flatlets and bed-sitters, with an increasing number of small one-man businesses creeping in, like the photographer next door. Watchmakers, jobbing printers, and one or two tailors. Worse than Petticoat Lane, he thought sourly.

Ma was calling from the bottom of the stairs. 'Come and have your breakfast in your dressing-gown, boy, while it's nice and hot. You can wash and dress afterwards.' Boy? He grinned wryly and climbed into a frogged and padded garment as heavy as a horse-rug, which had been a wedding present to his father from Grandpa Sam, and which Ma insisted on George wearing while he was home, in preference to the immoral red silk thing he had brought from the Marwari Bazaar. He had brought his mother and sister various silk garments also – blouses, dressing-gowns, pyjamas and saris – all as useless to these two women as they were beautiful, but all wrapped carefully in tissue paper and treasured.

He went into the gloomy dining-room, a mahogany-cluttered mausoleum that he hated above all other rooms, but in which Ma insisted on meals being served while he was home, in spite of his repeated pleas to have at least breakfast in the slightly more cheerful, and certainly warmer kitchen. Ma brought in his bacon and eggs and toast. She was a large and angular woman who, in spite of the black bombazine she had worn habitually since her husband's death twenty-five years earlier, did not look her age. She placed the plate before him and poured his tea. He would have preferred coffee, which was perennially hard to come by in India, but Ma seemed to regard the serving of the latter as smacking of disloyalty.

'The cup that cheers, but does not inebriate,' she said, and he winced. 'And there's the *Daily Mail*. I knew you'd rather read it than talk to your old Ma.' He grunted non-committally and reached for it, but she sat down opposite to him and planted her elbow firmly on it. 'What's this I hear about you and the Wilmott girl?' She wagged a finger at him archly.

'Who?' he asked, too innocently.

'Wilmott. Lives with her father and mother and an old rip of an uncle up behind the George Canning. Hoity-toity little baggage she is – '

'Oh, you mean the girl who passes here every morning?'

'There's lots of girls pass here every morning. I mean the one you've been making sheep's eyes at. What are you blushing for?'

He slammed his knife and fork down and shouted. 'For Christ's sake stop it, will you. First Dorothy, now you – '

'There's no need to take the Lord's name in vain.'

'I happened to be looking out of the window one morning when she was going by, and Dorothy started sniggering – '

'No need to shout, either. Get on with your breakfast before it gets cold.'

'You get on my nerves, the pair of you – '

'Only got your interests at heart, dear.'

'For God's sake, I'm forty, not fourteen – '

'Just wanted you to know, that's all. That family's no good. They owe money in every shop in Brixton and Tulse Hill, the father can't hold a job for more than a few weeks, the brother's been in trouble with the police and yet that little minx walks past here to the station every day as if she'd bought the whole road – '

He stormed out of the room and went upstairs to his bed-room and slammed the door and turned the key. His face, which saw even less sun in India than it did back here, was pale and blotched with rage. He'd have to do something about this. He still had two months of his leave to run, but he couldn't take any more. He pondered briefly on his chances of fore-going the rest of it, but he knew that was hopeless. HB's leave programme was as immutable as the stars in their courses. No, he'd just have to face up to the inevitable storm that would burst around his ears and tell these two straight that he was going off somewhere on his own. But where? And who with?

17

That was his whole trouble, and he had enough self-percipience to realize it – this awful dependence on the company of others, even others who couldn't stand him. School, the office, the Club, the Bachelors' Mess – even when he tried to buy his way in with rounds of drinks out of his turn. What was it that that swine Andrews had said? 'The trouble with you is that you can't stand your own company – and neither can anybody else.' Vicious bastard – but unfortunately he was dead right. Of all the places in the world this house that he hated so much was the only one where he was welcome – and these two women who smothered him with loving solicitude until he felt that he was drowning in syrup, the only ones who wanted him.

The knob was rattled from the other side and Ma said softly, 'Now don't be a silly boy. Come and have your breakfast.'

George took a deep breath and bit back the words that were forming at the tip of his tongue and substituted something milder.

He escaped from the house while Ma was out shopping and before Dorothy came home for lunch from her near-by school, and he waited at the stop opposite, with a weather eye cocked up and down Effra Road in case either of them came along before the tram. He had no clear idea of where he was going, except vaguely west and north. He'd probably eat a lunch for which he had no appetite, have a drink or two which, with his Indian-conditioned inner clock, he wouldn't enjoy before sundown – then he'd sleep in a cinema seat until the evening arrived with yet more time to kill. He regretted not keeping up his subscription to the Public Schools Club somebody had put him up for on leaving Dulwich. At least it would have been somewhere to go.

A car pulled up in front of him, and a man said, 'Can I give you a lift, old boy?' and George gaped at him. It was probably the first direct remark made to him by an outsider in ten days.

'I – I beg your pardon?' he mouthed.

'Don't mean to be pushing,' said the other. 'Empty car and

18

all that – like a bit of company myself. Going up to the West End, if you happen to be going that way as well.'

'Thank you – thank you very much indeed,' George said gratefully, and climbed in. 'Yes – yes – the West End – '

'Anywhere in particular?'

'Actually no. I'm just killing time.'

'You've got a lot of it to kill, haven't you? I believe you're back on furlough from the Old Shiny.' The man shifted gear noisily and the ancient Morris Cowley pulled away from the kerb reluctantly. 'Bloody old banger,' he said. 'But what can you expect for thirty quid? Young college boy bought it, and I'm delivering it to him. That's if he's got the Oscar Ashe in ready. You can never risk cheques in this business.'

'But how did you know I was on leave from India?' George asked.

'Oh, sorry – I've got the advantage of you. You're young George Quaife aren't you?' the other said. 'I remember your old dad – long before the war, when I was still a nipper – draper's shop at the corner of Acre Lane. That right?'

'Dead right – but I'm sorry, I'm afraid you *have* got the advantage – ' George looked sideways at the other's rugged profile, and saw one boiled and subsequently faded blue eye, half a stiffly waxed moustache and a somewhat red and corrugated nose.

'Sprunt,' said the man. 'Captain Bill Sprunt—Herne Hill Motor Engineering Works – Sales Department. Got a card in me waistcoat pocket but I can't take me hands off this flogging wheel in traffic.'

'How do you do?' said George. 'Do you live round here?'

'Off and on. Joined the Army as a boy – came out after twelve years – back in for the war – commissioned quartermaster – out again – been all over the place since. Just working up this business now – me and a partner. Tried to sell your sister a car last year. Almost did, too, but your mother put her bib – er – talked her out of it. Woman of strong character. Don't make 'em like that any more – thank Christ. No offence.' He turned and grinned, and George saw the rest of his battered countenance. He had that embalmed look of the typical old soldier which seems to hold age perpetually between forty-five and sixty-five.

'None taken,' said George. 'I know what you mean exactly.' 'As a matter of fact I was wondering if *you* were in the market for a bus. Got some really reliable used stuff in at the moment – not like this crate,' went on the Captain.

'Afraid not,' George said. 'As you mentioned – I'm only home on leave.'

'Just when you need one,' the Captain said earnestly. 'This place is getting more like America every day. If you want a bit of kerfifer nowadays you've got to have wheels under you. Spreadeagling them the dark end of Brockwell Park is not for blokes of our station in life – so what does that leave? Brighton, which means railway fares and hotel bills – cost the earth today. This way – couple of gallons of petrol – meal at a nice quiet little country pub – a haystack under the canopy of heaven, and you've had a bloody good night out for under two quid. Can't beat it.'

'Worth thinking about,' said George, amused.

'Damn right it is. I could sell you a real nice little job, then buy it back from you before you leave. That means you'll have been mobile for the difference – ' And he had almost succeeded in selling George the all but hypnotized Singer runabout, sight unseen, by the time they arrived in Brewer Street and pulled into a mews.

A youth in a leather coat and a pork-pie hat came out of a doorway and looked the car over with some apparent misgivings.

'It seemed different at your place last night,' he said.

'Same bus,' the Captain assured him. 'Lovely little job. Ask this gentleman here. Just come all the way from my works in her. Went like a bat out of hell, didn't she, Major?'

'Uh? Oh – yes – yes indeed,' George agreed.

'Had we both not been officers and gents,' the Captain went on, 'he'd have upped your bid by another tenner.'

'I'm afraid I've only got twenty in cash,' said the youth nervously. 'But here's my mother's cheque for the rest.'

'No cheques, sonny,' said the Captain firmly. 'I thought I'd made that quite clear. Rule of the house.'

'But Max knows me,' the youth wailed.

'I don't give a monkey's if Lloyd George knows you – and your bloody father – no cheques.' He winked at George. 'All right, Major – I'm relieved of my obligation to this gentleman now. The car's yours – for the forty quid you offered.'

'I *have* got the rest,' the youth said miserably, 'but I need cash. I'm taking Max out tonight and Oddy's won't take cheques either.'

'Take her for a spin instead,' the Captain advised. He gently abstracted a roll of notes from the youth's nerveless fingers and counted them. ' – fifteen, twenty, twenty-five and five makes thirty. There you are, squire – got yourself a nice little bus there. God bless her and all who ride in her – although there's not much legroom for that in the back. You want to get yourself a groundsheet. So long.' He took George by the arm. 'OK, Major, let's go and have a look at this Bugatti I was telling you about.'

'A little hard on him, weren't you?' George said as they walked down Brewer Street.

'Wouldn't trust him as far as I could throw a bull by the left knacker,' the Captain said. 'His bloody eyes were too close together. How about a gargle? I belong to a little club in Old Compton Street where licensed hours don't mean a thing.'

'I'd be delighted.'

'Nothing posh, you know. Fringe film mob from Wardour Street and out of work musicians mostly, plus a few old toms on the batter resting their feet before the night's prowl. Keep your hand on your wallet and count your change after every round.'

'You make it sound interesting.'

'I suppose it is in a sort of a way. You got to watch 'em though.'

The Captain turned into a doorway between a Greek restaurant and a barber's shop and scribbled in a dogeared ledger on a table at the foot of a narrow flight of stairs. 'Captain Sprunt and guest,' he called out.

'Cost you half a dollar for the guest,' a fat woman said

through a pigeonhole.

'I'm putting him up for membership,' the Captain said loftily, 'so Rule 7 doesn't apply,' and added, 'Up yours too, darling', as the woman called him a miserable old bastard.

The room at the top contained a dozen small tables and an assortment of bentwood chairs. There was a minuscule bar across one corner and a battered piano against the opposite wall. A profusion of theatrical and motion picture photos covered the puce wallpaper, and a sagging curtain hung over a door signed 'Madames et Messieurs'. The whole scene was inadequately lighted by one weak electric bulb in a Chinese lantern. Half a dozen dim figures sat at various tables, and a large man in a grimy white jacket lounged behind the bar. He came across to them as they sat down and flicked their table with a damp cloth.

'Two scotches and soda, Charlie,' said the Captain. He handed a pound note across. 'And that's for yourself. That young pie-can bought the drag. Couldn't get him above twenty though, so that cuts your commission a bit.'

'Ta,' muttered Charlie, pocketing the note. 'Know where Max is?'

'Who wants to know?'

'Dolly Dyson.'

'She's working – on her feet, not on her back like these toms you get in here. What's he want to know for?'

'Day's shooting at Denham day after tomorrow, if she can get off. Not just crowd work. He reckons he might fix a couple of lines for her. Could be worth a tenner in that case.'

'Jesus!' breathed the Captain. 'She'll get off for *that* all right, even if she's got to bury her old grandma again.'

'He'll be in here at six to sign up a couple of others. He'll want to know for certain then,' Charlie said.

'Let's use the phone,' said the Captain, rising. 'And bring them whiskies. Make 'em doubles. Won't keep you a moment,' he added to George, and made for Madames et Messieurs.

He came back after some minutes, beaming. 'Sorry about that, but you've got to get your finger out quick in this business. Max would never have forgiven me if we'd missed that.' He broke off as he noticed George's complete blankness. 'Pictures,' he explained. 'My young niece is trying to break in. Like trying to shove melted butter up a wildcat's arse with a redhot hatpin if you don't have a bit of pull somewhere. Bit difficult for her. She works in a posh hairdresser's in Dover Street, and although her boss is fairly easy she can't go taking days off just when the hell she wants. Damn good job she's got. Three-pound-ten a week, and she must make thirty bob in tips on top of that easy.' He looked at his watch. 'Don't mind hanging on here for another hour, do you? She's coming round as soon as they shut the shop at half-five.'

'Not at all,' George said. 'Glad of the company. Can I get you another drink?'

'You can and all, Major,' the Captain said heartily. 'A couple of doubles to wet the deal. Do they still call 'em bara pegs in the Old Shiny?'

'Double whiskies? Yes – that's the term.' George flicked his fingers at Charlie. 'Same again please – and have one yourself.'

'Ta, guv,' grunted Charlie. 'You're a gent.'

'India,' sighed the Captain. 'Gawd! I wish I'd never left there. Could have stayed out when my first engagement was up. Doing all right I was. Full sergeant at twenty-four, and a damn good job lined up for me on the railways. Live like a rajah and never soil your hands. Niggers to do everything. All you had to do was watch 'em. But you'll know all about that. What's *your* line, by the way?'

'Tea,' said George.

'That so?' The Captain was visibly impressed. 'That was the best tickle of them all in my days. You planter blokes – *Cor!* Drink like fish, fornicate like stoats, live to a hundred. Man's life – you lucky bugger.'

'Not *quite* like that,' said George modestly.

'You can't tell *me*, Major. I *know*. Jesus! If I only had my time over again – *that's* what I'd do.' He tossed his drink off in one. 'Same again?'

'Yes indeed,' said George. 'But do let me get them.'

'You're out of your turn.'

'That doesn't matter. I haven't had any decent company for

the last four months. I just feel like pushing the boat out.'

'Push away, Major,' said the Captain happily, and rapped on the table with his glass. 'Fingers out and chocks away, Charlie. Same again. No decent company, Major? Cor! Can't have that. Must get you fixed up with something. No – don't look round here, for Christ's sake. Tackle any of this stuff and you'd think you'd been bit by a camel next morning. I mean something nice that you could be seen in public with without her being moved on by the Law. Lumme, there's enough top-class spare kerfifer in London to paper the Great Wall of China – if you know your way about.'

'I wish someone would *show* me the way about,' said George wistfully. 'You know, Captain – '

'Bill,' corrected the Captain.

'I'm George – ah, here are the drinks – '

'Your health, George.'

'And yours, Bill – Where was I? Oh, yes – when I ran into you this afternoon I was so goddamned bored that I was thinking of asking the firm to send me back to India early.'

'How much longer have you got?'

'Nearly two months.'

'Hell of a pity we didn't meet earlier. I'd have got you fixed up with a car, given you a couple of intros in the right quarter and you'd have been home on the pig's back. Still, it's not too late even now – Same again, Charlie – no – my turn – I insist – yes – what was I saying? Yes – get you fixed up with a car. That's the crux of the whole thing – like I was telling you this afternoon. You just got to be on wheels these days. Your health, George – down the hatch.'

'Down the hatch, Bill.'

The place was filling and the noise level, muted until now, was rising. The Captain reached out and touched George on the forearm.

'That's him,' he muttered.

'Who?'

'Little fat poof over by the bar – just came in. Dyson, casting director's assistant for Ransom Films. You got to be a nancy boy or over seventy in that job. You d never stand the strain of handling all that kerfifer else.'

George looked across and saw a plump little man fluttering be-ringed hands at a group of girls who were besieging him. 'Damn it,' fumed the Captain. 'The little bastard will be picking someone else. He said six o'clock – You heard that berk Charlie say six o'clock, didn't you? It's only ten to now – oh, thank Christ for that – here she is.' He signalled violently and then pointed to the bar, and George saw the girl he had watched morning after morning walking along Effra Road, come into the room, wave an acknowledgement and move quickly across to the bar and join the others. The Captain mopped his brow. 'Lumme, I was having kittens in case she missed out on it. Up to her now.'

'Same again?' asked George unsteadily.

'Yes – oh, and get a gin and lime in for her, will you? She'll be ready for one. Good kid – must have run all the way – or got a taxi.' He was watching the group at the bar anxiously. The little man scribbled something on a slip of paper and handed it over the heads of the others to the girl. She turned and came across to the table waving it triumphantly.

'Nice work, Nunkie,' she said. 'You were right on the ball this time.'

'Aren't I always?' the Captain smirked. He climbed to his feet as George rose. 'Miss Maxine Wilmott, my sister's gal. This is George Quaife, lovie, old friend of mine – just over from India on leave.'

'I know,' smiled the girl. 'I see him nearly every morning on my way to the station.' She put her hand out. 'How do you do, Mr Quaife?'

Her hand was smooth and cool in his. His stomach, denied both breakfast and lunch, was in revolt against the not inconsiderable amount of whisky he had drunk too quickly, he badly wanted to pee, and he could feel himself blushing. He tried to return the greeting but he had to clamp his teeth tightly to hold back a thunderous reflux of fumes, and all he could manage before galloping frantically towards the Messieurs was, ''Scuse – gezzum drinks.'

Maxine looked after him with raised eyebrows. 'What's the

matter with *him*?' she asked.

'Pissed as a newt,' said her uncle. 'My fault. Nice feller. Stinking with money, like all them tea planters. Be nice to him, lovie. I'm trying to flog him a car.'

'What's my cut if you do?'

'Christ! Have a heart. Haven't I just got you a job in the movies? Five quid if I sell him the one I have in mind – two if it's anything cheaper.'

'Don't strain anything, will you?' she gibed. 'All right, I'll do my best. Funny looking character, isn't he?'

'Looks aren't everything,' the Captain said ponderously. 'Not in a bloke they're not – and particularly if he's a millionaire.'

'*Millionaire?*' She stared at him incredulously.

'How many cups of tea have you drunk today?'

'How the hell do I know? Couple at breakfast – one, two – oh, say about five at work – '

'There you are then. Multiply that by fifty or sixty million in this country alone, and then reckon out what these tea fellers must be making. Cor! You'd need an adding machine.'

'Then what's he doing living in Effra Road?'

'Family home. Probably the last aristocrats in Brixton.'

'Aristocrats my foot. His sister was a teacher at my school, and a nasty old bag she was. Always clouting me over the knuckles with a ruler.'

'Pity it wasn't over the arse with a slipper. You wouldn't have been so damn saucy. No – seriously, lovie, he's got plenty of rent, I'm telling you – so just give your old uncle a bit of a hand in this, will you? I could do with it. Things have been right on the ribs in the used car trade lately – what with these damned Baby Fords selling at ninety-nine quid, *new*.'

She smiled at him. 'Of course I will, you old devil – but I want a favour in return.'

'What's that?'

'This call at Denham on Thursday – make-up at *six-thirty*. I haven't a hope of getting there from Brixton that early. Will you drive me over?'

'I'll do my best, lovie,' he said doubtfully, 'but Panton has been pretty tight lately about letting me take out stock, unless it's for a genuine demonstration – or a delivery.'

'Then what am I going to do? A taxi would cost the earth, even if I could get one as early as that.'

The Captain could see George manipulating three glasses and a soda siphon at the bar. He rubbed his nose thoughtfully. 'I think I can see a little ray of light, lovie. Yes – sure I can. You ask me that very same question – can I drive you over to Denham on Thursday? – after the next round of drinks – then just follow my leads crafty like. I'd better go and help the berk before we have a bill for damages.' He rose and went over to the bar.

They came back to the table together, bearing the drinks between them, and George, standing and looking down at her, found himself catching his breath. Art and nature were combined in that exquisite face to perfection. Her light make-up was applied with the expertise she had learned in the salon – over an already flawless skin, and her deep violet eyes were not plastered around with the heavy mascara girls were beginning to misuse in the thirties. Her curling lashes were obviously her own, and her hair, slightly tumbled after her swift hatless transit from the shop to this place, seemed to owe nothing of its honey-blonde wave to rinses, tongs or fixatives. She smiled up at him, and he saw perfect teeth set in a mouth that was in exact proportion to her straight little nose and delicately rounded chin. Her figure he already knew from his daily study at the window was also perfect. He gulped and held her gin and lime out to her with a trembling hand. She took it from him and gurgled with pleasure. 'Gin and lime – just what I wanted. That was clever of you.' George gulped again and sat down.

'Cheers to the lot of us,' beamed the Captain. 'You know – I had a feeling when I got up this morning that this was going to be a lucky day. And it has been. Here's me made a sale to that boy friend of yours, Max – '

'Oh, he bought it, did he?' she said without particular interest. 'But he's not a *boy friend*. Just somebody I met at a party. Then I heard him telling Charlie he wanted a second-hand car – '

'*Used* car, lovie,' the Captain corrected. 'Then there's you landed a part in a movie – '

'That's worrying me a bit,' Max said. 'How on earth am I going to get across to Denham at six-thirty in the morning? Can you drive me, Nunkie?'

'Sure I can, pet,' averred the Captain, then broke off and looked dismayed. 'Oh hell – Thursday? No – no – 'fraid I can't. Damned delivery down in Tunbridge Wells. Oh, Lord – '

George's heart leapt. 'Could I run you across, Miss Wilmott?' he asked timidly, and her eyes widened with delight.

'Would you? Oh, you *darling* – ' she breathed. 'It means so much to me – '

'I haven't a car – not here in England, I mean – but perhaps Bill will hire me one – ?' George said.

'Afraid not, old man,' the Captain said regretfully. 'We're not insured for hires.'

'Well, sell me one? You were telling me earlier on that you had several – '

'*Sell* you one – sure – with the greatest of pleasure. I could deliver it to you before lunch tomorrow – '

'Do that then, please,' said George happily.

'Sure – sure – ' The Captain hesitated. 'But – I mean – you'll want to see a couple first – try 'em out and all that?'

'I'll leave it entirely to you,' George told him. 'You're the expert. Just pick out a decent one and bring it round with the necessary papers.' And the Captain felt that all the used car salesmen in heaven were singing an angels' chorus.

Max finished her drink and looked at her watch. 'I think I'd better be going,' she said. 'I've got a date, and I've got to go round to Ella's to change first.'

'Scrub it,' the Captain said, 'and we'll make a night of it up West here – that's if it's all right with you, George. Bit of dinner, few drinks, look in at the Pavilion after – '

'Absolutely fine with me,' said George eagerly.

'I couldn't do that,' the girl said regretfully. 'I don't know where to get in touch with him to cancel it.'

'Who is it? Pimply Percy? Aw, he'll be all right. He can play with his new motor car.' He beamed on them benignly.

'Of course I shouldn't be playing gooseberry on you youngsters
– but I'm going to – '

'But I *can't* stand somebody up just like that,' Max protested.
'Why not? He's only a young berk. Tried to stick me with a
rubber cheque this afternoon, didn't he, George?'

'Y-yes – ' George found himself agreeing. 'He certainly didn't
seem a very reliable type.'

'You'd find yourself being left with the dinner bill, and
paying for the theatre tickets afterwards,' the Captain went on.
'I know these blokes. Been dealing with them all me life – in
the Army and out. Plus-fours, posh accent and not two bob to
rub together. Charlie – same again.'

'Oo – I don't know – ' the girl said doubtfully.

'I do,' said the Captain firmly. 'It's all fixed. I wouldn't be
doing my duty by the family if I let you go out with that sort of
squirt.'

George caught her eye. She gestured hopelessly, shrugged,
smiled, then nodded. 'It's an awfully mean thing to do – but I
must confess I wasn't looking forward to it. I only said yes
because I didn't want to spoil a sale for this old devil.'

George turned to the Captain and muttered, 'Do you think
they'd cash a cheque for me here?'

The Captain looked at him in outraged incredulity. 'Cash a
cheque? *Here?* They'd scream blue bloody murder if you even
suggested it. Why?'

'It's just that I'd like it to be my party tonight and I've only
about a tenner on me in cash,' George explained nervously.

'Well now, that's damned nice of you, George – particularly
since it was me who suggested it,' the Captain said expansively.
'No problem – if you're sure you'd prefer it that way. I'm
carrying some firm's money on me. Give us your cheque for
thirty and you can have the lot – no, not here for Christ's sake
– in the gents later – Thanks, Charlie – right, you two – Here's
to a long and continuing friendship – Down the hatch.' They
clinked glasses.

Ma loomed over the bed and surveyed him without favour.
'Your tea's stone cold, right here where Dorothy left it,' she

29

told him accusingly. 'And your clothes are in an *awful* state.'

He opened his eyes, then shut them again quickly and nodded dumbly.

'Nice thing, I must say,' she went on. 'You sneak out of the house before lunch without telling a soul where you're going, then come home at three in the morning singing and carrying on with some creature in a taxi – your sister's got to come down to let you in – you use filthy language to her – then you're sick on the hall carpet. We've lived in this house for over fifty years, and I've always been able to hold my head up, even when your father made a pig of himself at the Masons' – George, are you listening to me?'

'No,' he shuddered. 'Go away, Ma, for Christ's sake.'

'Oh, no, you don't get out of it as easily as that, my boy. I want to know what you've been up to – '

'I haven't the faintest idea myself. I met some friends and apparently I had too much to drink. I'm sorry. Now will you please let me alone?'

'Not until I know – '

'Ma – please – ' he begged weakly.

'I want to know who you were with – '

He shot bolt upright and bellowed, 'Oh, fuck off!'

There was a shocked silence, broken only by the faint clicking of Ma's dentures as her mouth opened and shut slowly. He retreated beneath the bedclothes like a sick mole and she turned and tiptoed out, shutting the door behind her soundlessly. He emerged from cover again. His head was throbbing and his mouth and throat were ash-dry. He gulped down the cold tea left on his bedside table and then sat on the edge of the bed fighting waves of incipient nausea. What had happened? What the *hell* had happened? He remembered leaving that horrible drinking den and going to some restaurant or other, but after that things merged into a confused kaleidoscope. An argument —a stage somewhere with some character throwing knives at a girl strapped to a vertical board – and he wanted to show them how it was done in India, and he had tried to climb over the footlights and had fallen into the orchestra pit. He groaned. The sort of nonsense silly young office juniors get up to at

Firpo's restaurant in Chowringhee. But that was Calcutta, where it was perfectly permissible for a sahib to make a bloody fool of himself. What on earth would that lovely girl think of him? A middle-aged man, old enough to be her father, as that bitch Dorothy put it, behaving like an East End lout on a Bank Holiday pub crawl.

He dragged himself to the dressing table and shuddered afresh at what he saw in the mirror, then he went to his place at the window, wondering if she had passed yet. He got his eyes into focus with difficulty, and looked at his watch. It was nearly midday. A car pulled up in front of the house and the Captain climbed out. He walked up the short path towards the front door with a noticeable lack of military briskness. George drummed on the window frantically, and the Captain looked up.

'Don't ring,' George croaked. 'I'll come down there.'

'I've got your bus – '

'All right – Won't keep you a minute or so.'

'See you in the saloon bar of the George Canning. They're just open – and I could do with a couple – and so could you, by the look of you. Boy, did you have a load aboard! You were so pissed at the end I couldn't even see you.'

'Don't rub it in,' George moaned, and withdrew hastily to the bathroom.

The short walk to the corner pub cleared his head slightly. He joined the Captain at the bar and reached blindly for the pint of bitter the other had waiting for him. He drank deeply and felt marginally better. The Captain watched him with admiration.

'That's what I like to see,' he said. 'A bloke that can take his wallop.'

'Apparently I *couldn't* take it last night,' George said hollowly. 'From what little I remember I must have been behaving like a right damned fool.'

'Oh, the hell with that,' the Captain boomed. 'It was a *lovely* party. When you and that fat geezer was turning handsprings for pints – *on a marble floor* – I thought I'd bust a gut laughing. Nearly broke his bloody neck he did.'

'But what on earth must your niece have thought of all this?' George asked fearfully.

'Max? Oh, don't you worry about young Max. Nothing she enjoys more than a bit of a knees-up,' the Captain said. 'But as a matter of fact she'd gone by this. There were these two blokes from the studio, see? There was a party on somewhere and this producer was going to be there, and they reckoned that with a bit of luck they could get her a screen test. You were having an up-and-downer with this South African bush-whacker at the time, so she sent you her love and said she'd see you at five tomorrow morning. You made quite a hit there, George, I can tell you. She's got her head screwed on the right way, has Max. She can't stand these young jerks not dry behind the ears. She's always preferred older blokes, with a bit of balance and knowledge of the world – and *India!*' The Captain kissed his fingers. 'That's right up her alley. You know as a little 'un she'd have me going for hours telling her stories about the Old Shiny – and it was no good giving her a load of bullshit either. She used to read it up at school and at the public library. You know, she's seen that movie, *Lives of a Bengal Lancer* five times to my knowledge – *and* read the book. Absolutely fascinates her it does.'

'I hope she never sees Calcutta just before the monsoon,' George said. 'So what you're telling me is that she'd left before things got out of hand?'

'If you put it that way, yes – but they never got out of hand. You, me, them, *everybody*, was having a bloody good time – and really enjoying it – and if she'd stayed she'd have enjoyed it most of all. I told her a bit about it this morning before she left for work. Laughed her head off she did – and she was real fed up she wasn't there.'

'Well, don't tell her any more,' George said. He knew over-whelming relief.

'I don't think I'll need to.' The Captain nudged him slyly. 'You wicked old bugger – I've got an idea you're going to be seeing quite a lot of her before you go back.'

'What a hope,' George said gruffly, and felt himself going red – but his heart was singing.

'Well – I've got the bus outside here,' the Captain said. 'Lovely job it is. Standard Flying 14 – good as new – and an absolute gift. Had to argue like hell with Panton – that's the boss – well, you know – senior partner sort of – to get it down to half a monkey – '

'Two hundred and fifty?' said George a little doubtfully. 'I hadn't thought of spending quite as much as that.'

'Wait till you see it,' said the Captain confidentially. 'Besides, you'll get a lot of that back when we take it off you again – whereas a cheaper job will drop more in the meantime, if you see what I mean. How about another gargle?'

'Not any more, thanks. That's about filled the tank.'

'Well, a short? Whisky and soda?'

'Um – all right – just one.'

'Oh, about tomorrow morning – picking her up. It's just round the corner behind here – Barnwell Road – 16A – just give a toot on the horn. She'll be waiting at five o'clock. Sure that's not too early for you? Real sparrow-fart reveille – '

'No – that will be all right – Cheers.'

'Cheers – Well, I think I'd better give you a run round the block a couple of times. Ever driven a Standard before?'

'No. I've got a Ford 10 back in India – '

'Huh – this will be like caviar after skilly. Come on.'

He sounded the horn softly and a wraithlike figure came out of the front door and hurried across the dark pavement. He climbed out hurriedly to meet her, banging his head on the top of the car door. But it wasn't the girl. It was her mother, in a dressing gown and a turban over curlers, breathless with apologies.

' – won't be a moment – young girls nowadays – so sorry to keep you waiting – can I offer you a cup of tea – ?' she was gabbling, and he, tongue-tied with shyness, was trying to reassure her, and making matters worse.

' – so good of you to take her, Mr – er' the woman went on, – 'Sure you wouldn't like a cup of tea? – no trouble really – '

'Not at all – no – I mean – '

'Her uncle – my brother, you know – would have taken her

33

like a shot – but he's got this important business in Tunbridge Wells – '

Then mercifully the girl arrived and they drove off leaving the woman in an agony of fluster and refinement.

The girl said, 'Sorry about that. My mother always gets in a tizzy if anything unusual happens. *Have* you had anything to eat, by the way?'

'Oh, yes,' he lied. 'I – er – had – er – '

'I don't believe you. Anyhow, I haven't. There's an all-night coffee stall at Kennington Oval though, if you wouldn't mind stopping.'

'Of course. But how about the time? For you, I mean.'

'Oh, we'll do it easily in an hour at this time of day, so we can spare ten minutes. Do you know the way?'

'Yes – I got a road map and looked it up last night. Across Westminster Bridge, then make for Shepherd's Bush and out along the Uxbridge Road – '

'Clever you. I couldn't understand a map to save my life.'

His shyness was leaving him and was being replaced by an ease of manner that he had never before experienced in his limited dealings with women; an ease that was almost euphoric.

She said, 'What a gorgeous car', and snuggled down against the upholstery. 'Fancy being able to buy a car – just like that.'

'Oh, I don't know,' he shrugged. 'I never bothered back here before, because there didn't seem much point to it – just driving by oneself. Different out there, of course – you've got to have one.'

'You mean India?'

'Yes. Your uncle tells me you've always been interested in the darned place. I wonder why?'

'I don't know myself. But I've only got to close my eyes and I can see it all. Does that sound silly?'

'Not at all.'

'Elephants, tigers, peacocks, lean brown men – rajahs with lovely silk clothes, and smothered with jewels. Is it *really* like that?'

'Oh yes – yes indeed – one gets used to it, of course, after a time – '

34

'And the wonderful social life – the Viceroy's ball in *Lives of a Bengal Lancer* – the film, you know. Have you seen it?'

'I'm afraid not.'

'Oh, you ought to. All those lovely uniforms – and the evening frocks on the white women and those beautiful robes their princesses wear – '

'Saris they're called. But all Indian women aren't princesses, I can assure you. And some of them are anything but beautiful.'

'I know *one* that is. Princess Amina. I don't suppose you met her out there by any chance?'

'Not that I remember at the moment.'

'She's a starlet. You know – that means she's under contract to the studio, the lucky thing – and she's being watched and coached at the moment. She speaks English as well as you or I – '

'Lots of them do,' he said gravely.

'She always wears a robe – what do you call it – ?'

'Sari.'

'Sari – and she has a mark, like a spot, between her eyebrows that shows she's high class – '

'They call it "caste".'

'She was discovered when they were making this film *Elephant Boy* and they had an awful job to get her father to let her come over here. He'd be – well, if she's a princess, he'd be a king or something, wouldn't he?'

'Rajah. That's a native prince.'

'But she's not all stuck up or anything like that.'

'Where did you meet her?'

'At a party I was invited to once – but I've seen her lots of times on the set. She'll talk to anybody. Do you play polo?'

'I'm afraid I don't have a lot of time to.'

'Shoot tigers?'

'There aren't an awful lot of them about in my part of the country but the opportunity is there if one cares to take it.'

'It must be marvellous. I'd love a tiger-skin rug.'

'We'll have to see about getting you one.'

'You *mean* that? *Really* mean it?'

'Of course.'

35

'Oooo!' She grabbed his arm ecstatically and hugged it, causing him to swerve.

Dawn was streaking the sky when he dropped her, with a good ten minutes to spare, in front of the studio complex.

'What time do you finish?' he asked.

'Officially at six, but if they decide to carry on with night shooting and still need the crowd, it could be any time,' she explained.

'Well, I'll be waiting here at six then.'

She stared at him open-mouthed. 'You mean you'd wait here all day?' she asked incredulously.

'And all night, if necessary,' he said earnestly.

'But you *couldn't* – '

'Why not? I've got all the time in the world, on leave like this. Anyhow, I wouldn't actually wait here at this spot. I'll pass the time during the day and come back – '

'Well, it's ever so nice – I mean, it's terribly kind of you, but I couldn't take advantage like that.'

'You're not taking advantage. Let us say six then – and perhaps if you're not too tired we might have dinner somewhere.'

'I'd love it – but I still say it's taking advantage.' She looked at her watch. 'I'll have to nip.' She stood on tiptoes and pecked him on the cheek. 'You're a darling,' she said, and ran.

Chapter Two

Bradley said, 'There was a bloke in a car asking for you outside the studio when I came through.'

'I know,' said Max contritely. 'I hate standing anybody up like that, but Mike was bringing the princess along and he offered Jack and me a lift. We came out through the end gate so I didn't get a chance to tell him.'

'Naughty of you,' Bradley said softly. 'You wouldn't ever do that to *me*, would you?'

'Of course not – but you were telling me about this screen test – ?'

'Oh, yes. Nothing to it, really. You're supposed to do it without direction, but I'll take you through the script beforehand. It's usually three scenes with the same chap. He's just come back from the war – you thought he was dead – you're meeting him at the station. Then he's proposing to you and you're turning him down – then he's ditching *you*, and you're pleading with him. That sort of thing. They just want to see how you register and react – '

'I'll be scared stiff.'

'Nonsense. Bit of coaching from me and you'll sail through.'

'When do you think it could be arranged?'

'Oh, it will take a few days, of course. You'll have to keep it under your hat in the meantime – '

'Ooo – I wouldn't dream of mentioning it to a soul – '

'That's the girl. Which way now?'

'Just drop me at the end of Effra Road – Here we are – this will do.'

'Sure I can't take you any further – ?'

She looked at her watch in the faint gleam of the dashboard light. 'Not at – my God! – half-past two in the morning! My mother will be going scatty. Thanks – thanks a lot – it's been a lovely exciting day – and a *marvellous* party – so good of you to ask me.'

'There'll be lots more – when you're a star – '

'Oh, get on with you.'

'No, seriously – I think that with your looks and I believe latent ability, plus a weeny bit of luck and a word or two in the right place, we ought to be able to fix at least a starlet's contract for you. After that it would be up to you, of course.'

She sat back in her seat and closed her eyes. 'You think so?' she breathed. 'You *really* think so?'

'Oh, I *have* been wrong in the past,' he shrugged. 'Not often, admittedly, because I take pretty good care before I put anybody forward for consideration – after all it *is* my job, and I have my reputation to consider. Right – nighty-night. You go and catch up on your beauty sleep. You say I can get you on the phone any lunch time?'

'Yes – they're pretty decent – providing one doesn't have *too* many calls – ' She paused momentarily, expecting him to kiss her, but he just patted her hand.

'OK – then you'll be hearing from me. 'Night.'

He swung the car in a U turn, and the man in the back said, 'Jesus – I thought that line of corn went out with Mack Sennett and the Keystone cops.'

'Hello – I thought you were asleep,' Bradley said.

'Not bloody likely. I wouldn't have missed that for the world. You cheeky sod. But you didn't get anything.'

'I will, never you fret. A bit like that would have run a bloody mile if you'd put the hard word on her first time out. I believe in playing 'em like trout. Make 'em think you're going to grab a double handful, then stop, step back and look at them thoughtfully and say, "Um – your left's the better side. That would make a marvellous shot. Bit of indirect lime bounced off a mat white screen. Have to get Korda to have a look at you sometime. Right – run along now, dearie – I'm busy." Then later let 'em see you making a play for another piece, and if they squawk say, "Good God! I'm not after her, *or* you, for

38

tail. I'm only interested in discovering *talent*", and walk away.'

'Yes, but since you *are* after tail, you've got to change your spiel eventually, haven't you?'

'No – you let *them* change it. At first they're all professional – trying to convince you that they *have* got talent. You just shrug and yawn and say "maybe" – then they come right back at you with the only weapon the poor little cows have got – and in the end they're pulling *you* into the sack instead of the other way round.'

The man in the back chuckled. 'Crafty bastard. Hasn't one of them ever rumbled you?'

'What is there to rumble? Talent scouts don't wear badges. Anyhow, you never say you *are* a talent scout. You just show a mild interest in them at a party, like tonight. Ask them quite casually if they've ever had a screen test – if not, would they be willing to take one? *Would* they? Huh! You've got to keep 'em off with a big stick after that.'

'But sooner or later you've got to deliver *something*?'

'Not before *they've* delivered, boy.'

'What if they ever find out what your real job is?'

'What if they do? They certainly don't go round wailing "I thought he was a talent scout so I let him have a bit." No, all they do is avoid you thereafter and pretend it never happened – which suits your book fine once you've landed the bacon.'

'Hasn't your wife ever suspected anything?'

'Not as far as I know, thank God. A bloke's got to be bloody careful though. Drop you on Streatham Hill – that OK?'

The Captain stared at her aghast. 'You mean to say he was calling for you, and you never turned up?'

'I couldn't help it, I tell you,' Max said pettishly. 'By the time we'd got our make-up off and the costumes back to Wardrobe it was nearly seven – '

'But, Christ – didn't you go and *see* if he was still waiting?'

'I couldn't. I was asked to this party – and then this man talked about a screen test – and we drove out of another gate – '

'You're mad,' the Captain fumed. 'This bloke is not one of your pimply-faced poofs. He's *quality*, a man of substance – a tea planter, for God's sake. He's *stinking* with it. I *know*, I tell you. I've seen them out there – seen the way they live – race-horses, polo ponies, Rollses – '

'Well, *he* doesn't look it – and my career comes first.'

'Career my arse – '

'There's no need to be vulgar – '

'Listen, my girl – just listen a minute to your old uncle. It's *your* life – '

'Well suppose you let me live it my own way.'

'Chances like this don't come along every day. Look, lovie,' he pleaded. 'I'll see him and fix it up – '

'Fix what up?'

'Explain that you weren't chucking it all back in his teeth when he'd done you a favour – '

'I didn't ask him to. He offered. Anyhow, you keep out of it – '

'Well, that's a nice thing to say, after I went to all this trouble – '

'What trouble? You sold him a car, didn't you, and had a night out at his expense – and while we're on the subject, what about the fiver you promised me?'

'You'll get it,' he said with dignity, 'when I've completed the transaction at the office. In the meantime – '

'In the meantime,' she said, pushing past him, 'I've got to get to work, or I'll be late again. Oh, God, I'm tired.'

Her mother came through from the kitchen with a plate of cornflakes awash with tepid milk, and followed her up the narrow hall. 'You haven't touched your breakfast,' she complained. 'And God knows what time it was when you came in last night, or this morning I should say. If your father had woke up – '

'Oh, leave me alone, will you!' the girl screamed. 'All of you – or I'll go and get a flat on my own somewhere – '

'Not on what you pay *me* you won't, my lady,' her mother shouted as the front door slammed. She turned on the Captain. 'That's all this film business – and you with your stories, unsettling her and making her dissatisfied – '

'What the bloody hell has the film business got to do with *me* ?' he demanded indignantly. 'You're the one who should be taking the can back for it all, for not bringing her up properly. You and that husband of yours.'

'What about him ?' asked Mr Wilmott, coming downstairs.

'I was just saying to Kate here,' the Captain began placatingly.

'Yes, I heard what you were just saying to Kate here – and I've had enough of it, Captain Sprunt. I'll thank you to be out of my house as soon as you can get your stuff packed – what there is of it.' Mr Wilmott folded his arms and breathed heavily through his nose. He was a tall thin man with an air of drooping despondency constantly upon him. 'It isn't as if you were bringing anything in – '

'I was just saying to Kate here,' the Captain repeated with dignity, 'that I was now more than happy to be able to contribute a small something to the family commissariat.' He produced a crisp white five pound note from a comfortably thick wallet. 'Of course, Arthur, if you'd rather I went – '

'A man has his pride,' said Mr Wilmott, a little uncertainly, 'and he's got to be master in his own house.'

'Point taken,' said the Captain understandingly. 'Well, I've enjoyed my stay here with you, but all things come to an end.' He replaced the note and started to climb the stairs. 'I'll get on with my packing.'

'At the same time, blood's thicker than water,' added Mr Wilmott hastily. 'After all, you *are* my wife's brother, and I've no wish to turn you out, Bill.'

'Meaning to say *I* have,' said Mrs Wilmott angrily. 'Shut up for God's sake before you make matters worse. Bill, there's no question of you leaving – ' She held out her hand for the money. 'It's all that silly girl's doing. Thanks, dear. Now let's go through and have a fresh pot of tea.'

'And she *is* being silly,' said the Captain, as they sat round the kitchen table. 'Completely blind to her own interests. God damn it! The *Quaifes*. You remember them when we were all nippers round here ?'

'The drapers?'

'That's right. It seems like only yesterday, but it must have been all of forty years ago – getting a sixpence off the old chap for holding his horses at the front gate – and sixpence was sixpence in those days. Must have been the last people round here to own a carriage and pair – *and* the first to own a motor. An old Lanchester landaulette it was. I can see it now.'

'It was certainly very nice of him to pick Max up yesterday morning,' said Mrs Wilmott.

'Picked our Max up?' said her husband. 'What the hell are you talking about? He's been dead for years.'

'The son, you damned fool,' snapped his wife. 'Young George. Home from India or China or somewhere – '

'India,' said the Captain. 'Big tea man out there. Millionaire, over and over again.'

'How does he know Max then?'

'I introduced them.'

'How does he know *you*?'

'Oh, for God's sake – known him for years – met him out there when I was serving. Anyhow, he was good enough to come round here at the crack of dawn to take her to the studios – and he arranged to pick her up again after she had finished – and she goes and stands him up, the silly little bitch. Just leaves him waiting and buggers off to a party with a bunch of young twerps. *Gaw!*' He clenched his fists and glared at the ceiling.

'That wasn't very nice of her, I must say,' said Mrs Wilmott. 'What must he have thought of her?'

'I know what *I'd* have thought of her – but he's a decent, polite sort of bloke – a real gent. What we used to call a pukkha sahib out there. I could fix it again – I mean – he's barmy about her – you know – *really* – and no funny business either. That's what all the argy-bargy was about in the hall just now. I offered to do just that – see him and explain – '

'I wish you would, Bill dear,' said Mrs Wilmott earnestly. 'I mean, she's so silly. Fancy going and doing a thing like that.'

'What's the use? She practically told me to go and stick my head in a bag. "Career," she says. "Going to be a movie star,"

42

she says. "Bloke fixing up a screen test for her," she says.'

Mrs Wilmott's eyes shone. 'Well, it could be,' she said. 'She's a wonderful looking girl – even though I do say it myself.'

'It takes more than looks,' said the Captain profoundly. 'And you get nothing for nothing in that business. A girl won't get far unless she's ready to – well, you know – with all the bosses and directors and those sort of people.'

'By God! They better not try anything like that with *my* girl,' said Mr Wilmott fiercely.

'You wouldn't be there, Arthur,' the Captain said. 'Once the bastards get a girl inside one of those studios, anything can happen. I tell you, I know a hell of a lot of people in that business. The things I've heard – '

'And you let her go there?' Mr Wilmott demanded of his wife. 'What sort of a mother do you call yourself?'

'What could I do to stop her?' Mrs Wilmott whimpered. 'Don't forget she was twenty-one last month – and only this morning she was threatening to leave home and get a flat somewhere.'

'She'd only have to say that to me *once*, and she'd be out on her arse,' Mr Wilmott thundered.

'Make up your mind, Arthur,' the Captain said. 'One minute you're going to play hell and all with anybody who makes a pass at her – the next you're going to bounce her out on her arse. Can't have it both ways, you know.'

'What I'm saying is –' Mr Wilmott began, but his wife had now dried her eyes, and one look was sufficient to send him into rumbling silence.

'What ought we to do?' she asked the Captain.

'Nothing,' he advised sagely. 'Plain damn nothing – at the moment and on the surface, so to speak. Don't oppose her – don't argue the toss with her. Just let everything go on in the normal way. In the meantime I'll be seeing George. I'll smooth him down – explain everything. He'll listen to me. I'll have things going again between them before long, you mark my words.'

'How do we know that *he* won't be trying it on, like those film people?' Mr Wilmott asked suspiciously.

'I thought I'd made that quite clear,' the Captain said. 'He's an officer and a gentleman – '

'You said he was in tea?'

'He is – the other is a manner of speaking. Officer and gentleman *class* I meant. People like that don't go round trying it on – not with decently brought-up girls, anyhow.'

'Changed a bit since I was in the Army then,' Mr Wilmott grunted. 'The officers were the worst. Pissed half the time and after anything in skirts that came within a mile of camp – nicely brought-up or not.'

'I'm talking about real officers and the real Army, Arthur,' the Captain explained patiently. 'With all due respect you can hardly say that six months on Salisbury Plain in 1918 makes you much of an authority. Still, we don't want to start arguing amongst ourselves. It's Max's future we've got to be thinking of. He wants to marry her – '

'Has he *asked* her?' Mrs Wilmott whispered breathlessly.

'Not her, he hasn't. He wouldn't dream of doing so until he had spoken to *you*, but he told me the other night – told me in so many words – '

'That wouldn't amount to much if it was the night you and him was shouting the odds outside here,' Mr Wilmott said. 'You were both boozed up.'

'We'd had a few over dinner,' the Captain admitted coldly. 'But I'd hardly call that being boozed up. Anyhow, in vino veritas, as they say. He meant it all right – make no mistake about that. Now the question is, do you want me to handle it? Because you can take it from me that it's going to *need* handling, otherwise the whole thing goes up in smoke, and she loses a chance that may never come her way again. The chance of marrying money – *real* money.'

'Of course we'd want you to help, Bill dear,' Mrs Wilmott said, but it was obvious that small doubts were beginning to make themselves felt. 'At the same time money isn't everything. It's her happiness that counts.'

'If there's one thing I've learned in life, Kate,' the Captain said, 'it's that you can't be happy *without* money.'

'And that's nothing less than God's own truth,' said Mr

44

Wilmott with feeling. 'Yes, you go right ahead, Bill. Anything you can do to make the silly little devil see which side her bread's buttered, we'd be grateful for.'

'Still, if there *is* anything in this film thing,' began Mrs Wilmott wistfully. 'Remember she was runner-up in the Miss Streatham competition – and she was always so good in the school plays – '

'Forget it,' snapped the Captain. 'Listen, I know that film mob. Some of them have got themselves into my club. Not a sausage between the lot of them, except for a few of the top boys – and half the little titters in London are on a string to them. You don't want her to finish up like that – with young Quaife back in India, probably married to some General's daughter or something.'

'No, by God we don't,' said Mr Wilmott. 'Put a sock in it, Kate. Bill knows what he's doing.'

George made wet rings on the bar with his beer mug and shook his head sadly. 'Good of you, Bill, to offer to help, but I can't see that there's much you can do about it. Max is a lovely girl, but she's old enough to know her own mind, and to choose her own friends.'

'But that's just the point,' the Captain said earnestly. 'She *does* know her own mind, agreed – and you made a hell of an impression on her. She's talked about nothing else since.'

'I can't believe that,' George smiled.

'I'm telling you. This box-up the other night wasn't her fault. They were all kept back working late, and she couldn't get a message out to you.'

'That's not quite accurate. I saw her going past in a car with a couple of chaps and another girl.'

'Exactly – that's what I'm trying to tell you. They were shooting somewhere else and a couple of them got a lift over in one of the bloke's cars. She didn't think it would be for more than half an hour or so, but it dragged on.'

'I see. Well, whatever it was, the matter is closed now. No hard feelings. Have another.'

'Same again – but I don't think the matter *is* closed. Not

45

as far as she's concerned, anyway. I think you ought to see her – '

'Drop it, Bill. I find all this just a little embarrassing.' There was an unwonted edge to George's voice, and the Captain blinked, and was then profuse in his apologies, but long years of used car selling and kindred pursuits in South-east London had developed his persistence to a point where it was immune to snubs. 'Leave it to me,' he said, winked, nudged and so far forgot his erstwhile commissioned status as to tap himself on the side of his nose with a stiffly extended forefinger. 'I'll have a talk to her. Her old Uncle Bill knows what's best for her. Brings all her little worries to me she does. Wouldn't dream of going to her ma or pa with them. Something I've always had with youngsters, dogs and horses. Don't know what it is exactly – '

'Quite,' George broke in brusquely, 'but that wasn't what I wanted to see you about. This car – '

'What's wrong with it?' The Captain stiffened, like a stag scenting distant danger.

'Nothing, except that I think I paid far too much for it – but that doesn't matter. The thing is that I want to get rid of it.'

'Oh, no!' said the Captain, stricken. 'Now come on, George. You know what I was telling you – '

'Yes, I know all that, but the fact remains that it's a millstone round my neck. The police have been to the house, and scared my mother out of her wits. Apparently I'm not allowed to park on a thoroughfare in daylight hours, so that rules out leaving it in front of the house, and there's no carriage entrance since my sister had that ghastly privet hedge planted, so I can't put it in the garden.'

'I can rent a garage for you somewhere near by.'

'I'd rather you bought it back from me – as we arranged. I'm not likely to be using it again.'

The Captain cocked a sidelong eye at him. 'How much would you be asking?'

'I think it's up to you to make me an offer. You know what I paid you – and I've had it exactly five days.' George was

46

looking at him very directly. Too directly, the Captain thought.

'Well now – you see – buying and selling are two different things. The market is a bit dead at the moment.'

'That wasn't what you said originally. You told me that there would be no difficulty when the time came to buy it back from me.'

'Ah yes – but we were talking about later in the year, when there'd be more call for this type of job – '

'Oh, come off it,' said George sharply. 'We were talking about a little over two months hence.'

'Oh, sure, sure, sure,' the Captain agreed hastily. 'There'll be no difficulty about taking it *back*. None at all. It's just that I want to get you the best possible price for it *when* we take it back. You've got to know the market, you see. What we want now is a client who definitely wants just that sort of car. Same again?'

'No thank you,' said George coldly. He looked at his watch. 'I'm afraid you'll have to excuse me.'

'Just a minute,' the Captain said. 'Suppose you leave it with me for a few days? I'll run it around a bit, show it to a few prospects like – keep it round at my place so you won't be bothered about this parking nonsense – see what I mean?'

'Do that by all means,' said George. 'Just as long as you get rid of it. Good-bye.' He started to turn on his heel, then, as he saw the other's woebegone expression, his natural kindliness came uppermost. 'All right, Bill,' he said. 'No hard feelings – only don't try to be a little Mister Fixit between young Max and me. There's nothing to fix. She's a very lovely girl, and I'm well on the way to becoming a crusty old bachelor. The very idea of there ever being anything serious between us – why, it's just plain bloody ridiculous. Yes – all right – same again – but they're on me.'

Things were quiet in the Club.

'Just a hypothetical case,' the Captain was explaining earnestly to a solemn little man sitting the other side of the table. 'Well, maybe not *exactly* hypothetical. It concerns an old Army mucker of mine. You see, he got this job up in Finchley, selling cars on commission, and there's this nice little used bus – marked ninety quid. You could have got it down to seventy if you knew what you were about. Well now, this other fellow – overseas chap on leave – is in the market for a good used car, quick. He's a bit out of touch with prices, and has got plenty of rent. *Stinking* with it in fact. So this mate of mine happens to meet him sort of socially – away from the shop I mean. "You want a car?" he says. "I can let you have a beauty. Just come in – couple of years old, but showroom condition." The usual bullshit in other words. "How much?" asks the client. "Half a monkey," says my mate, meaning to go on, " – to anybody else, but I could get it for a hundred". The client had had a few jars by this time and he just shrugs and says, "Hm – two hundred and fifty pounds is rather more than I wanted to spend, but all right, deliver it to me in the morning." I tell you I – I mean my mate – nearly swallowed his glass. He said, "But you'll want to see it first, won't you?" But the client says, "Why? You're the expert, aren't you?" Then they fix up a sort of gentleman's agreement that my mate's firm will buy the buggy back at a reasonable price when the client goes back to India after his leave is up in a month or so's time. Nothing written – just verbal. My mate goes in to the shop next morning and tells his boss he's got a quick sale for seventy quid – cash – take it or leave it. "Take it," says the boss – so my mate does so, and the thing goes through smooth as butter – and he's a hundred and eighty lovely quid up, plus a tenner commission he gets on the sale at seventy.'

'Lovely grub,' said the solemn little man. 'What's his bellyache then?'

'The client changes his plans after two or three days and wants to turn the car in on the resale arrangement they'd made. Well, at the very most you couldn't expect him to drop more than fifty quid on the deal, so that would mean that I – my mate – would have to dub up a couple of hundred, and be stuck with a car that he doesn't want, and couldn't get forty quid for even if he busted a gut. What my mate wanted to know, is suppose the client got a bit shirty and happened to go to the firm, and it all came out? Is he liable for anything?'

48

'You mean your mate?'

'Yes.'

'Not if he bought the car from the firm, and then sold it as a separate transaction.'

'No – he didn't actually do that,' said the Captain nervously.

'You mean he sold the car on *behalf* of the firm for two hundred and fifty pounds, and rendered unto the firm seventy, keeping unto himself the sum of one hundred and eighty pounds for his own use and convenient advantage, while an employee of said firm? Stealing while a servant, the prosecution would call that. Eighteen months and a two hundred quid fine or a further six months in default I'd say – Oh, no – wait a minute. You've got form, haven't you? False pretences, wasn't it? Sorry. I mean your *mate's* got form.'

'There's no need to rub it in.'

'I'm not. I'm just stating facts. You can tell your mate that if that lot goes through bang to rights he's got three years' porridge up his shirt.'

'Jesus!' said the Captain hollowly.

'Thing to do is for your mate just to stall him along until he goes overseas again, and keep him away from the firm at all costs. You understand? It's the *firm* you've – I mean your mate – has committed an offence against. *They're* the people who would be filing the complaint against you. The other bloke wouldn't have a case if it was only a gentleman's agreement and not in writing. He'd be a first class witness for them though.'

'And the firm are just the buggers who *would* file a complaint. I could keep the *bloke* happy, if young Max would just co-operate,' the Captain said dolefully.

'Who's young Max?'

'My mate's niece.'

'We're getting a bit mixed up aren't we? If it's my professional advice you're after you'll have to be frank.'

'Yes, my sister's daughter.'

'The client is having it off with her, I take it?'

'She's not that sort of girl,' the Captain expostulated. 'Anyhow, between you and me, I don't think he'd know what to

49

do with a piece if it was served up to him on a plate. Real starry-eyed innocent he is. Well, I ask you – a berk who would buy a banger at asking price, sight unseen, isn't exactly a worldly type, is he?' He shivered. 'At the same time I've got an idea that he *could* turn nasty. Bloody nasty.'

'How old is your niece?' the solemn little man asked.

'Just turned twenty-one. Why?'

'Pity. If she was under age of consent you'd only have to catch him on the job and you'd have him by the short and curlies. Is he married, by the way?'

'No.'

'Another pity. In a case like this a threat to tell the wife all about it usually has the desired effect.'

'Anyhow,' the Captain said. 'We're wasting time even talking about it. He's got a rush of blood to the fork over her, but she just isn't interested, in spite of his money. This bloody talent scout has got her on a string now and she's just about gone off her rocker. I'd like to catch *him* on the job, by God. I'd Bradley the bastard – '

The little man jerked upright. 'Bradley?' he said. 'Did you say Bradley?'

'That's right. Why – ?'

'The Drag-and-Donkey king? Comes in here quite a lot?'

'He comes in here all right, but what the hell's "drag-and-donkey" mean?' the Captain asked.

'Contractor,' the now not quite so solemn little man explained. 'He supplies horses, donkeys, camels, bloody elephants if you like, and cars – posh numbers *and* breakaways for crash scenes. Anything at all in the special effects line. Biggest in the business. Started as a young diddikai round the studios, now he's worth a fortune. Lovely house in Wimbledon, married to a clapped-out actress, kids in posh public schools and all that. He's breaking his neck to put up a respectable front, but he can't keep off the women – young ones, and they've got to be lookers, by God.'

'Well, he's in the right business to get 'em,' the Captain sighed enviously.

'You mean talent scouting?'

'What else?'

'It's phony in his case. He just uses that as a hook. He's been warned about it by every one of the studios. Gets 'em a bad name if things leak out – and they have once or twice. He's been a bit more careful lately – but Christ, he's pulled some raw ones in the past.'

'And that's the skunk who's got my niece in his power?' the Captain declaimed. 'By God! I'll kill him.' He jumped to his feet.

'Sit down,' said the little man. 'You sound like an out-of-work scriptwriter.' He rubbed his chin thoughtfully. 'This could be interesting though. Very – very interesting – '

'Well, thanks for the warning. I'll have something to tell the silly little cow when I get home.'

'What good do you think that would do? Once they're on the hook, they're on the hook, my friend, and you could talk to them until you're blue in the face without getting them off it – for the simple reason they don't *want* to come off it.'

'It's a matter of family pride,' the Captain said. 'I mean, a man can't stand by and watch his own flesh and blood being made a fool of by some randy son of a bitch – '

'Your concern does you credit,' the little man said dryly. 'But going into things like a bull in a china shop is not going to help anybody. It's *him* you want to be getting after. You want to put the fear of God into him. Make *him* drop *her* – '

'All very well – but how?'

'That's something we'll have to work out. The immediate objective is, as I see it, to protect an innocent girl's honour, not to mention your family pride, and then to catch her on the rebound and get her snugged up with your client, who we hope will be sufficiently gratified as to relinquish any ideas he may have of nailing your twitching hide to the barn door, in the matter of the motor car. Am I correct?'

'I suppose so,' the Captain agreed reluctantly. 'But actually all I wanted to find out was whether anybody has a case against *me*.'

'Well, I've assured you of that. They have, my gallant Captain.' He chuckled throatily. 'Oh, yes, they've got a case all right. If the firm and the client get their heads together you're a dead duck.'

'Best thing I can do is to bugger off for a time until he's gone back to India and things have had a chance to settle down,' the Captain said moodily.

The little man shook his head. 'Last thing I would advise,' he said. 'You stay away for, say, a year and nothing happens – then, lulled into a feeling of false security, you come back, and the next thing you know the local law has pulled one off the files and slapped it across your bracket. They never chase small fish, my dear Captain. They just wait for them to swim back into the net. Oh, no – flight is the ultimate counsel of despair in a matter such as this.'

'Then what the hell do I do?' the Captain said wildly.

'Keep a cool head in the first place.' The little man glanced pointedly towards the bar. 'Perhaps we might – er – ?'

'Sure, sure,' said the Captain hastily. 'Charlie! Same again.'

'Thank you. Well now, look. I think there may be a possible way out of all this, with a minimum of discomfort to everybody concerned, with the possible exception of our Mr Bradley, who is a slag of slags anyhow – Thank you, Charlie – Your health, Captain. Oh, yes – as I was saying – I wouldn't charge you for my advice but I'd need a little for expenses, of course – '

'But there's no need for it,' Mrs Wilmott sobbed. 'You've got a good home here.'

'Sorry, Mum,' Max said with complete finality. 'I've got nothing against you, or Dad, or even that old bum of a brother of yours, but I just can't go on having my every movement questioned and criticized. I'm not going to the other side of the world – only to the other side of London, and I'll come and see you – often.'

'But *where* are you going? – *Where?* Your own mother has a right to know that, surely.'

'I'd rather not say at the moment. Not until I've settled in properly – then you must come across and see me.' She snapped the suitcase shut and smiled brightly at her mother. 'There now – no more tears. Damn that taxi. I told him to be here at three.'

'But what's it all going to cost?' Mrs Wilmott wailed.

'No more than I can afford. I'll be saving thirty shillings a week to you, remember, and I won't have fares every day.'

'I don't know what your father is going to say.'

'He can say what he likes – I'm twenty-one – '

The Captain called from the bottom of the stairs, 'Your taxi's here, pet,' then went up and carried her suitcase down. 'Oh, pipe down, Kate,' he said as Mrs Wilmott burst into a fresh paroxysm of weeping. 'She's not going to bloody Siberia. Where *are* you going, by the way?'

'Sorry, Nunks – I'm not even telling you – Not yet, anyhow.'

'Maybe you're right,' he nodded sagely. 'But I think you ought to have said good-bye to your old man. He won't even know you've gone until he comes home tonight.'

'It's because of him that I'm keeping it dark. I don't want him coming across and making a scene. 'Bye, Mum – Cheer up.' She kissed her mother and patted the Captain on the cheek and climbed into the taxi. He stood and watched it until it had turned the corner, then he gently propelled the tearful Mrs Wilmott into the house and pulled the front door shut. He crossed quickly to the side lane where George's car was parked, got in and followed in the path of the taxi.

An hour later he went into a telephone box and dialled a number. 'Is that you, Mr Metcalfe?' he asked. 'Good – no trouble at all. It's Redfern Place, just off Holland Road, number thirty-two. It's the first floor front flat. I saw her at the window as she was drawing the curtains.'

'Hm – and very nice too,' the little man said. 'Redfern Place? Big four-floor villas cut into eight furnished flats, with a porter in the basement – ?'

'That's right.'

'I know damn well it's right, my friend. A front flat would cost her five guineas a week plus light, heating and telephone – another guinea at least – unless, of course, she happened to have a generous landlord, and *she* has. The landlord of *that* particular house, and the three either side of it, happens to be our Mr Bradley. Not that he'd ever admit it to anybody, least of all her.'

'How the *hell* do you know that?' asked the amazed Captain.

'It was my guv'nor who put the conveyance through. That was when I was managing clerk to Braithwaite and Dempsey, the miserable bastards.' The little man chuckled happily. 'Good, good. Well now, I think we'll give the lovebirds say, forty-eight hours to get settled in, and then I'll discuss my plan of operation with you. Meantime, I'd like to meet the father of the wronged maiden – No, not at his home, nor mine – nor yet that sink of iniquity of a club. Make it Battersea Park, in your car, at half-past eight tomorrow night. And listen – don't tell Papa the address, in case he jumps the gun. Don't tell *anybody*. 'Night. You've done a great job.'

The Captain hung up feeling as if he had been patted on the head by the Colonel.

Mr Wilmott said, 'I'll kill him,' and growled in the back of his throat.

'Oh, for Christ's sake, you've said that fifteen times in the last hour,' the Captain said wearily. 'If you killed him you'd get topped for it – or do twenty-five years cracking rocks on Dartmoor, which would be bloody nigh as bad.'

'Nobody's going to make a kept woman out of *my* daughter.'

'Yes, you've said that too. Well, we're going to put a stop to it, aren't we?' the Captain went on. 'That's if you're sensible, and listen to me. Now this bloke is a lawyer – or as good as – some say a bloody sight better. He's managing clerk, or was, to a big firm of solicitors in the West End. They do a lot of work for the film companies – '

'I'll kill him,' said Mr Wilmott heavily.

'Aw – shit! Will you listen to me – I'm talking about my pal, not the bloke she's gone off with. He wants to meet you, with me of course, and a minder – that's a feller who sees that the other feller doesn't start any rough stuff. Then we're all going along when we know they'll be together – in the early hours so we'll catch them in – well, in the early hours. Then we'll sort this feller out and put the fear of God into him – and bring

Max home. No more trouble. See what I mean?'

'She had a good home here, and we always brought her up decent,' said Mr Wilmott and started to cry.

There was the little man and a very much larger one, and they waited in the shadow of an overhanging plane tree. The little man wore a long tight black overcoat and a bowler hat, which made him look rather like a ninepin in mourning. The big man wore a dark raincoat and a trilby pulled down over his eyes, and one had the impression that he would have large feet in thick-soled, well-polished shoes had it been light enough to see. He made the Captain feel ill at ease. A near-by church clock struck three.

The little man said in a low guarded voice, 'Right – they're in. He's been there since ten o'clock last night – '

'I'll kill him,' said Mr Wilmott mechanically.

'You'll do nothing of the sort,' the little man said sharply. 'Now, listen. We go in through the front door. This gentleman has a key that will manage that. We then go up the stairs – tiptoes please – and the flat door is facing us on the first landing. This gentleman will then unlock that door also, and we go in. Now we want no noise – no noise at all – and we certainly don't want any breaches of the peace – even though we can all appreciate a father's feelings. Got that? Good. This way then.'

They filed up the steps and huddled under the portico as a policeman passed the end of the street, flashing his torch into doorways.

'Quick, Terry,' the little man urged. 'That rozzer will be coming back this side in a couple of minutes.'

'Seven and a half,' corrected the big man. 'That's the end of his beat. He makes his point there with the bloke on the next. This used to be my patch.' There was a slight click in the darkness, and the heavy panelled door swung open silently, revealing a dimly lighted hall. 'There you are, gents,' said the big man. 'Walk on the edge of each step. It's always the middle that creaks.'

They went up to the first landing, and there were butterflies in the stomach and water in the knees of the Captain. The big man stopped in front of a door and looked inquiringly at the little man, who nodded. The big man bent over the keyhole. There was another click and they went through into a small hall. A night-light shone in a Chinese bowl. There were two further doors, one leading into a tiny kitchen, the other into a cosily furnished sitting room.

'Bedroom the other side,' the little man whispered. 'That door there. Now I think the two relatives ought to be the ones to go in, but make certain the injured father doesn't start a donneybrook, Captain. Bradley can fight like a bloody thrashing machine.'

'I don't think I ought to get mixed up any further in a family matter,' the Captain said hesitantly. 'I mean – her father's here – '

'Get on with it,' the little man said, pushing them forward. 'Terry will intervene if there's trouble.'

'I'll kill him,' said Mr Wilmott, but there was now the slightest tremor in his voice.

'Say that once again,' ground the Captain, 'and I'll pull out of the whole thing – ' and then tripped over a footstool and plunged headlong. His head came up against the bedroom door with a thunderous crash and Mr Wilmott, with the air of a non-swimmer about to dive into the Thames, took a deep breath and grasped the doorknob resolutely. He seemed rather relieved to find it locked. Terry, with an agility surprising in a man of his bulk, hurdled the prone figure and performed his little miracle once more with the skeleton key. He felt for the switch and the lights came on. Max was sitting up in bed holding the sheet under her chin and gazing fearfully at the group in the doorway. She was alone.

Mr Wilmott said with deep feeling, 'Thank God for that or I'd have swung for him.'

'Get out,' said Max through clenched teeth. 'Get out, the lot of you before I send for the police.'

Terry went forward and slid his hand under the bedclothes on the unoccupied side with an air of practised expertise.

'Warm,' he pronounced professionally. 'He's here all right. Try the bathroom.'

But they didn't need to because Bradley came out of his own volition in a multi-hued silk dressing gown. He said, 'All right – now suppose you tell me what this is all about?'

'These two are my father and uncle,' said Max, nodding at Mr Wilmott and the Captain. 'I'm sorry about this.'

'So am I,' said Bradley. 'It's usually the husband and the brother. What do you take me for? A bloody pie-can?'

'Quite genuine, Mr Bradley,' the little man assured him. 'This is Mr Arthur Wilmott, and his brother-in-law Captain Sprunt.'

'And who are you?'

'I'm acting for the family.'

'Acting as what?'

'In a legal capacity.'

'And this gink?' He jerked his head at Terry.

'He's a private investigator my firm employs on occasion.'

Bradley nodded slowly. 'I see,' he said. He took a cigarette from a box on the bedside table and lighted it. 'Well, now suppose you get the hell out of it before I start hollering copper. What do you think I am for Cri'sake? A bloody swedebasher up for the dairy show? Go on, beat it.' He kicked the side of the bed. 'That goes for you too, sweetheart. It hasn't come off.'

'I'll kill him,' said Mr Wilmott faintly.

'If you're insinuating that *I* had anything to do with this,' Max said furiously. 'I'll – I'll – ' She choked and burst into tears. 'Get out – all of you. I want to get dressed. *Get out!*'

They drove back to Brixton through the grey and murky dawn. Mr Wilmott said, 'There now, love, it's all over and thank God no harm's been done – we hope. You're coming home again, and the whole thing is going to be forgotten. There now, love – there now – ' and he kept on saying it until Max started screaming and the Captain kicked his brother-in-law on the ankle, hard.

Back at the flat the little man was being eminently reasonable. '*I* don't want any trouble,' he said. 'I'm more than willing to act as mediator between both parties, and I'm sure we can find

57

a way out of this with a minimum of bother all round. Unfortunately, however, the girl's family is angry – very angry indeed. You see, rightly or wrongly they were firmly of the opinion that she was about to be offered a starlet's contract, and they consider that her chances are now ruined. Then that old devil they call the Captain has been in touch with the *People's World*. They're thinking of running a series on "Traps of the Film Business" – you know, pretty young girls being exploited by wealthy tycoons – set up in places like this – love nests – palaces of beautiful sin and all that. I'm afraid if that comes off and first person accounts are given, names will be named. Some busybody has told them that you are not exactly persona grata round the studios at the moment – and I even believe that they know of this er – slight rift in your home life, and the possibility of your wife starting divorce proceedings – *if* sufficient really hard evidence was forthcoming.'

'All right, cut the cackle,' Bradley growled. 'How much?'

'Well – there are two of them – father and uncle – and I feel that the girl herself will require a little heart-balm to restore her *amour-propre*. Then the private investigator will be rendering his account – and there have been a few other incidental expenses. Let's say, in round figures – ten thousand.'

Bradley blinked hard, but otherwise showed no emotion. 'Look,' he said. 'I don't mind springing a couple of hundred just for the sake of peace, but have a bit of sense, man. I'm not *made* of money. How much of this would you be pouching for yourself?'

'Only my legal fees.'

'Oh, yes – let's keep it legal for Cri'sake. And what guarantee would I have that you, or them, wouldn't be coming back for more?'

'I will naturally get something signed by them that would protect you in the future.'

'You better, by God, or it's no deal – and I've got to see them sign it – and it's not going to be ten thousand, or anything like it. Come on, man,' he pleaded. 'Be reasonable. Make an offer – something we can both live with.'

'It's you who should be making the offer, Mr Bradley,'

the little man said. 'And I really think that you'd be wasting your breath at anything less than eight.'

'Call it five.'

'Eight. I'm afraid that's the very lowest figure I could take back to them. Oh, and of course I think they'd prefer cash. No cheques, Mr Bradley. Well, now – when would you like the meeting to be? I think, for your own peace of mind, that it had rather be sooner than later. Don't you agree?'

'Make it – let's see – yes – Tuesday,' Mr Bradley said miserably. 'I've got to raise this, and it doesn't grow on trees. Tuesday after lunch – say half-past two.'

'At your office?'

'Are you crazy? I don't want a shower of villains round my place of business. No, you'd better make it here – the whole lot of them – and I want a cast-iron guarantee that I'm not going to be blacked again – and then the bastards can crawl back into the sewers they came out of.' His eyes were misting slightly.

The little man inclined his head gravely, and went out smiling beatifically.

'I'm buggered if *I'm* signing anything,' the Captain said adamantly. 'Christ, you can get seven years for blackmail.'

'Don't use that word,' the little man said sharply. 'I've told you before.'

'Well, what is it? Bloody dominoes?'

'It's a gentleman's agreement.'

'In that case you don't need anybody's moniker on it.'

Bradley held up a small attaché case. 'Well, here it is,' he said. 'Eight thousand, like you asked for. But you don't get a penny of it until I know just what I'm getting in return.'

'You're getting our joint guarantee that neither Miss Wilmott nor any member of her family will trouble you again in this matter, Mr Bradley,' the little man said. 'You have my solemn word on that.'

'About as much use as a signed photo of Tallulah Bankhead,' said Bradley bleakly. 'All right, what about you others?'

'I'll keep my tripe-trap shut. Word of an officer and a gent,' the Captain promised. 'But no bloody signed chits.'

'And you?'

'I ought to have killed you for what you did to my girl,' Mr Wilmott rumbled. 'But I'm not a vindictive man and we've always brought her up decent, and since – '

'Nail a plank across it, Arthur,' the Captain said wearily. 'Tell the gentleman whether or not you're going to shout the odds about it once you've got the jingle.'

'I'm a man of my word,' Mr Wilmott said with dignity. 'No, I'll keep quiet.'

'What about the girl herself?' Bradley asked. 'Why isn't she here?'

'She's had a very upsetting experience,' the little man explained. 'She declined to be present but she authorized me to speak for her. She agrees not to talk about it in future. The matter is now dead.'

'And you?'

'Me? Oh, I'm only the mouthpiece acting on behalf of these others. It's quite safe with me,' the little man smiled.

'Well, who's actually taking the dough?'

'That will be quite safe with me also,' the little man said, and Bradley handed him the attaché case.

'What about that big yegg you had with you? What did you call him – private investigator?' Bradley asked.

'He had other business today, but I'll see he gets his share,' the little man promised. He rose. 'Well, I'm sure we're all happy that the matter has been brought to a satisfactory conclusion – '

'That's right, Metty boy,' said a bulky man with a heavy black moustache who came in from the kitchen. 'And you, Captain – long time no see. You, I take it, sir, are Mr Arthur Clive Wilmott. We haven't met before, but I am Detective Chief Inspector Beasley, and the gentleman unwinding himself out of the broom cupboard there is Sergeant Charlesworth – and this other gentleman is Mr Spence, the civilian shorthand stenographer. The rest of the boys are down below – quite a lot of them because I thought you'd be having old Terry Wain with you, and he's usually as drunk as David's sow at this time

60

of day, and likely to be awkward – This way, gents, if you please – straight down the stairs. I'd like you along at the station in about an hour, Mr Bradley. You will, of course, be Mr X from now on.'

The Captain croaked out of the side of his mouth, 'Not a bleeding word out of any of you until we've got a lawyer.'

Chapter Three

'I escorted the three male accused to Shepherd's Bush police station, where they were charged. The woman was arrested at her parents' home in Brixton some time later, and brought here. She said, immediately after being cautioned, "Oh, my God – no – I had nothing to do with it. It was them." ' Detective Chief Inspector Beasley closed the notebook from which he had been refreshing his memory, and the three magistrates went into close colloquy. The Chairman then asked if the accused were represented and the Clerk said no.

'Bail?'

'Our inquiries are not yet completed, Your Worship, but there will be no objection at a later stage, although they appear to be having some difficulty in finding acceptable sureties,' the Chief Inspector said.

'First defendant, how do you plead?' the Clerk asked.

'We plead not guilty and reserve our defence,' the little man said crisply.

'You may speak only for yourself,' the Clerk told him, and made a note. 'Metcalfe, not guilty. Next?'

'Not guilty, sir,' Mr Wilmott said in a high pitched squeak.

'Wilmott, not guilty. Next?'

'I'd like to say what happened,' the Captain began, with the air of a man who could explain all if given a fair chance. 'You see, Your Worship, it was like this – '

'You will have the opportunity of presenting your defence at the proper time,' the Chairman told him. 'In the meantime it would be in your best interests to say as little as possible until you are properly advised.' And the Captain mumbled a deflated, 'Not guilty.'

'Maxine Wilmott?' the Clerk queried.

There was room only for the three men in the cramped dock, so Max was sitting on a chair in front of it, hunched forward so that only the top of her head could be seen. Her fingers were plucking at a crumpled handkerchief. She made a strangled noise at the back of her throat and shook her head.

'Speak up please,' the Clerk said sharply, but she only shook her head again, and George, at the back of the public gallery, could see that her shoulders were shaking convulsively, and he wanted desperately to leap the barrier that divided the small and dingy courtroom and go to her side. A policewoman crossed and bent over her and said something, and Max raised a tear-stained face that appeared to him even more beautiful without the make-up that she had obviously not been given time to apply, and managed to articulate a faint, 'Not guilty.'

There was another huddle on the Bench, joined this time by the Clerk, who crooked a finger after a minute or so at the policeman who stood at the door.

'Mr X,' said the Clerk.

'Call Mr X,' bellowed the policeman, and Bradley, who had been waiting in the corridor, came in and was beckoned to the witness box. A court orderly put a bible in his right hand, and a dogeared card in the other, and Bradley read out in a gabble, 'I swear by Almight' God that the evidence I give will be truth, whole truth, noth' but truth', then looked rather bored.

The Clerk said, 'The court is in possession of your name and identity, but these will be protected by the use of the pseudonym "Mr X". You understand?'

'I do,' said Bradley.

'I ask the Press to take particular cognisance of this. Disclosure of the identity or publication of a photograph of this witness would constitute a grave instance of contempt, with the most serious consequences for publisher, editor and reporter concerned.' He turned back to Bradley. 'Mr X, you understand, I believe, that these are merely committal proceedings, and the Bench will most probably grant an adjournment before hearing detailed evidence, but in order for His Worship to determine whether or not a prima facie case has been made out, the court would like you to recount briefly the events of the early hours of the fifteenth instant.'

'Well,' said Bradley, 'I was in this apartment – '

'Which apartment?'

'One which I use occasionally if I have to be in Town late – on business. I've written the address down – you've got it there.'

'Quite correct. Proceed please.'

'These characters suddenly burst in – '

'Which characters, Mr X?'

'Those three over there.' He pointed to the dock.

'The three male defendants in other words?'

'That's right.'

'The woman?'

'Oh, she was there too, but she didn't come in with the others.'

'You mean she was already there?'

'That's right.'

'And what happened?'

'I turfed the lot of them out.'

'Turfed?' inquired the Chairman.

'Asked them to leave, Your Worship,' the Clerk explained. 'Yes, go on, Mr X.'

'Well, there was a certain amount of argy-bargy, but eventually I got rid of them.'

'All of them?'

'Yes – including the girl. But the little bloke – the short man on the end there – he came back about half an hour later. He made an offer.'

'An offer of what?'

'Well, he said they'd all keep their mouths shut if I paid them.'

'And what sum, if any, was mentioned?'

'He asked for ten thousand pounds.'

'What was your reaction to that?'

'Violent. I would have thrown him out, but it suddenly struck me that this was one that I had to get fixed – and fixed good, or I'd never get them off my back, so I stalled this fellow

64

along – told him that I had to have a proper assurance from each of them that they wouldn't be coming back for more, and all that sort of thing, and we arranged to meet, all of us, a couple of days later.'

'Where?'

'In the same apartment. Then I went to the police and – '

'And thereafter acted under their instructions,' the Clerk interposed quickly. 'Thank you, Mr X – just a moment please, in case the Bench have any further questions.' The Chairman shook his head, and passed the Clerk a note.

'You are remanded in custody until the twenty-third,' the Clerk told the accused. 'If acceptable sureties are forthcoming between now and then, application for bail may be made at any time, whether or not the court is sitting. Next case.'

George saw the four being shepherded down a flight of stairs behind the dock, and he slipped out of his seat and found his way to an office on the ground floor.

'I'd – I'd like to stand bail for one of those people in the last case,' he stammered to the sergeant at the desk.

'I don't think it's been fixed yet, sir,' the sergeant said. 'That'll be done by the Clerk and the DCI. Won't be long. Two drunks and an abortion, all pleading guilty, then they'll be rising. You a householder?'

'Well – I own a house. At least my sister and I do between us.'

'Have you stood as surety before?'

'No – I'm afraid I'm very ignorant of these matters – I – I mean – ' He was becoming tongue-tied and he could feel himself going scarlet. 'I have some money with me, but maybe not enough. Would a cheque – ?'

'Oh, you don't have to hand anything in – not yet you don't,' the sergeant smiled indulgently. 'That's only if they don't surrender to bail when called.'

'I see – ' said George blankly. 'You mean – ?'

'You merely sign an undertaking to be responsible for the accused at this stage,' somebody said behind him, 'and you are required to supply proof that you have sufficient means to pay the amount of bail into court should he abscond. The fact that you are a householder, or owner, is usually accepted without further guarantees.'

George turned and saw a man who put him strongly in mind of Stanley Baldwin – square, resolute, no nonsense – albeit rather redder of nose, with wing collar past pristine freshness, and over all a certain dustiness.

'Oh – oh – thank you,' said George gratefully.

'Not at all,' the other assured him gravely. 'I know how confusing these things can be to a layman. Confusing to *us*, indeed, until one gets to know one's way around these courts,' he added confidentially.

'You're a lawyer?'

'That's the generic term. Solicitor.' He fished a grubby card from his waistcoat pocket. 'Sinclair. I'm well known in these regions. Ask the sergeant there.'

'Not 'arf,' grunted the sergeant.

'Of course you'll have your own man-o'-law, but if there's anything I can do to help, purely unofficially of course, until he turns up – '

'I haven't a lawyer as a matter of fact – '

'Relative of one of the accused?'

'Oh, no – I just happen to know Miss Wilmott – and I'm sure there's some ghastly mistake – I just – well – wanted to help – '

'I'm sure you can,' Mr Sinclair said. 'But there are many more congenial places than this to discuss matters.' He took George's elbow and shot a meaning sideglance in the direction of the sergeant, then gently piloted him out of the room.

'You bet there are,' the sergeant remarked laconically to the constable. 'The saloon bar of the Horse and Hound being one of them. Sinkie's got himself a right mug there, the crafty old git.'

'He needed one. He hasn't had a dock brief for months,' the constable said. 'Tried to bite me for half a dollar yesterday.'

'Now you just relax,' Mr Sinclair was saying, setting an example over a double brandy and water. 'This can be a most distressing experience seeing – er – someone we care for in

66

this predicament. Thing is to get her out of it – as quickly as possible.'

'You think you can?' asked George anxiously.

'Well, not me personally – I mean, I'm not retained by you – I'm just giving you a little advice from my not altogether limited experience in these matters, if you see what I mean.'

'*Could* I retain you?'

'Oh, now,' mused Mr Sinclair, stroking his chin reflectively. 'I'm afraid I've got a pretty full list at the moment – '

'Could you recommend another solicitor?'

'A dozen – quite good ones – and probably far less expensive than I – I'm not cheap, you know – on the other hand I do know this particular aspect of the law rather better than most, if you'll excuse a little professional egotism.'

'I wish you could,' George said wistfully.

'Um – lemme see.' Mr Sinclair took a notebook from his pocket and riffled through the pages. 'I'd better have a few particulars, Mr – er – ?'

'I'm so sorry – Quaife – George Quaife – '

'Married, Mr Quaife?'

'No – '

'You live with your sister I thought I heard you say?'

'I *stay* with her, and my mother, when I'm in this country. I'm home on leave from India at present.'

'Army?'

'Tea – '

'That so? Splendid life a planter's I should say.' Mr Sinclair's interest visibly increased. 'Yes – very well, Mr Quaife. I don't mind helping out in a special case such as this. Now, I take it that you are not concerned with the other three defendants?'

'Not in the slightest. I bought a car through Sprunt – that's her uncle, but I've never met her father or that other chap.'

'The other chap happens to be a damned little fraud who has had the impertinence to pass himself off as a solicitor on occasion,' said Mr Sinclair splenetically. 'Actually a one-time solicitor's clerk, who has been imprisoned for fraud. Name of Metcalfe – nasty piece of work. The same goes for Sprunt. Theft and false pretences I think in his case. The father is a complete stranger to me, but *he* doesn't look a very prepossessing type either. Good – far better chance of getting the girl off if we can separate her from the villains.' He looked at his watch. 'Well, His Worship and the rest of the Bench will be lunching upstairs here, and the Clerk of the Court will be drinking his in the back room of the Cat and Fiddle. The court will sit again at quarter-past two. I think I'll go round and see the Clerk, and then we'll have to get hold of the Chief Inspector. Let me see – I'm afraid I hurried away from my office this morning before the banks were open – I might need a little for immediate expenses – '

'Oh, please let me – ' George said, reaching for his wallet.

'Good – good – That will save some time. I may not need anything at all, but I'd better take – er – ' He cocked an appraising eye at the wallet, 'say, fifty, to be on the safe side. I'll let you have a detailed account at the end of it, of course. Right – I'll see you in the lobby outside the courtroom at half-past two. Chins up in the meantime.' Mr Sinclair hurried out of the saloon bar as light of heart and foot as a miner who has just stumbled upon the mother lode.

'Right, miss,' the sergeant said. 'Just sign here for your property, will you? Handbag, powder compact, lipstick, little thingummy box, couple of doodads, sum of seventeen and fourpence-ha'penny and the belt off your raincoat. Thank you. Now you understand your commitment to the court, sir? The lady is remanded until the twenty-seventh. Anyhow, Mr Sinclair knows the form. Good-night.'

They came out into the evening gloom.

Max said in a small beaten voice, 'I don't know why you're doing all this for me.'

'Well – we're – er – I mean to say – Well – we're friends – ' stammered George.

'Right,' said Mr Sinclair. 'You know your way? Richmond – just over the crest of the hill. Cropley Arms. The landlord's an old friend and client of mine – I'm happy to say all my clients remain my friends. He'll be expecting you – you'll be very comfortable there, Miss Wilmott, and nobody will disturb

68

you. Sign the book as Mrs Curtis. I'll call you there each day. We'll be meeting between now and the date of the next appearance, Mr Quaife. I've got your address and telephone number. Now good-night to you both, and don't worry.' He closed the door on them and George drove off. Max was crying quietly. He took one hand off the wheel and put his arm round her shoulders.

'Don't – don't, Max,' he said gently. 'It's going to be all right – I promise you.'

'What must you think of me ? What must *everybody* think ?' she sobbed.

'I think you've been through a very unfortunate experience,' George said. 'And I'm damned certain none of it was your fault. Mr Sinclair told me of the talk he had with you in the – in the – '

'Cells,' she said, and shuddered. 'Oh, it was awful – *awful*. I thought I'd have died of shame. That beast – that *beast* Brian Bradley. First he told me that he was fixing this screen test for me – then he said I'd have to have a better address than Brixton, and that he knew of this flat that belonged to a friend of his and it would be vacant for three or four weeks, and that I could have it rent free – just until after the screen tests and the signing of contracts – and – and the publicity photos and all that – and I believed him – I *believed* him – What sort of idiot must I look – ?'

'The *bastard*,' ground George.

'Then he came round that night – he had another key – and – and – I told him he'd have to go – and I was getting really annoyed – and – then Dad and uncle Bill and these other awful creatures came crashing in – and – and – '

'No more, dear – no more,' George begged. 'You mustn't distress yourself. We're going to get you out of this – I promise you – I *promise* – '

'But I'll never be able to face anybody again – the people at work – the neighbours – '

'There's no need for you to go back – either to your place of work or the neighbourhood – '

'But I've got to,' she cried. 'I've got to work – and I've got to live somewhere – and now my mother will be on her own if they put Dad away – Oh – ' She broke into a fresh storm of weeping.

'Please, Max – please – don't. You'll make yourself ill. Leave it to me – leave it all to me,' he urged. 'I'll take care of everything.'

'Why should you?'

'Because that's what friends are for. Someone to rely on when the going gets tough.' He was aware of sounding like a Hollywood B movie, but there was a world of sincerity there also, and it was getting through to her.

'After all I did to you the other night – ' she mourned.

'You did nothing to me the other night.'

'I did – I *did* – and it was because of *him*. I knew you were waiting, and I stood you up – just because he said he could get me a screen test. It serves me right – everything that has happened.' She turned in her seat and buried her wet face in the rough tweed of his sports jacket like a small sick animal, her fingers convulsively clawing at his arm. 'But I didn't do what he said I did – You know? – lead him on and then try and get money out of him. I *didn't*. You don't believe that, do you? *Please* – you don't believe that – ?' She was becoming frantic again.

'Good God Almighty no,' he swore. 'And neither does anybody else – '

'But they *do*. There was a bitch of a policewoman on duty last night. She didn't say anything – not directly to me – but I could see her sneering all the time, and I heard her say something about "little whores" to one of the bobbies – '

'She didn't mean you.'

'*Oh yes she did* – and everybody is going to think the same. It has been in all the papers – even in the *Brixton Messenger* – my mother told me – "Local Girl on Attempted Blackmail Charge." Oh, Mr Quaife, what on earth am I going to do?'

'Mr Quaife be damned. My name is George,' he said brusquely. 'And you're going to dry your eyes, and when we get to this pub you're going to have a stiff drink, and after that a good dinner. Now come on – that's an order. You didn't know I was a soldier, did you? I am. Calcutta Light Horse – that's cavalry – like your Territorials over here. Very smart crowd the old CLH – you should see us on parade – ' He was jabbering now.

'I wish I could – I wish I was ten thousand miles away from here – '

'Well, perhaps some day you will be. We go out on paper-chases on Sundays – mounted, you know – ' He stopped. 'Yes – perhaps some day you will be,' he said slowly. 'That's if you want to. India's a wonderful place. I know it sounds disloyal to my family, what's left of it, but I'm always glad to see Tilbury disappearing over the stern of the ship – '

'If ever I got away from here I'd never come back,' she said passionately. 'Never – never – *never*.'

'There's no reason why you shouldn't get away,' George said quietly. 'That's something we could talk about later. Now let's see – I think we turn left for Richmond here – '

'George – what if they find me guilty?' She was trembling like a leaf and her voice was a cracked frightened whisper.

'They're not going to,' he said firmly. 'If I thought for a moment that they were, I wouldn't let you appear. I'd whisk you away somewhere.'

'But you'd lose a thousand pounds then, and probably go to prison yourself.' She was staring at him through the darkness, her face a white blur. He laughed and aimed a mock punch at her jaw, sideways, then touselled her hair – and he was amazed at his own temerity. It was the first time he could ever re-member taking a liberty with a 'nice' girl.

'You old silly,' he scoffed. 'As if a thousand quid mattered. But we're talking nonsense. Sinclair is going to try and have the case against you dismissed, so you probably won't even have to appear again – or if you do, it will only be to be acquitted.'

'Oh, God,' she breathed. 'Do you think he'll manage it?'

'He's pretty certain of it, and I understand that he's the best lawyer in London in this sort of case.'

'But what must it be costing you? And how am I ever going to pay you back?' she wailed.

71

'I only pretended to slug you then,' he said gaily. 'But you talk about cost and paying back and all that, and I'll do it properly.'

The Cropley Arms was frankly a pub, albeit a cosy one set in a small walled garden a stone's throw from the Star and Garter Homes, but the occasional letting of a couple of small bedrooms on the upper floor justified its elevation to hotel status. George went into the saloon bar alone. It was empty except for a fat man behind the counter.

'I believe you have a room reserved for Mrs Curtis,' he said.

'That's right, guv,' said the fat man. 'That's you just arrived in the car outside, is it?'

'Yes.'

'Good. I'll send the girl out for the luggage. Can I be getting you anything in the meantime?' He gestured towards the glass shelves behind him.

'There is no luggage,' George said awkwardly. 'Not at the moment, I mean. That will be coming along later.'

'I see.' The fat man pushed the register across the bar. 'Just the one of you like?'

'Yes – can you manage dinner for two though?'

'Sure – ' And then the idea came to George for the first time.

'On second thoughts I'll stay overnight too,' he said, and felt himself going red again.

'That'll be *Mr* and Mrs Curtis then if you don't mind,' said the fat man. 'Doesn't matter to me as long as things are kept quiet, if you see what I mean, but the missus gets raspy if she thinks there's a bit of that-there going on. Welsh,' he added confidentially. 'You know what *them* buggers are like.'

'We would require separate rooms,' George said coldly.

'Oh, sorry,' mumbled the other. 'No offence. I didn't quite understand when Mr Sinclair rang. Two rooms – certainly, sir.'

'And I'd like a private sitting room please. There'll be certain conferences over the next day or so.'

'Well, there's only the snug besides this and the dining room – of course I could book it to you alone – but I'm afraid

72

that would mean having to charge you extra and – '

'That will be all right,' said George shortly. 'You can serve our dinner in there – and I'd like a large whisky and water – and a brandy for the lady.'

'Yes, sir – certainly, sir – right away, sir,' said the fat man, and George, mollified, said, 'Have one yourself – and put a bottle of champagne on ice for me.'

They had soup, a good steak, a pêche melba for Max and a slice of Stilton for George, then they sat over coffee and the brandy he insisted upon rather than the sticky liqueur she named. She brought a surprisingly good appetite to the meal, and that, and the two glasses of champagne she drank with it, had brought the colour back to her cheeks and a sparkle to her eyes, and the terrors of the earlier day were in temporary retreat.

She said, 'I've never stayed in a hotel before,' and hunched her shoulders contentedly. 'It's nice.'

'This is not a very grand one,' George smiled. 'Although they do seem to be doing their best to make us comfortable.'

'Do they have hotels in India?'

'Oh, yes. Some of them are very good. The Taj Mahal in Bombay and the Grand and Great Eastern in Calcutta are supposed to be at least the equal of first class London hotels.'

'It must be wonderful,' she said dreamily.

'You mean the country? Yes – yes – I suppose it is. It grows on one. I felt desperately strange and lonely when first I went out there – but that soon passes.'

'It's always fascinated me,' she said. 'I don't know why.'

'Yes, so your uncle told me,' he said, and realized that it was the wrong thing as her face clouded.

He reached across and took her hand. 'Stupid of me,' he said. 'Forget it. Put it out of your mind. It's going to be all right. I'm going to phone my home now or my mother and my sister are going to wonder what's become of me. What about you? Would you like to call your mother and tell her you're quite safe?'

'We're not on the phone,' she said.

73

'I could ask my sister to go round,' he said, and knew deep relief when she reacted violently.

'Oh, my God no!' she gasped. 'That would send the balloon up proper – *properly*. Staying at a hotel with the posh Mr George Quaife – on top of everything else? I think she'd rather I was safely in the nick.' She covered her mouth with her hands. 'Oh, wasn't that an awful thing to say? I didn't mean that you – well – that you'd – ' She struggled to repress a giggle, and then came the blessed release of laughter to them both.

'Didn't mean that I'd what?' he demanded, a shade archly.

'You know perfectly well what I mean – so don't try to make me say it again. Any rate, I know that you wouldn't – '

'If you mean what I think you mean, don't you be so sure, young woman. In fact you should be thanking your lucky stars that I'm a steady old codger nearly old enough to be your father.'

'Fiddlesticks. You're not old, and you look as hard as nails.'

'Nice of you to say so. Actually I *am* pretty fit. Of course we have to keep in trim out there.' He was in the saddle now and the devil was driving. 'Funny thing that. We notice it when youngsters first come out East. We older men are always in so much better shape. We just have to be.'

'For polo and things like that?'

'Yes – and point-to-point and shikar.'

'What's that?'

'Shooting – tigers, panther, that sort of thing. One goes off into the jungle for days on end – sometimes on foot, with just a couple of servants – bearers and so on – other times on an elephant – all depends on the time of the year. But whatever you do, you need a clear head and a steady hand. We drink hard, play hard and *stay* hard. That's the motto of the planter.'

'Go on,' she said, her eyes aglow. 'Please go on. I could listen all night.'

'That would probably be safer for you, but it's time you were in bed,' he said. 'Go on – off with you before I start getting ideas.' He rose and held both hands out to her and pulled her from her chair. She came forward to him and raised her face, her eyes closed. He kissed her gently, and then found

74

himself trembling.

'That's enough of that,' he said gruffly. 'I'm sorry – really sorry – I should have had more sense.'

'What are you sorry about?' she asked softly.

'I didn't bring you here just to cash in on it – to take advantage of the situation, I mean,' he said. 'I think I'd better push off. I'll be back quite early in the morning, and I'll take you out to do a bit of necessary shopping – you know, a toothbrush and a nightgown and a few odds and ends like that.'

'Don't go,' she begged. 'Please don't go. I'd be scared stiff left here on my own.' She was clinging to him, panic-stricken.

'Look, this is entirely my fault,' he said. 'I should have taken you home to your mother. If anybody ever found out that we'd stayed at the same hotel, even in different rooms, there's only one conclusion they would draw from it.'

'What the hell does that matter now?' she asked ruefully. 'They'll all have drawn their conclusions long ago. But I see what you mean. It wouldn't be very nice for you, would it?'

'It doesn't matter in the least as far as I'm concerned. I'm a man,' he said. 'But it *does* matter to you.'

'I don't care – anyhow, who's to know?' She was still clinging to him. 'Please don't leave me – Please. I've had such a shaking up over this – I just couldn't face being on my own. Oh – *please* – '

'All right – don't cry,' he said softly. 'I'll stay.'

Mr Sinclair said, 'Lovely. We've just got to keep our fingers crossed now, but I think I've got old Chievelly, the Clerk of the Court, round to my view.'

'What about the magistrates themselves?' George asked.

'The Chairman is an eminent pork butcher who doesn't know his posterior from his elbow, legally speaking. He'll do as the Clerk advises him. The other two on the Bench are only there to make up numbers. They don't count. No, Chievelly's our man.' He buried his nose in his glass and slewed an appraising eye round at George. 'I'm afraid it's all costing a bit though,' he added.

'You mean to square him?' George asked innocently, and Mr

Sinclair recoiled in horror.

'My dear sir!' he exploded. 'Square a British court? Unthinkable. No – I meant in the way of expenses. I've had a lot of running about to do after Chievelly. He's not in court the whole time, naturally – he's got a very busy private practice as well – and I've just had to tackle him when I could find him. Of course I've got one or two clerks in various offices squared as you call it, to keep me informed of his whereabouts – couple of pounds here – couple there. It all mounts up.'

'Don't worry about that,' George told him.

'Oh, I won't – but I'd prefer you to know the position now, in order to avoid anything in the nature of a nasty shock later.'

'What do you think the whole thing will total up to?'

Mr Sinclair fingered his chin. 'Well, if as we hope, the lower court decides that she has no case to answer and dismisses her, there will only be another, say, fifty pounds for expenses, and my fee. I'll keep the latter as low as possible, of course, but I'm afraid the Law Society, on whom be peace, would not allow me to accept less than – um – a hundred guineas?'

'So that's another hundred and fifty. Two hundred altogether, counting the fifty I let you have the first day,' George said.

'Of that order,' continued Mr Sinclair, just a little cast down. He had been hoping that the original douceur had been forgotten. 'Give a pound or so – take a pound or so.'

'That will be perfectly all right,' George said, relieved. 'I thought it would have come to more than that.' And Mr Sinclair smothered a grimace of chagrin.

'I think, though,' he said thoughtfully, 'that to make an absolute stone-cold cert of an acquittal, that I ought to take counsel's opinion – and that could be a little more expensive.'

'What does that entail exactly?'

'There is a ship,' Mr Sinclair said, spreading his hands graphically. 'A sound ship, a seaworthy ship – splendidly afloat in *harbour*. You know – you positively *know* – that she'll remain splendidly afloat at *sea* – but the consequences of her sinking would not bear contemplation. So you eliminate all elements of risk – and you send a diver down to examine every inch of her bottom before she sails just in case of a hitherto undetected leak. Counsel is the diver.'

'And what would he charge?' George asked. 'Please don't think I'm cheese-paring, Mr Sinclair,' he added hastily, 'but I'm approaching the end of my leave and I've had one or two unexpected expenses.'

'I quite understand – I quite understand,' said Mr Sinclair sympathetically. 'Well – er – I have a friend – a very able leader in chambers in the Middle Temple – he'd make a special case of it if I put it to him frankly. He's in the three hundred guinea bracket, but I think I could get him down to half that. I've retained him in quite a number of cases in the past – and there's a certain gratitude involved. But, of course, you needn't do this. I feel I can get her off on my own. Counsel would just make, as I say, an *absolute* certainty of it.'

'Retain him,' said George positively. 'That's if you can get him down to a hundred and fifty.' And quiet content reigned in the heart of Mr Sinclair.

'I think you're wise,' he said. 'Another little drink – and this time they are on me – no, no – I insist.'

George, lying in bed blowing smoke rings at the ceiling, and watching Max brush her hair at the dressing table, said, 'I still think you ought to let your mother know you're safe.'

'Like hell I will,' said Max viciously. 'What has she ever done for me, except cadge every bob I ever earned that I didn't have the sense to hide?'

'But she *is* your mother.'

'Worse luck.'

'And she did come to see you when this thing broke.'

'She came to see my father, to whine and howl, and to bite her old deadbeat of a brother for money. All she did as far as I was concerned was to tell me I was a disgrace to the family. *That* bloody family! Don't make me laugh.' She turned and looked at him with fear-widened eyes. 'George – you *are* going to take me away from all this? I mean – you're not going to change your mind?'

He said, 'Come *here* – and leave that damned hairbrush *there.* Now, listen to me go through it all once more – just *once* – and listen carefully,' he went on when she was lying beside him again, 'because this is the last time I'm going to tell you. Tomorrow we go to court, and you're going to hear the police prosecutor say, "the Crown has no evidence to present against Miss Maxine Jane Wilmott – because all three of the others have exculpated her". Do you know what that means?'

'No, but it sounds rude,' she giggled, her face muffled against his neck. 'Go on.'

'It means that they have had the decency to tell the prosecution that you had nothing to do with it. *They* will then no doubt be sent for trial – but *you* will walk from that court without a stain on your character.'

'What a hope,' she scoffed, with a further lightning change of mood. 'Win, lose or draw, my name will be plastered. It is already. Oh, George – it's that that frightens me. Even if we are married in India *someone* is going to find out – and we *both* get dragged through the mud then. And what is your family going to say? – and the people you work for?'

'I don't give a damn what my family says. The company – well, they *can* be a bit sticky. But that will all be fixed up.'

'That's the bit I don't understand,' Max said. '*How?*'

He sighed. 'All right – I'll tell you again. It's a thing called a deed poll, and you use it to change your name, legally. It's perfectly simple – old Sinclair has already got the form from the Crown Stationers. You fill it in under your present name, in front of a commissioner of oaths, and state, "I, Maxine Jane Wilmott, intend from this day onward to be known as Jane Curtis." You sign it in front of him and one further witness – the thing is stamped and sealed – two copies – You keep one, and the other goes round to Somerset House and is attached to your original birth certificate – and filed with another five hundred and fifty million other bits of bumph that collect the dust there.'

'But I thought you could get into trouble for changing your name.'

'If you use an alias for unlawful purposes, yes – but otherwise you can call yourself what the devil you like, *without* a deed poll. The only trouble is in that case you'd have difficulty in getting either a marriage licence or a passport. *With* a deed poll you *are* Jane Curtis – and you can get both in that name. Now have you got all that?'

'Yes – go on.'

'All right – so, having got your passport, we book your passage to India – and I, the other end, in Calcutta, will already have the marriage licence. Miss Jane Curtis arrives, and stuns the whole city – we are married – the company coughs up quite a handsome flat for us – '

'Do we have servants?'

'Of course we have servants, you chump. You can't live in India without them'

'How many?'

'Khansama, khitmagar, couple of bearers, an ayah for you, and a sweeper.'

'*Six*? I don't believe you. Now tell me what that all means in English – the Indian names, I mean.'

'I've got something better to do at the moment. C'mere.'

'George – You are *awful* – awful.'

'This crime has been made the more odious,' intoned Mr Justice Mottesley, 'by the fact that the girl used in the sordid ploy was the daughter of one of you, and the niece of another. The fact that she has been dismissed from the case largely as a result of your exoneratory statement in no way lessens your guilt. She was possibly unaware of your intent to blackmail Mr X when she went to bed with him – I hope she was – but this is a court of law, not a court of morals, and it is you we have to deal with. Anything known?'

'John Eric Metcalfe. Three cases of fraudulent conversion between nineteen-thirty-one and nineteen-thirty-six, M'Lud. Fined fifty pounds on the first, six months and eighteen months imprisonment respectively on the others. One case of theft in nineteen-thirty-four, two years. William Sprunt, twelve months for fraud in nineteen-twenty-eight. Arthur Wilmott, no previous convictions.'

'Metcalfe, I regard you as the ringleader and possibly the instigator of this crime. Your previous punishments failed, quite obviously, to have any salutary effect, lenient though they appear to me in hindsight. You will go to prison for five years.' He made a note, then resumed, 'Sprunt, you also failed to take a lesson from your previous conviction. Three years. Wilmott, you were apparently the junior partner, but your role, although only that of the scullion in this thieves' kitchen, is, in my view the most contemptible by reason of your being the decoy's father. I have to take into consideration however, the fact that you have a hitherto clean record. One year. Take them down.'

A woman screamed in the public gallery.

'Five hundred pounds,' said George handing over a cheque. 'I understand that takes care of counsel also?'

'That's right,' said Mr Sinclair unblushingly. 'He didn't have to appear, but I had to retain him just the same, and that was what his brief was marked. Twice that to anybody else.'

'Oh, I'm not complaining,' George assured him. 'But I've got to be a little bit careful now. It's the end of my leave and I've had a lot of expenses I hadn't budgeted for. I'm going to leave Miss Wilmott here at the Cropley Arms – '

'*Miss Jane Curtis,*' Mr Sinclair corrected. 'You've got to get used to that.'

'Sorry – Miss Jane Curtis – '

'When will you be sending for her?'

'About a month after I arrive back in Calcutta myself.'

'No reason why you shouldn't be married here and take her with you, you know. The deed poll is through, and there's still time to have her passport changed from Curtis to Quaife, or be included on yours. Special licence can be arranged in twenty-four hours.'

George shook his head. 'I'd love to,' he said regretfully, 'but it just wouldn't work out. You see, my company is one of the very old concerns, with rules as rigid as those of the army. They look after us quite well, but we've got to toe the line, and ask formally for permission to get married. The managing director's wife is as strict as any Colonel's Memsahib. No – I'll have to apply for permission, and arrange for a company flat to be made available, and then book her passage that end. They pay for that, thank God – and then, finally, I'll apply for a marriage licence. There's a special arrangement dating right back to the East India Company days governing the marriage of English girls arriving out there. She's got to be accommodated and sponsored and chaperoned and Lord knows what else, from the time she arrives until the actual wedding. A married pal usually does all that – '

'I see. Well, you know your own business best, of course. Oh, by the way – I've got a letter for her here.' Mr Sinclair took an envelope from his inside pocket. 'It's from either her father or that old devil of an uncle of hers. He slipped it to Mellish, their lawyer, in the cells before they were carted off.'

George took it and weighed it speculatively in his hand for a long moment. It was sealed, and the one word 'Max' was scrawled in pencil across its grubby face. Mr Sinclair seemed to guess his thoughts.

'You needn't give it to her if you think it might distress her,' he said.

George shook his head. 'I've got no right to censor her letters,' he said. 'Curiously enough she was quite fond of both of them. It's her mother she didn't get on with. No – I'll give it to her.' He held out his hand. 'Thank you, Mr Sinclair,' he said earnestly. 'Thank you for everything. I don't know what we'd have done without you.'

'We pass this way but once, my boy,' said Mr Sinclair piously. 'So it behooves us to do what we can to aid our fellow men – the *first* time our paths converge. There is no second opportunity – unfortunately. Good-bye, George – and God go with you.'

'Say it again,' said George.

'My name is Jane – my name is Jane – my name is Jane,' said the girl.

'Jane what?'

'Curtis. I won't forget again – I promise.' She looked at the ring on her engagement finger and started to cry.

'*Now* what's the trouble?' he asked, taking her in his arms.

'It's beautiful – it's so *beautiful*. But it must have cost y u a fortune – '

'You mustn't put price tags on everything, Max – er – Jane,' he said. 'Not the things I give you, anyhow. Now listen to me, darling, because there's a lot I must tell you before the boat train leaves – '

'Why can't I come with you to the station?' She moved to the window and stood looking down into the small garden. The evening sun was on her face, bathing it in a soft glow, and he caught his breath as he did so often when some fresh aspect of her flawless beauty was revealed. He came and stood behind her, his hands on her bare shoulders.

'You don't think I don't want you to, do you?' he said softly. 'Of course I do – but Mother and Dorothy will be there. They come down to Tilbury whether I like it or not. Personally I don't give a damn – but you said yourself that you wanted this to be a clean break.'

She nodded slowly, and the tears started once more. 'You're right, of course,' she said. 'But, oh God, it's going to be lonely when you've gone.'

'It's only for a couple of months, and Henry and that old Welsh Rabbit of a wife of his will be looking after you – then you'll be sailing yourself. You'll enjoy the voyage, I promise. Hordes of randy young subalterns and even randier Majors and Colonels coming back off leave. You'll have to watch those.'

'What about the planters? Aren't they randy?'

'Not half – but they're usually as tight as owls by dinner. It's after dinner that danger lurks. Now listen – I'm sorry that I can't advise you about clothes. I know damn all about women's fashions – '

'Don't you worry about that,' she smiled. 'The P & O brochure tells you everything. English summer clothes after Port Said – and nobody wears stockings. I've got it all planned.'

'And I feel an awful louse because I can't leave you much money for shopping,' he went on, frowning.

'Seventy-five pounds, not much money?' she scoffed. 'Listen, you idiot – I had to dress for a year on less than that – and I

82

didn't look such a frump, did I?'

'You've always looked wonderful – but I still wish I could leave more. It's only a temporary shortage, until next month's pay comes in, of course – '

'You've been spending it like water,' she said. 'That boozy old shark Sinclair – God knows what he must have cost you. Then that wretched car my bloody uncle stuck you with. What did you get for it, by the way?'

'Not much,' he grinned ruefully. 'They found the darned thing had a cracked chassis that the gallant Captain must have overlooked – Anyhow, forget it. Incidentally, Sinclair gave me a letter for you from one of them.' He took it from his inside pocket and held it out to her. She recoiled as if it was a snake. 'I don't want it,' she almost spat. 'I won't read it.'

'Please yourself,' he shrugged. 'But fair doos – the poor old bums. They've got plenty on their plates – and quite honestly, I don't think they ever intended you any harm. That little swab Metcalfe was the villain of the piece. I'm sorry for them.'

She nodded slowly and opened the letter and read it, then turned away, and there was a long silence.

'You're quite right, George darling,' she said quietly. 'You're always right. You're always so kind – so gentle – '

'Here,' he protested, pleased but embarrassed. 'You make me sound like bloody Saint Thingummybob. I can be an absolute bastard when I like. Don't you ever doubt that.'

'I won't,' she smiled. She tore the letter into small pieces and dropped them into the wastepaper basket. 'I'll always do just as you want me to – I promise.'

'And that would bore the pants off me. Christ, you've got to have a mind of your own.'

'Oh, I will – I promise that too. I'll answer this letter. They were just saying, both of them, how sorry they were. And Dad asked me to go and see Mum. I'll do that.'

'Will you tell them where you're going? About getting married?' he asked a little anxiously.

She shook her head. 'No. No – I don't think that would be wise – not for some time – nor about changing my name. I'll just say good-bye – and that there are no hard feelings – not on my side – and that I'm going away to make a new life for myself – and that some time in the future I'll see them again – when the scars have healed. I read that somewhere. That's just how I feel – scarred. And they've got to have time to heal.'

He took her in his arms again. 'And you say *I'm* kind and gentle.' He kissed her slowly. 'When do you want to go and see your mother?'

'Some time – sooner the better, before my good resolution fades.'

'I'll take you tonight.'

'But you haven't got the car any longer.'

'I'll get a taxi.'

'It'll cost a *fortune*!' Her voice rose in a horrified squeal.

'There you are – price tags again. Come on – get your clothes on, you scarlet woman.'

He waited in the taxi near the George Canning while she slipped away into the darkness. She was back within ten minutes, and he was relieved, though a little guilty. 'You weren't there long,' he said. 'How did she take it?'

She shook her head. 'She wasn't there. The woman next door says she's gone to her sister's for a few days. I left a note, and my latch-key.' She held his arm in both her hands and rested her head on his shoulder. 'I did try, didn't I? I did do my best.' She sounded like a small child, anxious to please.

'You did your best, darling,' he agreed. 'You're entitled to forget now. The past is dead – *dead*.'

Chapter Four

She leaned on the rail and watched the Essex mud flats re-ceding. The first lights were flickering palely against the grey winter sky, and the northerly wind was whipping the colour into her cheeks and blowing her hair into disarray. She snuggled deeper into the upturned storm collar of her travelling coat, savouring once again the guilt she had felt when she had bought it, for a sum that would normally have covered her entire winter wardrobe. It was probably wanton waste, she reflected. Heavy coats had no place in India, but she hadn't been able to resist it – nor the sheer will-sapping luxury of the cashmere sweater that she wore under it – the soft West of England tweeds – the good brogues and gloves – all things which, as George had told her, would be packed away after the first week at sea, to be replaced by summer frocks. But she was glad she had so equipped herself. All the other women on board seemed to be dressed similarly. She had a natural dress sense, an instinctive flair, and a discerning eye, and she had learned from the smart women who came to the Dover Street hairdressers, and from the pages of the fashion magazines that they read and discussed while under the dryers. No, nobody would be able to fault her clothes. She had a well-balanced wardrobe in which quality had taken precedence over quantity. And her luggage was in keeping. She had once read somewhere that luggage should never be glaringly new, so she had spent some enjoyable hours in the Railway Lost Property salerooms and had bought a good trunk, two hide suitcases and a dressing case, all becomingly battered and with a few intriguing labels giving them a patina of expensive travel.

She had been disappointed to find that George had booked her tourist class, but a quick glance through the passenger list outside the purser's office had reassured her. It would appear that only the very senior, and commensurately old, travelled first class. There was a plethora of Generals, Colonels, Judges and Commissioners on A Deck, together with their wives, but Captains, Lieutenants and plain Esquires, who, for the most part, appeared to be travelling unaccompanied, were in the humbler accommodation. There seemed to be quite a number of single girls travelling also, and she assumed that these were part of the Fishing Fleet that George had told her about; the daughters, nieces and younger sisters who came out to India in the 'Cold Weather' in search of husbands, and she wondered how many would strike lucky before arriving in Bombay. Well, that was one bran-tub she didn't have to dip into. She felt her engagement ring through the finger of her glove and smiled to herself. Yes, safety and security were the real prizes, particularly when conjoined with an assured social position – and what could possibly be more assured than that of Memsahib, as they called married white women out there? The surname went first, according to George, 'Quaife Memsahib' she would be after the short chrysalis interlude of 'Curtis Miss-sahib'. A far cry from 'Maxine Wilmott' – an even further one from 'the defendant Wilmott' of just a few short weeks before. She shuddered. That was all behind her now, thank God. The memory was fast fading, and she no longer woke in the darkness of the night sweating with terror –

The last glimmer of daylight had gone now, and the wind seemed to be increasing and she could feel the slight rise and fall of the deck beneath her feet becoming more pronounced as the ship came out of the estuary. She hoped that she wouldn't be seasick. She hadn't been on the one occasion she had ever been on a ship before – a day trip to Calais from Dover – although lots of others had, because it had been a particularly rough crossing both ways.

The promenade deck was almost deserted – just a couple of early starters leaning on the rail a few yards away – a girl, pretty enough but with a dumpy figure, and a young man in an outlandish sheepskin coat which came down to his ankles and seemed in the dim decklights to be covered in some sort of

86

beadwork – and a tall spare man who was striding round the deck as if his life depended upon it – the dedicated keep-fitter who would do his three miles a day from Tilbury to Ballard Quay come hell or high water. George had told her about these earnest types as well.

Someone came out on to the deck from the saloon entrance, hesitated, then crossed to the rail and leaned on it a foot or so away from her – a dark figure that she took to be a smallish man in the uncertain light until, after a fruitless rummage through several pockets the newcomer asked her if she had a match, and she realized that it was a woman in a peajacket and slacks.

'I'm sorry, I haven't. I left my handbag in the cabin,' she said.

'You don't want to do that too often. Not if you've got money in it,' the other said. 'Damn Goanese stewards – they'd pinch anything. I had a wristwatch go on the way over from Bombay.'

'You've been in India before?' she asked, and the other laughed.

'Oh, yes – I've been in India before. Don't you remember me? Party at Brian Bradley's place. *I* recognized *you* as you came aboard.'

She managed to ride the shock, like a boxer who takes a near knock-out but somehow stays on his feet as a matter of instinct.

'I don't know anybody by the name of Bradley,' she mumbled. 'You've made a mistake.'

'Sure, if you'd prefer it that way,' the woman said. 'But you've got nothing to worry about as far as I'm concerned. The bastard did *me* dirt too, you know.'

'I'm sorry – I don't know you – I *don't*,' she said. There was a note of hysteria in her voice.

'Princess Amina – as was.' The woman laughed shortly. 'I was dolled up like a Marwari bikriwalla last time you saw me. Remember now?'

'Yes – I remember,' Jane said dully.

'Well, don't let it get you down, for Christ's sake. I only made myself known in case it came as a shock later on when

87

there might have been other people around. I'm Mandy Scanlon by the way – I mean that's my real name. What's yours?'

'Jane Curtis.'

'OK, Miss Curtis – we'll meet as strangers if we meet at all. I'm a Returned Empty.'

'What's that mean?'

'Oh, just a silly joke. Girls who go out on the Fishing Fleet and don't make it, come back to England as "Returned Empties". I'm doing it the other way round. I didn't make it in England, so I'm going home – to India.'

'But I thought you had a contract,' Jane said. 'A career ahead of you – '

'A contract, but no career,' Mandy said wryly. 'I happened to be doing a bit of crowd work in an Indian film in Bombay when one of Korda's talent scouts spotted me, and thought I had something. They gave me a starlet's contract, sure – seven quid a week for one year – and they brought me over and the Publicity Department really went to work on me – but it never came to anything. I thought it was going to once, when Brian Bradley came along, but he was just giving me the old run around.'

'So you're not Indian?'

'Half. Maybe only a quarter.' She laughed again dryly. 'You'll see lots of us out there. My old man was a corporal in the Somerset Light Infantry so I'm told. My mother? – God knows. I hardly remember her. I was dumped on the convent steps in Bangalore, and brought up by the nuns. I once swore that if I ever managed to get out of India I'd never go back – but there's damn all for me in England, except maybe go on the bash. On the other hand the fact that I *have* been back to England might give me a bit of standing in Indian films – like the babus who put "failed BA" on their visiting cards. What about you? I mean what are you doing? Tell me to go to hell if I'm being too nosey.'

'I'm going out to be married,' Jane said.

'For sure or on spec?'

'For sure.'

'Lucky bitch. Army?'

'Tea.'

'Even luckier bitch. The Army's fine for social standing, but most of them are as broke as church mice. It's the box-wallas who've got the money.' She sighed. 'I wish *I* could pick one up.'

'You mean a husband?' Jane said. Her fear was abating in the face of the other's earthy philosophy. 'I shouldn't have thought that would have been difficult – with your looks.'

'Dark, Eastern, mysterious? We're ten a penny out there. It's your type of blonde who makes it. Anyhow, I couldn't marry an Englishman – not one of any standing.'

'Why not?'

'Good God! You *are* an innocent, aren't you? Because I'm an Anglo-Indian – a half-chat, a chillicracker, a blackie-white – The first is the polite term – the others are what they call us behind our backs.'

'I can't believe that – I mean that you couldn't marry who-ever you wanted to.'

'Can't you? You wait until you've been out there a bit. You'll see the system in operation then. In fact you'll see it before you get off this ship. All the nice young pukkha sahibs trying to make it with me on the boat deck at night – all palsy-walsy – until we get to Bombay – then they'd look right through me if I was silly enough to make an approach. Can't blame them really. That's the way they've been brought up – and their daddies and grandpas before them.'

'I think that's horrible,' Jane said.

'You do now, maybe. You'll change though, like the rest. Even the bloody missionaries get a bit uncomfortable when we're around, although they'll mix with the lowest caste Indian quite happily. They're doing God's work then, converting them. We're already in the fold – Catholic or Protestant – and there's no need to chase a bus once you've caught it.'

'What about the Indians? How do you get on with them?' Jane asked.

'Not at all. That's our own fault though. We kid ourselves that we're more European than Indian. I could wear a sari and be thought glamorous in England. I wouldn't dare do it in India though – or on this ship.'

'Why not? I thought you looked absolutely lovely in one.'

'Maybe – in *England*, like I said. In India a woman takes her caste from her father in the first place – and she's got to marry within that caste. A white man has no caste in Indian eyes – therefore his daughter is casteless also. A European girl, wearing European clothes, gets the respect due to her because of her *race* – and we Anglo-Indians come in for a bit of it also – or we like to think so. If we dress *Indian* though, we're just casteless – and they regard casteless women as whores. This must sound a bit complicated.'

'It does.'

'You'll learn. Anyhow, it all adds up to the fact that we're not British because they won't have us – and we're not Indian because we won't have *them*.'

A gong sounded softly in the distance.

'That's the dressing gong,' Mandy explained. 'Although you're not supposed to dress the first night out. Come and have a drink, and I'll point out some of the talent.'

'You know some of the passengers, do you?'

'Not a bloody soul – but that's one big advantage of British-Indian society. Everybody fits into their own individual pigeon-hole – and the pigeon-holes are unmistakable.'

They sat in a corner of the smokeroom, and Mandy ordered two gimlets. 'You can do this the first night at sea,' she said. 'Come into the smokeroom unaccompanied, I mean. Not afterwards though. If nobody invites you in here you sneak into the moorghi khana – that means henhouse – the ladies' lounge – and buy one for yourself. Dead loss that.'

'There you are,' she went on as two youths came in from the deck. 'Typical first timers – all pimples and bumfluff, straight from Sandhurst. The other one in the corner – subaltern or junior Captain – been out there for one tour, five years – going back after his first leave – same with that one who has just come in. They're all bachelors – '

'How do you know that?'

'Age. They can't get permission to marry under thirty. If

they do, without permission, they don't get marriage allowance, or quarters or passages for their wives – so none of them risk it unless they have money of their own – and damn few of them have nowadays. Most of these are Indian Army – that's something quite different from the *British* Army.'

'I thought they were all the same,' Jane said.

'My God no. The Indian Army has Indian soldiers and British officers, and they're out for life, except for leave. The *British* Army has British troops as well as the officers – and they only come out for five or six years at a time, then they get posted Home again. You don't get many British Army travelling P & O. They've got to go by troopship generally. Aha! – here come the boxwallas – you watch the oil and water separate now,' she said as another group of young men entered.

'I can't see any difference,' Jane said. 'What does "boxwalla" mean exactly, anyhow?'

'The real boxwalla is a pedlar who goes round the bungalows with odds and ends in a box on his head – soap, needles and cotton – buttons – knitting wools – things like that, but the Army calls anybody in business a boxwalla, no matter how big a job he's got. The boxwallas get their own back by calling the Army the BBBs. That's rude. It means the "Balls and Bullshit Brigade". Hello – here comes a dog-collar. He'll be a priest. The Protestant missionaries don't drink – not when anybody's looking at them – ' Mandy broke off and looked a little preoccupied, then she clapped both hands to her stomach and said, 'Oh, hell – I think I'm going to be sick.' She got up and left hurriedly, and Jane, to her chagrin, realized that she, also, was beginning to feel queasy, so she went out on deck again. They were round the North Foreland now and the ship was feeling the cross-currents of both Channel and North Sea but the fresh air and the fine spray the wind was whipping the length of the promenade deck revived her for a moment, until the rising and falling of a cluster of lights ashore hastened the inevitable, and she hung miserably over the rail and gave her all.

She was only dimly aware of a strong grip on her arm, and a

quiet voice saying, 'That's not a good thing. You'll just go on being sick that way. Try walking.'

'Go away – Leave me alone,' she moaned, but the grip tightened, firmly but not brutally, and she found herself matching the pace of the newcomer, and the agonizing waves of nausea were receding, although it was a long time before she risked opening her eyes. When she did it availed her little as the deck was now completely darkened and she made out only a tall figure muffled to the nosetip in overcoat, scarf and pulled-down cap. She assumed it was the earnest walker she had seen earlier – an elderly man, spare and lanky – and now that her first resentment had abated, she was grateful to him.

'I'm all right now, thank you,' she said faintly.

'Good – I'll leave you at the saloon entrance and you can make a quick dash for your cabin before it comes on again,' he told her. 'You'll probably find you're over it by morning. It's always a bit choppy going round the corner as we are at the moment. Good night.'

She found her double berth cabin with difficulty. Hers was the upper bunk and she viewed it anxiously, but then she met her cabin-mate for the first time – a young and very pretty girl who seemed to be making better weather of it than herself.

'Hello. Not feeling so good? I'm Tessa Storland,' she chattered. 'Would you prefer the lower berth? Please go ahead. I'm reasonably all right – so far.' Jane nodded her thanks dumbly, stripped off her outer clothes and dropped them in a heap and crawled into the bunk gratefully, and the other girl pulled a counterpane over her, switched off the light and departed quietly.

The strain of the last few weeks plus the debilitating effect of seasickness had exhausted her, and she stayed in the cabin for the next thirty-six hours, and the other girl helped her undress, and brought her Bovril and dry toast and kept the large and motherly stewardess at bay until, on the third day, she felt able to face the world again, provided nobody made a loud noise in her hearing or mentioned solid food.

'A hot shower,' advised Tessa. 'Followed by a cold one.

Sounds horrible, I know, but it's what all the old ko'i hais swear by for both hangovers and seasickness, which they say feel much the same. Come on, I'll help you along to the bathroom before all the hearty boys start stirring.'

'What hearty boys?'

'Oh, the usual mob. Subalterns and young boxwallas.'

'You seem to know all about them. Have you been out to India before?'

'I was born there. Usual thing with Army families. The kids spend their first six years out there, then they're brought Home and left with relatives until they're old enough to go off to school.' She was helping Jane into her dressing gown. 'You see your parents thereafter only when they come on leave.'

'You must miss them?'

The girl shrugged. 'At first, yes, but then they become a bit shadowy and blurred round the edges, and you start to dread the leave periods, because you know what a devil of an upset it's going to be again when it's time for them to go back. My father is a bit senior now, and he gets leave every two or three years and comes back for conferences and things like that, and of course my mother comes with him, so I've been seeing quite a lot of them lately.'

'That must have been nice. And now you're going home for good?'

The girl looked slightly puzzled. 'Home? Oh, I see what you mean. Funny thing that – we never refer to India as "Home" even though one may be born there and live all one's adult life there. England is "Home". We usually spell it with a capital "H".'

'You don't like India?'

'I love it. If you've once lived there, even if only as a child, you never completely get it out of your system. I haven't seen it for twelve years, but I know that I'll cry when I see the coast at Bombay, with the Ghats in the distance behind it – and I get that smell of hot earth and wet jungle and – and – Oh, I'm so sorry – ' She broke off, confused. 'I'm talking absolute nonsense.'

'You're not. Please go on,' Jane begged.

93

'Another time – Here's the bathroom. I'll see you back in the cabin.'

Jane came out on to the promenade deck at midmorning, and a steward cocooned her in a travelling rug and settled her in a long chair, and another brought her a cup of hot bouillon and since the day was beautiful and she was a creature of magnificent health and proportionate recuperative powers, her recovery was swift and euphoric.

A man stopped in front of her chair and grinned cheerfully at her. 'Hello,' he said. 'Better?' and then seeing her look blank, went on, 'I did the sergeant-major act on you the first night out, and walked you round the deck.'

'That *was* kind of you,' Jane smiled. 'I must have looked an awful sight.'

'I've yet to meet anybody who could look glamorous when seasick,' he said. 'Anybody using that next chair?'

'No.'

'Mind if I do?'

'Not at all.'

'Thank you.' He sat sideways on the chair, facing her. 'My name is Robert Powell.'

'I'm Jane Curtis.' The name was coming quite naturally to her tongue now. She wondered why she had imagined him to be an old man. He would be about thirty, she decided. Tall – perhaps a little under six feet, but not much. Not conventionally handsome by any means, but he had the sort of face she had always found attractive – strong, a good jawline, deep-set very blue eyes – good humoured, with radiating crinkles at the corners – a firm mouth. He was wearing tweeds that looked just right on him – well worn and comfortable – but at the same time tough, durable and eminently serviceable. Like the man himself, she decided.

'And what part of India are you going to, Miss Curtis?' He leaned forward and looked at her left hand. 'It *is* "Miss", isn't it? I can't see if you are wearing a wedding ring under that other one.'

'I'm not – this is just my engagement ring. I'm going to Calcutta,' she said.

'What's the lucky man's regiment?'

'He's a tea planter.'

'Forgive me. I'm in the North – the Punjab – and we have nobody up there who isn't in the Army – except a few civilians in Government service – and we are rather apt to imagine everybody is in the same category. Tea? That will be Assam. I envy you. I once spent a shooting leave there. Beautiful country.'

'Have you been in India long?' she asked.

'Ten years. I'm just returning from my second leave. My God, how time flies. It doesn't seem any time since I was coming out for my first jolt.' He shook his head and sighed. 'That means I'm more than a third of the way through my career already. No time at all now to the day when I'll be listening for the first cuckoo in Cheltenham and writing to *The Times* about it.'

'Is Cheltenham your home?'

'No – not yet, anyhow. That's just one of the scrapheaps for retired Indian Army people. It used to be the South of France but that's getting too expensive.'

'Doesn't anybody ever retire in India?'

'Very few. It would be the sensible thing really, because at the end of one's service one is far more at home there than in England – and it's a damned sight cheaper – and the climate is better – But no – except for a few eccentrics in places like Kashmir they all head Home like pigeons when their time is up, and wallow in nostalgia until they die. You never completely get India out of your system.'

'That's the second time I've heard those exact words in the last two days,' Jane said.

'I'm afraid you'll hear them a lot more before you chuck your topee overboard.'

'Chuck my what overboard?'

'Sun-helmet. It's something the British soldiers do ceremonially when they come through the Suez on their way home for the last time.' He stood up as Mandy came along the deck and halted in front of their chairs. Jane felt faintly resentful because the easy flow of their conversation was now checked.

95

Mandy said, 'Hello. How are you? Oh, boy – have I been sick!' and mimed the act of nausea very graphically, and Jane felt hot with embarrassment, but Powell laughed, genuinely amused, and said,

'You should have seen this one hanging over the rail there.'

'This is – ' Jane began, and then realized that she had forgotten both their names.

'Mandy Scanlon,' the other girl said. 'You're Major – er – ?'

'Bob Powell – Only Captain I'm afraid.' He picked up the folded rug from the chair. 'Sit down and I'll wrap you in this thing.'

'But I can't take your chair – ' Mandy said, sitting just the same.

'That's all right – I'll pull another one up.' He tucked the rug round her. 'Have you had any bouillon?'

'God no. It would make me sick I think.'

'It wouldn't. It'll settle your tum. Jane's just had some. I'll go and find the steward.' He walked off and Jane felt absurdly pleased at this natural use of her name.

Mandy said, 'Uh-uh – It didn't take *you* long to get mobile. A real pukkha sahib – proper gentleman – that one. I'll even drink that damn jallap when he brings it back. I'd rather have a brandy and ginger ale though – but the bar's not open until twelve. How did you get hold of him?'

'I didn't,' Jane snapped. 'He stopped here and talked to me.'

'Same thing,' said Mandy, unabashed. 'What did I tell you? Man oh man! Do they go for blondes out this way! You don't have to do a damn thing. It's us poor darkies who have to work at it.'

'I think you're being silly. I don't suppose for one moment that he noticed – ' She broke off, and Mandy pounced.

'Noticed what?'

'Well – what you were talking about – '

'That I'm Anglo-Indian?'

'Oh, if you like.' Jane felt her patience ebbing. 'All I know is that I found him awfully nice – and he was nice to you also – but if you keep on moaning and whining no wonder people get fed up with you.'

96

Mandy shrugged and smiled twistedly. 'Maybe you're right. Sorry. You better hang on to this one. There's some heavy Fishing Fleet competition aboard.' She threw the rug aside, got up and walked away quickly.

Powell came back with a cup of bouillon. 'Hello,' he said. 'Has she gone for good?'

'I don't know,' Jane said. 'I don't think she's feeling very well.'

He sat down. 'We were talking about retirement in India or something, weren't we?'

'Yes.'

'What a hell of a subject. Let's talk about you.'

'There's very little to talk about,' she said quickly.

'I've got an "insatiable curtiosity" about people. Where's your home?'

'Richmond,' she told him. She had prepared herself for this.

'Are you a working girl, or do you just help mamma with the flowers?'

'I worked in an office – a solicitor's office – in Town.' She was ready for that question too.

'Good for you. You'll find yourself missing that terribly. Work, I mean. That's the curse of India. The men are away all day and the women have absolutely damn all to do.'

'I thought they played tennis, and rode and had a wonderful time.'

'That only fills an hour or so in the early morning and in the cool of the evening,' he said. 'I'm talking about the bulk of the day when you're hiding from the sun in your bungalow. Some of the jungee Memsahibs interest themselves in good works – Indian welfare and things like that – but it's only a stop-gap. There *are* working women out there, of course – nurses, teachers, missionaries – but those are specialized fields. For the girl who has had an interesting job at Home, and earned her own money and enjoyed the independence that goes with it, it must be hell.'

'You're not going to frighten me. I'm going to enjoy every moment of it.'

'I'm not trying to frighten you, my dear,' he smiled. 'I'm

only giving you a warning. You will, undoubtedly, feel very homesick at first, and you'll suffer from the most terrible boredom unless you are prepared for it. It does seem such a pity. India can be the most interesting place on earth if one only takes advantage of it.'

'How? I mean, what do you advise?'

'An all-absorbing hobby – photography, sketching, painting – bird-watching, animals, Indian architecture, history. God Almighty, there are a thousand things – '

'But one would have to know something about them beforehand. I mean, you can't say, "Right – I'm going in for tiger-shooting."'

'I didn't suggest tiger-shooting – or shikar, as they call it. That's one of the things I loathe – a gaggle of bloody fools on elephants shooting at, and often only wounding, a beautiful animal that hasn't a chance of survival – driven by hundreds of coolies beating on tins. Lovely deer slaughtered the same way, and – ' He stopped and looked embarrassed. 'I'm sorry. I'm a bit cracked on that subject.'

'You don't shoot at all?'

'Occasionally, for the pot – but I'm not awfully keen even on that. No, I'm no Nimrod.' He stood up. 'Come for a walk and meet a few people. You're safe from the bitchpack.'

'What's that?'

'A stupid invention. There's no such thing. It's based on the fallacy that girls on the Fishing Fleet gang up on the best looking of their group and tear them to pieces – one at a time – so that when the ship arrives in Bombay only the very plainest is left, and she has the pick of the bachelors as they go down the gangway.'

'So I'm safe?' she said indignantly. 'Thank *you*!'

'Safe because you're engaged already, so you don't constitute a danger. Hell, I wouldn't give a brass farthing for your chances of survival if it wasn't for that ring.'

They circled the deck until eight bells and the accompanying toot on the siren signalled noon and the opening of the bar, and she learned that gin and lime, which was considered 'tart's tipple' in London, was known as a 'gimlet' in Indian bar society, and was respectable, and that small white onions were preferred to olives in cocktails.

'But you don't *eat* them?' she said, wrinkling her nose. 'What must they do to one's breath?'

'Take away the stink of curry and Bombay duck – that's very ancient dried fish done up with garlic,' he told her. 'You're in India now, my girl – or on its doorstep. Dancing with some of our more senior hostesses after dinner can be like wrestling with a vulture in the hot weather.'

By common consent and shipboard courtesy their chairs remained inviolate from that first day, and they met there after breakfast – and talked and walked, and when the sea had become a white-flecked blue and the sun was warmer than any she had ever experienced in Herne Bay even in August, he taught her deck tennis and shuffleboard, and they danced every night on deck to an amplified contrivance called a Panatrope, and twice a week to the music of a Goanese band – and in a riotous party of subalterns, with Tessa, Mandy and four 'Fleeters' to even things up, they went ashore in Marseilles and ate bouillabaisse and explored the Vieux Port – and bought useless junk in Simon Artz's cluttered store in Port Said, and later watched the desert glide past and finally melt into a brazen sunset and then total darkness. They were on the boat deck that night and it was the first divergence from the path of easy camaraderie that had characterized their relationship up until then – something which she had found strange, because platonicism had had no place in her world to date. One went out with a boy in the first place – and he almost automatically 'tried it on' – and the girl repulsed him, and the boy left the field and tried elsewhere – or, if he was genuinely attracted, he returned to the fray and 'tried it on' again until, after a seemly interval and a gradual lowering of her defences, they 'went steady' – and a certain liberty was allowed. It was as stylized as the courtship of the mayfly. But Robert had not 'tried it on' and it had piqued her because it had seemed an affront to her femininity. Of course, opportunity was lacking – she had heard the standard shipboard joke which parodied a racing stable studbook – 'Fornication by Second Class, out of the

Question' – the implication being that only in the first class were there such conveniences as single berth cabins. Still, whispered gossip had it that certain enterprising subalterns had made it with the more amenable of the Fishing Fleet in an empty cabin that could be secured from the second steward for a monetary consideration. She would never have agreed to this sordid arrangement, not because of any lack of libido on her part, but because here again iron-hard convention ruled. An engaged girl simply did not go the whole way with an interloper. If she did she was either 'easy' – or worse, 'common'. Boys talked – and boasted – in the world she had left, and she had no reason to believe that they didn't in this new one. Still he *might* have tried, she thought wistfully, when, after a passionate embrace behind a lifeboat, he suddenly broke away with a mumbled apology, and hurried off into the darkness.

But things were back to normal next morning when they sought their chairs, and they were even able to discuss it dispassionately.

'I'm really very sorry about last night,' he said. 'I shouldn't have done it.'

'Done what?'

'Now don't act dumb. You know perfectly well what I mean.'

'It doesn't matter.'

'It does. Out here it does, anyway. In England where the sexes are even one can be rather more free and easy, no doubt – but in India, where the ratio is one wench to five hundred blokes, it's different. Blokes have to travel – go on duty tours – up to the Frontier and that sort of thing – and the bags and baggages have to be left behind – and only a real bastard takes advantage – and a pretty lousy sort of woman. Oh, it *is* done – of course it is – but I've seen some awful tragedies as a result. I'm always lecturing you, aren't I?'

'Go on. I like to hear about these things.'

'What I mean to say is that a married man during an enforced separation, miles from anywhere, is apt to mull over things and to give way to morbid fantasies in the long hot nights.'

'I can't stand jealous men.'

'Don't be a self-righteous little prig. What might seem to be needless jealousy in a temperate climate is understandable at a hundred and ten in the shade, when a man's got prickly heat and he's just getting over malaria, and he starts thinking about the little woman up in the cool hills with a lot of predatory lounge lizards on the prowl. Only the man who is one hundred per cent certain of his wife is safe from what the French call cafard.'

'Is that why you never married?'

'What do you mean "never married"? You make it sound as if I've reached the end of the road already. Actually I'm just moving into the marriage zone now – and I'd love to take the plunge, but I don't think this is the ideal time for it – not for a soldier I mean.'

'Why not?'

'Because like everybody else in the business I'm pretty certain that there's going to be a war within the next twelve months.'

'With Germany you mean?'

'Who else? Yes – Germany, and Spain and Italy probably thrown in for good measure.'

'But it was agreed between Hitler and Chamberlain when they met in Munich that – '

'I have here a piece of paper signed by Mr Hitler and myself in which we have agreed that never again shall Britain and Germany go to war – Hooray!' He laughed bitterly. 'Yes, *I* saw that newsreel too.'

'But that will be in Europe, surely? It won't make any difference out here, will it?'

'Good God – How naïve some of you civilians are. Listen, my little one – the last war was pretty cataclysmic. This one will be proportionately worse – because of the technological advances since then. Air power, chemical and biological warfare – all that sort of thing.' He broke off. 'I'm not only scaring you, but I'm boring you as well, which is inexcusable.'

'You're not,' she said urgently. 'Please go on. I'm so ignorant of these things, and I do want to know. I *do*.'

'You haven't picked much of a teacher. I have no authority

for any of this. I'm just giving you my opinion. Yes, I think it will make a difference in India. It may change a lot of our present thinking – but that in itself mightn't be such a bad thing. We've been living in a mid-Victorian vacuum since 1857.'

'In what way?'

He yawned. 'Every way. Take our own social system.' He jerked his head in the direction of Tessa, passing at that moment with a young subaltern. 'That one – Nice enough child – pretty in a vapid sort of way, and with the brain of a peahen – but her position is assured. Top of the heap – because Daddy's a General. She'll marry some bloke, preferably one with a General or two in his pedigree also, and he will be an automatic first choice for the next crop of Generals. But if that same bloke was seen in public with, for instance, Mandy, gorgeous creature that she is, he'd get a stern warning from his CO – the first time. If it happened again he'd be out on his ear. It would be perfectly all right for him to sleep with her – in private – but he mustn't dine with her – in public.'

'She told me that herself. I thought she was exaggerating.'

'It's absolutely true.'

'Poor Mandy. What's ahead of her then?'

'Oh, there are plenty of people she *can* marry. Any Anglo-Indian at all, which means that she's got the lower echelons of the police, customs, railways and British soldiers up to the rank of sergeant to choose from – and even some boxwallas – although many commercial companies can be as sticky as the Army.

'I think it's wicked,' she said indignantly.

'So do I – so do a lot of other people – but that's the way it is, and that's the way it will remain – unless a war does change it all. The awful thing is that you will find yourself not only accepting it wholeheartedly, but supporting the system before you've been out a month.'

'Never,' she said flatly.

He laughed. 'I'd like to meet you in a year's time and bring the subject up again. Listen, my dear – you're talking to an expert. I am a keen and ambitious soldier and I intend going right to the top. I have certain initial advantages – the foremost being that I am an Etonian – that's three aces in any poker hand to start with – but there's a slight qualification in my case. I was a Colleger. That means I was there on a scholarship – everything found. You see, my father is a dairyman in Finchley – that's a sort of closed shop for the Welsh in London. If that were known in certain circles in India it would make me as untouchable as the poor bloody A-Is. So you see, I have no protective wing to spare for *them* – I need it all for myself. Do you know why I am telling you this?'

She shook her head.

'I'm telling you because a chap in my position becomes very sensitive to feel and atmosphere, and develops the same sort of ear as Professor Higgins in Shaw's play *Pygmalion*. I think your background and mine have much in common – No, don't confirm or deny that – I've done enough breast-baring for both of us. I'm giving you this advice; don't strive too hard to fit in. Be a bit of an odd ball at times if you like, but always play it sweet and simple. Don't, for God's sake, give yourself a background that could be checked and found wanting in Debrett. People will seldom ask you directly where you come from and what your family does or doesn't do, for a living – too many of them are hiding things up themselves – so just skirt round the subject – one becomes very skilful after a certain amount of practice.'

'Is it – is it so noticeable?' she asked shakily.

'No – not at all – except when you try to speak very precisely. It *can* sound a little precious then. Soft pedal a little on make-up during the day – and never wear jewellery before lunch, except your engagement ring. Things like that you will pick up naturally as you go along. Anyhow, your husband will be telling you all this – especially if he had to go through the process himself.'

'Actually he comes from quite a posh family,' she said, and he winced.

' "Posh" is out,' he said firmly, 'even though it originated right here. It means "port out, starboard home" because that is the eastern side of the ship going through the Red Sea –

nice and bright in the mornings but shady in the hot after-noons. Never use it in any other context though – It ranks with "pleased to meet you" and "ever so nice".'

'Oh heavens,' she said faintly.

'A resounding "bloody Hell" is permissible, indeed prefer-able, when expressing dismay,' he told her solemnly. 'But there's no need to be dismayed. You're doing all right. Carry on the way you are now. Behave yourself if possible – but if you do backslide at any time, never be found out. Learn a bit of kitchen Hindi and never have an English-speaking servant. Ride horses even if, like me, you hate the damned things. Swear like a longshoreman if you wish, but never miss morning Church on Sunday. Get mildly tipsy after sundown if you feel like it, but not too often, and never when entertaining in your own home. Just keep to those few simple rules and you'll be a Bara Memsahib yourself in no time at all – and as such, socially inviolate and absolutely safe the length and breadth of India. Come and have a drink.'

Chapter Five

The ship had, within the last hour, become a different place. It was no longer a detached piece of England peopled by semi-aliens. It was now part of this vast sub-continent and everybody but herself had come home. She, for the first time, felt lost and frightened and she was dreading the moment when she would have to leave this safe and familiar steel womb for the uncertainty of the shore. George, damn him, always managed to fall short just at the moments when she most needed him. She had to get a passport – and equip herself for the voyage on what really had been insufficient funds. Seventy-five pounds sounded a lot, but it hadn't gone far, she reflected. And her passage – Yes, it had been comfortable and pleasant and she had no doubt enjoyed the voyage more in the tourist class than she would have in the stuffy formality of the Saloon – but it *had* been a bit of a let-down, she thought, for the fiancée of a tea planter – And now the damned fool had failed to meet her.

'Of course,' his letter read, 'since I have just returned from Home leave I am vulnerable for extra duty, and with the new season's tea coming downriver from Gauhati by the shipload, it is a furiously busy time for all of us. I am desperately sorry, sweetheart, not to be in Bombay meeting you, but I know my little girl [she shuddered] will understand. See the Thomas Cook man who will come on board as soon as you arrive, and he will give you your ticket and reservation slip on the Calcutta Mail for the same night. It is one of our best trains and it leaves Victoria Terminus, Bombay, every night at 11.30 p.m. The journey takes two nights and one full day, and I'll be waiting for you bright and early on Howrah Station, Calcutta, at 8 a.m. on the second morning. You will find travelling here vastly different from England, but I know you will enjoy the novelty of it and the new scenes and strange people – [Just like his bloody sister giving a geography lesson]. I am enclosing fifty rupees, that's a little over four pounds, for incidental expenses. Do not tip luggage coolies and the bearer who will bring your chhota hazri – that is early morning tea – to your compartment, more than four annas – that is fourpence and more than enough although they will, of course, complain that it isn't. The flat is not quite ready for occupation yet but some old friends of mine, Reggie and Louise Hawkesley, are very kindly putting us up for the first few nights in theirs. I know you will like them both and L. will be able to give you some very useful tips about housekeeping here – '

She looked down at the quay and felt a fresh upsurge of terror. What a fool she had been to come out. This was not for her. She longed for the safe drabness of Brixton again. Some beggars were being chased by policemen in blue uniforms and yellow turbans, swinging vicious clubs – men, women and children – thin and miserable in tattered rags – and one, an old woman with a hideously disfigured face, tottered blindly over the edge into the water between the ship and the quay and a crowd gathered above her, yelling, screaming, laughing, until the policemen's clubs scattered them and she was fished out on the end of a bamboo pole like a filthy bundle of wet rags.

Robert came and stood beside her. 'You'll get used to it,' he said quietly. 'The apes and elephants and peacocks and bejewelled rajahs are still here – but there's a hell of a lot of this sort of thing also.'

She shivered. 'I don't want to get used to it,' she said. 'I hate it.'

'You'd better see the purser about reserving your cabin for the return trip then,' he said dryly. 'Don't be silly, Jane. This has been here for ten thousand years. You arrived fifty-five minutes ago. Boy friend not turned up yet?'

'He's been detained on business,' she said dully.

'That can happen too. I told you, didn't I? The bags and baggages get left behind an awful lot in India. You're going to lead the life of Reilly out here, my dear – money, cars, horses, servants – you need never do a hand's turn for yourself again that you don't want to do – God Almighty! What more could a gal want? But hubby has got to bring the berries home to make it all possible – and that calls for hard work, and doing what the boss says. Come on – snap out of it.'

She smiled wanly and said, 'Yes, I know. I'm being a fool – but it *is* frightening.'

'Of course it's frightening – so is looking over the edge of Niagara, or into the crater of Vesuvius – but it's also vital and fascinating. What are you doing? Going over to Calcutta on the Mail?'

'Yes – at half-past eleven tonight. I've got to find the Cook's man. He'll have my tickets.'

'Don't worry – I'll collect them for you,' he said. 'Will you have dinner with me ashore first?'

Her heart leapt. 'Oh, I'd love to.'

'Good. We'll go to the Taj Mahal – the most fabulous pub in all the world, in my opinion. You'll see the other side of the coin there. Where's your luggage?'

'It's all gone down to the Customs, the steward tells me.'

'Right – give me your keys and my orderly will see it through for you.' He pointed down at the dockside. 'There he is, the bloody rogue.' A tall Indian sepoy, magnificently turned out in starched khaki drill and a high pagri wound over his black, bobbed, ear-length hair, saluted and grinned up at them with a flash of white teeth.

'He's handsome,' Jane said.

'He's damned lucky,' Robert said. 'He shouldn't be here at all. He was due to be hanged last year in Landi Kotal.'

'What on earth for?' Jane was open-mouthed with horror.

'Oh, somebody had been mucking about with his woman while we were out on manoeuvres, so he took a knife to him.'

'You mean *murdered* him?'

'Not half, although *he* wouldn't have called it that. He'd have said "hallal". That means "lawful killing".'

'Well, how did he get away with it?'

'Oh, through the Colonel and me – and the Regimental

Association – pulling hard for him – and a couple of highly expert perjurers swearing that they saw the other chap drawing a knife first, and so making it self-defence. Good thing actually. If he ever misbehaves I threaten to go back to court and tell the truth – and then – ' He circled his throat with his finger and made a jerking motion upward, ' – that would be *it.*'

'You are *awful*!' she said.

'Never say that again,' he told her. 'It ranks with "posh" and "pleased to meet you".'

'I'll remember. Oh, Robert – I wish you were coming to Calcutta – or I was going to wherever it is *you're* going.'

'God forbid,' he said fervently. 'I'd probably finish up with my throat cut, and your husband in the same boat as Sher Mohammed down there. A bit of innocent dalliance is delightful on shipboard – but it should always end right here – at Ballard Quay. Remember that whenever you go on leave.'

'But you *are* taking me to dinner ashore?'

'That's purely incidental – because my train, the Frontier Mail, doesn't leave until midnight, and we've got time to kill.' He held out his hand. 'Keys. Then go and wait in the smoke-room if you can fight your way through the bar-flies loading up on duty-free gin. I'll collect you there.'

She nodded happily and turned away, to face Tessa Storland who had come up behind them.

The girl said, 'Oh, Jane – I'd like you to meet my parents. Mummy – Daddy – this is Jane Curtis, my cabin-mate.'

The man was short and stocky with a clipped white moustache and the dried, leathery look of a lifetime spent east of Suez. She had seen a dozen like him perambulating the first class decks – and the woman was typical – no taller than her husband, but with a thin angularity making her appear so, and the same leathery look, which in her case was the more noticeable because of her blue-rinsed hair – a new fashion even in London, and in this case badly done, Jane noted. But her eyes were kind, albeit very direct and piercing, and the whole face softened when she smiled.

She put out her hand. 'Thank you, my dear, for looking after my gel,' she said.

'It was the other way round,' Jane told her – and just managed to bite back a concluding 'moddom'. 'I mean, *she* looked after *me*.'

'A job I wouldn't have minded myself,' said the father, taking her hand. 'By George, you're a pretty girl. A *damned* pretty girl. What's your station, my dear?'

'A long way from you, you wicked old man,' Tessa said. 'Calcutta. And this is Robert – '

'Powell, Lady Storland,' said Robert, bowing slightly – and to the father, 'Second-Ninth Punjabis, sir – we met when you had the Wana Brigade.'

'Before I was translated to higher things,' said the General, shaking hands. 'Yes, of course, I remember you. You were at school with Ian, weren't you?'

'Marginally,' said Robert. 'He came there just as I was leaving for Sandhurst. There's a good six years between us. How is he now, sir?'

'He's an idle young bugger with champagne tastes on a beer income,' said the General fondly. 'Stationed in Dhond at the moment.' He turned back to Jane. 'Well, what are you doing? Going straight to Calcutta?'

'Yes, tonight – '

'Twenty-three-thirty from VT,' said the General. 'That gives you plenty of time to dine with us, and we'll put you on the train afterwards.'

'Oh, thank you,' said Jane, confused. She looked sideways at Robert. 'But we – I mean – '

'He'd got in first, had he?' chuckled the General. 'Don't blame him. You too then – at the Yacht Club at seven – all right?'

'That's very kind of you, sir,' said Robert. 'Thank you. If you'll excuse me now – I'm just getting Jane's saman through Customs.'

He steered her through the crowd towards the gangway. 'That was your first Memsahib,' he said. 'What do you think of her?'

'She was very nice. I didn't know she had a title. Tessa didn't tell me.'

'One doesn't. It's not a title in its own right, of course. She's a "Lady" because her husband is a Lieutenant-General. It's an automatic knighthood that goes with the rank. Yes, she's all right – but I'd hate to cross her. It was she who got the old boy up into the dizzy heights. He'd never have made it on his own. Take a good look at her and you'll see Tessa in about twenty-five years from now.'

'They're not the slightest bit alike,' Jane said.

'Not at this moment – but they will be. And somewhere, dreaming under the pagoda tree, is a subaltern or a captain who will be the spit and image of Pa eventually – after he has been married to Tessa for the same length of time.'

'You, for instance?' she said, and he shook his head.

'No, not me. I intend to make it on my own two feet. That no doubt sounds priggish, but I really would loathe that type of marriage.'

They came to the bottom of the gangway and she listened, awed, to Robert giving complicated instructions to the sepoy in an outlandish tongue.

'I've told him to take your stuff and mine to the station when we've got it cleared,' he explained. 'There are rest rooms there where we can dress.'

'Dress?' She looked down at the very pretty frock that she had kept inviolate for this day.

'You're in India now, carrying the white man's burden. You'll dress for dinner every night of your life except Sunday – when you "change" – which means a short frock for you and an ordinary tie for your husband instead of a black one.' He laughed. 'Don't look at *me* like that – I didn't make the silly rule.'

'Yes, I knew all that,' she said. 'But I would have thought that it would have been relaxed when one was travelling.'

'Actually on the train itself, yes – but if you're dining with a General and his Memsahib in Bombay – and at the Yacht Club – ' He whistled. 'Dine dirty and God wouldn't love you any more.'

They pushed through to the Customs benches and found themselves alongside Mandy, who was spitting machine-gun

Hindi at the Indian searcher who was rummaging through her cases.

'Angrezi kaho,' said Robert softly behind her, and she turned on him like a wildcat.

'Yeh ulu hamara saman – ' she began, then recognized him. 'Oh, you, is it? Damn language – I've forgotten every word of it. Never did know much anyhow. This goddamn black fool is going through every bit of my luggage. Will you tell him that I'm not carrying drugs or gold nuggets or any bloody thing like that.'

'There are regulations, madam,' the searcher said stiffly in English. 'You will find them printed on this card. Please read – English one side, Hindi and Gujrati the other. I am thinking that the lady is knowing all three very well. Open these other two cases please.'

They found and cleared their own luggage quickly and handed it over to Sher Mohammed. 'Let's grab a taxi,' Robert said, and took her elbow.

'Oughtn't we to go and help Mandy?' Jane suggested.

'Not by any means,' he said flatly.

'So it *is* true?'

'What's true?'

'Just what she told me – that you looked through them once you landed in India.'

'I didn't look through her. I told her to speak English to the Customs babu. She was using "gali" – that's low abuse – so naturally he was making things as difficult as possible for her. They *will* do that to the Indians – then, when we're around, they pretend they don't know any of the local languages, just to prove how English they are. I'm sorry for them – very sorry – because they do get it in the neck from both communities – but at the same time they bring a lot of it on themselves.'

Victoria Terminus, that huge Gothic sprawl from which all Indian journeys start, fascinated her. It was noisier even than the docks, and more colourful, but she was over her initial fear now. She stood in the entrance colonnade and gazed at the vast assembly platform that crawled, writhed and pulsated with life like pond water under a microscope.

'Euston – with palm trees,' said Robert. 'Come on, and keep a tight hold on your handbag – right up against your chest. You've got to wade here – literally.'

They crossed the concourse, stepping over prone figures and heaps of luggage – bundles wrapped in palm matting and coarse blue cotton rugs – brass cooking vessels – babies – sleeping mats – tin boxes – hubble-bubble pipes.

'One half of India is always travelling,' he told her. 'The other half is seeing them off or meeting them – and when they travel they take everything they possess with them. When you're as poor as they are a brass lota or a cotton dhurri can represent a pretty sizeable chunk of your capital – so you don't leave it lying around to be pinched.'

Sher Mohammed was standing guard over a venetian-slatted doorway. He saluted and spoke in Punjabi to Robert, who shrugged and pushed through the door and held it open for her.

'He's very put out,' Robert said. 'There's only this one waiting room left.'

She looked around her and marvelled. 'How many more does he want? There's room for a dozen here, and even a bed.'

'Oh, waiting rooms are rather different in India. They are more like hotel accommodation – there's a private bath through that door for instance – and once you've shown your first class ticket and paid your five rupees you're entitled to its exclusive use. Very handy if you ever miss a connection.'

'They do make life easy for one out here,' Jane said.

'*If* you have a first class ticket.' He pointed back over his shoulder with an outstretched thumb. 'If you haven't – well, you've seen for yourself.'

'You mean the people lying on the platform? Yes – but they're Indians. I mean, white people wouldn't be expected to – well – ' She looked confused. 'You're laughing at me.'

'No, not you entirely,' he said. 'Just the inevitability of it all. You took me to task when we landed, for cold-shouldering Mandy – but within half an hour you're accepting the sahib and Memsahib's God-given right to a private room, while

Johnny-with-a-black-face kips on the stones outside.'

'You *are* laughing at me.' She was white and tight-lipped with anger. 'I know I'm ignorant, and that I say the wrong things – like "posh" and "ever so nice", and I call gimlets gin and limes, but that doesn't give you the right to poke fun at me. Who the hell do you think you are? Keep your bloody private waiting room – I'll look after myself, thank you.' She ran past him to the door, but he reached it before her and she finished in his arms, her face pressed hard against his chest, in a storm of weeping. He felt behind him for the key, and turned it – then he led her to the bed and sat facing her on the edge.

The weeping finished in a series of gasping sobs, then the storm had passed, as suddenly as it had broken. He gave her his handkerchief. She dabbed her eyes and blew her nose and smiled wanly.

'Sorry,' she said.

'No need to be,' he told her. 'It's much better to let off steam than screw the safety valve down. Time and place are all important of course. If you ever feel choked about things in future, or think that somebody is taking the mike out of you – which I wasn't incidentally – smile sweetly and slip off to your room unobtrusively – and pull faces at yourself and kick the jerry until you feel better – but never, never, *never* let anybody see that they've got under your skin. That was the great advantage Eton had over most other schools – one had a room, with a bed and a burry to oneself – a big consideration for a small bloke who was liable to slip into a Welsh-Cockney patois in moments of stress.'

She shivered. 'Oh, I'm scared the whole time. Those people – Tessa's parents – they were so terribly nice and kind – but you can imagine the way they'd look at you if you – you know –'

'Put a foot wrong?' He shook his head. 'Actually they wouldn't high-hat you whatever you did – not because they're nice and kind so much as the fact that it wouldn't be considered well-bred.'

'I'm dreading tonight. I wish we were having dinner together quietly, like we planned.'

'So do I. I'm afraid I was caught out. But there's no need to dread it. You'll enjoy it. Your main problem will be keeping the General-sahib's hand from sliding higher than your knee under the table.'

She stared at him. 'You don't mean to say he's like that?'

'Not half. Randy Storland, they used to call him on the Frontier in the old days.' He laughed. 'Don't look so shocked. He's no worse – or better – than any other ancient military gent. Most of them get a bit stopped up in their old age. Probably something to do with all the curry they eat, and the fact that the real Bara Memsahib is about the most sexless thing you'll find east of Suez. Experts say it's because so many of them are doing self-inflicted penance for all the shenanigans they got up to when they were *chhota* Memsahibs. Burnt-out cases, in other words.'

'But you said that people didn't do that sort of thing out here,' she said. 'Because husbands feel bad about it when they're separated and – '

He chuckled. 'Did I say that? It must have come straight out of my subconscious. That's part of the lecture all young subalterns get from their COs when first they arrive out here – poker-faced and solemn, without batting an eyelid. It's a wonder the good Lord doesn't send down fire to blast some of them.'

'But you *did* say it – and I thought you meant it.'

His face straightened. 'All right,' he said quietly. 'Yes – I said it. Like the fox that couldn't reach the grapes – I didn't like grapes, I was saying – and they were sour anyhow. Time and place, my dear, both wrong, and even suppose I had been able to work some sordid little ploy, there was always the chance that someone would find out – someone who you might run into on your station some time in the future. That's the stuff of gossip on the long hot nights that I told you about. I couldn't risk exposing you to that sort of thing – so I fell back on the Holy Joe spiel in case you thought I was a eunuch.'

'I'm glad of that,' she said simply. 'I thought it was because you didn't like me.'

'My God,' he said hollowly, and reached out for her.

The Club servants wore striped vests and cotton breeks and phrygian caps, like the powder monkeys of Nelson's days. A light breeze ghosted across the harbour from the open sea past Karanja, and rustled the fronds of the palms that fringed the open-air dining patio. The music of the twelve-piece band was soft, and the fairy lights round the dance floor were like jewels against the night sky – and the dinner had been magnificent – and she wanted the magic of this perfect evening to go on for ever. But end it did, at eleven, amid regrets from the quite sizeable group that had grown round the nucleus of the General's little family party – a youngish Brigadier, a middle-aged Colonel, an ADC from Government House – all womanless – and then some younger people from the ship, but she knew with absolute certainty – that she, Maxine Wilmott – Jane Curtis, she corrected quickly – was the belle of the ball. In fact the General, who had a splendid ear for a cliché, used those very words himself, and talked about glass slippers and pumpkins, and Robert winced comically, then winked at her.

They went back to Victoria Terminus in a convoy of cars, and the way was made smooth before her because India's bone-bred sycophancy ensured the full treatment for a protégée of a General-sahib, and nowhere does news spread faster than on a railway station. So they were received at the entrance by the stationmaster himself and his head babu, and an Inspector of Railway Police, the guard of the train and the Goanese 'bootlah' of the dining car, and escorted to her carriage, where her bed had already been made down, and the General himself showed her the working of the impossibly complicated system of Indian train windows, which come in many layers – glass to keep out hot air, but not the light – fine mesh which is supposed to admit air while excluding flying insects, but which usually works in reverse – and finally, heavy venetian slatting designed to keep out train thieves.

And Tessa was repeating over and over again, 'Oh, you *must* come and stay with us in Gonah – whenever you like – the sooner the better – it's a lovely all-weather station – never too hot, and beautiful and cool in the mornings and evenings – and there are dances and picnics and the races – and loads and lashings of boys – and six horses, and Daddy is getting me my own car – '

'Jane will be a respectable married woman in a day or so, dear,' said her mother, then smiled and added, 'But the invitation stands just the same. Do come and visit us whenever you feel you'd like a change. Calcutta, I'm afraid, can be very trying.'

'I'll second that, by George,' boomed the General. 'Soon as you like. There's going to be a war, and you youngsters want to get all the fun you can before the balloon goes up.'

She saw Robert standing behind the noisy group, on the edge of the patch of light cast from the windows of her reserved compartment. He caught her eye, smiled, then winked slowly and gave her a covert thumbs-up sign – an affectionately conspiratorial little gesture that brought an absurd lump to her throat, and she felt tears rolling down her cheeks. Lady Storland appeared to be the only one who noticed them, though, and she put her arm protectively round Jane's shoulders and said quietly, 'You've had an exciting and tiring day, my dear. In you go, and make certain you've bolted the door – and leave the windows the way the General has fixed them.' Then she kissed her on the cheek and gently pushed her on to the train. Somewhere a bell was ringing and there was a blast from the whistle, and they were moving – past other groups of Europeans, white uniformed police, baggage coolies in red surtouts, black faces, brown faces, whites of eyes, teeth, multi-hued saris, red terracotta water chatthis – a final green signal light at the end of the platform, then the black Indian night, and the initial fear that attended her arrival was back and she was lying face downward on her bed sobbing.

But she slept well that first night, cool under a sheet, with the electric fan directed downward on to a metal container of ice, and with the dawn her fears receded and the habitual interest she brought to all that was new had returned. The toilet annexe, solidly mahogany and uncompromisingly Victorian, with its huge washbasin, thronelike lavatory and glass-shuttered shower, all clinically clean, delighted her. She bathed and then knelt on her berth, wrapped in a big swadeshi towel, and watched the magic that is India in the early morning flow past. Flat dusty country that stretched to the horizon, broken only by clumps of kika thorn, with goats standing on their hind legs to browse on the upper bark. Here and there a copse of bigger, greener trees with usually a well somewhere near, where women drew water in brass pots which they carried away on their heads, walking like princesses. Cattle – cattle everywhere – stunted and thin – villages, all alike, mud-walled, flat-roofed, blue smoke from the cooking fires layered above them in the motionless air, until the passage of the train disturbs it momentarily. Children – playing in the dust – riding on their mothers' hips – running for a brief moment along the edge of the railway embankment almost under the wheels, naked, pot-bellied, large-eyed, open hands held up imploringly.

They were slowing down, and then crawling over a long box-girdered bridge spanning a river course. The stream had shrunk to a rivulet through black sand in the middle, where men and women stood waist-deep banging clothes against flat rocks, then, without warning, they were sliding into a station, and the pandemonium that greets all trains in India was lapping round the compartment. Hands, hands, hands, old and wrinkled, young, pink-palmed, shrivelled like monkeys' paws, beating on the windows, shaking beggars' bowls – and always behind them huge pleading eyes that followed however one moved, like those of Kitchener on the recruiting poster. She retreated into the toilet compartment where the window was of frosted glass and hurriedly pulled on some clothes. Somebody was pounding on the door, and peering nervously out she saw the head and shoulders of an Indian bearer carrying a laden tray, flat-palmed at ear height, and behind him the train guard. She slipped back the bolts cautiously and tried unsuccessfully to open the door by pushing it outwards, but the Anglo-Indian guard grinned and pushed it in towards her and said, 'Oh, my God, miss – not in Blighty. Doors open inward in this damned country. Chhota hazri now and I'll get a sweeper in to dust and clean up and put another maund of ice in the tank – Chalo tum – safkaro ek dum jaldi! – jaldi! – jaldi!' And things were happening. Her bedding was folded and whisked away, a jarroo handbroom was raising clouds of dust, and somebody was sliding miniature mountains of ice through the door, and the bearer was setting out her tray on the centre table – a silver-plated tea service, toast, and peeled oranges impaled on forks.

'Breakfast in one hour, miss,' the guard said. 'At Akola. Are you wanting to go to dining car, or having it in compartment here?'

'But what's this?' Jane asked, nodding at the tray.

'Oh, this only chhota hazri. That meaning tea, fruit – eye-opener they call it.'

'I don't think I'll need anything more,' she said.

'Oh, my God!' The guard was dismayed. He consulted a list. 'All paid for at Calcutta end – hire of bedding roll, bath towels – two chhota hazris, two breakfasts, one tiffin, one afternoon tea, one dinner. If you are telling anybody in Calcutta that you are not getting this I am losing job. Please, miss – sign for it, then chuck it out of damn window if you are not wanting.'

'All right,' she agreed, smiling.

'Good,' he said, relieved. 'If you go to the dining car you'll see other people from Blightyside. Very nice – and I'll put a man in here while you are away, to see that no loosewallas get in – that's train thieves, very bad – '

The heat of the day was steadily increasing but she break-fasted on papaya and fresh lime, which one loves or loathes on first taste, finnan haddock, bacon and eggs, fresh rolls, honey and coffee, toying with each, afraid to refuse, because she was aware of the 'bootlah' watching her and meticulously ticking off each item as it was served. A fat man in a freshly laundered tussah suit stopped by her table and said, 'Excuse me – you wouldn't be by any chance Mrs Wallingford's young sister, would you?' Jane shook her head, and he went on apologet-ically, 'So sorry. I understood she was coming over from

Bombay today, and I promised I'd keep an eye open for her. You arrived on the *Strathnaver*, I take it? I saw your send-off at VT Impressive.' He sat at the table across the aisle from her and flicked his fingers for the waiter. 'Usual silly question. What do you think of the place?'

'Very nice,' said Jane, and could have kicked herself. That was one of the things Robert had blacklisted. ' – of you to ask,' she added primly. 'Of course it's rather early to start forming opinions yet.'

'Exactly,' he agreed solemnly, and fumbled for a card. 'Very rude of me to thrust myself on you like this. Put it down to an old man's impertinence – '

'H. J. R. Rossall,' she read, and in one corner, 'Bengal Club.'

'How do you do,' she remembered to say, wondering whether she was expected to keep the card or return it. 'I'm afraid I've left my cards in my compartment. My name is Jane Curtis.'

'Delighted to meet you. Mrs or Miss?'

'Miss.'

'That won't last for long, I'm willing to bet,' he said, looking at her approvingly.

'No. I'm being married almost immediately.'

'Inevitable. Who's the lucky man?'

'George Quaife.'

'Army?'

'No – tea.'

He looked slightly puzzled. 'Quaife? Quaife? I should know him if he's in tea. Where about?'

'Calcutta.'

'Oh – office man.' She sensed disparagement in his tone so she inclined her head coldly and turned away and looked out over fields of bone-dry maize. Watching his reflection in the glass of the window, she thought he looked crestfallen. The waiter brought him some fruit juice, but he waved any further breakfast away, and when the train stopped at a wayside halt to allow passengers in the dining car to go back to their compartments, he mumbled, 'Nice to have met you, Miss – er – ' and stood aside to let her pass in the aisle, and she smiled sweetly and went off, leaving his card on the table.

It was her second victory. She remembered George telling her something about the Bengal Club. He almost genuflected when he mentioned it. It was strictly for the 'Bara Sahibs' – the big men at the top of the tree. Well, she'd toppled the first one – and she had received a warm invitation from a General, and a 'Sir' to boot, *and* from his wife, a Lady, with a capital L, to go and stay with them. And all within her first twenty-four hours in the country – the country which was, what was it that Robert called it? – Yes – 'the last ditch of Victorian snobbery'. She would make the grade – up to George's level in the first instance – then past it, taking him with her if he had the nous to follow, and didn't try to hold her back – without him if necessary. Right to the top. The Bara Memsahib. She would watch, and listen, and note, and learn. She wouldn't – what was it again? – oh, yes – 'put a foot wrong'. She must remember some of these phrases of Robert's – the ones that were so apt, and which came so easily to his tongue. The language of this new world of hers – a language which would never be understood in Brixton.

The day passed quickly and without loneliness or boredom, because her really phenomenal powers of observation and resultant interest held her spellbound at the window. The constantly changing countryside, once the monotony of the central plain was behind them, awed and delighted her – hills, jungle, dry river beds – a string of camels, nose to tail, carrying bales of hay – the fleeting glimpse of a gazelle bounding into a clump of bamboo – and above all the stations – colour, smells, noise – and the constant feeling of déjà vu that was upon her. She exercised her privilege of lunching and having tea in the compartment, but, after another shower and a change into a fresh frock, she walked along the platform at the dinner halt and took her meal alone at a table some distance from that of Mr Rossall, to whom she bowed distantly in passing.

She lay awake for a long time that night, watching the stars and an almost full moon through the window. Robert had a journey as long as hers ahead of him, but in a different direction – north as against hers to the east. He would be in a train similar to this at this moment. She wondered if he was thinking of her

– or was that brief hour in Bombay just one of those things as far as he was concerned? An opportunity seized, exploited and as quickly forgotten. 'Just moving into the marriage zone,' he had said. Then why, oh why – ? But then her inherent pragmatism came to her aid and she forced it from her mind. Life lay ahead, not back over her shoulder. But one thing she had learned from the encounter – she would give nothing away as freely in future to *anybody*. She knew the value of her assets, and they were not for squandering on passing affairs, however attractive she might find dalliance at the time.

She saw him at the end of the platform peering myopically into first class compartments and fending off hotel touts and baggage coolies with flailing arms. He looked even more tall and gangling in his grey tropical-weight suit and the ridiculous little flat sun-helmet she had heard referred to as a 'Bombay bowler'. It was her first sight of the business dress of the boxwalla and she experienced a distinct sense of let-down. She had always pictured white men in this country as lean, brown and nail-hard, in uniform, or shirt-sleeved, breeched and booted. He saw her leaning out of the window of her compartment, and he ran through the crowd towards her, wrenched the door open and sprang inside. He enfolded her in a bearlike hug, missed his aim and kissed her on the left eye, ruining the better part of an hour's handiwork on the lurching train earlier.

He said, 'Oh, my God – if you only knew how I have been longing for this day. Let me look at you.' He put his hands on her shoulders and pushed her to arms' length. 'As beautiful as ever – more so,' he murmured, and for some reason it sounded like a speech delivered by the leading man of the Brixton Amateur Dramatic Society.

She disengaged gently and said, 'Good to see you – but you're thinner than when I saw you last.' And that sounded even more stilted.

'Have you had a good voyage?' The stammer that afflicted him in moments of stress was making itself felt, and he knew he was reddening.

'Lovely, thanks – but it's nice to be here.' That damned 'nice' again, she thought.

'There's only me to meet you. Old Reggie has to hold the fort for both of us, and Louise flatly refused to play gooseberry. She's waiting for us at the flat. Have you had breakfast?'

'Chhota hazri – I didn't feel like anything more.'

'Oh, picking up the language, are we? Good – good – Coolie hai! Sirf ek admi mangta,' he called out, then spoilt it by reverting to English. 'Just one man – Only the luggage in here and no bedding roll. That reminds me.' He slapped himself on the pockets and produced a slip of paper. 'Hire of your bedding and towels – I must remember to claim a refund of the deposit. Meals? Did you have them all?'

'Yes, thank you.'

'Except breakfast this morning, I think you said.'

'Oh, of course.'

'That's five rupees eight annas.' He made a note on the slip. 'I might as well claim it back as let these thieving devils have it. Come on – chalo – pick up this saman and get out to the car park, jaldi, jaldi.' He herded the coolie with the luggage out on to the platform, together with another four who were trying desperately to share the load with him. 'Sirf *ek*, damn you – only *one* man. You're not making your fortunes out of *me.*'

They went out through the barrier on to the assembly platform, but although it was even bigger, noisier and certainly smellier than Victoria Terminus, it struck her as drabber. Somehow the magic seemed to have gone out of things in the last few minutes, and she suddenly felt miserable and forlorn, and the more she tried to fight it off and match his awkward ebullience, the more the words stuck in her throat – and she wanted to cry.

They crossed the concourse and he made for an old and battered Morris and superintended the loading of the luggage into the back. There was too much to go inside and one of her suitcases had to be tied to the spare wheel on the back, and the coolie snapped the leather handle and was driven off, tipless and wailing, by the furious George.

'My God,' she thought. 'He's mean – *mean*.'

They drove across the pontoon bridge that spanned the Hooghli in the shadow of the huge cantilever construction that was soon to replace it, and he, with something definite to say, was jabbering like a guidebook.

'The burning ghats down there on the bank,' he pointed out. 'That's where they cremate their dead – in the open on piles of wood. Look, you can see one now – where the cloud of smoke is coming from. They scatter the ashes on the surface of the river afterwards – This bit is called the Hooghli – it's one of the arms of the Ganges, so that makes it sacred. There's Government House ahead of us. Away to the left is Clive Square – and Clive *Street* – that's *our* empire – the tea kingdom – of course this place was built on tea – and jute, the stuff they make sacks out of. Here's the Maidan – a damn great park, as you can see – nearly two miles long and half as wide, right through the centre of the city – with Fort William, that's the military head-quarters, over there on the right – Ochterlonie Memorial – that Cleopatra's Needle thing there – and Chowringhee on the left – that's our Regent Street, Bond Street and Knightsbridge rolled into one – Louise is going to take you to see the shops there – '

He paused for breath as they negotiated the traffic in Auckland Road before crossing on to the Maidan, and she wished he would go on talking because it covered her own complete conversational deficiency. When he did resume, it was to repeat, 'God, if you only knew how I've been longing for this day – but I'm afraid there's a fly in the ointment. I've been wondering how to break this to you. I think I'd better plunge.'

She said, without interest, 'Why? What's wrong?'

'I have to go away – tomorrow – for ten days – which means, of course, that the wedding will have to be put off until I get back. Oh, my dear, I'm sorry – but there's absolutely nothing I can do about it.' He turned his head to look at her, and narrowly missed a bullock cart, then, in correcting, grazed a rickshaw, and shrieked at the human beast of burden pulling it. 'Sorry about that,' he went on. 'The wretched traffic gets worse every day – Oh, yes – about going away – damn bad luck, but I can see the Company's point of view, and they've really been very decent about everything.'

She felt an immediate relief, akin to that of a condemned prisoner who is granted a stay of execution, which, while not amounting to a full reprieve, does at least offer a brief respite.

She said, 'Don't worry about me. I'll be all right.'

'You're a darling,' he said, delighted, and reached for her hand. 'I've been dreading having to tell you – '

'Watch your driving for God's sake,' she told him. 'You nearly hit another of those cow cart things.'

'Oh, never mind about *them* – they're used to it. Yes – the Company has been marvellous. I should have been up in Gauhati a week ago. We have a saying here – "Time and tea wait for no man". This is the busiest time of the year and we have to have a sahib at each of the checkpoints when the stuff comes down, or half of it's pinched. Anyhow, it's really a blessing in disguise because it will give you a chance to get the flat straightened out – Louise will help with that, of course – and she'll look after you in the meantime – Damn nice people – This is Mayo Road – running into Chowringhee – Metro Cinema there – as good as any Odeon or Plaza in London – *Top Hat* – Fred Astaire and Ginger Rogers, on at the moment – straight from Hollywood – Don't think it's been on in England yet – ' And then, mercifully he had to concentrate on his driving again, and she was saved from screaming.

'Park Street,' he said, turning left out of Chowringhee. 'Not far now. That's the Bengal Club down there, where all the Bara Sahibs foregather. We'll belong there one day, you see.'

He pulled up before a three-storeyed house sandwiched between two taller buildings. It was yellow-washed, with black and brown rain streaks giving it a leprous appearance, and the faded paint on the doors and iron-grilled windows was flaking off in strips. There was a space in front between the pavement and the front door that had possibly once been a garden, but which was now bare of any type of vegetation other than two bedraggled palm trees. A small girl with a naked baby boy sitting astride her immature hip regarded them solemnly. She gave the baby a slight shake and he salaamed them – skinny wrist to forehead, palm to the front.

'Here we are,' said George with evident pride. 'Of course I should carry you over the threshold – '

'But what is it?' asked Jane, bewildered.

'Home,' he said. 'Ours – at least one flat is. The Hawkesleys have the next door one – we're both on the top floor, which makes it much cooler in the hot weather.' He climbed out and said, 'Hamal bulao!' peremptorily, and added apologetically to Jane, 'Wretched hamal's kids. He *will* let them play in front like this. I'll have him fined five chips when I get to the office.' He opened the door on her side and held out his hand. 'Welcome home, sweetheart. It may not look very grand from the outside, but they're jolly good nevertheless. I was very lucky to get one because although I'm fairly senior as an employee, I'm the most junior as a married man – or will be, ha ha.'

A wizened little man in an ill-fitting blue uniform and an untidily wound turban came out of the front door carrying a wreath of tired marigolds. He said, 'Salaam, sahib – salaam, Memsahib – may God bless and bringing plenty sons – ' and lassooed her with the wreath.

Startled, she said, 'What the hell – ?'

'Sorry,' said George. 'I should have warned you. They always garland one on arrival and departure. This is the hamal – that's the porter – of the block. Achcha – bring the saman up to Hawkesley-sahib's flat – jaldi – jaldi.'

'Do I give him anything?' whispered Jane.

'Not yet. I'll give him another ten rupees a month when we actually take the flat over. That's a fortune to these people for doing precisely nothing.'

'What about the children – ?'

'Christ no,' said George hastily. 'You'll be waylaid by them every time you come in or go out if you do that. Come on.'

He took her by the elbow and led her into the hall. It was completely bare except for a wobbly table at the foot of the concrete staircase, and it smelt of curry.

'Indian lawyer in the flat on the right,' George said as they passed. 'But he's quite a decent chap and gives no trouble. Frobisher and Hine's manager on the left – bachelor – bit of a nance they say.' They climbed to the first floor. 'These four –

that's the two on this floor and our two on the next – are Company. Walters, godown supervisor, this side. Married – three kids – noisy little devils who should be Home at school, but he and his wife drink like fish and say they can't afford it. Turton on the other side – Inland Waterways – not a Company man actually, but he handles the paddle steamers that bring the tea down from Gauhati and Chandpur, so we accommodate him. Married – no children – wife visiting her family up-country.' He lowered his voice. 'Anglo-Indian, but she'd never admit it of course.' They came to the top of the stairs. 'And now – I was just going to say "someone who needs no intro-duction" – Louise – Jane.' He beamed, holding out a hand to each of them, and Jane saw a small gipsyishly pretty woman waiting for them. She came forward and said, 'Pleased to meet you, Jane. Hope you've had a decent trip.'

Jane said, 'How do you do? Yes, delightful, thank you.' It sounded cold and formal in her own ears, and evidently in the other's, because Jane saw her bridle slightly, but George was obviously blissfully unaware of this initial non-rapport.

He said, 'You'll never know how much I owe these two, darling. You'll meet Reggie later – he's standing in for me at the moment – doing two men's work – with never a grouse – and Louise has been keeping an eye on the decorators in our flat – That's it there – like to have a look at it before we go in to Louise's?'

'Later, George,' she answered wearily. 'I've got an awful headache.'

'Oh, you poor kid,' he said, concerned, and put his arm round her protectively. 'I bet you're dying for a cup of tea – decent tea – *Company* tea – not the muck they serve on the trains.'

Louise said, 'Oh, Gawd – anything but that. Bloody stuff – I never touch it on principle myself. Come on in – don't stand there.'

The flat, shuttered against the morning sun, was gloomy, and a dispirited electric ceiling fan was doing little to stir the stale, hot air. It was furnished exclusively in battered bamboo, faded cretonne and Benares coffee trays.

'Of course the lower orders don't get air-conditioning,' Louise explained. 'That's for the Bara Sahibs. These lousy electric punkahs are good enough for *us*.'

'Now don't start that again,' George chided gently.

'No, that would be ungrateful, wouldn't it?' She turned to Jane. 'These two, Reggie and George, *make me sick. They just won't stand up for themselves.* These are Class Four quarters – for *Anglo-Indian Supervisory* Staff. We're entitled to *Class Two*, or *at least* Class Three – those are for *LREs* – which *we are not.* We're *Covenanted Staff* – recruited on contract *in Blighty* – ' She seemed incapable of speaking without emphasis, and incapable of emphasizing without spitting. Jane moved back a little out of range.

'Oh, come on, Louise,' George protested. 'You'll be scaring her off before she's had time to see things for herself. This is only a temporary arrangement until the new quarters are ready in Tolleygunj – '

'That's what they told *me* – when I arrived out *three years* ago. Tolleygunj? *Tolleygunj my bloody arse!*'

'Hey! Go easy, old girl!' George was genuinely shocked.

'Sorry.' She shrugged. 'You'll have to get used to me, Jane. I believe in *telling 'em straight* what I think. They don't *like* me for it maybe – but they know what they can do *about that.* Bedroom through here. That *bloody hamal* bringing up your bits and pieces? That's another one who's going to get it *right in his bloody black neck* before long – I'm *telling* you –' She stormed out and they could hear her shouting '*Jaldi! Jaldi! Jaldi!*' as she went downstairs.

George grinned. 'Heart of gold really,' he said ruefully. 'Although she does tend to shock people on first meeting. Let's have a look at the bedroom. Ah yes – very nice. You'll have to get used to sleeping under a mosquito net. Bathroom through here – remember to lock both doors when you're using it. It's between the two bedrooms and serves both.' He turned to her and held out his arms.

She sat down on the edge of the bed and closed her eyes. 'You don't happen to have an aspirin, do you?' she asked, and gained another respite as he went out, concerned, to find

Louise. She looked round the small room, and shuddered. It might have been her own in Brixton. Only the untidily festooned mosquito net and the electric fan struck an alien note. The pitch-pine dressing table and slightly askew wardrobe were identical, as was the squeaky iron bedstead on which she was sitting. She felt that if she ran her fingers along underneath the side members she would rediscover the hard little mounds of chewing-gum she used to deposit there and forget as a child.

George came back with the aspirin and a glass of water. 'Here you are, darling,' he said. 'I feel a brute, but I really must dash off now. I've got a hell of a lot to do in the office before going tomorrow – but of course I'll see you this evening. I'll be dining here with you all – then I'll be off to my virgin couch in the Chummery – that's the Bachelors' Mess in Theatre Road – not far away.' He almost giggled. 'I'm afraid we're all very Victorian out here. It just wouldn't do to doss down here or even in our own flat next door until I'd made an honest woman of you – although the down-to-earth Louise says we're crazy. "She'd tell 'em," she said. "*Whether they liked it or not.*" Heart of gold, like I said.' He bent over and kissed her gently on the cheek. 'Oh, my darling – if you only knew how I've longed for this day – even though it's only going to make things worse for the next ten. Still – won't be long now. Bye-bye.'

He went out, closing the door softly behind him, and she found herself clenching her fists until the nails were digging into her palms. 'God Almighty!' she whispered tensely. 'What the hell could I have been thinking of? I can't go through with it – I can't.'

But she had rallied somewhat by the afternoon and she went out with Louise into Chowringhee, and the shops, the crowds, the colour and noise of the Hogg Market, the tangle of cars, trucks, trams, buses, bullock carts, horse carriages and rickshaws that make up Calcutta's traffic awakened her interest again. They went into Firpo's for tea, and sat on the balcony and looked out across the Maidan towards Fort William.

Louise said, 'I'm sorry for you.'

'Why?' Jane asked.

'You've got it all to come. I've only got another two years before leave. If that monkey of mine wants to come back for some more, *he can come on his own.*'

'You really dislike it as much as all that?'

Louise lit a cigarette, drew in smoke slowly and then exhaled violently.

'*Every bloody minute of it,*' she spat. 'Oh, not the country – ' The bearer was placing their tray before them. ' – not these black buggers either. I can put up with *them* – and put 'em in their place *smartish* if they get uppity at any time – although, fair doos, they don't very often. No – it's the bloody *Memsahibs* I can't take.'

'The Memsahibs?'

'Yeah – the wives of the Bara Sahibs – the *bosses.*' She pressed her thumb hard on the table as if squashing a bug. 'They'd like to keep us – the likes of you and me, there – *there* – like that. Toffee-nosed lot of bitches – '

'But isn't – your husband – I mean – well, he's one of the bosses, isn't he?' Jane said.

'He's in the same grade as your old man,' Louise told her. 'Oh yes – he's a boss, in a *sort* of a way. Everybody who hasn't got a black face is a boss out here. But there's bosses and *bosses*, if you see what I mean. Reggie and your George are in "Overseas" – Reggie in Sales – George in Accountancy. They've each got a couple of Anglo-Bangloes under them and a dozen babus. But, when all's said and done, they're just pen-pushers. They get more money out here than what they'd get for the same job at Home, and the blackie-whites and the full niggers have got to kowtow to them if they want to keep their jobs. Big fish in small ponds, if you see what I mean. But real authority – standing – social position – *never*. Not for their grade. The goldplated nobs in this racket are the directors and the planters – not the poor bloody Reggies and Georges.'

'But surely they can get promotion in time?' Jane faltered.

Louise shook her head firmly. 'It's a father-and-son, uncle-and-nephew world,' she said. 'The big jobs, the posh houses, first class passages Home every second year, bungalows up in the Hills in the hot weather, and hobnobbing round Government House, that's all reserved for the little bastards before they're even born. Oh, they tell the Chhota Sahibs – that means *little* bosses – that if they work hard and say "yes, sir – no, sir – three bags full, sir" for long enough they'll be *considered* for the big time, but *I've* never heard of one of them making the grade. It's something the directors learned off the Indians. The Brahmins, that's the highest caste, tell all the other lower castes that if they are meek and mild and obedient they'll all be born again as Brahmins themselves in a couple of million years or something. And the poor devils believe it, and go on doing all the hard and dirty work, while the "Heavenborn" as they're called, sit on top of the heap as a matter of right. They say it's only the Hindus that have the caste system, but you wait until you see it working among the whites out here. *Jesus!* The directors and their Memsahibs slumming among us lot once a year at the Company Dinner. Us lot giving the blackie-white kids a Christmas tree and a bun fight – the blackie-whites running a rice kitchen for the all-blacks in famine time, which is about every second year. Because we all love each other? *Like hell.* That's to keep everybody on their proper rungs.'

Jane was fighting back tears. 'It's not as bad as all that, surely?' she choked. 'You're pulling my leg.'

'You wait,' said the other grimly. 'I thought the same when I first arrived and saw the form. It's not as bad as all that, I said. They weren't going to get *me* down. *No fear.* I didn't want to belong to their damned clubs – and I wasn't going to talk posh just to please them. *We* did the same as you two – met and married without asking permission first, while Reggie was on leave. The directors don't like that. I'm not hiding anything – Reggie married beneath him as they say. He had this big job in India, and I worked in a factory in Dagenham and we were both on holiday in Margate – but *he* did the chasing – not *me*. No, *sir* – I wasn't asking favours off *anybody*.' She shrugged and lit another cigarette. 'Well – there you are. I'm telling you all this for your own sake, so you'll know what to look out for. It might even be tougher for you. You're pretty and you talk upper-ten, so you'll probably get your nose rubbed in it even harder than I did. But don't let it get you down. Stand up to 'em. Fight for your rights.'

She went for another walk later, with George, in the cool of the night after an ill-cooked dinner, badly served by a sulky Indian Christian factotum who argued with Louise in pidgin English, and which ended in a final explosion when she threw a plate at him and retired screaming to her bedroom.

'Hot weather coming on, you know,' said Reggie apologetically. He was a cheerfully inept little man, and the frank admiration with which he had greeted Jane hadn't helped matters. 'She's always a bit hairtriggerish at this time of the year.'

'The Maidan,' said George as they crossed Chowringhee, in the manner of a schoolmaster conducting a party of bright children round the Tower. 'We skirted the corner of it when I was bringing you from Howrah – but this is a different part. Fort William there – that's where the Black Hole of Calcutta was – and there's the racecourse straight ahead of us – and the Cathedral down to our left. The number of times I've taken this walk at night when it's been too hot to sleep – and now I'm walking here with my little girl   '

'George,' she said in a tight, tense voice, 'I can't stay in that flat with that bloody woman while you're away. You'll have to make some other arrangement.'

'It's so difficult,' he said, distressed. 'I mean – they invited you. Just try it, sweetheart. She really has a – '

'Say "heart of gold" just once more, and I'll scream,' she told him. 'She's a common factory tart and she's done nothing but try to make me miserable all day. For God's sake book me into a hotel somewhere.'

'I can't,' he said desperately. 'I'm sorry, darling – but I just haven't got the money. All that extra expense before leaving England – then I had to pay your fare out – oh, I can claim it back when we're actually married – but that won't be until next month. Please – please, darling, try to stick it out. It will only be for ten days, then we'll be in our own little nest – '

131

'You can lump "little nest" in with "heart of gold",' she ground. 'That's the eleventh time you've said it today. All right, if you can't, you can't. I don't want to sound ungrateful, but being boxed into a rabbit-hutch with a bitch like that for ten whole days, when I thought I was coming to a home of my own, is a bit of a let-down.'

They walked on over the damp grass in silence for a long ten minutes, then he said stiffly, 'I'd better see you back now, unless you'd like a drink in Firpo's first.'

'No thank you,' she answered, as stiffly.

'I'll be catching the five-fifteen from Sealdah tomorrow morning, so I won't be seeing you again until I return. I'll write every day, of course – but the Hawkesleys aren't on the telephone, unfortunately, so I can't call you. You'd better have some money – '

'Not if you can't afford it.'

'*Please*,' he said, stung, and pressed some notes into her hand. 'There's only a hundred rupees there, I'm afraid, just for incidentals.'

'Thank you,' she said quietly. 'You're making *me* feel a bitch now. It must be catching.'

They came back to the flat, and Reggie, with winks and nudges and smirks, and many oblique references to jumping the gun, and beating the parson, forced drinks upon them that neither wanted, until, once again pleading a headache, she managed to make her escape after a peck on the cheek from George, with Reggie tactfully pretending to get more ice from the kitchen.

She lay awake for a long time listening to the squeak-clunk rhythm of the slowly turning fan, against a background of whining mosquitoes and, in the distance, the howl of the jackals that slink on to the Maidan each night after the traffic has stilled.

She shivered again. Oh no – this was not for her.

Chapter Six

The crunch came on the third morning, stemming as most major crises do, from a quite minor incident. Jane knocked a cup off her chhota hazri tray.

'That's one of my best set,' Louise said sourly, when she apologized later.

'I'm sorry,' Jane answered. 'If you'll let me know where you bought it I'll replace it.'

'Selfridges – so how the hell *can* you replace it? The only decent bit of china I've got – and *three* bloody cups broken in the last month – '

'You can hardly blame me for the other two.'

'Who's blaming you?'

'You appear to be.'

'If you came out in the morning for your tea instead of lying back like Lady Muck waiting for it to be brought in to you, it wouldn't have happened.'

'That's a bit unfair, isn't it? I didn't ask for it to be brought in. Please don't again.'

'Getting orders in my own house, eh?'

'Oh, don't be silly – ' and so on in the same vein until Jane struck her colours and beat a retreat to her room. She came out an hour later and walked round to the Park Street post office, where, after a long battle with the hopelessly inefficient Indian telephone service she managed finally to get through to the Storlands' bungalow in Gonah.

'*Who?*' said Tessa, over the mush of static. 'Speak up, please – I can't hear you.'

'*Jane Curtis*,' Jane shouted. 'You know – the *boat* – '

'*Jane!* How lovely! Where are you?'

'Calcutta – '

'– wedding? – didn't see anything in the papers – '

'Hasn't come off – my fiancé had to go up-country. He won't be back for some time – '

'Why don't you come and see *us*?'

'Oh – could I? I'm so fed up with this place – '

'Of course you can! – train back to Bombay – change at Kalyan – send me a wire – meet you – '

'You *angel*!' shrieked Jane, and burst into tears of relief.

She counted her money in the taxi on the way to Howrah Station. She had been husbanding her slender resources, and she had a total of three hundred and twelve rupees.

'A hundred rupees is seven-pounds-ten,' she reckoned, counting feverishly on her fingers. 'Three times that is – is – Blast it! – about twenty-two pounds – a bit more if you take the twelve in – Oh, God – don't let the fare be more than that – '

It was, in fact, two hundred and four rupees eight annas, which included hire of bedding. Meals, she decided prudently, she would pay for as she had them. She hired a waiting room and took another taxi back to Park Street, and told the driver to wait. And to her relief Louise was out.

'Dear Mrs Hawkesley,' she wrote on a sheet of the pink, scented stationery she had bought in London:

I am going to stay with friends I met on the ship. You have been most kind but I don't wish to put you out further. Please thank Mr Hawkesley for me. I shall be writing to Mr Quaife direct.
Yours faithfully,
Jane Curtis.

She left this propped up on the centre table, stuffed her clothes into her cases and returned to Howrah where she pondered long over her letter to George, settling finally for,

Dear George: I don't know what to say exactly except that getting married is such an important thing that I think we ought to give it a bit longer before rushing into things and I hope you will not think me ungrateful because you have been so kind in everything. Things haven't been easy,

Louise has been a bit of a bitch and it would have been better if you had put me into a hotel like I suggested but that wasn't your fault so don't blame yourself. I am going to stay with some friends I met on the ship in Gonah and I will write to you from there. Don't worry about me. I will be alright but I really and truly think in fairness to both of us that we ought to give things a bit more time before rushing into things and I am sure everything will be alright in the end. Love, Jane.'

She found the journey back as exciting as the one out, perhaps even more so because of the element of uncertainty this time. Coming to Calcutta she knew what lay before her. George and security – and, although she wouldn't have admitted it even to herself at the time – dullness. Now the security was no longer there – but in its place was a challenge – something she had to face up to herself with such weapons as a not niggardly Nature had provided her – weapons she had already tentatively tried and not found wanting.

She got off the train at Kalyan in the early hours of the second morning, and waited two hours for her connection, sending a telegram to Tessa, breakfasting and watching the changing scene in the fields around the ugly little station in the meantime, while the sun climbed above the Western Ghats, bringing back the greens and yellows of the rice paddies and the scarlet of the flame-of-the-forest trees. In the waiting room, among the detritus of papers, out-of-date magazines and other useless literature left by the passing tide of travellers she came across an illustrated Government of India handbook, and in idly riffling through the pages she happened on an article about Gonah. It was, she learned, a military station on the western edge of the Deccan Plateau, one hundred and twenty miles from Bombay and some two thousand feet above sea-level; the climate was pleasant and healthy; the Headquarters of West Deccan Military District was situated here together with the Army School of Signals and the newly raised Army School of Mechanization, and two Indian and two British infantry regiments, an Indian cavalry regiment and their ancillary services.

She stood on the edge of the platform and watched the train approaching down the long, straight stretch from the west. Yes – *this* was the India she had always dreamed about. Calcutta? Her lip curled. Calcutta was only Brixton, once removed.

Tessa was jumping up and down on the platform like a small and demented rubber doll. She hurled herself forward as Jane stepped down from her compartment.

'Oh, isn't this absolutely wonderful!' she babbled. 'Just what this wretched station needs – a few more wenches. No competition is far worse than too much. Ram Lal! – saman jumakaro – ek dum – jaldi!'

A magnificently accoutred chaprassi took charge of several lesser minions and her luggage was collected and wafted away, and a path through the crowd was opened for them by an Indian policeman wielding his truncheon, and the station-master salaamed, and another policeman cleared the way to Tessa's little car and caused crippled beggars to slink aside and melt into the shadows. Tessa was still babbling but Jane hardly heard her. She was comparing this reception with that of a few days earlier in Calcutta.

Tessa paused for breath as she drove out of the station into the traffic of the main cantonment road, and then asked the question Jane had been waiting for. 'But what happened about the wedding exactly?'

'He had to go up-country immediately,' she explained. 'Actually he should have left much earlier. Of course we could have had a registry office thing the same day, but I jibbed at that and said I'd rather wait.'

'Good for you. What's the new date then?'

'I jibbed at that, too. I said I wanted more time to think things over.'

'Then it's all off?'

'Not as far as he's concerned – but – Oh, damn – I hate hurting him, Tessa – but I really think I have made a mistake. I should have been stronger in England when first he proposed – but he wouldn't take no for an answer. He just wore me down. I've had my doubts all along – but I decided to give things a last chance to settle themselves – but then, as soon as I saw him again – I knew – I knew – I couldn't go through with it.' She choked and swallowed.

'So you *have* chucked him?'

'Yes and no – That sounds feeble, I know – but what I mean is I told him I wanted time to consider. I've had that time now – nearly thirty hours of it on the train – and I've decided it's just no-go. It wouldn't be fair to either of us. I'm going to write and tell him so – and ask my father to arrange my passage home. Do you think that's terrible of me?'

'I think you've got *guts*,' said Tessa enthusiastically. 'Bloody men who won't be told – they make me furious. I've been back just over a week and I've had three proposals already. Fun at first, I suppose – and a bit flattering no doubt – but what *bores* they are when they hang round looking all spaniel-eyed after you've told them *no*, and meant it. You'll have to watch it here, by God. They'll be round like flies.'

'I *will* watch it,' said Jane with feeling.

'But don't let your people whisk you away too soon,' Tessa begged. 'I mean, stay for a few weeks at least – '

'Well – that's terribly kind of you,' Jane said doubtfully. 'I'd love to see a little of India before going home – but what would *your* people say?'

'They're only too delighted to humour me,' Tessa said. 'I'm afraid I've been sulking a bit. You see, I wanted to go up to university at Home, but they're obsessed with this war thing with Hitler in Europe – bombs and gas and the Lord knows what else – so I've been dragged back here kicking and screaming, because they think India is going to be safe. Oh no – don't worry about the parents – Daddy, in particular, was very bucked when I told him you were coming over.'

'Well – it's terribly – it's terribly kind of you,' Jane said. 'I'll write to George straight away. Thank you, Tessa dear – you've no idea what a relief it is to be able to talk to somebody. I felt so *alone* over there – Oh, there were plenty of *people* – men mostly – one had to fight them off – but nobody to *confide* in – to ask for advice – '

'Don't worry any more about it.' Tessa took one hand from

the wheel and covered Jane's. 'Here we are – this place is your home for as long as you want to stay.' She swung the car into a gateway set in a high stone wall, and a turbaned sentry crashed to attention and presented arms. A long drive wound through an avenue of ancient banyan trees, and smooth lawns lay the other side, and there were beds of zinnias and marigolds, and a flagstaff, with the Union Jack stirring in the early evening breeze, and finally a long low bungalow, deep-verandahed and smothered in scarlet and purple bougainvillaea, with brass cannon flanking wide stone steps.

'Welcome to Flagstaff House,' said Tessa, climbing out. 'I'll show you to your room and you can freshen up and then come along to tea – that'll be in the drawing room at the end of the verandah here. We never change before seven by the way, then Mummy always insists on long frocks. Nothing to do with protocol – it's just because this place is alive with mosquitoes after sundown and they give bare legs hell.'

'I see,' said Jane. 'Tessa – will you do me a favour?'

'Certainly. What is it?'

'If you see me putting a foot wrong in anything – anything at all – do tell me.' She turned frank eyes towards the other girl. 'You see, all this is very new to me. We live quite simply at home in Kent – just the one maid – and since Daddy is up in Town most of the week we seldom change for dinner.'

'Lucky you,' said Tessa. '*We* don't have a maid when the family is on Home leave. Mummy and I do the lot. Change for dinner? Smash and grab in the kitchen most of the time.'

'Yes – but things *are* a bit formal here, aren't they? What I mean is, if you see me doing anything wrong – wearing the wrong clothes at any time – too much make-up – you know – things that would be quite all right in England, but out of place here – '

Tessa laughed. 'Good God! Fancy you asking *me* that. I used to watch you on the ship – and then copy you – and so did most of the other girls. Don't worry, Jane – just be natural. There's nothing grand about this place – except when the Old Man is entertaining officially, and we'll probably dodge that if we're lucky.'

'Yes – but you will tell me, won't you?' Jane insisted anxiously.

'Of course I will,' Tessa promised. 'Just as I would expect you to tell me my slip was showing – if one wore slips out here.'

Her bedroom was large and high-ceilinged, with jalousied doors opening on to the verandah and affording a wide vista of garden. There were two ceiling fans – running fast and silently – and through an inner door Jane could see an enormous upended tin bath.

Tessa said, 'I think you would have had push-pull and all mod cons in Calcutta, wouldn't you!' and laughed at Jane's bewilderment. 'Right – you asked for it – so here your education begins. The bathroom – or gusl-khana as the locals call it – is primitive in the extreme, but at least we each have one of our own. That throne thing there with a lid, is the loo. There's no running water or anything like that – so you use it and then open that other door there and bellow, "Mehta!" and a dark gentleman comes along and empties it. Same with the bath. You just yell, "Gusl tiar karo!" and a different gent comes and dumps hot water into that tin tub. The hole in the wall down there at floor level is – '

'The waste hole,' Jane said, delightedly. 'That's where snakes come in. Yes – I've heard all about that from my uncle. He was a cavalry officer out here.'

'Good – well, you need no further coaching from me,' Tessa said. 'I think it's all disgusting. We've been here for nearly five hundred years and we haven't installed proper plumbing outside Bombay and Calcutta. I believe even the Viceroy has to use a thunderbox when he's up-country.' She giggled. 'No wonder we Indian-born barrack-rats were regarded as savages when we went Home to school. Poor little devils. Half of us weren't properly housetrained.'

They walked along the verandah. Jane suddenly halted and closed her eyes, lifted her face and inhaled deeply. Tessa watched her for some moments in silence, then she said, 'You're hooked.'

'What do you mean?' Jane asked.

'That smell. It's a compound of all our pathetic English flowers fighting for existence in this hot earth. The malis – that's the gardeners – are watering now and it brings it out.'

'But why am I hooked?'

'Few people notice it – but if they do, they never forget it. It was the one thing that could make me cry with home-sickness when I was at school. You'd get it very occasionally on a hot summer's evening in England.'

Jane nodded slowly. 'You're right,' she said. 'I won't forget it, ever – and whenever I smell it again it will bring me back to this garden. I don't know how to thank you, Tessa.'

'Oh, nonsense. As I said before, I'm only too glad you've come.' They came to the French windows of the drawing-room. 'If we're lucky there'll only be Mummy and the ADC who's rather a drip. People only drop in for tea informally on Mondays and Thursdays – ' She peeped cautiously round the edge of the window. 'Oh, and my brother – but he doesn't count.'

A long-legged youth uncoiled himself from the depths of a chintz armchair. He was wearing polo kit and trying to balance a cup, saucer and plate, but the manoeuvre was abortive and he spilled tea down his white breeches. He spat an underbreath four-letter word venomously, and then went pink from jawbone to sandy hairline.

Tessa said, 'This is Jane. This is my brother, Ian. You see what I mean now about barrack-rats not being housetrained.'

The flush deepened to a mottled tomato red and the boy muttered incoherently and went from the room quickly. His mother said mildly, 'You shouldn't, Tessa. You know how awkward he is with girls on first meeting. Do excuse him, Jane. He'll suffer agonies over this.'

She knew a moment of wild elation. She, Max Wilmott, routing and putting to flight an Adonis in polo kit! But she had enough intelligence just to smile shyly and say nothing, and the older woman warmed to her. 'He's so uncomfortable with women, at first,' she confided. 'They get so little oppor-tunity of meeting any in that God-forsaken camp of theirs.'

'Damn right he's uncomfortable,' Tessa said. 'It's our

wretched educational system. You know what the Americans say about our boys' public schools – "Great for raising poofs and longshoremen, but they fall over their feet when they meet a dame." Same with girls. We little angels used to smoke and swear and drink – if we could get our hands on any booze – but we were frightened stiff of boys. It's unhealthy. All schools should be co-educational. Don't you agree, Jane?'

She was saved from answering by the entry of another polo-kitted figure – a dark young man who halted in the doorway and brought his spurred heels together with a click and murmured, 'If you'll pardon my kit, ma'am – '

'Well, at least they didn't make a longshoreman out of *you*, did they?' Tessa said sweetly. 'This is Jane Curtis – Terry Felton-Neave, the ADC.' Jane made a mental note to find out what the initials stood for.

Tea extended over to the drinks period, and the General came in with an elderly Brigadier and a hatchet-faced woman who was introduced as the only lady vet in India. 'God! Who'd want another?' Tessa whispered. The General greeted Jane uproariously and then stood beside her with his arm paternally round her shoulders. She glanced nervously once or twice towards Lady Storland to see how she was taking her husband's camaraderie, but if she noticed it at all she certainly didn't seem to be resenting it. All the same, Jane thought, I'd better watch it. That arm was just a *weeny* bit on the affectionate side. She managed to slip gently out of the circle later, when the General was discussing equine tape-worm with the lady vet, a subject on which he appeared to be an authority. More people were arriving, including one or two of the Fishing Fleet from the ship, and she found herself repeating her story without confusion or the slightest hesitation. ' – miles and miles up in the jungle – so it was a case of special licence at the registry office, or wait until he returns. I opted for the latter, because it seemed such a shame not to use my wedding dress and veil after bringing it all this way. I was terribly grateful when Tessa invited me over in the meantime – ' And nobody seemed to be questioning it.

She moved to the side of the room as it filled, and engaged in what was becoming her favourite avocation – watching, listening – and learning. There was nothing to be frightened of here, she decided. Nothing more rigid about this protocol than that of the Streatham Locarno, where you *really* had to watch your Ps and Qs. She heard an officer's young wife talking about a point-to-point in which she had ridden recently; ' – my bloody animal dumped me in the shit at the third brush fence,' she had said. That would have been social suicide for any *nice* girl at a tennis club dance at Home. No – it was just the little things one had to watch – 'Pleased to meet you' – 'ever so nice' – 'you *are* awful' – the things Robert had warned her about. She wondered how her accent sounded in others' ears. She wasn't particularly worried about it. Her speech was the only thing that had earned the approval of George's sister at school. It had never been marred by a Cockney whine or elided vowels even as a child – and then a couple of years working among people who, if not exactly cultured were at least well-spoken, had smoothed and polished it. No – she was certain that she *sounded* all right. It was what she actually *said* that mattered –

She saw Ian come into the room and peer round as if looking for somebody. He caught her eye and tried unsuccessfully to dissemble by turning away and making conversation with another guest, but Jane knew that he was looking for her so she made it easy for him by going out on to the now quite dark verandah, and sure enough within minutes he had come up behind her.

He said, 'I say – I'm awfully sorry about the language – but that damned tea was hot.'

'I didn't hear a word,' Jane assured him, and then they were both laughing naturally.

'I hate poodle-faking,' he told her. 'Normally I steer clear of Ma's drawing-room binges until drinks time – but I wanted to meet you.'

'That was sweet of you,' she said. She had noticed that 'sweet' seemed to be a widely accepted portmanteau adjective in this circle.

'Not at all. Sheer curiosity – ' He realized immediately that he had made a gaffe and once more he was floundering, but she rescued him again by laughing. 'I'm always putting my foot in it,' he mumbled ruefully. 'The thing I came out to ask you is, do you ride?'

She was prepared for this, because she had heard the same question asked of one of the Fishing Fleet, and had noted the readily accepted answer. 'I'm hopeless,' she said. 'Badly taught at school by a fool of a woman, but I'd love to start again seriously.'

'Good,' he said eagerly. 'You must let me teach you. The Old Man has some quite decent stuff in the stable here. I'm out in the blue unfortunately – in Dhond, twenty miles away, but we only cop one duty weekend a month out of the training season, and I could drive in most evenings.'

She though it prudent to temporize. 'I'm afraid I haven't brought any riding things with me,' she said regretfully.

'We only wear jodhpurs and shirts here,' he told her. 'Tessa could lend you some of hers – you look much of a size – or Ram Gopal, the bazaar darzai, would run you up a pair in a couple of hours. That's fixed then – tomorrow. I'll be in about four.'

She found herself torn between triumph at this easy conquest and terror of making a fool of herself. She remembered, vividly, herself and Alice Dutton – in bathing suits at Herne Bay – being inveigled on to ponies, and some joker had burst a paper bag behind hers, and it had bolted with her up the beach and finally thrown her into the middle of a Cockney family's picnic lunch. She shivered. 'I don't think so,' she said. 'Not tomorrow. Perhaps some other time.'

'I see,' he said glumly, and sighed. 'Oh, well – it seemed worth trying – '

'Worth trying what?'

'Trying to get in early. You'll be bombarded by all these bloody lounge lizards and staff wallahs in here. A bloke out in the mofussil like myself won't stand a chance. Sorry to have bothered you.' He turned away abruptly, and, unaccountably, she felt a stab of pity. She reached out and touched him on the arm.

'Oh, *please*,' she said. 'I wasn't putting you off – I really

wasn't. It's just that I'm scared – scared of horses I mean –
otherwise I'd love to come. That's the truth.'
He stared at her, then broke into a delighted grin.
'You're not pulling my leg?' he asked. 'You really mean that?'
'Yes – '
'Good.' He put out his hand. 'Put it there. I'll tell you something. Kids in this country are put into ring-saddles at the age
of two – that's a felt contraption with a circular bar round it
for the miserable little blighters to hang on to. Most of them
hate it at first. I know I did. Later when I'd outgrown the ring
I used to get thrown regularly. I loathed the sight of horses –
and I never went near one after I had escaped Home to school.
Then came Sandhurst – and all the hoary old jokes in the riding
school, which was of course compulsory. You'd get chucked,
and the cretin of a Rough-riding Sergeant would bellow,
"Mister Storland, sir! Who gave you permission to dismount?"
You might have broken an arm or something, but that only
made it all the funnier – for the hearty boys.'
'Well, now you know how *I* feel,' she said. 'I was thrown
badly once too.'
'I know exactly,' he nodded. 'If you only knew how refreshing it is to hear somebody admitting it, instead of pretending
to be up to National Hunt standard. Most of the silly cows in
that room at this moment are talking about horses. They go on,
and on, and on, until one could foam at the mouth and run –
because that's the done thing. You could murder your mother
and perhaps still be accepted in society – but you jag a horse's
mouth or draw blood with your spurs and you're *out*. It's all
a pose.'
'And yet you want to teach *me*?'
'Yes,' he said quietly. 'I want to teach you – and I'll tell you
why. I passed into the hands of an old cavalry buster in my
second year. He was typical – hard-drinking, foul-mouthed and
as tough as an old saddle – but he was a born teacher, and no
mean psychologist. He realized I was scared, and that I'd
been badly taught, and that I was hating every minute of it.
But he also knew that in the Army the horse is king – in spite
of all their talk of mechanization – and he knew that I'd have

144

to come to terms with it. So he just completely *un*taught me – and then *re*taught me – right from scratch. He gave me my confidence back in other words – and now I ride, play polo after a fashion, and hunt – and I really enjoy it, although I try not to be a bore about it. So what do you say? Will you trust me to teach you? I promise you you'll not be frightened, *once*.'

'So that I'd be better than any of those silly cows in there?' she asked.

'Better than most,' he promised. 'I can't answer for the lady vet. I haven't met her before – but with a face like that the poor bitch would have to be able to do *something* well.'

'It's a deal,' Jane smiled.

'Splendid. I'll talk to Tessa about clothes, then I'm afraid I have to be going. We've got a confounded Mess night on. Until tomorrow then.' He turned and went back into the drawing room, and Jane watched him neatly dodge his parents and then speak briefly to Tessa before going out.

Since the parents had an official engagement that night, the girls dined alone, magnificently attended by five servants – khitmagar, abdar, two bearers and a mesalchi.

'And there are a couple outside pulling the punkahs,' Tessa said wryly. 'Daddy loathes electric fans in the dining room – and of course there'll be the khansamah, that's the cook, and about four helpers in the kitchen. That's the white man's burden. But what can one do? I remember when I was quite small a woman arriving on the station – the wife of the Medical Officer. She was a doctor herself but, of course, she couldn't practise in her own right out here – so she had lots of time on her hands, a thing she'd never been used to before, and she got into mischief – '

'With other men you mean?'

'No. That wouldn't have mattered as long as she was discreet. It was much worse. She went down to Bombay and bought a portable oil stove and some English pots and pans and started to do their own cooking. She was very good at it apparently, but the whole station was up in arms – white as well as black.'

'Why? What harm was she doing?' Jane asked.

'The khansamah said she was robbing him of his livelihood – even though he was still being paid his wages – and he left in high dudgeon, and since they always stick together, the rest of the servants quit too – and there are some you can't do without – the sweepers and mehtas, the Untouchables whose work no other Indian can possibly do. Still, she stuck it out, but then the strike spread to other households, and people who had just been amused by a harmless eccentricity at first, got very angry indeed. There were indignant meetings in the Club, and a round robin was sent to her expressing everybody's views – but she had the bit between her teeth now and she told them all to go to hell – and carried on turning out the most heavenly meals, and saving hundreds of rupees a month on her normal household bills. Daddy had her husband up and told him to tell her to stop it – but the husband said, "You have a go, sir. She won't stop for me." So Daddy tackled her – and she told him to go and take a running jump – she wasn't breaking any laws – civil or military.'

'What happened in the end?'

'She was invalided Home with the worst type of amoebic dysentery. The local bhut-hakim – that means witch-doctor – put a spell on her.'

'You surely don't believe that?' Jane asked, wide-eyed.

Tessa shrugged. 'It happened,' she said. 'Oh, there were lots of theories. The servants' guild used to break into their cook-house at night and put all sorts of revolting things in their food – that was the favourite. Anyhow, whatever caused it, I know that when I'm a Memsahib I won't start trying to put the world to rights. Things have been running their own way out here far too long for that.'

'You *are* going to be a Memsahib?'

'What the hell else is there ahead of me?'

'You said that you wanted to go Home to university.'

'Pipe dreams. I couldn't do it without money, and Daddy wouldn't loosen the purse-strings for something he didn't approve of. "Higher education for women? What the devil for? Put 'em to bed and give 'em plenty of babies. Boy babies for preference because you can put 'em in the Army and you

146

don't have to give 'em dowries." They talk about the natives and their medieval customs – God, these old Indian Army pukkha sahibs haven't advanced an inch since Genghis Khan.' She laughed dryly. 'Oh, yes – I'll marry, and spend the rest of my life out here agonizing over my poor little chickabiddies at Home in some ghastly school, but refusing to give up any of the fleshpots and go back to England to make a home for them. Yes – I'll be a Bara Memsahib like the rest of them – salaaming my lord and master, but treating everybody else like dirt – intriguing, gossiping and backbiting. I said the sahibs hadn't advanced since Genghis Khan. The Memsahibs have been static since the Queen of Sheba.'

'But they're not *all* like that,' ventured Jane. 'I mean your mother for instance – '

'If I had to pick a prototype for all the others I'd pick Mother,' Tessa said. 'Look – both of them were Home last year, when I first brought the university project up. "Oh, no dear," said Mamma. "It would be so pointless. You'll be coming back to India next year and marrying some nice boy and dedicating your life to the Service." I nearly spewed. I tackled the Old Man after that – on his own. He was rather more honest. "No, India's the best place for you youngsters. This war that's coming along is going to be noisy and nasty here in Europe." "What about all those who can't cut and run?" I asked him. "Bloody hard luck on them," he said. "But it's the next generation of our *own* people my first obligation is to. Don't be difficult, sweetie." But I kept at him, and in the end he said he'd agree to my going up to Cambridge if Mummy would stay Home for the next three years, if there was no war. Huh! Mummy stay in England as a nanny-cum-chaperone to her darling daughter when her place was out here at the top of the stack? Not bloody likely.'

It was rank iconoclasm to Jane. She felt like a devoted novice, not yet understanding the mysteries but still revering them, listening to one of the elect defiling them. But since she was not sure enough of her ground to take up the cudgels, she just made softly sympathetic noises. Tessa started to rise and two servants darted forward to draw her chair back while the remainder struggled for the privilege of assisting Jane. Tessa waved them aside impatiently. 'See what I mean?' she asked Jane. 'It's this sort of thing that stifles one out here. Servants prostrating themselves at every turn. We get used to it as children and become spoilt brats unable to do a thing for ourselves, then we face a rude awakening when we go Home – and, finally, when we come back, seeing things in their proper perspective and refusing to be deified, we're thought rude and ungrateful by the Indians, and dangerous radicals by our elders. One just can't win. Come on – let's go to the cinema before I bore you stiff. This is the third time I've returned since I was a child, and it always affects me the same way.'

The cantonment was clean, brightly lighted and well policed, with a marked absence of the appalling poverty that has always been a feature of Calcutta, and there was a heavy scent of frangipani, mango blossom and night jasmin on the warm air. Tessa kept up a running commentary as she drove.

'Three clubs,' she explained. 'This one we're passing now is the Gymkhana – junior officers and other bright young things, but our elders and betters turn up for the dance every Saturday night. There are tennis courts and rather a nice swimming pool here, with the polo ground behind it. Just a bit further along, behind those banyan trees, is the West Deccan. That's for Colonels and above and, of course, their Memsahibs. Serious things of life there – bridge, how to govern India, and who's next for full General? The racecourse is just outside cantonments, with the Jockey Club next door. Very jolly during the racing season, but quite dead for the rest of the year unless you play golf, because they run that too. Do you play, by the way?'

'I always find it rather a bore,' Jane said solemnly.

'So do I. Both the game and the people who play it. Here's the main street – Curzon Parade, it's called. All the best shops are here – Bansi Lal, Cheapjack and Eduljee. When you're buying anything you play one off against the other to get the price down. Of course, you never pay their asking price – I think they'd be disappointed if you did. Bargaining is a way of life with them. And here's Marchioni's. You'll find an Italian restaurant in practically every cantonment in India – which is

148

just as well, because they are about the only places the poor damn Tommy can go, besides the cinemas. The pukkha sahibs have their messes and clubs – the sergeants have the same on a lower social level, but the soldiers have nothing.'

She turned into a forecourt in front of what looked like the Brixton Odeon on a slightly smaller scale. A neon sign proclaimed it to be The West End Electric Palace. They parked and went inside and it was only then that Jane saw that the brave façade covered a long open-sided shed with a screen at one end and a raised platform at the other. In between were half a dozen rows of very civilized tip-up seats separated by a formidable bamboo pallisade from further rows of wooden forms, then a large square of beaten earth. On the platform were arranged a number of cane lounge-chairs with small tables beside them. Electric ceiling fans whirred overhead.

'Here you see the system working in miniature,' Tessa said. 'We're on the top shelf here – at two rupees – reserved for the Lord's anointed – that's us. Troops in the seats immediately in front, at one rupee – then *respectable* Indians on the forms at eight annas – and the lower orders squatting on their hunkers on the ground in front for four annas.'

'But we didn't pay at all,' Jane said. 'How's that?'

'Nothing so vulgar as a box office for *us*. The Parsee manager will just debit Daddy's account. The mob come in by a side entrance and buy tickets in the ordinary way.'

'Well, the same thing happens at Home,' Jane said defensively. 'You've got dear seats and cheap seats – What's wrong with that?'

'At Home, just so long as you've got the money you can sit where the devil you wish,' Tessa said. 'In theory that applies here too – but I often wonder what would happen if Private Bloggs's wife smacked down two rupees and came and sat by Mummy. I'd like to be here to see it – ' She paused, and added, 'No, I wouldn't. Mummy wouldn't do a thing, except raise her eyebrows slightly – but the manager would be looking for another job tomorrow. Anyhow, it's all hypothetical. Mrs Bloggs wouldn't get in in the first place – not even if she smacked down ten rupees. I'm sorry – am I spoiling anything for you?

'In a way, yes,' Jane was emboldened to answer. 'I mean, you seem so bitter about everything – and I think things are ever so nice – I mean so well arranged and – '

But Tessa didn't appear to hear that, because they had climbed the few steps to the platform, and heads were turning and young men, some in mess kit and others in dinner jackets, were hastily pulling in legs to let them pass, and in some cases climbing to their feet, and she was returning greetings, here with a smile, there a wave, and occasionally a mock scowl. Two of the men pulled chairs round for them so that they could get the benefit of one of the fans without actually sitting underneath it, and one asked Tessa if he could get drinks for them, so she had no option but to introduce them to Jane, although the latter had the feeling that she didn't want to.

'Jane Curtis,' Tessa said shortly. 'Staying with us – Ricky Mallow and Tom Sixsmith. No, no drinks, thank you – we've just dined. And now shut up both of you. We want to see the picture.'

How did she get away with it? Jane wondered. It had been the same on the ship. Tessa was good-natured enough but, as she had again demonstrated clearly tonight, she was subject to moods, and she could be thoroughly rude to people on occasion for no apparent reason. But the boys kept coming back for more. Like George. *He* kept returning to kiss the boot that kicked him in the mouth. Those tactics didn't work at Home though, she reflected. Tick a boy off for something there, however well deserved it might be, and you'd find yourself spending most of your time in the Ladies powdering your nose on dance nights. Louise, too. Shrewish little bitch – she led her poor damned husband a hell of a life, and she'd picked on George the night he'd dined there something awful – but they had taken it as meek and mild as lambs. Was it because women were so scarce out here? And if so, were these not then the correct and accepted tactics to adopt? She'd have to watch carefully. She didn't want to scare any of them off, but, at the same time, it would be folly to be too sweet if it was likely to make one appear easy to get. Poor old George. Decent enough chap – but God, how dull. And the nerve of it! Telling her he was a *planter* – stinking with money and all that – when all the time he was some sort of clerk. If she married him she'd find herself down in those seats in front. Not quite on the bare earth, or even the wooden forms – maybe the rupee tip-ups. She smiled secretly. No, thanks. This was her place – up here on the platform, with handsome young men pulling chairs around for her, and trying to ply her with drinks –

The lights came up for the interval and she realized that she hadn't taken any of the picture in at all. She was aware of practically everybody up here on the platform waving to Tessa, and a few of the men, but certainly none of the women, found some excuse or other to join them – either to talk to Tessa or the two youths with them, which, in the ordinary way of basic politeness, meant introductions – and then suddenly she was sure that it was she who was the target – absolutely sure. It was a heady sensation, and one that frightened her not a little for the first few moments – like hearing her name called out as a winner of the Miss Brixton contest – but then she came to grips with the realization. She could make it here. She *would* make it. But, by God, she'd have to be careful. Mustn't put a foot wrong, she told herself. *Watch* it, Max – *Jane* – no high-hatting Tessa – really polite and deferential to Ma – a sweetie-pie to Pop, with always a touch of breathless admiration. Watch – watch all the time. Watch and learn.

The young men gathered round them like flies after the National Anthem – played right through, with all Europeans, of both sexes, standing rigidly to attention and not fighting to get to the exits as they did at Home. Drop into the Club for a nightcap? A drink at Marchioni's? – quite a decent band there at the moment. Tennis tomorrow? What about old Jacko's gin-swill at the Pool on Sunday morning? Tessa batted them all lightly aside on the score of Jane's tiredness after her train journey, and they drove out through their milling ranks.

'Veni, vidi, vici,' Tessa said dryly. 'You certainly made a hit there.'

'But it was you they were all talking to,' Jane protested insincerely.

'Come off it. You know damned well they were cocking their sights at *you*.'

'I'm sorry,' Jane said meekly.

'What the devil have you to be sorry about? I'm delighted. It's going to be fun sitting back watching them all trying to cut each other's throats.'

'I don't want to make trouble.'

Tessa laughed. 'Don't worry. I promise you you're not treading on *my* toes – but I can see the Fishing Fleet forming a vigilante group before you leave this station.'

'Well, in that case I'd better not stay – ' She sounded distressed.

'What bloody nonsense!' Tessa exploded. 'I'm only pulling your leg. Ian tells me that you're going riding tomorrow.'

'He wants to teach me.'

'We'll have a fitting-out parade in the morning then. Now there's a lad you could be very good for, poor kid.'

'Why "poor kid"?'

'He's always been so overshadowed – at home by the Old Man – at Eton and Sandhurst by everybody – and now he's having a bad time in his regiment.'

'What a shame – '

'Oh, a lot of it is his own fault. He should stand up for himself more. He certainly should have stood up to the Old Man years ago and refused to go into the Army.'

'You mean he's unhappy in the Army?'

'Not particularly – I don't think he cares much one way or another now. That's the whole trouble. Apart from horses he doesn't seem to be interested in anything, so he's picked up a reputation for laziness and indifference with his CO and Adjutant and they're making life hell for him.'

'Can't your father do anything about it?'

'Good heavens no. A parent, certainly an Army parent, would never dream of interfering in a matter like that – except perhaps to tell them to pile it on more. They make me sick, the lot of them.'

'I'm sorry. If there's anything I can do – ' Jane ventured.

'There is,' Tessa said quickly. 'Give him a break. If the

bright and hearty boys see him making the running with you, he'll gain izzat – and that would give him quite a lift, and do a lot to restore his self-confidence.' She laughed again. 'I'm told that in Bombay dirty little boys offer the services of their sisters to the sahibs. I seem to be reversing it. But you know what I mean. He'll probably bore you to tears – '

'Oh no – '

'– but if you go around with him a little, I really would be awfully grateful.'

'Of course I will,' Jane said eagerly. 'And he wouldn't bore me at all. I think he's ever so – I mean I thought he was quite fun – What's "izzat" by the way?'

'It's Hindi for "honour" – "prestige" – that sort of thing. One shouldn't mix languages – but each has words that the other hasn't, and it's handy at times. Thanks, Jane. I really am grateful. In the early days as kids at Home he always looked after me – and I hate to see him being picked on now.'

'I'll do my best,' Jane said earnestly. 'I really will.'

Ian said, 'Damned good – I mean it. Of course you'll need to keep it up. We ought to do a couple of hours every day I'm home here. You do like it, don't you?'

Jane nodded and smiled eagerly. 'Of course I do – '

'And you're not frightened?'

'Not while I'm with you, although I'd be scared rigid with another teacher.'

'Instructor,' he corrected. 'Yes, it's a good thing to stick to *one* – certainly in the early stages. Some of the hearties are inclined to force the pace a bit – start jumping too soon, before the pupil's balance and grip have been developed – ' He dropped to the ground and helped her to dismount, waving away the syce who came forward to take their horses. 'Always ungirth and remove the bit yourself after a ride, and make sure your mount hasn't hurt himself in any way – girth-galls – cut fetlocks – jagged mouth.' He went through the simple routine with both horses, and she eased the seat of her breeches away from her hot and aching behind surreptitiously, and hung on his every word.

'Right,' he said when he had finished. 'I think we've got the makings of a darned sound horsewoman in you – provided we stick at it. Good hot bath now, with a spoonful of ammonia in it – then how about drinks and dinner at the Club? There's a dance tonight,' he finished hopefully.

She hesitated. 'But your mother? I mean – missing dinner here – Wouldn't she be annoyed?'

'Good God,' he laughed. 'The Old Woman doesn't feed at home half a dozen times a month, and she's quite surprised when we do. But don't worry – I'll warn out with the khidmagar.'

'Oh, *please*,' Jane breathed, looking up at him. 'I'd *love* to – ' and Ian's chest expanded visibly beneath his damp shirt.

Chapter Seven

Mr Greenhalge stood at the jalousied window of the directors' conference room and looked down into Clive Street. He grunted with annoyance as one of the distinctively yellow-painted Hollins-Bland Company cars came into view, crawling at a snail's pace through the congested traffic. Six of the damned things, rear doors removed to allow for quick ingress and exit, constantly circling the two blocks of Calcutta's tea empire, because parking was prohibited anywhere in this area, and when the bidding started at the Tea Exchange the brokers had to get their asses down there fast. Half a head gained on a rival could make the difference between half a million rupees lost or won at the end of the day. But it certainly pushed up overheads. Everything pushed up overheads. This bloody fellow and his wretched woman's passage out – and now trouble over their flat, with Braganza, the best tea-taster and blender in the business, threatening to quit and go to Brooke-Bond if he didn't get better accommodation – He turned and glared as a tap sounded at the door.

'Come in,' he snapped. 'And for God's sake close both doors after you or we'll lose the benefit of the air-conditioning.'

George came in and blinked nervously at the figure that was black and faceless against the light. 'You sent for me, sir,' he said. There was a frog in his throat, and in trying to clear it he coughed and gagged.

'Yes – I sent for you, Quaife,' Mr Greenhalge said ponderously. 'I think some sort of explanation is due. Don't you?'

'I know it seems a little strange, sir,' George said desperately, 'but as I explained to Mr Muir – '

'Suppose you explain to me.'

'Well – there's been a – a sort of a – a temporary hitch, you see – '

'I *don't* see, Quaife. That's why I'm asking for an explanation.' Mr Greenhalge started to enumerate on his fingers. 'In the first place you decide to get married while on leave, without the traditional courtesy of introducing your intended wife to the London directors – '

'It was a last minute decision – '

'Allow me to continue. You then apply on arrival back here for a passage for the lady – well knowing that while established wives and families are generously, even, I might say, *lavishly* taken care of in the matter of leave travel, it is the rule that *fiancées* are the responsibility of the individual concerned until such time as the marriage has taken place. You know that, surely, Quaife?' Mr Greenhalge had reached the third finger.

'I'd spent rather more than I intended at Home, sir,' George said wretchedly. 'I was very short of ready cash.'

'That, of course, is your own affair,' Mr Greenhalge said, tapping the fourth finger. 'I mean, the Company pays you an adequate salary. How you outlay it is entirely up to you. You're no longer a boy, Quaife – not a feckless first-time-Home junior. However, to continue, we overlooked the irregularity, and let you have the passage money. We went further. We allotted you married quarters out of your turn – causing a good deal of unrest among other, in some cases, more senior employees. You then ask to be excused up-river duty, a thing most of your colleagues look forward to and enjoy – '

'I asked for a few days' *postponement*, sir, because she was arriving out, and I naturally wanted to be here to receive her – ' George was conscious of his vocal cords knotting in an imminent stammer.

'*Naturally*,' Mr Greenhalge conceded. 'But there is such a thing as *duty*, Quaife. Some people hold the belief that duty comes first in *all* matters. You were never in the Army, were you? No, of course you weren't,' he answered himself. 'However, be that as it may, we *did* allow you to stay over to meet

156

the lady. We *did* cut your up-river stay by five days at the busiest time of the whole transhipping period. We *did* take workmen off quite important maintenance duties in the go-downs in order to get your flat ready for occupation. But – ' Mr Greenhalge threw his hands up in a gesture of complete bewilderment – 'where *is* the lady?'

'She – she's visiting f-f-friends, sir. She – she – she – ' His cords stuck fast.

'I see.' Mr Greenhalge closed his eyes and nodded slowly, his expression that of an understanding parent humouring an idiot child. 'Visiting friends – I see – I see. Rather odd, I should say, for the bride to dash off to visit friends on the eve of her wedding. Still, that, like the matter of your salary, is your own affair. The Company, Quaife, *interests* itself in the welfare and, er – life-style of its employees, but it does not presume to *dictate*. Not so long as the employee in question carries out his duties satisfactorily, and behaves in a seemly manner.' He paused, then continued portentously, 'But you, I am afraid, have not been giving of your best lately. Not since your return from leave. And your behaviour has been – well as I said – just a little odd.'

'I – I – I'm sorry, sir,' George muttered. 'I know it's a bit difficult to understand – but – '

'*Very* difficult, Quaife,' Mr Greenhalge amended gravely. 'I must therefore ask you to do the following – ' He commenced the finger-count again. 'One, provide proof of your marriage within the next few days, or refund the passage money advanced to you. Two, pursuant upon one, regularize your occupation of the flat allotted to you as a married man – or relinquish such occupation. Three, and this is by far the most important point, in your own interests even more than in those of the Company, do put your back into things rather more than you have been doing lately. Mr Muir tells me that he hasn't been altogether satisfied with things in your sub-department for the past few weeks. This might be taken as a friendly, but still official, warning. I would hesitate to invoke Article Nine of your contract – but – Well, let's not talk about that – *yet*. That is all, Quaife. I will see you again in ten days –

that is on the twenty-third – and I hope that you will have got things sorted out by that time. If you require a few days off to accomplish this, you may take them – and they will be deducted from your local vacation entitlement.'

Mr Greenhalge turned and resumed his study of the Clive Street traffic. George mouthed an incoherent 'Y-y-yes, sir – thank you, sir – ' and went swiftly.

He walked along Clive Street, through Dalhousie Square, past Government House and across the Maidan, a long dragging mile and a half through the turkish bath humidity of the pre-monsoon evening, until his shirt and grey business suit were soaked with sweat, not heeding the string of rickshaw coolies who pulled their ramshackle vehicles hopefully in his wake, nor the beggars who tugged at his jacket. What could he do? he thought hopelessly. What the hell could he do? He didn't even know where she was. Two letters – the first posted at Howrah, the day she left, and this one today, three weeks later. No address – just the postmark, 'Gonah Cantts' as a clue.

Dear George,
Please excuse no letter up till now but I have been thinking. I am afraid it is no good we made a mistake but don't think I am not greatful for all you have done and the trouble you went to but it just wouldn't work out and it wouldn't be fair to you nor to myself. It is just as well we found out in time so theres no harm done. Thank you for everything and I hope you meet some nice girl who will make you happy. Yours sincerely Jane.
PS I am staying with some Army friends who I met on the ship an officer and his wife and there family so you are not to worry. J.

It was in his pocket now – sweatsoaked and illegible – but he didn't need to read it again. Every one of the trite, mincing, misspelt, unpunctuated words had burned itself into his brain.

He crossed Chowringhee, not hearing the clanging of a tram's warning bell, nor the hooting of taxis and the frenzied blowing of a policeman's whistle which halted the traffic before he was mashed to a pulp. A hand gripped his arm and Reggie yelled in his ear, 'What the bloody hell do you think you're doing? I've been chasing you since you left the office – Come on with me, you dam' fool.'

He suffered himself to be led the rest of the way to Park Street, blinded with the ochre-stained sweat that trickled down from the lining of his topee and mixed with tears of self-pity, thankful that Reggie, with an unwonted understanding, was for once silent. They went up to the flat, colourwashed now in a hideous magenta and stinking of new paint. Louise came forward from the door of their apartment, but Reggie shot her a look that held her. He lowered George into a chair and went to a drink cupboard and came back with an unopened bottle of whisky, a syphon of soda and a bowl of ice. He mixed strong double pegs and sat down opposite the other. 'Get that inside you, and don't try to talk yet,' he said tersely, and George obeyed mechanically – and held out his glass for a refill.

'That's the idea,' Reggie said approvingly. 'If you take my advice you'll get as pissed as a newt – and when you've got over your hangover tomorrow things will look different. They're not worth it, George. Not a bloody one of them, and that goes for that bag of mine – in spades, doubled. Bottoms up – and down the bloody hatch.'

'That's all very well,' George said miserably. 'But they're going to fire me if she doesn't come back.'

'Bloody nonsense. They can't do that.'

'They can you know. Greenhalge was quoting Article Nine to me.'

'But Article Nine is only concerned with your work – you know – like going on the sherbert and brothel-bashing and not doing your job.'

'He said I'd been dodging the column and trying to get out of things because – sh-sh-*she* – was coming out – and I got this flat on false pretences – and an advance of her passage money – and Muir told him I was neglecting my work – ' George finished his drink and started to cry again. Reggie replenished his glass.

159

'If you ask me, old boy, you're well shot of the bitch,' he said. 'Tell 'em to stuff the bloody flat, and refund the passage money. It's only eighty-five quid in English money, anyhow, at Company rates.'

'I haven't got it.'

'You've got some savings, surely to God?'

'Not a brass stiver.'

'Where the hell's it all gone? You were loaded when you went on leave.'

'I had – had – a – some legal trouble. That cost quite a bit – then I bought a car for more than the damn thing was worth and dropped a packet over it – and – well, one or two other things – '

'Like her engagement ring, for instance? Louise reckons that must be worth a hell of a lot.'

'Christ! I can't ask for it back,' George said, shocked.

'Why the hell not? You had a contract with her – she's broken her end of it – OK – she kicks back anything she's had on the strength of it. Give us your glass.' Reggie filled it again.

'You don't understand,' George said sadly. 'Down the hatch.'

'Down the hatch. Who doesn't understand? I'm a realist. You're a sucker. If it was me I'd say "Come on, sweetie, *give*" – and I'd get it off her finger toute suite. That's what *you* ought to do.'

'How the hell can I? I don't even have her address.'

'We know the station, don't we? – from the letter you got this morning. Gonah, isn't it? Military Cantonment in Bombay Presidency.'

'Yes – but I still don't know the name of the people she's staying with.'

'It would take you ten minutes to find out – once you got there. Give us your glass – '

'Thanks – But I couldn't go barging in, just like that – '

'Why not? Listen, cocker. The way things are it's all un-finished business. Finish it, for Christ's sake – one way or the other. See her – face to face – and say, "All right – cards on the table. I'm willing to overlook certain behaviour on your part – and we start again – or, if you don't want to start again, hand that ring over – plus eighty-five quid fare money, or I'm going to sue you – and how would *that* look out here, honey-girl?" God – she'd be scared out of her frilly French frou-frous. You'd have her crawling to you.'

'Couldn't do it,' George said owlishly. 'No gentleman could.'

'Balls. You'd only have to worry about being a gentleman if you were dealing with a lady.'

Louise was pounding on the door and demanding to come in. Reggie bellowed, 'Fuck off!' and opened a second bottle. 'Here, give us your glass, and try listening to some sense for a change. Muir told me that Greenhalge said you could have some time off to get things sorted out. That right?'

'Right.'

'Good. So you do just that. Get your body over to this place Gonah. Go to the Cantonment Executive Office and ask for the address of Miss Jane Curtis. Doesn't matter who she's staying with she'll have to be in the visitors' book. See her – frighten the shit out of her – then bring her back *on your terms* – or get the ring off her – Flog it to Lund and Blockley, the jewellers, and give these Shylock bastards their passage money. Everybody happy – and you'll still be single, you lucky bastard.'

'Down the hatch,' mumbled George, and swallowed another half-tumblerful. 'Thinga – thinga 'bout it.'

'You will and a pig's arse,' said Reggie. 'You'll *do* it. I'll put you on the Bombay Mail tonight.'

'Have to go in – into the office – and fix things up first – Go tomorrer – '

'*Tonight*,' Reggie insisted. 'I'll do all the fixing that's necessary. Where's that damn bearer of yours? Ko'i hai! Boy! Get some clean clothes for the sahib, and his saman. He's going Bombayside, ek dum. Come on! Smack it about – Jaldi-jaldi!'

'Banks closed – got no blurry money – ' George temporized.

161

'Don't worry about that. We can cash a cheque in the Club bar. You're bloody well going if I have to hog-tie you.' Reggie poured out yet another murderous peg. 'Here – get this down you.'

George moaned softly and passed out.

Chapter Eight

TRAGEDY ON BOMBAY MAIL
European Killed

Nagpur: Wednesday

The body of Mr George Quaife, a 41-year-old bachelor and an employee of the Hollins-Bland Tea Company, Calcutta, was recovered from the permanent way by the DD & CI Railway Police on Tuesday morning. Lieutenant J. R. G. Kendrew of the 3rd Baluch Regiment, told District Officer R. F. Montieth-Cookson, sitting as Coroner in the Sub-Divisional Court, that the deceased shared his first class compartment on the Bombay Mail the previous night, and that when he boarded the train in Howrah he had appeared to be overcome by the heat, and was somewhat unsteady on his feet. He, the officer, had helped the deceased to make his bed down, and had then gone to sleep himself. When he awoke at about 5 a.m. the carriage door was open but the deceased was nowhere to be seen. The officer pulled the alarm cord and the train was halted and the line searched for a distance of two miles without success. The train then proceeded on to Nagpur Central and a police patrol under Sub-Inspector H. J. Pereira left immediately by light engine. Mr Quaife was found on the line near Rohta, and Assistant Surgeon Anthony de Mello stated that life had been extinct for some five hours.

Mr Montieth-Cookson, sitting with two assessors, ruled out any suspicion of foul play and gave his opinion that the deceased had unfortunately mistaken the outer carriage door for that of the toilet compartment in the darkness, and returned a verdict of Accidental Death. He thanked Lieutenant

Kendrew for his timely action in stopping the train even though it was by then tragically of no avail, and expressed the sympathy of the Court with the relatives of Mr Quaife, who it is understood are all resident in England. The funeral took place the same afternoon in the European Cemetery, Nagpur, the Reverend R. J. Waddesley, Indian Ecclesiastical Establishment, officiating.

Jane put down the *Times of Western India*. She wished genuinely that she could have felt some sort of emotion – just a tinge of regret – that she could even shed a tear. But she experienced nothing except a sense of relief – and release. Poor old George. How like him. She had to fight to repress a grin. Out of the carriage door instead of into the loo. What was he doing on the train anyhow? Coming to look for her? Thank God he didn't reach here if that was indeed the case. She wondered if anybody would connect her with this. Hardly, she reassured herself. She certainly couldn't remember ever having mentioned his name, either here or on the boat He might, of course, have left a letter – but in that case surely it would have been referred to at the inquest? Anyhow, only suicides left letters, or so she understood – and there was apparently no question of suicide here. No, she had nothing to worry about – now. Nothing at all – *now*. The possibility of his turning up and making a scene had always been at the back of her mind like a nasty little cloud in an otherwise clear sky. But the cloud had gone – *now*. The last link with the past was finally severed. Maxine Wilmott was in truth dead – *now*. More than dead. She had never existed.

She opened a drawer in her dressing table and took out the engagement ring that she had removed from her finger the day she left Calcutta. She had meant to send it back to him, but had not been able to screw up the requisite resolution. It was the most intrinsically valuable thing she had ever possessed, and the thought of returning it irked her acquisitive little soul. Well – that was solved – *now*. It was hers. Perhaps she could start to wear it again – on another finger? Heirloom – Something her dear old great-grandmother had bequeathed her? No – too modern for that. Besides, Tessa had seen it previously and would recognize it for what it was – or had been. She put it back in its box. That was something for the future. Diamonds were a girl's best friend, as the song said.

Something rattled against the jalousie of her bedroom window. She crossed to it and looked out. Ian was standing on the path in the act of throwing another pebble.

She said, 'What are you doing here? You told me that you were Orderly Officer today.'

He came nearer, signalling for silence. 'I don't want to wake the Old Man up,' he muttered. 'Have you had breakfast.'

'No – only chhota hazri. Why? What's the matter?'

'Nothing. I just wanted to see you. I'll wait for you at the gate, and we'll go down to Marchioni's for bacon and eggs.'

'I can't do that,' she protested. 'What on earth would your mother think if I didn't show up for breakfast?'

'What the hell does it matter? She doesn't think at all before lunch. Come on – get a move on. This is important.' He was curt and peremptory, but she could sense the pleading behind the words. She hesitated. Wouldn't this be putting a foot wrong? Missing family breakfast – and the General's heavily paternal greeting – pinched cheek and playfully smacked bottom – and Lady Storland's daily duty roster, helping with the flowers and in the amateur clinic she ran in the servants' lines –

Ian was muttering again urgently. 'Look – this might be the last chance I'll have of talking to you privately. *Please* – it's important.'

Her curiosity piqued, she nodded, though still with a show of reluctance. Reluctance had become the main weapon in her armoury in these last few weeks – not coyness, and certainly not arbitrary refusal – more the charming shyness of Edwardian girls – *nicely brought-up girls* – pursued by the hairy hearties of those days – which meant that instinctively she had hit exactly the right key in this country that remained consistently thirty years behind Home in manners and codes of conduct.

She joined him in the road and walked the few yards to where his car was parked. 'Would you like to drive?' he asked, and again she nodded, without reluctance this time. He had

165

been teaching her over the last three weeks, and she had been an apt and intelligent pupil. She slid behind the wheel and started the engine.

'You still haven't told me how you wangled the day off,' she said.

'I gave Mike Bartley fifteen chips to do my Orderly Dog for me,' he answered as she pulled out into the roadway. 'Watch it. You were too fierce on the clutch then.'

'Are you allowed to do that?'

'Do what?'

'Pay somebody else to do your duty for you?'

'So long as the Adjutant approves, yes.'

'And did he?'

'Did he what?'

'You're just pretending to be stupid,' she said. 'Did he approve?'

'What the hell does it matter? The son-of-a-bitch never approves of anything I do – nor does the bloody CO.' He sounded like a sulky schoolboy.

'It *does* matter,' she chided. 'I'd be ever so – I'd be terribly worried if I thought you were in any sort of trouble.' Her eyes were fixed on the road ahead, but she was conscious of him studying her curiously.

'Do you mean that?' he asked slowly, 'or is it the sort of little-mother-big-sister crap I'm given all the time at home?'

'Of course I mean it.'

'Why?'

'Oh, Ian, you're just being – being – you know – silly,' she said angrily, 'and if you don't stop I'm going to get out and walk back.'

'I'm not being silly. I really want to know why you'd be worried if I were in the mullock. Why?'

'Well, wouldn't anybody be?' She was wary now, feeling that some sort of trap was being laid for her.

I don't give a damn about *anybody*. I'm asking *you*.' They ha'd arrived outside the Italian café. She parked neatly and waited for him to make a move, but he didn't. He sat hunched in his seat staring ahead of him through the windscreen, and the inevitable blind beggar led by a small naked child came up and keened to them of famine, sickness and the immutable vindictiveness of fate, and Ian swore at him in Hindi, which was unusual, because he himself had told her of the superstition attaching to the cursing of beggars and the kicking of sweepers.

'You *are* in a bad mood, aren't you?' she said, and opened the door on her side. 'Thanks for the drive. I'm going back home for breakfast. I'm hungry.'

He put his hand out past her and closed the door again.

'Just a minute,' he begged. 'Look – I'm trying to say something, and I feel a fool.' He took a deep breath, then blurted out, 'Will you marry me?'

Receiving proposals was one of the most recurrent of her daydreams, and in them she always had the right answer pat. It was never anything so prosaic as a plain yes or no. It was neat, witty, sometimes barbed, according to who featured in the fantasy at the time. Mostly they were refusals; in fact she had only ever unequivocally accepted Robert and Gary Cooper, though sometimes she had temporized and kept them in an agony of suspense. It was that type of answer she was desperately scrabbling for in the scrapbag of her memory now. Her first impulse was to accept him out of hand. She, Max Wil – damn – *Jane Curtis*, the daughter-in-law of a Sir and a Lady! A magnificent military wedding here in Gonah. She had seen one the previous week – full dress uniforms – the wives in garden party hats and white gloves – the Regimental band in scarlet and gold – Flagstaff House lent for the reception, and the Governor's carriage to take the happy couple off to the station afterwards. Perfect, she had thought at the time, until that same evening she had heard the General discussing it with his wife. 'Bloody young idiot, marrying as a subaltern,' he had snorted. 'If he'd been one of mine when I was commanding, he'd have been out on his bottom ek dum.'

'They are in love,' Tessa had defended, and had been blasted for an empty-headed little fool who didn't know her hocks from her rump.

No – pity – but this would have to be the one that got away. Ian was a subaltern – and one not in the highest favour with family or regiment at the moment – but, at the same time, certainly not one to be rejected out of hand.

He was holding both her hands in his now – and was babbling. She withdrew them gently and shook her head sadly and in that simple action the mot juste came to her – one of her better ones – straight from Ethel M. Dell. 'No, Ian, dear – I can't say yes – not at this moment – but I'm honoured – more honoured than I can ever tell you. We must leave it there – for the present at all events – *Please*.'

'But why, for God's sake?' he demanded wildly.

'Your parents for one thing – your Colonel for another – '

'What the hell has it got to do with any of them? I'm of age. I'm not going to be told who I'm to marry – or not marry. Anyhow, why should they be against it? We haven't even told them yet.'

'And we're not going to,' she said with unwonted firmness.

'You mean you're turning me down?' he said miserably.

'No – not exactly. But I know your father's views on married subalterns – and so do you. They've been too kind to me for me to pay them back like this.'

'Kind my foot. It doesn't cost them anything to have you here – and Mother dear gets a secretary and general factotum for sweet damn all.'

'What a horrible thing to say.'

'It's true. Come on – you haven't answered my question. Yes or no?'

'I'm sorry, Ian – you've got your career to think of – '

'Damn the career. I hate the Army. Once and for all – yes or no?'

'Please – please – ' she begged. 'Let me think about it – '

'For God's sake, woman, we're not discussing buying or selling a bloody horse.' He took her by the arms and shook her. 'Do you love me?'

'I don't know – Ian – I honestly don't know – and I certainly didn't know *you* felt this way either – '

'Balls. You must have realized it. What the devil do you think I've been hanging round home for, and risking a carpeting damn nearly every day – either from the Old Man or the Colonel – if it wasn't to see you? I tell you, I'm as miserable as hell when I'm away from you – '

'But you musn't be. Ian, please listen to me. I'll be leaving here shortly – as soon as Daddy has arranged my passage – and we might never see each other again – so it's so silly for you to feel like this – ' She fumbled for her handkerchief and turned away.

'Don't you understand?' he groaned 'It's just that that's getting me down. If we don't do something about it, and quick, I'm going to lose you.'

'What *can* we do about it?' she asked in a small choked voice.

'All *you've* got to do is to say yes,' he told her. 'I'll do everything else that's necessary. I'll tell my parents – and my Colonel – and write to your father – '

'No,' she said quickly. 'Don't do that. Leave that part of it to me.'

'So it *is* yes?' he said joyfully, and spun her round to face him.

'What else can I say?' she whispered, her face pressed into his damp shirt. 'Ian dear – *please* – people will see us – '

'The hell with them!' he shouted. 'Oh, my darling – my darling – my darling – '

'The little bitch!' raged the General. 'She can pack her bags and get to the devil out of it – now – today. And as far as my laddo is concerned if I catch him hanging about this house just once again without my express permission I'll kick his arse and tell his CO to confine him to lines.'

'Yes, dear,' Lady Storland said gently. 'But that would be the very thing that would make him resign his commission.'

'And do what?' snorted the General. 'Sell secondhand cars in Great Portland Street? The bloody fool can't even make a career of the Army, where everything is silver-spooned for him. He'd starve outside.'

'I don't think that would worry him much in his present frame of mind. No, I really believe that this is where we will have to finesse a little.'

'And while we're doing that they're getting married and making a cock-up of everything I'd planned for him. God

169

damn them for a couple of below-stairs, conniving little – ' He spat and poured another bara peg.

'How clever of you, dear,' Lady Storland said. 'I see you've noticed it too.'

'Noticed what?' The General regarded her suspiciously over the rim of his glass.

'Below stairs is the operative phrase. Lower middle class, I should say – beautifully covered, but her guard drops from time to time. The odd word – the wrong gesture on occasion. But she's intelligent enough to realize it – and she seldom makes the same mistake twice – '

'All right, all right,' snapped the General. 'What does that signify, other than that you're a bloody snob?'

'Aren't we all, dear?' smiled Lady Storland. 'Including Ian, although he'd go to the stake rather than admit it – '

'It cost me enough to make the fool one,' rumbled the General, 'but what are you getting at? Come to the point for God's sake.'

'Just this,' flashed Lady Storland. 'If you go off at half-cock and fly into their faces, Ian will send in his papers, get a special licence and marry her – ' She snapped her fingers. 'Like that. They'll be on board ship sailing for England within the month – '

'Well, what do you advise?' the General said uneasily.

'Don't oppose him. Tell him, most certainly, that you don't approve of married subalterns, but that if he's determined to do it, then he must agree to keep it a secret for the time being – until you can sound the Regiment out and generally smooth the path ahead for him. You can even hint that you'll increase his allowance to ease things until he gets his captaincy.'

'That'll be the day,' the General gloomed. 'I don't see where it'll get us though. We couldn't fob him off indefinitely. He'll still marry her.'

'It's time we want,' Lady Storland said. 'Time to make a few inquiries. I'm *certain* there's something hidden there – some – some – Oh, I can't put it into words. It's an intuition. Haven't you noticed that she never receives letters from Home? She mentions her father sometimes – he's a banker or a stockbroker or some such thing, and, I gather, quite wealthy. Well, surely he'd write to her, wouldn't he? Friends? And this mysterious wedding that was called off at the last minute? Not a word from the man – whoever he might be. The more I think of it the odder it all appears.'

'But one can't go making inquiries about somebody out of the blue, just like that – I mean – well, where would one start?' The General scratched his head – and poured another whisky.

'Wartnaby?'

The General stared at her. 'My lawyer? What's he got to do with it?'

'Don't you think it might be a good idea to write to him and ask him to look into things – very discreetly? It shouldn't be difficult. We know her name – and her home is in Herne Bay, I gather. He could put an inquiry agent – private detective or whatever they call them – on to it, surely?'

'Cost the earth,' grumbled the General.

'It would cost Ian, and ultimately the Family, much more if she *is* undesirable and they married.'

'Um – yes – I suppose so – '

'And while the inquiries are going on, if Ian happened to be posted to a non-family station on the Frontier – '

'You're a wicked woman,' grunted the General, 'but you don't get the credit for *that* one. It was what I was going to do anyhow.'

'Nay bother at all,' Ian said exultantly. 'I sprung it on Ma first, of course.'

'How did she take it?' Jane asked.

'You can never tell with the old girl. She didn't bat an eyelid – just said, "Let me break it to your father. You know his views on married subalterns." I expected something like that from *her*, of course, but when the Old Man sent for me and called me a silly young bastard and then gave me a whisky and an affectionate punch in the ribs, I just couldn't believe my ears – ' Ian shook his head in bewilderment.

'They've both been absolutely sweet to me,' Jane said. 'But

I still can't understand why we've got to keep it dark.'

'Only for the next couple of months or so,' Ian explained. 'It's what the Army calls duck-shoving. Sounding things out. I mean, if my CO raised objections the Old Man would want to have time to arrange something else for me – a posting to one of the Corps, or Staff College or something like that. It would look much better if the move came before the announcement rather than the other way round. He wants to do something with the Family Trust, as well, which is *bloody* decent of him.'

'What does that mean?'

'Twisting the Trustees' tails for an increased allowance for *us*, my poppet. Something to keep the wolf from the door until I get my third pip.' He gazed at her fondly. 'I just can't believe that all this is happening to *me*.'

'Isn't it sweet of them? – your parents, I mean – '

'Yes – it makes me feel a swine because of all the rotten things I've said about them in the past. Which reminds me – I *must* write to your father formally. Do let me have your home address.'

'Let me break the news first,' Jane said earnestly. 'Just like your mother did. I know Daddy so well. He could be terribly grouchy if it was sprung on him. On the other hand, coming from me he'd probably be as nice as pie.'

'Whatever you say, darling. We don't want the old boy to stop your allowance or anything like that, do we?'

'Good heavens no,' said Jane, aghast.

Tessa said, 'I think you could have done much better, duckie. Oh, yes – he's my brother and all that and I did ask you to give him a tumble – but he *is* a bit wet, isn't he?'

'He is not!' Jane said indignantly. 'That's a horrid thing to say.'

'Well, I'm not going to fight you over the issue. I'd certainly keep him well up to the bit though, if I were you. If the Old Man could make Lieutenant-General I suppose there's hope for Ian eventually.' Tessa grinned wickedly. 'Watch my sainted Mother closely, and take a tip from her book. Sweetness, gentleness, guilelessness – and a hog-spear held a quarter of an inch from his bum at all times.'

'Oh, Tessa, – you're *awful*,' Jane said. 'But I'll forgive you, because I'm so happy. Of course you do realize that it has to be kept a deep dark secret for the moment, don't you?'

'So I gather – until the Old Man has sweetened Reggie Corke, Ian's CO – and more importantly, Reggie Memsahib. The usual gambit. What absolute bloody rot. As if it mattered a damn.'

'It's tradition,' Jane said stiffly. 'And that's terribly important. I want to be a good wife, Tessa – a good *Army* wife – who'll help her husband with his career – and never put a foot wrong.'

'It hasn't taken them long to make a Memsahib out of *you*, has it?' Tessa said with a touch of bitterness. 'And I had a feeling that you were somehow different.'

'I don't *want* to be different.' The cry was torn from her. 'Oh, Tessa, don't spoil things for me – please – *please* don't spoil things!'

Ian received his marching orders a week later. 'Razmak!' he wailed to his fellow subaltern, Mike Bartley. 'Bloody place! Why *me*?'

'Keep you away from the women,' Bartley said with satisfaction. 'It's time the men had a shot at that glorious piece of kerfifer. The boys have been hogging it for too long.'

'Watch it,' Ian warned him grimly.

'I will,' Bartley chuckled evilly. 'Like a bloody hawk. Wow!'

Ian drove in to Flagstaff House, stiff with resentment, and bearded his father, with a singular lack of tactical skill, before drink time that evening.

'What do you want *me* to do?' the General asked him. 'Call GHQ and tell them not to send my little son to the Frontier? Don't be an idiot, my boy. I don't mind practising a bit of nepotism with your Commanding Officer and his wretched wife in a strictly personal matter, but I'm damned if I'm going to interfere with a posting in the normal course of your duty. Good God! I'd never be able to hold my head up again. Pull rank to keep your hide unpunctured by the odd Pathan bullet? Not bloody likely.'

'But we agreed – ' began Ian.

'We *agreed* nothing,' the General snapped. 'Against my natural wishes and desires I withdrew my objection to your marrying at this stage of your career, and even undertook to help you where I could – provided you, in turn, promised to behave like an adult and not a puling schoolboy – and kept your mouth shut until I had carried out a preliminary reconnaissance. I'm actually doing that now, but if you start squawking about a posting which has obviously been designed to give you a little much needed active service experience, and which most youngsters of your age would give their ears for, I'll drop the whole thing and let you stew in your own juice, by God. Do I make myself clear?'

'Yes, sir,' said Ian miserably.

'Good,' said his father. 'Help yourself to a whisky, and pour me one at the same time. This posting has nothing whatsoever to do with our bit of business,' he went on unblushingly, 'although I wouldn't be surprised if old Reggie hadn't wangled it because he thought you were poodle-faking round this house too much. *I* certainly had nothing to do with it – but I quite approve of it nevertheless. Damn it, it will only be for a few months I imagine – and by the time you get back we should have got everything sorted out. See what I mean?'

'Yes, sir,' Ian said again, with more resignation than conviction.

'Good – well, stop looking like The Soldier's Last Farewell. I wish to God they'd send *me* up to the Frontier for a few months away from your mother.' The General held out his empty glass. 'Pour me another.'

Jane didn't see Ian off from the station. He wanted her to, but Lady Storland said public farewells were strictly for Other Ranks, so they repaired to a secluded corner of the garden, where she cried a little on his shoulder and he displayed the stiff upper lip he had been practising in his shaving mirror for the last few days.

'It won't be for long, darling,' he said gruffly. 'You'll –
you'll write every day, won't you?'

'Every day – I promise,' she choked.

'And you'll look after Toby for me?' Toby was his lean
and lecherous bull terrier.

She nodded and smiled bravely.

'And – well – er – I don't want to tie any strings to you –
but – '

'The Club?' she said. 'Don't worry, darling. I told you – the
place just doesn't interest me – not if you're not there – '

'It's not that I'd ever dream of doubting *you*,' he said earnestly,
'but some of the chaps here are awful bastards, and – well, I
mean to say – if our engagement had been officially announced
you'd have some protection, but as it is I wouldn't put it past
some of them to regard you as one of the Fishing Fleet – and
fair game.'

'How horrible,' she shuddered, and clung tightly to him.

Then he kissed her for the last time, turned abruptly and
strode manfully away across the lawn.

Tessa said a week later, 'But you can't live the life of a nun,
for God's sake. Not even that little twerp could expect that.'

'I promised him,' Jane said demurely.

'Then you were a damned fool. Well, you can forget it for
one night. I'm counting on you to make up even-stevens at my
party. There'll be a pal of yours there, by the way. Robert
Powell – from the ship. Remember him?'

Jane swallowed hard. 'Yes – I remember him,' she said.

'I told him you were here. He was most interested,' Tessa
went on. 'He's been sent on a Signals course, and he was at the
Club last night. Now come on – you can't let me down.'

'All right,' Jane agreed reluctantly. 'Just this once.'

He had become leaner and browner than she last remembered
him, but the slow friendly smile was unchanged. He took both
her hands when they met on the Club verandah and said, 'What
a lovely surprise. Let's sit this first one out while you tell me
all about everything.'

'There's not much to tell,' she shrugged. 'I realized that I was making a mistake when I saw my fiancé again – and thought the only honest thing to do was to tell him so – and break things off.'

'Poor chap. How did he take it?'

'He was – well – a bit upset – '

'And I bet that's the understatement of the century. But how did you manage to fetch up here?'

'I rang Tessa from Calcutta. I was upset myself, naturally – and I wanted to talk to somebody. She invited me over – and Lady Storland begged of me to stay on for a while, and I thought it was silly to come all this way and then go back to England without seeing at least a bit of India – '

'Very sensible of you,' he approved. 'You must let me show you some of it. How long are you staying?'

'Nothing's quite settled yet,' she said uneasily.

'Good. This course of mine is only a refresher, so I'll have lots of spare time on my hands. Have you been out to the lake yet?'

'No – '

'That's as good a place as any to start. How about a picnic there tomorrow? I'll borrow a car.'

'I – I'm afraid I can't – '

'Booked up, are you? Hardly surprising. You must be a gift from the gods to this station. All right then – what's your first vacant date?'

'Robert – I'm sorry,' she said desperately. 'But – I – I haven't any vacant dates at all – I mean – '

He whistled in mock dismay. 'Wow! I *am* getting a brush-off,' he said, and then saw that she was fighting back tears – genuine ones – and he became serious immediately. 'Here, you chump – there's no need for that. Come on, let's find a kala jagah.' He took her elbow and led her unprotestingly round the verandah until they found a couple of low cane chairs screened from the open french windows of the ballroom by a bank of palms. He settled her into one of the chairs and sat down facing her in the dim half-light. 'Now, what's the trouble?' he asked quietly.

'No trouble,' she assured him, but there was a distinct tremor in her voice. 'It's just seeing you again like this – ' And then she was crying in earnest. He leaned across and put his arm comfortingly round her shoulders.

'Is what happened in Bombay worrying you?' he asked gently. She shook her head and sniffed, and he passed her his handkerchief. 'I mean, did it have anything to do with your not getting married?' She shook her head again, decisively. 'I want to know,' he persisted. 'Did it?'

'No.'

'Then what *is* the trouble? There must be something. Come on – tell me.'

'I have told you – It's just seeing you again – '

'But damn it all, woman – I want to see more of you – lots and lots more.' He pulled her hands away from her face gently. 'Stop snuffling into that handkerchief. You'll make your nose red. Now listen to me – carefully. I've done a lot of thinking since that day – futile and profitless thinking, because as far as I knew you were now married and done for. When Tessa told me last night that you were here and that the other thing was off, I nearly stood on my head. Are you listening to me?'

'Yes,' she sobbed.

'Then for Christ's sake stop snivelling. I've got nothing to offer you except a poverty-stricken Captain's pay, but I'm ambitious, with wits and guts enough to get somewhere. Do you understand what I'm trying to say?'

'No.'

'Then you're thicker in the skull than I thought. I'm proposing,' he told her. 'Proposing – and dreaming how marvellous it would be to be married to someone like you – someone to whom I wouldn't have to pretend – who I'd be able to take to a North London dairy when we were on leave, without apologies and mean little equivocations. I've had a lifetime of it – of not being able to accept invitations to other chaps' homes at school, because I was ashamed to take them to mine – of pretending I'd spent holidays abroad, when actually I'd been helping my father to deliver milk. Do you know, you're the only soul in the world – this world – the Army world –

that I've ever told about my background and antecedents – not because I'm ashamed of them but because I know only too well that it would be social and professional suicide to let the cat out of the bag until I was sufficiently far up the ladder that it no longer mattered. That's the wretched code we live under out here.' He paused, then said slowly and distinctly. 'Now, knowing all that, will you marry me?'

'I'm engaged to somebody else,' she moaned.

He was silent for a long moment, then he said, 'Who?'

'Tessa's brother.'

'Young Ian? I see. Nothing more to be said then – except to wish you every happiness.' He rose. 'Come on – off you go to the powder room and make some repairs. You look as if you've been dragged through a hedge.'

'No – no – please – ' she implored. 'Wait a minute – '

'There's nothing to wait for, my dear,' he said firmly.

'There is – there *is* – How was I to know how you felt about me?'

'You have a point there – but you might have told me the score before I went hoofing on and making an ass of myself.'

'I couldn't. It had to be kept secret until the General has talked to Ian's Colonel – But, Robert – please – I can't go through with it now – '

He stared at her in amazement. 'What the hell do you mean by that?' he asked.

'I could break it off – if you really – '

'*What?* Oh, no – *no*. One broken engagement is regrettable – two would be disastrous.' He laughed shortly. 'I don't mind facing the foe and seeking the bubble reputation in the cannon's mouth and all that – but I'm not spitting in a General-sahib's eye by cutting his son out. Oh, no. I ain't *that* heroic. Come on – off with you, or the others will wonder where we've got to.'

'I can't go back and face anybody now. Take me home – please take me home, Robert,' she pleaded.

'Home being Flagstaff House, I take it? With you looking like a rape case? Not bloody likely, poppet.' He pulled her to her feet. 'Here's a spot of advice for you which might stand you in good stead since your lot is now cast out here. Learn to

178

put a face on things. A good Memsahib never shows emotion – *any* sort of emotion – *ever*, in public. She saves that for the bedroom – her own, or somebody else's. Hop it. I'll see you inside.'

'I'm not going to marry him now, I tell you,' she screamed.

'You please yourself about that,' he told her calmly. 'But please understand that you're not ditching him on *my* account. I think we'd both better forget that we ever had this tête-à-tête. I certainly will.' He turned on his heel and went into the ball-room.

Tessa saw her the next morning at breakfast, which, in Tessa's case, consisted of iced nimbo-pani, because she had a hangover.

'What happened to you?' she asked. 'I don't remember seeing you after we arrived. You didn't get yourself laid on the polo ground or anything like that, did you?'

'What a shocking thing to say,' Jane said severely. 'No – I felt I was letting Ian down – after I'd promised to keep away from that wretched place – so I came home and went to bed.'

'Aw, shit!' said Tessa.

And Jane kept her word thereafter and stayed close to the house – going out only in the mornings to exercise the General's horses in turn, with Toby trotting obediently behind her, in a manner which gained the General's wholehearted approval.

'She's got good hands and she keeps that beautiful arse of hers well down in the saddle – and even that sodding dog of Ian's does what she tells him,' he said to Lady Storland. 'I do hope Wartnaby gives her a clean bill. The boy could do much worse, you know.'

'Um-m-m,' said Lady Storland dubiously. 'I wonder. Good with flowers, although I don't think she's ever had a formal lesson in her life. Drives the car well – much better than that damned Army driver of yours. Intelligent – always there when one wants her – and she never seems to look at another man. But – I don't know – I've still got this feeling.'

Tessa had long given her up as a boon companion. 'I thought you were going to be fun to have around,' she said sorrowfully, 'but you're a Memsahib already – even before you're married. You're going to be just like Ma, God help you.'

'I hope He will,' Jane said piously. 'I certainly can't think of anybody else I'd rather be like.' And once again Tessa said something filthy.

She saw Robert one morning. He was riding a borrowed horse on the bridle-track that threaded through the peepul trees that lined the Mall. He cantered up beside her and touched the brim of his hat with his riding-crop and they exchanged politenesses, and he told her that his short course was ending the following week and he would be returning to his regiment, and she smiled tautly and hoped he'd had a pleasant stay in Gonah, and the only departure from inconsequentiality was when he suddenly said in genuine admiration, 'Christ! To the manner born. You've *got* it, girl – a damned sight more certainly than I have. Good luck to you – and goodbye.' He touched his hat again and went off up the track at a forbidden gallop.

The mail orderly was arriving on his bicycle as she reached the stables, so she took his bulky package in and placed it on the General's desk. It was bigger than usual today, because the weekly air mail was in. She flicked through the letters and sighed as she found the daily missive from Ian, which she was finding an insupportable task to answer. Then she went off to shower and change.

Chapter Nine

London: 3rd July 1939

Dear Sir John, (the General read) In accordance with your
instructions I retained the services of Argus Investigations
Ltd., a reliable firm of inquiry agents who have worked for
me in the past, and since I was able to supply them with the
name, ship and sailing date of the person concerned, it was a
relatively simple matter for them to trace further con-
nections through the P & O Company, Passport Office and
finally Somerset House, where it was ascertained that one
Maxine Jane Wilmott changed her name by deed-poll on 26th
February last, to *Jane Curtis* following upon a case of
attempted blackmail in which her father and uncle were
sentenced at the Old Bailey to one year and three years
imprisonment respectively, which they are serving at
present, the woman being acquitted by the lower Court for
lack of corroborative evidence. (*See Press cuttings enclosed.*)
There is no record of the family ever having lived in the
Herne Bay area, their home actually being in Brixton. The
Argus agent called upon the mother, ostensibly with an
offer of employment in a film studio for her daughter. He
found her in straitened circumstances and extremely em-
bittered. The family is quite unaware of the girl's change of
name or her present whereabouts, their last news of her
being a letter in which she said she intended to take up a
post in a hairdressing establishment in the North of England
and wanted nothing more to do with them. The agent, of
course, did not enlighten them.

I append the account from Argus Investigations, for
fifty-five guineas, plus thirty-five pounds, eighteen and

sixpence, expenses, and shall be happy to receive any further instructions you may have in the matter.

With kindest personal regards to yourself and Lady Storland,

I am

Yours sincerely

P. J. R. Wartnaby.

'My God!' said the General hollowly. 'That was a close one. Could you imagine what the *News of the World* would do with it if they knew? We'd be the laughing-stock of India. What's she doing in this country, anyhow?'

'Instinct,' Lady Storland said. 'The same thing that brings the vultures and kite-hawks here. Good pickings. The little harpy has made London too hot to hold her at the moment, so she's ranging further afield. I *knew* it – I knew it all along –'

'Well – out she goes, neck and crop – *today*.' The General breathed heavily through his nose.

'Finesse, John,' cautioned Lady Storland.

'You and your finesse,' snarled the General. 'Bugger the finesse. *Out!*'

'Yes – and where does she go?'

'What the hell do *I* care – just so long as she's away from here?'

'Use your sense,' Lady Storland said acidly. 'If she has no money what on earth does she do? Sit on her suitcase outside and cry? That's the very way to attract attention. She'd probably do it just to spite us.'

'How do we know she hasn't any money?'

'We don't. Actually I hope she hasn't – because if she had she might make a bolt for the North and tell Ian *her* version of the story – and they'd get married out of hand. Don't overlook the fact that she wasn't convicted of anything. She could quite easily convince that fool of a boy that she was a persecuted victim.'

'She didn't need to be convicted of anything,' the General said, and fluttered the Press cuttings at his wife. 'Have you read these? The father is a shiftless, lazy, unemployed bum –

the uncle a gaolbird with a record as long as your arm – the mother appears to be a trollop – and our little Jane was actually arrested while in bed with this Mr X feller, whose keep she was.'

'All the more reason why the whole thing has to be handled with extreme delicacy,' said Lady Storland firmly. 'We've not only got to get her out of this house and off the station. We have to get her out of the country. Agreed?'

The General grunted a reluctant affirmative.

'Good – then listen to me. I suggest that we face her with this, and tell her that if she will just go quietly we will not only give her her fare to Bombay and something over to keep her until she sails for England, but that we'll pay for her passage as well – and that in addition to that we'll give her our word of honour that we'll keep it dark – absolutely silent, even to Ian. We'll get her to write him a short note to say that she's changed her mind – and she can then slip away with nobody any the wiser. What do you say?'

'Umm,' mused the General. 'Yes – I suppose you're right – but I'm damned if I'm going to cough up her fare to England though. I can get her a DEW ticket.'

'What on earth is that?'

'Destitute European Woman, it means. It's to stop the possibility of white women going into prostitution out here. Remember that corporal's wife who bolted and went on the bash in Bangalore last year?'

'Of course – but won't it leak out if you do anything officially?'

'No. The authorities always keep it very much *sub rosa*. It's not good for British prestige for the locals to know that our women sometimes run off the rails.' He grunted dryly. 'I don't know what old Gandhi would think of Simla in the rutting season.'

'All right then. I'll send Ramu to tell her that you want to see her.' Lady Storland rose.

'Give me ten minutes,' the General said. 'I want a good stiff drink first.'

'At ten in the morning?'

'I don't give a damn what time it is. I don't relish the job.'
'Who would?' Lady Storland asked. 'But you mustn't in any way weaken. You must be absolutely firm. You must insist that she's off this station immediately and that – '
'Oh, sod off, woman!' the General said sourly. 'Unless you'd prefer to do it yourself.'

Lady Storland departed with dignity, and the General kicked an elephant-foot ashtray across his study and then poured himself a large whisky. He was standing at the french windows looking out into the garden when Jane arrived.

She said brightly, 'Hello, Big Bad Wolf. Ramu said you wanted to see me.'

'Sit down,' he said in a flat emotionless voice, without turning. 'I'm afraid you'll have to brace yourself for a nasty shock.'

'Not – not Ian?' she faltered.

'Not Ian. You. Some information regarding you has arrived.'

'What – information?' She got the words out with difficulty.

'Your name – Wilmott, isn't it? Or was before you deed-polled it. The blackmail case – your father and uncle going to jug for it. Want me to go on? It's all there on the table – the Press cuttings – full details – ' He turned and looked at her. 'Poor little bastard,' he thought. 'Like a mynah bird fixed by a cobra. Petrified.'

'I – I didn't – do anything,' she choked. 'I mean – it wasn't my fault – '

'Don't distress yourself unnecessarily,' he told her. 'Never mind the rights and wrongs of it now. The thing is that only my wife and I know anything about it – and there's no need for anybody else to know – '

'It was *him*, wasn't it?' she whispered tensely. '*He* told you – It could only be him. He – he tried it on with me the other night, the bloody swine – tried to get me to be untrue to Ian. I smacked his face – and came home early. You ask Tessa – ' Her voice was rising. 'It was *him*, wasn't it? It was only him who knew. And who the hell does he think *he* is anyhow? The son of a lousy Taffy milkman, for all his poshness – the *bastard!*' She ended in a scream.

'Stop that,' the General said harshly. 'I'm trying to help, but if you're going to behave like an hysterical fishwife I'll leave you to your own devices. I don't know who you're referring to, but I assure you that the information came from England – and certainly not from anybody who was in a position to "try it on" with you the other night. I repeat, nobody but my wife and I know about this – as yet – and, unless you're stupid, nobody other than us *need* know.'

'What about Ian?' she asked dully.

'He needn't know, either. I suggest you write him a short note when you're a little steadier, and tell him that you've changed your mind. Have you any money?'

She shook her head.

'All right then,' the General went on. 'I'll let you have what you require, and if you take my advice you'll get off to Bombay tomorrow morning. I'll give you a letter to – to – well, a friend of mine down there, who will arrange your passage Home – and will fix up somewhere for you to stay until you sail. It will not cost you anything.'

'I don't want anything from *you*,' she said passionately. 'From anybody. And I'm not going to be pushed around. I can look after myself. I'll get a job. I'm not going back to England – not until I'm good and ready.'

The General shook his head. 'You don't understand, my dear,' he said. 'Regulations governing white residence in this country are very rigid. They have to be – particularly where women are concerned. You would only be allowed to stay here as a wife or dependent daughter – or if you yourself were in an approved job – that is nursing or teaching or something like that – something that calls for professional training, which I don't think you have. There are no jobs in offices or shops. Be sensible, Jane. Go Home – start again – forget all this. I'm sorry – sorrier than perhaps you'd believe – but the social code of this country is tough – and cruel. What happened back in England may not have been your fault, but you'd never live it down out here. All doors would be closed to you. Believe me – I'm telling you this for your own good.'

She sat hunched in her chair like an animal made vicious by fear, that has retreated into a corner.

'I'd manage all right if I was given a chance But I never have been. Never. You wouldn't give me one now, would you? Your sort never does. You'll tell everybody.' She spat the words at him.

The General moved across the room and stood looking down at her. 'I've given you my word,' he said. 'Once you leave here the matter is forgotten. It will never be mentioned again – unless, of course, you're foolish enough to try and get in touch with Ian. If that happens, then I shall have no option but to tell him.' He pointed to the Press cuttings on the table. 'I'm afraid those reports don't make very savoury reading. And now perhaps you'd prefer to go to your room. You'll have some packing to do. My wife will send your meals in to you.'

Then suddenly the fight had gone from her. She covered her face with her hands and he could see the tears trickling through her fingers. Her whole body was racked with sobs.

'Oh, God, I'm sorry,' he said. 'Really – really sorry. But this is India, my dear. You're better off out of the damned place.'

There was nobody she knew on the station next morning, for which she felt deep relief. She looked out over the sunscorched landscape as the train sped towards the top of the Ghats, and once more felt the tears blinding her. It was all so different from her triumphant arrival, this dismal retreat. But from some unsung and unchronicled forbear she had inherited a strain of resilience that had been lacking in both her parents, and after an hour of despondence and self-pity she washed her face and repaired her make-up and took out the General's letter which she had glanced at only cursorily when it came in with her breakfast before leaving Flagstaff House. It was typewritten on plain paper and was concise in the extreme.

Dear Jane: On arrival at Victoria Terminus, take a taxi to: *The District (Sub-divisional) Commissioner's Office, Fort, Bombay,*

186

and hand him the enclosed letter. I have already spoken to him on the telephone, and he will be expecting you.
My wife and I wish you well in the future.
Sincerely,
J.S.

The enclosure was heavily sealed with red wax which she realized would defy all attempts to open without it being evident afterwards, so she put it to one side and counted the ten-rupee notes that were clipped to the letter. There were fifteen of them, which eased her immediate anxieties. With what she had managed to save after having a couple of cotton frocks and a simple evening gown run up by the bazaar darzai she now had two hundred and fifty rupees – just under twenty pounds – little enough to be facing the world afresh with, she thought ruefully. She would have to be careful on the ship. But, of course, she had the ring also. That ought to be worth a hundred pounds or so in London – And, since with her resilience was allied a proportionate philosophy, she then went to sleep.

Bombay sweltered in its pre-monsoon humidity. She stood in the forecourt of Victoria Terminus fighting off hordes of coolies who were clamouring over her luggage, near to tears once more, but this time of rage and frustration. She finally found a taxi, and the driver said, 'Ha-ji, Memsahib, knowing all places dam' quick,' when she gave him the address. Then he took her in succession to the Presidency Court, the Custom House, the Bombay Salt Tax Directorate and finally the Salvation Army Citadel, before finding the correct office by process of elimination, a few hundred yards from the starting point – but the amount on the meter was by then a frightening twenty-two rupees.

The District Commissioner's office was large and imposing, deeply verandahed and palm-shaded, and a slight breeze from the harbour gave an illusion of coolness. She sat and waited in an anteroom, conscious of whispering Indian clerks watching her through venetian slatting, and she found herself shivering in spite of the heat, because there was something in the atmosphere of this place that brought back memories of the

187

Shepherd's Bush police court. But the elderly Anglo-Indian chief clerk who eventually dealt with her case was politeness itself. More – he was apologetic.

'All boats are very full at present, Miss Curtis,' he told her. 'Defence and Commercial Secretariats have first call on un-booked berths, so Indigent European – ahem – *sponsored* passengers go to the bottom of the list. I am very sorry, but you will have at least one month's wait here. But please don't worry,' he went on hastily as he saw her look of blank dismay. 'We will put you in comfortable accommodation – and, of course, all expense is met by this office. You will not be troubled.'

Then she signed various forms, shrinking within herself to see her category put down as 'destitute European woman', but she rallied sufficiently to be able to refuse rather wasp-ishly the old man's offer of ten rupees for taxi money to her hotel.

'Not exactly a hotel, you see,' he explained. 'More – what you would call Blightyside a – a guesthouse. That's right – a guesthouse – Mrs Furtado, the lady who runs it, is a very nice lady – oh, very nice. She will look after you.'

Braganza Mansions, in spite of the plural, was a single building; a long, low bungalow with small rooms opening on to a broad, deep verandah on three sides, with an entrance hall, parlour and dining room on the fourth. It stood in a dusty compound off the Colaba Causeway in which shanties of palm matting, sacking and rusty corrugated iron proliferated, and swarms of naked children and lean and scabrous pi-dogs fought for existence. It had started life, so local legend had it, as a brothel for the European clerks of the East India Company in pre-Mutiny days, and had been in turn since then, a Sailors' Home, a Methodist Mission, a Government stationery store and a Remand Centre for Wayward Girls, until now, under the suzerainty of Mrs Furtado, a stout Goanese widow, it was frankly a cheap boarding house, enjoying quasi-official status by the permanent reservation of six rooms for the con-venience of subordinate civil servants passing through Bombay, soldiers' fiancées arriving out from England to be married and, less frequently, cases such as Jane's, Homeward bound.

She met Jane herself – a rare gesture – and stared over the girl's shoulder as she paid the taxi driver. She let out a shrill squeal of indignation and grabbed the money out of the man's outstretched palm, selected a few small coins and threw them in his face, then handed the balance back to Jane.

'Dirty black thief,' she fulminated. 'Charging you more than double.' She was, in fact, several shades darker than the driver, in spite of the pure white face-powder which mingled with her sweat and formed a thick coating over her plump cheeks and treble chin. 'Come in, lovie, and don't let nothing worry you while you're here. I'll show you your room.'

It proved to be some eight feet by twelve, with a french window opening out on to the verandah, and a drooping net curtain screening a doorway which led to a dark and noisome cavern containing a battered tin bathtub, an enamel chamber pot and a powerful stink which battled with the overriding smell of curry and Bombay duck which pervaded the entire demesne in an almost particulate cloud. The furniture consisted of a very ancient brass bed with a dusty mosquito net suspended from the sagging ceiling cloth above it, a table with a piece of scratched mirror on the wall behind it, a wooden chair and a second curtain across a corner doing duty as a wardrobe.

'There you are, lovie,' Mrs Furtado said kindly. 'I've given you one of the best, on the civvy side. I'm not supposed to, as the stingy bastards only pay the lower rate for Homeward Transients. Private bathroom, as you can see, but I'm not charging you for that. Breakfast eight to nine, tiffin one to two, dinner eight o'clock, dead on. Chhota hazri and tea is an extra – four annas a time. You pay that yourself – *them* soor ka bachas won't. Come and go as you please – you're not a Delinquent or a Deportee, so I don't have to report on your ins and outs. OK? Right – be seeing you at dinner and I'll introduce you to some of the others. Don't, for Gawd's sake, leave nothing valuable lying around – and lock your door when you're out during the day and when you go to bed at night.' She went, and Jane stood and looked around her in silent misery. This, she decided, was worse than her night in the cells.

She was still sitting on the edge of the bed three hours later, staring at a stream of cockroaches that crossed and recrossed the cracked cement floor, and a huge, scaly tac-tu lizard that lurked in a dark corner near the 'bathroom' door and shot out a long tongue from time to time, to haul it in again with a writhing cargo of insects stuck to it, after which there would be a ghastly crunching sound, followed by a reflective silence, until it made its next foray. And some small animal was moving about unseen the other side of the ceiling cloth, shaking down a fine rain of dust. She thought of cats, rats, then inevitably snakes, until she could bear it no longer, and she ran out on to the verandah in mute, dry-mouthed terror.

To the west, across Back Bay, the sun was going down behind Malabar Hill in red and orange glory, and the lighthouse at Colaba Point had begun to flash whitely, and some superbly handled dhows were making their way into harbour on the evening breeze, and somewhere nearby the shrill keening of a muezzin was calling the Faithful to evening prayer – all sights and sounds that would have thrown her into an ecstasy twenty-four hours ago. But now she saw only the filth and poverty of the dwellers in the shanties, and the ubiquitous beggars who appeared silently from nowhere and stood with outstretched hands the other side of the broken railing of the verandah, and mangy pariah dogs, and a small child defecating in the open. So she came back into the room and bit on her handkerchief to stop herself from screaming.

'Oh, God,' she prayed. 'Get me out of this – out! If I've got to pay for something I will – some other way, another time – but get me out – now!'

Mrs Furtado came along later and said, 'Goddalmighty, lovie, you don't have to sit in the dark like this. We've got the electric,' and a naked bulb gleamed pallidly behind a ghastly blue lampshade. 'Why don't you come along to the parlour? We've got company.' She nudged Jane jocosely. 'Two of the boys from Colaba Barracks – Sergeants. Really nice boys – you'll like 'em. They don't get much chance of meeting girls from

Blightyside – not often. Come on, sweetie,' she coaxed. 'No good moping.' And since it was at least an escape from the room, Jane followed the fat woman round the verandah past dimly lighted french windows, stumbling over boxes, broken chairs and other assorted rubbish until they reached a large lean-to room which jutted out like an excrescence from the main building.

'The public rooms,' Mrs Furtado explained grandly. 'The boys and girls staying here can have their friends in, see what I mean? And sometimes the sergeants from Colaba come along, like these two tonight – but I don't have Tommies in – not privates and corporals – Oo-ah *no.*'

The walls of the room were formed of latticed bamboo, and there was here no ceiling cloth, that haven of a myriad creeping horrors common to most pre-Mutiny dwellings, so one could see tree rats and tac-tu lizards scuttling along the rafters. Two or three low-powered bulbs did their inadequate best to lighten the gloom but succeeded only in bringing the sheer desolation of the place into starker emphasis. There was a sprinkling of bare wooden tables, a few chairs and some forms round the walls, a couple of dispirited palms in terra cotta water-chatthis, and a piano on which a young Anglo-Indian was one-fingering a tune in inexpert accompaniment to a portable gramophone the other side of the room which was blaring the Donkey's Serenade. Two Europeans sat at one of the tables with glasses and a bottle between them, and as Mrs Furtado ushered Jane in, one of them yelled at the pianist to pack it in, for Chris' sake.

Mrs Furtado said sharply, 'Language, Chalky – there's ladies present,' and they both swung around, then got hurriedly to their feet. 'Sergeant White and Sergeant Poole,' she went on. 'Chalky and Dan to their friends. And this is Miss Jane Curtis – and now call me a liar. What did I tell you, eh?'

Sergeant White, a jaundiced, thin-faced man, said, 'Jesus!' in deepest wonder, wiped a damp hand on the seat of his trousers and then held it out. 'Pleased to meet you, miss.' Jane winced as she felt her hand gripped in his hot vice. The other, younger, man took her hand in turn but neither squeezed it painfully nor spoke. He just stared.

Mrs Furtado was prattling on with great satisfaction, 'Didn't believe me, did you?' She turned to Jane. 'I told 'em I had a young lady staying here, a *pukkha* young lady, I told 'em. Fresh out from Blighty I told 'em – and now she's going back again because she doesn't like it out here, and I don't blame her. I wish I'd had the sense to go back myself years ago.'

'Where to?' asked Sergeant White, who had now got his breath back. 'Goa?'

'Clever bastard,' snarled Mrs Furtado. 'Don't take no notice of this one, lovie. Been out here too long. The sun's got him. Now here's a nice boy.' She turned back to the younger man. 'Dan. Talk to *him*, dear – and you, you old goondah, Chalky, just mind your manners and leave them alone.'

'Come and dance then,' Chalky said and grabbed the fat woman round her massive waist and whisked her into a frenzied jig. Some more Anglo-Indians, all male, looked in through a bamboo-chick curtain that screened the dining room from the parlour, laughing, shouting and clapping in time with the music.

'Bit noisy,' Dan said apologetically. 'Chalky's had a couple of drinks, but he doesn't mean any harm. Can I get you a drink, by the way?'

'No thank you,' Jane said, and started incontinently to cry.

He took her by the elbow and led her gently to the outer door. 'Let's get out of all this for a bit,' he said quietly and she went without protest.

They crossed the compound, out on to the main road that ran parallel with the waterfront. 'There's some seats the other side,' he told her, 'and it's cool overlooking the harbour – and quiet.'

They sat there for some time, she sobbing softly at first, he with his arm around her shoulders, not talking or attempting to comfort her, until after a while she dried her eyes and smiled ruefully.

'I'm sorry,' she said.

'Why should you be? Everybody gets down in the dumps at times – especially in this country,' he said.

'I *hate* the place!'

'So did I when first I came out – but it sort of grows on you after a bit. But you should worry. You're going Home soon, aren't you?'

'Yes – thank God.'

'How long have you been out?'

'A few weeks.'

'You didn't give it a chance, did you? I mean, you haven't seen much of it. It took me three years to get Streatham out of my system –'

'Get *where* out of your system?'

'Streatham – that's where I come from.'

'That's practically next door to *my* home,' she said, and experienced a feeling of relief at the absence of any further need to cover up, evade or lie. 'Brixton.'

'Well, I'll be damned. Did you ever get over to Streatham?'

'Yes, of course. To the Saturday night hop at the Locarno – every week, except when our tennis club had something on. When were you there last?'

'I just told you – three years ago. I spent my embarkation leave there. Do you know Morton's, the Cash Chemists in the High Street?'

'I've seen it. Why?'

'That's where I used to work. I got my MPS there.'

'What does that mean?'

'Membership of the Pharmaceutical Society – I'm a chemist.'

'I thought that woman said you were a sergeant or something.'

'So I am – now. I'm a dispenser at the Military Hospital.'

'Is that better than working at Morton's?'

'All depends how you look at it. There was no job for me when I'd finished my apprenticeship, so I joined the Army – RAMC. My qualification got me quick promotion. Yes – I think all in all it *is* better. See the world – and the money's not bad – rank pay plus trade pay just about equals what old Morton would have given me for counter-jumping – and I get free keep here as well.'

'Will you ever be an officer?'

193

He laughed. 'Lap of the gods. I'd probably make Captain-Quartermaster if I stayed in long enough. I'm not sure that I'd want a commission though. I'm happy as I am. But we're doing a lot of talking about me. What about you?'

'What about me?' she asked cautiously.

'I mean – well, it's unusual to find a girl like you out here on her own. I was wondering – '

'There's nothing to wonder about,' she said coldly.

'Oh, I wasn't prying – '

'I came out to marry somebody. A boy from near home – He was in a very good job – beautiful house, cars, horses, every-thing – but when I saw him again I realized that I didn't love him. I *liked* him – *respected* him – but that is not enough. So I called it off – and now I'm going Home again. Does that answer your questions?'

'I wasn't asking any.'

'I thought you said you were wondering about me.'

'Well, maybe I did, but that was only to stop talking about *me* – ' He broke off and turned to her and took both her hands in his. 'There's something wrong, isn't there? Is there anything I can do to help?'

She shook her head and withdrew her hands and stood up. 'I'm just being silly,' she said brightly. 'Don't take any notice of me.'

'Ever ridden on the back of a motorbike?' he asked, apropos of nothing.

'Lots of times. Why?'

'Because I've got one here. I thought, if you felt like it, we could take a run along to Greens and have some dinner.'

'But what about your friend?'

'Chalky?' He laughed. 'No need to worry about *him*. He can either find his own way back to barracks, or doss down here. What about it? The grub will certainly be better than anything old Maudie Furtado would give you – and it will be much quieter.'

Her hands flew to her hair, then dropped and smoothed her frock down. 'But I look such a sight – '

'You look all right,' he assured her. 'In any case you'll get blown about a bit on the bike. You can straighten up at Greens. It's quite a nice place, but not posh like the Taj – I mean you don't have to be dolled up in evening dress, although a lot of people do.'

'Well, if you're sure – ' she began doubtfully. 'I'd better get my handbag and a comb and a few things – '

'Yes, and a scarf or something for your hair. You nip off and I'll go and fix it with Maudie.' He took her by the arm and led her back through the littered compound. 'I'll meet you here again in a few minutes.'

She tried to repair the ravages to her face in the scratched mirror on the wall, shuddering at the effect of the sickly blue light and finally giving it up and snatching her handbag and a Bokhara kerchief that Ian had given her, and hurrying out. Then she remembered Mrs Furtado's warning and went back and found a huge iron key hanging on a hook, and locked her door.

Dan kicked his motor into life as she approached through the darkness and yelled over its roar, ' – give us your bag – I'll stuff it in the front of my shirt – Don't worry – won't go fast – ' and she hefted herself up on to the padded pillion.

She leaned forward, her face against the thin linen of his jacket and her arms around his waist, and they sped up Colaba Causeway towards Apollo Bundar. She recognized the Gateway of India and across from it the entrance to the Yacht Club, and she knew a brief moment of panic at the thought of a chance meeting with anybody from Gonah, before dismissing the thought impatiently from her mind. What the hell did it matter now?'

Dan swung left into a small triangular garden between the bulk of the Taj Mahal Hotel and a smaller, older building on the edge of Gateway Square, and parked between two cars in a driveway.

'Greens,' he said. 'Like I told you – not as posh as the Taj next door, but lots of people like it better – and the food comes from the same kitchens, at half the price.'

It was two-storeyed, deeply verandahed and balconied, and overhung with arching palm trees, and the dining room and outside patio were softly lighted, and a muted band was playing somewhere in the background. She turned and looked back across the harbour. The Gateway loomed in front like an oversize Marble Arch, and the lights of the Yacht Club were not a hundred yards away, so the view was similar to that of her first night in India, with, once again, a full moon in a cloudless, star-emblazoned sky. She felt an immediate lift of heart and she impulsively took Dan's arm in both her hands. 'Oh – It's ever so nice!' she said, and didn't feel the need to correct herself.

She found the cloakroom and washed her hands and face in ice-cold water, and a white-saried ayah stood by clucking in admiration as she made up her face afresh and rearranged her hair with a few professionally deft touches. She examined herself critically in a full-length mirror. Her frock, unchanged since morning, was a little creased, but it wouldn't be too noticeable in this dim lighting. This lad wouldn't mind anyhow. Nice boy. Good-looking in an ordinary sort of way. Well-spoken – quite refined in fact. But then chemists always were, weren't they? You had to have a good education for that job – almost like doctors. Pity he wasn't an officer – 'There you go again,' she muttered to herself angrily. 'Give over, for God's sake. Try being yourself, just for once.'

He was waiting for her on the verandah. The place was busy but not crowded and he had already secured a good table on the patio. They sipped gimlets and she left the ordering to him, and he chose iced papaya, pomfret – the superb Bombay fish that was available in Gonah in very limited quantities only when the weekly refrigerated van came in – moorghi chop – pineapple fool – and petits fours with Turkish coffee – with an unhurried expertise that compared more than favourably with Ian's undecided bumbling.

He said, 'Any preferences as far as wine is concerned?'

'A Chablis with the fish,' she answered promptly. 'Nothing with the curry. It masks the palate.' She had gleaned that from Robert.

'It hasn't taken you long to learn that,' he said, impressed.

'My father is an expert,' she told him. 'We have a huge cellar at Home.'

'I thought it was all mild-and-bitter round Brixton,' he grinned.

'We don't live there all the time,' she flashed. 'It was the family home before the district got so run down, but we only stay there now when Daddy has to be in Town on business. The rest of the time we live in Herne Bay.' And even as she was saying it she was raging inwardly at herself. Why? Why? *Why?* – when there was no further need to pretend?

'I'm afraid my family lives at thirty-nine Chestnut Grove, S.W. sixteen – *all* the time,' he said. 'My old man is only a tailor's cutter.'

They danced between courses, and again after coffee. She was desperately tired but she was prolonging things because the prospect of returning to that room terrified her. But then the band played 'God Save the King' and everybody rose, and the bearers were stripping the tables.

He said, 'I don't know how to thank you. This is the best evening I've had in India – the best anywhere.'

'It's been lovely for me too,' she responded with genuine gratitude. 'You rescued me from that awful place.' And he seized on the last sentence.

'Look – if you don't mind my asking,' he said. 'Why are you staying there? I mean – it's a pretty rotten dump for someone like you.'

'I got a shock when I saw it,' she admitted, 'but someone recommended it to me.'

'How long are you going to be here before you sail?'

'I don't know. It seems that all the ships are booked up.'

'That's right,' he said. 'Everybody's talking about this war that's likely to break out at any time in Europe, so they're shoving all the spare odds and sods Home for training duties. The troop-ships are full months ahead and they're commandeering all the space they can grab on civvy boats. If you haven't got a priority you could be here for ages.'

She nodded and gulped, 'What on earth can I do then?'

'Get out of Maudie Furtado's for a start,' he said earnestly. 'You see – she's the widow of a Goanese probation officer from the police court in Girgaon and she gets all the delinquent girls that are sent on remand – and right little whores some of them are – barrack-rats, absconders from orphanages, bar girls – all sorts. Most of them have been on the bash, and they stay on it at Braganza Mansions – with Maudie collecting a percentage. Who the hell ever suggested *you* going there?'

'Oh – somebody – somebody I was talking to in Calcutta,' she said.

'He must have been mad. This place – Greens – you'd be much more comfortable here. Why not move in?'

'Is it expensive?' she faltered.

'I don't know. Hang on – I'll go and ask at the desk.' He went off and she sat quaking for five minutes until he returned.

'They can do you a nice single room and bath for twenty rupees a day,' he told her. 'That's about thirty bob – and it includes chhota hazri.'

'I – I – can't afford it,' she said desperately. 'Not if I'm going to be stuck here for a long time.'

'But your family? Surely – '

And she was once more away, sowing the whirlwind. 'I haven't told them yet. You see, Daddy had a bad heart attack recently and I don't want to worry him. I intended to go Home and break it to him gently. You see, he didn't want me to come out in the first place. All this must sound awfully mixed up I know – '

'No, I see what you mean,' he nodded. 'But he'd have a worse heart attack if he saw you in Maudie's. Look – please don't get me wrong, but I've got a bit saved up – '

'No – *no*,' she declined quickly. 'It's sweet of you, but I couldn't dream of it – '

'You could let me have it back later – '

But she was shaking her head decisively, and she meant it – certainly at that moment.

'All right then,' he said resignedly. 'But at least you must let me drop in often just to make sure everything is all right – and to take you out and show you a bit of the countryside. It's really interesting, some of it.'

'I'd love you to do that,' she said eagerly.

'Good – it's a deal,' he told her.

He walked her back through the compound to her room and unlocked the door for her, switched on the light and grabbed by the tail the somnolent tac-tu that she had told him about, and flicked it out into the darkness. Then he helped her to let down and tuck in her mosquito net, and he waited until she was safely settled before leaving.

'I've got a day off tomorrow,' he told her. 'There are two dispensers and we do alternate spells of duty. I'll be round in the morning. Nine too early for you?'

'Earlier the better,' she said. 'But are you sure I'm not putting you out? I mean – if you've got something better to do – '

'Better than taking you out? My God!' he said feelingly.

There was the inevitable awkward moment – he plainly wanting to kiss her but not wishing to appear to be taking her for granted – she, almost tearfully grateful, but wanting to preserve her aloofness. She resolved it by standing on tiptoes and kissing him chastely on the cheek, and murmuring, 'Oh, thank you – thank you – *thank you!*'

'Lock the door,' he told her gruffly. 'And don't worry. I'll be back on the dot tomorrow.' And he went off in a haze of delight.

Music was spilling thinly from the parlour as he walked round the bungalow. He looked through the lattice and saw Chalky asleep with his head on a table, and two or three other sergeants from the Colaba Garrison dancing with some Anglo-Indian girls. Mrs Furtado was dispensing drinks at a makeshift bar. She greeted Dan warmly and noisily as he came in.

'My God, man,' she yelled. 'Fast worker, eh? Whips her off in first five minutes. Chalky says he's going to kill you, leaving him flat like that – then he goes and gets drunk again – damn bum.'

'Come outside,' he muttered. 'I've got something important to tell you.'

'What? That you made it?' She nudged him in the ribs and cackled. 'The quiet Danny boy, eh? Still waters run deep. You bugger, you. What about a little present for Auntie

Maudie for fixing it for you?' She followed him out into the darkness.

'Listen to me,' he said tersely, 'and listen bloody carefully. Four blokes have picked up doses in this gin mill of yours in the last three months.'

'What the hell do you mean?' she demanded. 'They never got it here!'

'Oh, yes – I know,' he said. 'They were squared to say that they'd been down to the cages in Grant Road – but if I had a talk to Major O'Riordan and another to the APM, you'd have this dump put out of bounds in a pig's whisper.'

'What are you after?' she whined. 'I never done nothing to you. You want money? I don't make enough to pay the damned city rates, for God's sake.'

'I don't want anything,' he told her. 'I'm giving *you* something – something for nothing. A bit of advice. That young lady in there – Miss Curtis. She *is* a lady, understand? So no arsing about. If I hear that she's been annoyed in any way at all – that you've been sending blokes along to her room or anything like that, I'll have you busted the same day, you stinking old bag – for spreading VD among the troops – for flogging booze without a licence – for putting young kids on the bash – the *lot*. Savvy?'

'Who the hell do you think you are?' she screamed. 'Jesus Christ? And who do you think *she* is?'

'I told you. A lady – an *English* lady.'

'Lady my arse! I'll tell *you* something now. She's a Destitute European Woman being run out of the country because she don't have a cowrie to scratch herself with. A DEW under IPC Schedule G, sub-para 273B. You think I don't know the law, sonny boy? I was raised on it – both sides of it – ' She stopped as she ran out of breath.

'Sure, I know all that,' Dan told her. 'You've got a good job, one way and another – with the civvy police squared, and a bottle of whisky and a bint to the Provost Sergeant from time to time – but Major O'Riordan happens to be the chief pox doctor in these parts, and he doesn't like his medical returns mucked about – and Colaba is military territory, and you're just inside the boundary. You wouldn't stand a chance. You've been warned.' He turned and walked away out of the light, leaving her panting between fear and fury.

Jane was waiting on the verandah next morning, when Dan arrived. He cut the engine of the motorbike and sat looking at her. She smiled shyly at him and he felt his heart turning slowly over and over.

He said, 'Would you like a swim to start off with?'

'Oh, heavens yes. That wretched tin bath in there is horrible and I've been bitten all over by mosquitoes or something,' she complained.

'Let's see a couple,' he said, and she held out her forearm.

'Bugs, I'm afraid,' he told her after examining two red bumps, and she shuddered and looked as if she was going to be sick.

'Oh, don't worry about them,' he laughed. 'Nobody does in India. I'll give you something that will keep them away tonight. Had breakfast?'

'A cup of vile tea and a shrivelled banana.'

'Good – then we'll go to Breach Candy and have bacon and eggs and fresh rolls and coffee.'

'Oh God! That sounds marvellous,' she said. 'Where's Breach Candy?'

'On the coast, to the north of Malabar Hill. Over there.' He pointed across Back Bay. 'The very best bit of Bombay. Have you got a bathing costume?'

'Yes – Wait a minute.' She darted back into her room and rummaged through a suitcase for the smart two-piece Jantzen that had been yet another of Ian's presents. As she came out and locked her door, she saw Mrs Furtado standing at the end of the verandah and she waved to her cheerily, but the woman, arms folded, scowling, in a grubby wrap and with her hair in curl-papers, made no response.

'No need to be polite to that cow any longer,' Dan said as Jane climbed on to the pillion. 'I had a little talk with her last night. She knows the score now, as far as you're concerned anyway.'

'Oh, she hasn't been rude or anything like that,' Jane told

him. 'The other extreme, in fact.'

'Exactly. I know her sort. She'll grease her way into your confidence if you let her, then try and get you involved in this damned dive of hers.' He kicked the starter savagely. 'Don't give her any encouragement, and above all don't tell her anything at all about yourself.'

'I'm not likely to do that,' Jane said. 'Thanks for warning me though.'

They crossed the narrow peninsula through a network of tortuous alleys, roaring on open throttle through small bazaars and maidans, in and out of strings of bullock carts, past clanging trams and finally out on to Queen's Road with Dan delivering a shouted commentary over his shoulder.

'This is where all the nobs live – European and Parsee – stinking with money, all of them – That's Sonapur Lane, leading up to Crawford Market – wonderful place – have to take you some time – buy anything in the world there, at half the price of the shops if you know how to go about it – Elphinstone Fountain in the middle there – supposed to be ornamental but the wogs use it as an open air bathroom, and wash their clothes in it – can't blame the poor devils – Here we are – this is Marine Drive – it curves right round the waterfront of Back Bay – that's Government House at the end there. Up on the hill ahead of us are the Towers of Silence – the Parsees put their dead out on top of them for the vultures to eat – their religion won't allow them to defile earth, water or fire with dead bodies – sorry, I shouldn't have told you that until after breakfast – Leave Marine Drive here – right – next left – and now we're on Breach Candy Road – '

She leaned forward against his broad back, the sun warm on her own back, the breeze of their headlong rush through the morning air cooling her face, neck and bare legs and tossing her hair into disarray, savouring the sensuous pleasure of it all.

All too soon the ride was over, but there were even greater delights still to come. Green lawns and gardens in a half-moon round a gleaming white beach, with a narrow inlet running in through smooth rocks, crystal clear, from the incredible blue of the Arabian Sea – the whole picture framed by curving coconut palms – sun-drenched, hot, but with a total absence of the characteristic humidity of the rest of Bombay. She stood entranced, the sheer beauty of it catching her by the throat, while Dan jacked up the motorbike and unstrapped a basket from the back. An old Indian came out of a small gate office and glanced at them sharply in turn, then nodded and made a curt salaam and went back in again.

'Oh, lovely – lovely – lovely,' she breathed.

'Not bad, is it?' Dan conceded with elaborate understatement. 'Funny place. Europeans only. A British Tommy, who is usually regarded as something lower than a snake's navel, can come in, but the Maharajah of Patiala or old Gandhi himself would be stopped dead at the gate. They won't even let an Anglo-Indian in – not if he looks like one. And the bloke who enforces it is that old wog who just gave us the once over. He's an Untouchable himself, but one look at you and he'll tell you the colour of your grandma's eyes.'

They stayed there for the whole day – eating at the small restaurant when they were hungry – swimming – dozing in the shade and generally lotus-eating – with Jane dreading the approach of evening and eventual return to Braganza Mansions, because Dan was due back on night duty at eight o'clock.

'But I'll be off again at eight tomorrow morning,' he told her. 'If you're not doing anything in particular we could take a run out to Juhu. There's a beach there – miles and miles of it – you know, everything in its wild state, if you see what I mean, instead of tarted up like this place. What do you say?'

She laughed shortly. 'Doing anything in particular? That's a joke. I'd love it – but isn't it taking advantage? I mean, aren't *you* doing anything in particular?'

'Don't talk daft,' he said.

The short twilight had passed and it was quite dark when they got back. He unlocked the door for her and gave her back the key – and this time there was no awkward moment, because she took the initiative, and clung to him passionately, unwilling to let him go, fearing the gloom of the night ahead of her in that room – crying, unreasonably, like a frightened child about to be left in the dark – promising anything to stave off the last fatal moment of departure. 'Don't go – oh, please don't go,' she begged.

'Christ,' he groaned. 'You don't think I'd be pushing off if I had the choice, do you? I've *got* to go, love – it'd be bloody nearly a court martial offence if I didn't turn up on duty – on the pegs, not allowed out – probably busted as well. But I'll be back – you bet – tomorrow – and the next day – and the next – every day – and I'll take you out of this dump – I promise you – out for good. You changed your opinion today, didn't you? About India, I mean. You said you loved the place – and you didn't really want to go Home. All right then – you don't have to. We could get married – hundred per cent married establishment for Technical Sergeants – I'm drawing good pay, and we'd have marriage allowance on top of that and lovely married quarters – I love you, Jane – Yes, I know – I only met you yesterday, but I knew immediately I saw you. Christ, it knocked me flat – ' He was babbling incoherently in his eagerness.

She said brokenly, 'But you don't know anything about me – you don't – '

'I don't want to – no more than you want to tell me – I don't care – marry me, Jane – marry me,' he pleaded. 'I've never asked a girl that before – ever – It's you – only you – There'd never be anybody else – not if I never saw you again from this minute – Marry me, Jane.'

'All right,' she whispered. 'If you want me to – that badly. But don't leave me here alone tonight – please – I'm frightened – '

Chapter Ten

'If he'd been an ordinary NCO like me, he might have got away with it,' Chalky White was explaining. 'Sheer bad luck it was, him being the duty dispenser and this bloke being brought in with spinal meningitis at three in the morning, and the MO wanting some special dope mixed up quick, and Danny AWOL. That means Absent Without Leave.'

'What will happen now?' Jane asked anxiously, and Chalky shrugged.

'Gawd knows. The client kicks the bucket, and the doc does his block and shoves Danny on a fizzer. He's in close arrest at the moment. He told me to give you this.' He handed her an envelope. 'I'd better be getting back or I'll be on the hooks meself. Any answer to that?'

She opened the envelope.

Darling (she read), There's a bit of bother going on here, but don't worry, it will be all right. I won't be able to see you for a couple of days, but here's a hundred rupees and I'll send some more as soon as Chalky can get down to the bank for me. I will write properly later today. Now don't worry. I love you.

Dan.

'Just say – say, "all the best",' she said. 'I'll be writing – '

'I'll be back this evening,' he told her, and added hopefully, 'If you get fed up or lonely or anything like that – you know – until Danny's back in circulation – I'm always around – '

'Thank you.' She smiled wanly and watched him wobble across the compound on his push-bike, then she went back into her room and sat on the edge of the bed staring into space. What on earth was she going to do now? It wasn't fair, she thought tearfully, these foul swipes of fate, every time a way seemed to be opening ahead of her. She looked around the room, dark and gloomy even at high noon, and shuddered. He was going to move her into Greens today. That was the last thing they had arranged before he left at dawn. Just for the few days it would take to obtain his CO's official permission to marry, and to secure married quarters. Should she risk it? Take a chance and shake the dust of this horrible place from her heels? She had enough to pay her way there for ten days or so, and he said he would be sending her some more. But suppose things went wrong, and he was in serious trouble, and the money ran out, and she was still waiting for a passage? What then? Oh, God – *what was she going to do?* She certainly couldn't face another night here – not alone. That awful lizard, or a near relative, was back, and after Dan had left she had a feeling that the occupant of the next room was watching her over the top of the dividing wall which didn't quite go right up to the ceiling cloth, and the disreputable bearer who had brought her chhota hazri had seemed to leer and wink.

It was after midday. She hadn't any appetite at the moment, but her sense told her that she would need food before long, and she couldn't face the dirty, curry-redolent dining room –

The ring, she thought. Surely the time had arrived to turn it into ready money – or at least get an estimate of its value. She could take it to more than one jeweller. There were several around the Taj and Greens. It would give her something to do for the rest of the afternoon – and she could have a meal, and do some serious thinking – and maybe there'd be better news when she got back.

She gathered up her things and went out through the compound on to the causeway and was fortunate enough to see a vacant taxi almost immediately, and she said 'Greens' sharply and authoritatively in the manner of one who knew where she wanted to go without any nonsense – like Lady Storland when she dealt with the lower orders. And the driver said, 'Ha-ji, Memsahib – ek dum, ceda jata,' and took her there without meter-padding side diversions.

But her very temporary courage deserted her when she looked through the plate glass doors of Lund and Blockley.

206

There was an American tourist ship in harbour and the shop was full of people buying six-armed goddesses, and jewelled elephants and no-see-no-hear-no-talk monkeys. No – it would probably be better to try a native shop first, she was telling herself when she turned away and bumped into the woman who was just entering. Jane muttered an apology and side-stepped, but the other caught both her hands and shrieked, 'Jane! What are *you* doing here?'

It was Mandy, more darkly beautiful than ever, and magnificently dressed and groomed.

Jane gulped and said, 'It's a long story – '

Mandy looked down at her bare ring finger and nodded in sympathetic understanding. 'Got a bit unstuck, did it? Never mind, lovie. Better fish in the ocean than ever came out of it.'

'I gave *him* up,' Jane was stung into telling her.

'Sure, sure, sure,' said Mandy. 'But what are you doing in Bombay?'

'Waiting to go Home, but the ships are all booked up – '

'Lucky you. I wish to God I was going back – although I can't really grumble at the moment. Where are you staying? At the Taj?'

'No – '

'I'm just going there for tea. Will you come with me, and tell me all about everything – ?'

'If you like.'

'Oh, goody. Wait a minute while I leave this watch here for repairs – dropped the damned thing on the bathroom floor this morning – Oh, it's lovely seeing you again – '

Jane went into the shop with her. She thought for a moment of seizing the opportunity and saying to the Parsee assistant, 'Oh, while I'm here you might value this ring for me – for insurance purposes, you know.' But she knew Mandy would recognize it, and she hadn't had time to think of a convincing cover story. They came out, with Mandy chattering excitedly and Jane hardly hearing her, so busy was she preparing answers for questions she knew perfectly well would follow.

' – really lovely boy – but then, all Americans are, aren't they – especially pilots – and then when his divorce comes through back in California we're going to be married and to hell with this dump – you can have it – elephants, peacocks, bloody Maharajahs – the lot – '

They walked the short distance to the Taj, through the lobby and up on to the deep, cool balcony of the Harbour Bar, and Mandy ordered prodigally – cucumber sandwiches, Swiss pastry and China tea – with hardly a break in the flow, which was now a spate.

'Just like that. There was this louse of a producer, Biswan Dass, and I was told that the only place you could see him was here – in the Harbour Bar – between six and seven in the evening – so I took a risk, with my last ten rupees, and came in for a drink – and it is a risk, lovie – all right for you, but if the house detective thinks one of *us* is on the prowl she gets hutjao-ed out, jaldi-jaldi – and there was this lovely hunk of man – huge – fair hair – blue eyes – sitting on a high stool by the bar – and he just said "Hello, beautiful. Can I get you a drink?" You know, the sort of thing you'd spit in most guy's eye for, but somehow the way he was looking at me made it different from the usual bar pick-up. And I made it more different still, and said I'd have a tomato juice and nothing more – and things started from there. Oh, Jane – he's lovely – really lovely.'

'So you're going to be married?' Jane said enviously.

'Like I said – when his divorce comes through. She caught him when he was a college boy and knew nothing of life, and he's been terribly unhappy. Oh, you'll love him, Jane, when you meet him – '

'Where is he now?'

'Away flying. He's a commercial pilot. Charter work, you see,' she explained knowledgeably. 'All over the place – Calcutta, Madras, Delhi – but this is his headquarters, and we've got this beautiful flat on Marine Drive – '

'You mean you're living with him?'

'Why not?' Mandy said defensively. 'We're as good as married – '

'Oh, I wasn't criticizing.'

'I should think not. Not Hank. I wouldn't have a word said about him. But here's me chunnering on about myself. What about you? What happened?'

'I just decided I didn't love George,' Jane said. 'And broke it off. I didn't like hurting him – but it was the only honest thing to do.'

'My God – I wouldn't have had the guts. When one of *us* catches a fish, she doesn't chuck it back until she's got hold of a bigger one – but, of course, with your sort of looks you could have your pick – '

'Oh, yes – there have been others around – lots of them – an officer – son of a General – a lord – that was up in Gonah. I got no peace, so I came down here – then there was this captain, a doctor. I had to tell him only last night that it was no go. I wanted to get back to England – '

'Lucky you. But where are you staying? Who with?'

'Oh, at a place called Braganza Mansions,' Jane said, caught unprepared.

Mandy sat bolt upright, as if electrified. *'Where?'*

'It's not much of a place – but, of course, I didn't know the names of any Bombay hotels, and the taxi driver took me there when I arrived – '

'But good God!' Mandy shrieked. 'That's where they send the jig-a-jig girls! Don't I know it? I got remanded there when I was fourteen. Old Maudie Furtado is the biggest madam in Bombay. Jesus! You must come out of there double quick. What's wrong with this place?'

'It might be a bit expensive. You see, I don't know how long I'll be staying here before sailing – '

'You broke?'

'Good heavens no, but I have to be careful. You see, my parents didn't want me to come out here in the first place, so I haven't told them yet that the wedding is off. I want to go Home under my own steam.'

Mandy nodded understandingly. 'Of course – I see. All right then – there's two bedrooms at the flat. You can come and bunk down there.'

Jane's heart leapt, but she smiled gently and shook her head. 'Sweet of you, Mandy dear,' she said, 'but I couldn't take advantage of your kindness like that.'

'Oh, pish! You'd do the same for me in London, wouldn't you?' Mandy said generously. 'Braganza Mansions! The soldier boys call it the Fornicatorium. She'd have been closed down years ago, only she's got the cops and the Court people squared. Finish your tea and we'll get out there and pick up your saman.'

'You must let me pay for tea,' Jane offered tentatively.

'Like hell. It all goes on Hank's bill. He's got an account here – and everywhere else in Bombay. He's *stinking* with money.'

They went out into the forecourt, and a splendidly uniformed Pathan hamal blew a whistle and a large shining American car drew up before them.

'Colaba Causeway, ish-tation ko nasdik,' Mandy told the Sikh chauffeur, plainly enjoying Jane's open-mouthed admiration of these thaumaturgics. 'Company car,' she explained. 'Always at my beck and call. Lovely, isn't it?'

At Braganza Mansions, Jane tried to call a halt outside the compound, but this was an opportunity that Mandy was not prepared to let go. 'Undar jao,' she commanded, and they drove in, scattering dogs, children, chickens and goats. Mrs Furtado, aroused from her customary siesta by the noise, came out on to the verandah and stared in gummy-eyed wonder at the car, then she recognized first Jane and then Mandy, and cackled shrilly.

'A bit early, aren't you?' she gibed. 'The boys don't get paid until Friday.'

'Dirty-mouthed old cow,' Mandy shot at her. 'Haven't they closed you down yet?'

'No – but they might think about it if they see *you* hanging around,' said Mrs Furtado. 'What you doing now, baba? Number five wife to a Lascar bosun?'

'Teri ma'ka,' Mandy said obscenely. 'We want this lady's luggage – '

'Lady?' sneered Mrs Furtado. 'I've seen better ladies in the Grant Road cages. A Schedule G transient – '

'Which is your room, lovie?' Mandy asked Jane. 'That one? Good. No, don't you bother to get out of the car. Partab Singh

– Miss-sahib ke saman jumakaro – ' And she continued to insult Mrs Furtado in a mixture of English and kitchen Hindi while the chauffeur collected the luggage and stowed it in the boot. 'Do you owe her anything? No? Then let's get the hell out of it before we catch something nasty. Agi jao, Partab Singh.' And they drove out leaving Mrs Furtado shrieking wildly after them.

'Sorry about that,' Mandy chuckled as they drove across to Marine Drive. 'It's not often that I get down to gali – that's dirty gutter talk – not nowadays anyhow – but seeing that filthy old bitch again brought it all back. Good job I ran into you, lovie. There's no saying what might have happened to you if you'd stayed there long.'

The flat was in one of the new highrise buildings that were beginning to scar the beautiful sweep of Marine Drive – a place of synthetic marble, plate glass and chrome, with hamals disguised as American bellhops in brass buttons and pillbox caps. Mandy swept Jane through the lobby and into the elevator like a grande dame ushering peasantry into the castle – kindly but with bursting pride.

'Bit better than Braganza bloody Mansions, eh?' she beamed.

'Lovely,' the awed Jane agreed. 'But your – er – friend? Won't he be annoyed?'

'Annoyed? What's he got to be annoyed about? No fear. If I say I'm inviting a friend here – a friend from Blightyside – he'll say fine. He's American – big, big, big. You wait till you meet him.'

The flat was on the fifth floor, huge, air-conditioned and vulgarly sumptuous, with sweeping views across Back Bay and out to sea. Mandy whirled her through on a lightning tour of inspection – the two bedrooms, each with its luxurious Western bathroom *en suite* – drawing room, big enough to hold a trade convention in – the king-sized refrigerator in the dining room, stuffed to bursting point with every type of alcoholic refreshment, homogenized milk and Coca Cola – but, characteristically, no kitchen. 'All the grub comes up topside on the service lift,' Mandy explained proudly. 'No damn stinking cookhouse up here. You want to eat, you just grab the phone there and tell the cook. *American* food. I tell you, lovie, these bums out here never knew how to live until the Yanks came.' She sniffed. 'The British didn't teach them anything. They just went wog themselves – talking Hindi, eating curry and God knows what – '

'Are there many Americans here?' Jane asked. '*I* haven't met any.'

'Just in Bombay – a lot here already and more arriving every day. It's this war that's coming soon. It's bringing a hell of a lot of business here. You want to hear Hank talk about it. He says American money is going to put this place on the map.' She paused, smiling, and looked at the other girl. 'You haven't lost any of your looks out here, lovie,' she said thoughtfully. 'You seemed to have picked some up. Got a bit sunburnt. Suits you. Me, I've been dodging the sun all my life. Fatal for an Anglo-Indian girl to go dark. We ought to be finding *you* a nice American boy friend. What do you say?'

'Oo, you *are* awful,' Jane giggled.

They dined alone that night in the flat, on guzpacho, Maryland fried chicken, sweet corn, and ice-cream, with tinglingly cold lager and beakers of café-crème, while Mandy bemoaned the weight she was putting on alarmingly. 'That's one thing about the Yanks you've got to watch,' she said ruefully. 'The Limeys don't mind a girl being a bit rounded, and, of course, the Indians love it – but Americans like us streamlined. You don't seem to have to worry though.'

'I ride a lot,' Jane said grandly.

'So do I,' Mandy grinned. 'Hank's a tiger for it – but it doesn't seem to do much good. Well, now – what would you like to do? Cinema? That's about all there is, I'm afraid. We couldn't risk going to the Taj or anywhere like that at night without a man. People get wrong ideas.'

But the worry and sleeplessness that had been assailing Jane for the past few days and nights were taking their toll, and now, with this temporary surcease, she felt an overpowering weariness and wanted nothing more than to sleep – and sleep.

'OK, lovie, you do that,' Mandy said sympathetically. 'Tomorrow Hank will be here and it will be different. Anything you want, just press a button or grab a phone. You're riding high on the hog now, as the Yanks say.'

Jane slid back the double-glazed windows of her bedroom and stepped out on to the terrace, passing from sterile air-conditioned coolness into the langorous warmth of the Indian night. Across the bay she could see the beam of Colaba light-house, with the darkened bulk of the barracks to the north of it, and she thought of Dan for the first time since her headlong rush from Braganza Mansions. Poor Dan. A nice boy – and she was genuinely grateful to him. He had pulled her through that first awful twenty-four hours. But the thing was ended now. She certainly couldn't marry him – not a sergeant. He couldn't expect it – not really. She hoped he hadn't got into any serious trouble. Sweet of him to send her that hundred rupees, but of course she couldn't possibly accept it – not now. She must remember to send it back to him – some time. She took a deep breath and then slowly exhaled. She knew a sense of relief that was almost exaltation. It had worked again, as it always had in the past. When things were at their blackest; that night in the police station; when she had seemed to hit bottom in Calcutta; the hideous first few minutes in the General's study; then, finally, Braganza Mansions. Yes, it had worked again. She couldn't define 'it' – she had no single word for 'an infinite capacity for survival' in her limited vocabulary. She knew it wasn't entirely blind luck, because a lot of it was due to her own energy and sound common sense, she told herself with some pride.

'Like that bit of poetry in school,' she thought. ' "There's a sweet little cherub that sits up aloft and keeps watch on the life of poor Jack." ' She smiled. 'Poor Jane. That's me. Hang on, cherub. Don't ever let me down.'

They were having breakfast on the terrace, Jane in a swim-suit, revelling in the morning breeze from the sea, Mandy carefully insulated from her enemy the sun in a neck-to-ankle Bokhara wrap that made her look like some exotic bird of paradise. Someone was talking interminably on the radio about an Anglo-Polish pact signed the previous day in Warsaw, and Mandy switched it off impatiently.

'Bloody Indian radio,' she complained. 'Either talking or playing wog music. Never anything decent. My God, I'm bored.'

'With all this?' Jane looked around her at the palms and bougainvillaea in tubs, and the beach umbrellas and luxurious cane furniture – with two bearers, here called 'house boys', standing by at a side table attentive to their every want. 'You don't know when you're well off.'

Mandy shrugged. 'Oh, yes – I know that all right. And I know what it's like to be broke, and hungry, and to be running from the cops. They're bastards in this town – the European and Anglo-Indian ones. I know what I'd choose if I had to. This, every time. But, oh, my God, it can get on your nerves. What the hell can I do? What friends have I got? Other Anglos, who I wouldn't trust and who certainly wouldn't trust *me*, because I've got a bit more than them at the moment? No thank you. I can't go to any of the pukkha white clubs – not that I'd want to, because the bloody old cows there give me the pip, but I hate being kept out, all the same.'

'You're mad,' Jane said shortly. 'You were dancing on air yesterday when you were showing me all this. What's got into you?'

'Just what I said. Nothing to do when Hank's away – no friends – '

'Thanks,' said Jane dryly.

Mandy reached across and squeezed her hand. 'I didn't mean that – you know I didn't. I mean friends on one's own level – whose houses you could walk into at any time without waiting to be asked – and know you'd be welcome – and who would walk into yours, and you'd be glad to see them. Like you do Blightyside.'

'But surely you could find people like that here, if you tried?'

'No. Not here. If Anglo-Indians are respectable they are more formal than the pure whites. If you want to call on them, or want them to call on you, you leave bloody silly cards with your name on 'em, and then wait until they leave theirs on you.'

'All right then,' Jane said impatiently, 'Get some printed and do just that.'

Mandy's face twisted into a wry smile. 'And what do I put on them? "Miss Mandy Scanlon – at present shacking up with Mr Henry Dexter"? Cards are only any good if you're respectable, lovie. You know something? I'd swap everything I've got my hands on at this moment – this flat – car, uniformed chauffeur, servants, open accounts in all the pukkha shops – for the seven pounds a week and the bedsitter I had in Earls Court.'

'Then why didn't you stay there?' Jane said, exasperated.

'No contract. You know that.'

'You didn't *have* to stay in films.'

'What else for a girl like me? No education, no training. Modelling? Tried that, but they told me I was too fat. So what's left? Oh, yes – I know what you could say to that, and get a good laugh out of it – but that was the one thing I didn't want to do. Not the bash. Anyhow, you damn nearly need a union card for it in London nowadays.' She lit a cigarette and smiled wanly through the smoke at Jane. 'Don't take any notice of me,' she said. 'I always get on edge like this when Hank is away – and it gets worse when it's time for him to return. I keep asking myself what in God's name I'd do if he didn't come back some time. What if he just flew on and out – back to his wife – or took up with somebody else? It's my last chance, Jane. I feel it – That's the wog side of me – being able to get a look at things that are going to happen – or you *think* are going to happen.'

'You're giving yourself the willies for nothing. Use your sense, Mandy.' Jane waved her hand round the flat. 'If he's given you all this he must think something of you. I mean, he's hardly likely to walk out on you now – not just like that.'

Mandy nodded eagerly. 'Yes – that's something I tell myself when I've got the kala janwar mera khanda par. That means the black beast on my shoulders. He wouldn't set me up like this, would he? Not if he didn't mean to marry me and take me back to America when his divorce comes through.'

'Of course he wouldn't. This must have cost him a fortune.'

'Thousands of rupees. If it was just a quick roll on the old charpoy he wanted he could have got any short-time Charlotte for a couple of hundred rupees a month in a single room in Dhanraj Mahal, and lived at the Club for the rest of the time like all the other pukkha sahibs. No – he's the sort of man who wants something to come home to. Somebody waiting for him, with his slippers and a drink ready – who'll listen to him when he's having a gripe about the things that have happened to him during the day. He's not interested in a Chinese honeymoon – "me likee you – you likee me – Finish!" – He's not that sort, thank God. He's a gentleman – a pukkha gentleman. Oh, wait until you meet him, Jane.'

'When is he due back?'

'Any time today, tomorrow, or even the next day. That's one of the things you have to get used to – not knowing when to expect him – and when the time stretches out, that's when you start thinking – and worrying – '

'Well, don't worry any more,' Jane told her. 'He's not going to walk out on you. Of course he's not. But – but – ' She hesitated. 'Are you sure he's not likely to be angry when he finds you've got a lodger?'

Mandy grinned. 'He'd be *bloody* angry if the lodger was a fellow,' she said. 'No – I know Hank. He'll be only too pleased for me to have company while he's away. He told me that himself more than once. Less chance of me getting into mischief, he said.'

'Well – as long as you *are* sure – ' Jane said, uncertainly.

'I'm sure,' said Mandy, positively. 'But if you don't mind amusing yourself today, and maybe tomorrow – I mean, I can't come out with you, and I'll have to keep the car ready to send to the airport at Santa Cruz if he phones – '

'Don't let me interfere with anything at all,' Jane told her. 'I can find plenty to do.'

But it was harder to kill time than she thought. She put a wrap over her swimsuit and crossed Marine Drive to the beach in front of the flats, only to find that below the sea wall it degenerated into a stretch of liquid filth overlaid with a detritus of cans, broken bottles and plastic containers. She shuddered and came back and found Mandy about to wash her hair, and she was only too happy to bring her professional expertise to bear on the task, but that only filled an hour. She went out walking then, in spite of Mandy's horrified protests.

'My God, girl!' she squealed. '*Walking?* In the *sun?* Hot as hell and you'll have every beggar in Bombay trailing along behind you. Take a taxi.'

'Where to?'

'Wherever you want to go.'

'But I don't want to go anywhere in particular.'

'Then stay indoors, for Chri'sake. Lovely and cool – plenty to eat and drink – You know what you pay for *one* air-conditioned room in Bombay now the Yanks are here? Five hundred rupees a month – and we've got the whole damn flat.'

'Have you got anything to read?'

'Read? What do you mean, *read*? Oh, books and things? Hell no. I gave all that up when I scrammed from the convent. Bloody nuns used to ram The Life of Saint Philomena and things like that down your throat whenever you weren't doing goddamn needlework for some lousy Memsahib or other. I swore I'd never read another book as long as I lived – and that's one promise I've kept. What's wrong with the radio?'

'What you said yourself – wog music or somebody talking. So long – see you later.'

She turned right when she came out of the lobby – as a matter of instinct largely dictated by the fact that going the other way she would have Colaba in front of her. She was beginning to feel a little uneasy. Suppose she ran slap into Dan? How would he react? She ought to have her story ready in advance. But what story? The same as for George? Not certain of her feelings, therefore the only honest thing etc. etc.? Hm – sending a letter – without a forwarding address – to a timid civilian is one thing – Facing an angry soldier in the flesh is quite another. He might blame *her* for everything. Wasn't her fault. He shouldn't have stayed if he thought the wretched Army was going to cut up rough. How was *she* to know?

Something plucked at the back of her frock, and turning,

she saw a woman, emaciated and filthy, holding out a tiny monkeylike baby towards her – and behind the woman was a man with advanced elephantiasis, his hideously engorged scrotum supported in a sacking sling, and a legless child was dragging itself crablike along the burning pavement behind him, and others were converging from hitherto unseen corners like dung-beetles from an overturned cowpat. Trembling with horror she quickened her pace, but most of them managed to keep up with her, and she could see others ahead waiting to join with them. She panicked and broke into a run – and then deliverance was to hand in the form of two blue-clad, yellow-turbanned Mahratta policemen, their whirling truncheons smacking down on unprotected heads and skeletal shoulders, and the road was suddenly clear again except for the legless child who had rolled sideways and was whimpering in the gutter. Jane turned and ran every step of the way back to the flats. Safely cocooned in well-policed military cantonments, seldom on foot, or if so, with a stalwart male escort, this was an India she had scarcely been aware of previously, and it terrified her.

She burst into the apartment, and a tall, fair man pouring Bourbon over ice cubes with one hand and caressing Mandy somewhat intimately with the other, turned and glared at her, then his jaw dropped and he said, '*Holy shit!*' in tones of deepest wonder. Mandy pulled away in some embarrassment and said reproachfully, 'Mind your language, Hank – she's not used to it. And stop doing that – This is Jane. You didn't believe me, did you?'

Hank took a deep breath. 'No,' he said softly. 'I didn't believe you. I didn't know they made 'em like this any longer. Hi, Jane. Welcome aboard.'

'How do you do?' Jane said, and smiled shyly. Mandy was looking from one to the other uncertainly, as if, for the first time, doubting the wisdom of this introduction.

'Can I fix you a drink?' Hank asked, breaking quite an appreciable silence.

'Thank you – I'd love some lime juice.'

'No likker? I mean – no gin or anything with it?'

Jane shook her head. 'No thank you – I'm afraid I haven't much head for it,' she said apologetically. 'I mean, it makes me quite dizzy.'

'That's fine – fine,' he reassured her. 'You don't like likker, Christ – you don't have to drink it. You're the first girl I've met out here though who didn't have the capacity of a Wyoming teamster.' He carefully cut and squeezed fresh limes over ice cubes, then added sugar and water. 'Try that for size,' he invited.

Jane sipped and smiled her thanks. 'Lovely,' she said, and Hank took another deep breath and followed it with an even deeper swallow from his glass, then grinned beatifically. 'Say – this is nice,' he said, unspecifically. '*Real nice.*'

Jane, feeling the ground firm and solid beneath her feet, said, 'Look – it's been worrying me I can't stay here any longer – '

'Aw, hell – why not?' Hank said, his face falling.

'Well – I mean – two's company. I feel an intruder – taking advantage of your kindness – '

'For God's sake,' exploded Hank. 'Is *that* all? I thought something had offended you – my language maybe. You're not butting into anything. And you're not taking advantage of anybody's kindness. Mandy said you were waiting for a boat to England. Fine – you wait right here. She wouldn't have it any other way – would you, honey?'

'No. I was telling her that myself – I love having her here. It's company while you're away,' Mandy averred stoutly, her momentary uncertainty seeming to have passed.

'So that's settled. Good. Now how's about us all going out to Juhu to swim, and then eat lunch?'

'I – I thought you'd want to rest, since you just got in,' Mandy said, slightly put out.

'I've been flying that damn box and breathing gas and glycol for eight hours,' Hank said. 'I want some fresh air and cool sea. C'mon now, both of you – move it.'

They drove north from the city along the palm-lined Salsette Road, with the hood of the convertible down, Partab Singh at the wheel, and Hank asprawl in the middle of the rear seat with an arm round each of the girls.

They swam and lazed and ate and drank, and came back in the evening soporific with sun and sea air, to rest a while before dressing and going forth again to dine and dance at the Taj Mahal – and that set the pattern for the remainder of the week that Hank was in Bombay while his aircraft underwent its half-yearly check. Until the last day, when he went out to the airfield alone to complete some paper work, leaving the girls to their own devices. He came back early, in a more than jovial mood, and announced a party for that night.

'Jimmie James's birthday,' he told them 'He's had lobsters flown in from Colombo, trout from Kashmir and God knows what-all. He's our operations manager,' he explained to Jane. 'Nice guy – but don't let him kid you into going walkies. The son-of-a-bitch has got wandering hands, hasn't he, Mandy?'

'Son-of-a-bitch is right,' Mandy retorted. 'I don't like him – and I don't think you ought to have Jane there, not without a definite partner to look after her.'

'I'll look after you both,' Hank said, and winked at Jane.

'The last party you got as drunk as a skunk,' Mandy said, 'and I nearly got undressed by him in public. You couldn't look after yourself, let alone me. No – I don't want to go.'

'You're going,' Hank said quietly. 'He's a friend of mine – and he also happens to be the guy who allots assignments – and I get paid a flying-hour bonus. If you hurt Jimmie it's going to hurt me, honey – right where it hurts the most – in the wallet.'

'Count me out of it,' Mandy flared. 'The hell with your wallet.'

'Sure,' said Hank, still quietly. 'We'll be leaving at eight o'clock, Jane.' He walked through the room and then they heard him singing under the shower. Mandy was curled in a chair, crying.

'What do I do, Jane? What the hell do I do?' she pleaded.

'You go,' Jane said flatly.

'I hate his friends. They're all American and Australian – and they're tougher on coloured people than the damned British.'

220

'You still go,' Jane told her. 'This way you're asking for trouble. If you like I'll say I've got a headache, and drop out.'

'That wouldn't help,' Mandy said miserably. 'He'd be madder than ever then. No – one goes, both go. But watch him – Jimmie James, I mean – and some of the others too. There'll probably be about ten men, and maybe another couple of women at the most, besides us two. And things can get nasty – very nasty – '

'I can look after myself – so can you.'

'You bet I can – with a hatpin or a broken bottle – at a certain sort of party. But this is different. You can't win. If I let James or any of the other drunken goondahs maul me around, Hank'd start a fight. If I stopped them, and made a fuss about it, he'd be just as likely to call me a missionary-trained half-chat who was insulting his friends.' She stood up. 'Oh, well – the hell with it. We both go. But watch it, lovie – watch it.'

But the spat had passed as quickly as it had been engendered, and they met in the Harbour Bar shortly after eight – three other pilots of the small but lucrative company Hank worked for, two Canadians and an Australian, the chief mechanic and his assistant, both American, the Bombay manager, also American, the wives of one of the pilots and the mechanic, and the girl friend of the manager, who Jane could not categorize, a large and brassy woman with streakily dyed hair and a prominent gold tooth, but whom Mandy summed up succinctly in a muted aside, as 'a Piccadilly pro imported by a rajah – out on her ear when he died – moved in with this sugar daddy'. Their host, a Scotsman, was a small ginger man with bad breath and a braying laugh which unfortunately synchronized on occasion, usually in his more confidential moments, and in the face of his listeners.

Jane was received in the manner to which she had become accustomed as a right, but which she invariably managed to meet with just the right admixture of shyness, modesty and childlike trust. The men stopped talking, and stumbled to their feet, there was a concerted intake of breath which developed here and there into an involuntary whistle of sheer admiration. The women watched with circumspection.

James said in an exaggerated Highland accent, 'Since I'm the Birthday Boy, will ye no sit here beside me, lassie, and show me what an ill-spent youth has caused me to miss,' and thereafter proceeded to pay her compliments and semi-asphixiate her from a range of two feet, until she was rescued by some of the other men who almost picked her up bodily and bore her downstairs and across to the Yacht Club.

'But the others – ?' she managed to gasp.

'Coming,' one of the pilots told her. 'But we had to get you away from that little jerk. This is where he's throwing the party. We had to meet outside because some of the guys aren't members, and have to be sponsored.'

Jane knew a brief moment of panic in case she should meet any of the Gonah residents, but then remembered that this was midweek and not a period when out-station visitors were likely to be present, and anyhow she had had a glass of champagne and was accordingly brave, lighthearted and very happy – once again in the India she had always pictured. Her India.

The special table had been set at the edge of the patio, a glory of lobsters, salads, fruit, flowers and champagne in ice buckets, and a birthday cake surmounted by three huge church candles with a facetious notice stating that each represented twenty-five years. She was whirled into a dance by one of the men, then another cut in, and another – and it was some time before the rest of the party arrived, and there was much popping of corks, and the band struck up Happy Birthday Dear Jimmie, and others had joined them in a crescendo of deafening and unmelodious singing that was followed by a samba in which everybody present joined, so that the party was split up and separated as they snaked round the patio, through the bar, cardroom and indoor dining room, then out again and round the boathouses and slipway – and somewhere she lost a shoe, but it didn't seem to matter because most of the women were dancing barefoot by now.

It was long after midnight before she noticed the absence of

Mandy. She found her way to the side of Hank and said, 'Where's Mandy? I haven't seen her since we left the Taj.'

He shrugged and said, 'You people make the rules, honey – not me.'

She felt icy at the pit of her stomach. 'What do you mean?' she asked.

'They wouldn't let her in.'

Jane stared at him in horror. 'But – what happened? Where is she now?'

'Gone home in a taxi. Here – ' He took her elbow and led her out into the garden, and down to the water's edge.

Jane said, 'I can't stay – not after that. Oh, Hank – how must she be feeling – ?'

'God damn,' he swore. 'It wasn't my fault. I didn't know the son-of-a-bitch had laid it on for the Yacht Club – the tightest anti-Jim Crow joint in India. I thought it was to be held in the Taj.'

'Let's go,' she begged. 'Or if you want to stay, please get me a taxi and I'll go on my own.'

'Sure, sure,' he agreed. 'But there are a couple of things I'd like to tell you first. I've been trying to all week, but she never gave us a chance. Jane, listen, for Pete's sake. Call me a hairy dog afterwards – but I want you to know.'

'What?'

'Well – the way things are. You see – oh, hell – this is hard to explain. Look – there was no harm in setting her up in the apartment. It's done every day out here. She'd been around and she knew the score. I didn't lie to her. I didn't promise her anything I couldn't deliver – '

'You told her you'd marry her,' Jane accused.

'Like hell I did. I told her I *was* married. Sure, it was on the rocks and we were thinking of a divorce – but the bit about marrying her afterwards came from *Mandy*, not me. I couldn't marry her. Jesus! – my home town is Atlanta, Georgia – and they're as tough there as they are here. Mixed blood just doesn't get by. Jane – are you listening to me?'

She nodded dumbly.

'It had to end – in fact it's *got* to – this week – but I didn't want it to finish this way. I'm not a monster, Jane – She's a hell of a nice kid, and I wouldn't want to hurt her – but I have to leave Bombay, and go somewhere else. Jane – do you know what I'm trying to say to you?'

'No.'

'I'm trying to ask you to go with me – '

'What in God's name do you think I am?' she demanded indignantly.

'Yes, I know – that sounds pretty raw – but whether you say yes or no it doesn't make any difference as far as Mandy is concerned. It's over, Jane – *finished*. I've got to complete my contract with these people in this other place – then I can either sign on for a further five years – or I've got another job open for me back in the States. Either way there's a hell of a lot of dough in it – not that I suppose that would make any difference as far as you're concerned.'

'But I don't understand – ' she began.

'I know – I'm putting it badly,' he said. 'But please listen – just a bit longer. I'm asking you to go with me. As far as the locals will know, you'll be my wife. Meanwhile I'll put a firecracker under the lawyer's tail back home, and get this divorce thing through. It should take, maybe, three months – six perhaps – then we get married quietly somewhere – and go back to the States. Jane, what do you say?' He took both her hands in his.

'But – what – what an awful thing to do to Mandy – ' she whispered.

'I told you – it doesn't make any difference to Mandy one way or the other. I've got to be going – whether you come with me or not – '

'You hardly know me – we met less than a week ago – '

'I know I love you,' he said earnestly. 'On my side, that's all that matters. On yours, I'm hoping that you might feel a bit that way about *me*. Maybe I've got a hell of a gall, you coming from a fine old British family and all that, and me from very ordinary folks. But I'm going to get somewhere, Jane – somewhere up there on top. I'm doing all right now – but I'm going on further. I made one bad mistake – and married a tramp. I'm not making another. I want a home, a wife I can be proud of, a family. Jane honey – will you take a chance on me? Will you give me a break?'

'Where is this other place – ?'

'Madras. They want me to take charge of things over on that side. It's promotion – but as far as Mandy is concerned I'll have been recalled to the States, and the company will confirm that to her. Don't worry – I won't be leaving her broke – and the rent of the apartment is fixed up until the end of the month – '

'Oh, Hank – We'd be hurting her – hurting her terribly – '

'She never need know – about you, I mean. Me? Well, like I said, I'll be on my way anyhow.' He took her in his arms. 'Now listen to me. If we do it this way – '

Jane stirred and sat up as Mandy tiptoed into her room next morning. The dark girl put a finger to her lips warningly.

'Sh-h-h! He's still sleeping,' she whispered. 'Did you have a good party?'

'Yes – in a way,' Jane said hesitantly. 'Mandy – I wanted to leave early when I heard – I – I – ' She choked on the words.

There was no rancour in Mandy's smile. 'That's all right,' she said. 'I told the silly fool what would happen, but he would insist on trying to get me in. He wanted to bring me home, but that would have been a pity once the party had got under way.'

'It's so unreasonable,' Jane said angrily. 'They let that awful creature with the dyed hair in without question, and she got drunk and behaved badly – '

'She's white,' said Mandy simply. 'It makes a difference. It won't matter though, not when we get to America. Listen, lovie – you won't mind amusing yourself this morning, will you? Hank is taking me out to buy me a present – ' She dropped her voice conspiratorially. 'He won't tell me what it is, but I *think* it's a jade bracelet I saw in Eduljee's the other day, and started to drop hints about. O-o-oh! Lovely. I'm a very lucky girl.' She ran her hand lightly over Jane's hair. 'We'll have to see about getting a nice American boy friend for you – not one of their drunken Goodtime Charlies – a *nice* one – like

Hank – with a wedding ring at the end of it. Be seeing you, lovie – about lunch time.' And she went out.

Jane rose and packed quickly, then she bathed and dressed and gave herself over to the task of composition once again.

Dear Mandy (she wrote), You've been terribly sweet but I don't think it is fair to take advantage of your kindness any longer. Some friends, I think I told you about them once, rang me up and invited me to their place up-country just after you left, and they are calling for me in a few minutes so please excuse this short note. I can't spell the name of the place but I'll write after I get there. Once again thank you for everything and give my love to Hank and lots and lots of it to yourself.

Jane

Then she sent for a taxi and had herself driven to Victoria Terminus, and since she had a first class ticket to Madras Central, she had no difficulty in booking a waiting room for her sole use until train time that evening. She was becoming, she thought with no small satisfaction, an experienced traveller. Indian trains held no terrors for her now – nor did Indians. She even had a few words of the language – like 'idhar ao' which means 'come here' – and 'hut jao', its opposite, forcibly expressed – and 'mujhko lao' – 'bring me' and several more imperatives, plus a few terms of ladylike abuse. And she knew how much to tip and, more importantly, when not to tip – how, and from whom, to summon support and assistance by use of a wide-eyed look of innocent bewilderment – thanks expressed by a shy smile – and the congé, when necessary, with a cold little stare. Quite the Memsahib, in fact, she summed up.

Hank was waiting on the platform for her at Madras, having flown in the day before, a vastly different figure from that of poor old George at Howrah, she thought, as he pushed through the crowd towards her – bronzed, tall, muscular, wearing his laundry-faded khaki shirt and shorts with an air. He gathered her up in a bearlike hug and swung her off her

feet. 'Hi, honey,' he said. 'How's my gal?' There was a car
waiting for them outside – like the one in Bombay, big, shiny,
and American – and they drove out through the town and
along the coast towards Adyar. He passed her a small velvet-
covered box. 'Had to guess the size,' he said. 'We can get it
altered in the bazaar if it doesn't fit.' It was a plain gold wedding
band, and it fitted well enough – and since he never did things
by half, there was an emerald and diamond engagement ring
with it, a brooch and a matching set of ear-rings.

'Anyone wants to know, we were married a couple of years
ago, in Canada,' he told her. 'They won't though — not over
here. More commercial people in Madras than Army. They
take you as they find you, and mind their own goddamn
business. Great crowd – you'll like them, and, boy! are *they*
going to like *you*. But watch it, honey – I'm a jealous son-of-
a-bitch – I can't help it.'

Characteristically, she did not ask after Mandy, nor what
had been the manner of their parting, but he told her nevertheless.

'We went back to the apartment after you had left, and found
your note. It kind of worried her at first, but not for long. I
guess she's not the worrying type. I left the next day in the
ordinary way. I told her I'd be away a bit longer than usual
this time, and I mailed a letter to her from Calcutta yesterday,
saying I'd been called back to the States unexpectedly – and I
put five hundred bucks in it. No bones broken. So we forget
about it, eh?'

It was a new experience for Jane – a totally different India
from that which she had seen hitherto. The people were
smaller and blacker, and the city, though busy, lacked the
frenetic bustle of either Calcutta or Bombay – and certainly
had none of the military atmosphere of Gonah. The buildings
were lower and older, and the blight of the skyscraper was
totally absent. It was hot – hotter, it seemed, than Bombay, but
there was a brisk breeze from the sea to temper it. Yes, she
decided, she was going to like Madras.

'No apartment here, I'm afraid, honey,' Hank apologized.
'It's a sort of a beat-up bungalow that must have been thrown

together five hundred years ago. No plumbing – but one hell of a nice garden – and there are about twenty black joes to run the place – cooks, bearers, water-boys, sweepers, gardeners – the lot.'

'But how have you been able to arrange all this in a day?' she asked.

'Day hell,' he laughed. 'I've been flying in and out of this dump for the last couple of years. This is a company shack.'

They swept up the drive and she got out, and when he started to apologize again she halted him with an upraised hand. The bungalow was almost a replica of Flagstaff House – a riotous mass of bougainvillaea screening a deep verandah, banyan trees and graceful palms – with flame-of-the-forest and jacaranda in full bloom – and beds of zinnias and marigolds – and there was a billiard-table lawn that malis were sprinkling from oxhide waterbags – and the smell of water on hot earth that Tessa had spoken of came to her – and something that could only have had its roots in pure atavism clutched at her heart and misted her eyes. She turned to Hank and rested her head on his shoulder.

'Oh, Hank darling,' she murmured. '*This* is it. This is what I have always dreamed of. This is what I've heard my uncle, the General, describe so often. I've come home – Yes – I've come home.'

And Hank said huskily, with deep feeling, 'That's my li'l gal. Let's go in and have a drink.'

The servants stood in line in order of precedence, and to her delight she found herself naming their functions correctly as she walked down the rank like an empress receiving the fealty of her vassals, nodding graciously in acknowledgement of their salaams, 'Khidmagar? Shabash. Khansamah? Shabash. Bearer? Shabash. Mesalchi – Mali – Dhobi – Mehta,' just as she had heard Lady Storland enumerating when paying the staff at the end of the month. Hank was lost in admiration.

'Goddamn,' he said. 'I can never remember all those coon names, and I've been out here a hell of a time.'

'I told you, dear,' she said kindly, 'when one's family has

228

been in Indian service for generations, like mine – it becomes a matter of instinct.'

'Sure – see what you mean,' said the impressed Hank. 'Same with our people back home. You can always pick the old plantation aristocracy from the crackers and sharecroppers.' He picked her up and carried her over the threshold. 'I guess Lady Luck isn't going to mind us beating the gun a mite. *My little Memsahib.*'

Part Two

Chapter Eleven

Winter 1943

Jane came out of the grocery department of Spencer's followed by a chokra carrying a laden basket. Bunty Wheeler, just entering, pulled a face and said, 'American plutocrat. Have you left anything for us depressed classes?'

'Well, *you're* going to eat some of what I've bought,' Jane said. 'And there's plenty left.'

'What have you got?' Bunty halted the chokra and peered into the basket. She reminded Jane of a Brahminy kite foraging in a rubbish heap. 'Good God! Beluga caviar! Where the hell did that come from? I thought the bloody Russians were living on rats and grass.'

'That didn't come from here,' Jane told her. 'A pal of Hank's flew half a dozen jars in from Teheran. I've been keeping it in their freezer. I hope it's still eatable.'

'What else? Tongue – smoked salmon – half a Stilton – a Fortnum and Mason game pie. No wonder the people at Home accuse us of fiddling while London burns.' Bunty clucked disapprovingly.

'Is not buying British going to help them?' Jane asked acidly. 'And I'm neither American nor a plutocrat.'

'Of course not, sweetie,' the other soothed. 'Merely married to one. How is he, by the way?'

'Very well, thank you,' Jane said stiffly.

'Hey!' protested the other. 'Don't get miffy with old Auntie Bunty. I was only leg-pulling – and being a bit covetous at the same time. When do you want us there tonight?'

'Come as you please. It's no good setting a time with the men so uncertain. It's a buffet anyhow.'

'Eat, drink and get stinking, for tomorrow the Jap cometh,' Bunty said. 'But you still haven't told me how Hank is. "Very well, thank you" merely means "mind your own damned business".'

'He really is much better,' Jane said hurriedly. 'Look – do excuse me – I've got an awful lot still to do before tonight.' She flashed a bright smile at the older woman and ran across to the parked Buick, waited while the chokra stowed the basket in the back, threw him a four anna piece, and started to drive slowly out of the compound. A middle-aged European came out of a doorway beside the big store and lifted his hand in a polite but unmistakable signal to stop. She pulled up, her heart sinking, and switched on the smile again.

'Good afternoon, Mrs Dexter,' he said pleasantly. 'I hope you found everything you wanted.'

'Yes thank you – '

'It's getting more difficult every day – for imported stuff, I mean – and of course, the prices – ' He whistled softly in dismay. 'Nowadays we get little or no credit either. It's cash on the nail – or somebody else, mostly the Parsees, get the supplies.'

'I don't know what we'd do without you,' Jane said gratefully.

'Well – I do my best – but – er – Mrs Dexter, I was wondering – It's over three months now – '

'I know,' Jane said, stricken. 'It really is awful – but the mails – you understand? I mean, they were bad enough before – but now, since Pearl Harbor it's taking even longer for anything to reach us from America. My husband's salary is terribly in arrears. But it *will* arrive – any day now – If you could just be patient a little longer, Mr Paterson – '

'Of course,' Mr Paterson conceded courteously. 'But it *is* a big balance now, you know – and your purchases today have brought it up to over three thousand rupees.'

'A party tonight – for business reasons – '

'I see – but I really must ask you, with the greatest regret, to confine your purchases to basic necessities until such time as you are able to settle, Mrs Dexter. You see – it isn't as if you were Army people – ' He trailed off awkwardly, and Jane, stung, pounced in icy fury.

'No – we're not Army people, Mr Paterson. We're mere civilians, who in the past have usually spent more in a week in your store than the average Colonel draws in a month. Don't worry. Your bill will be paid.' She brought her foot down heavily on the accelerator and the car shot forward, leaving the man floundering in apologies.

But it was only a gesture on her part, she reflected grimly. The problem still remained. Why in God's name was the wretched company holding his salary and bonus up? Other men got laid off sick on occasion, but they weren't treated like criminals. Let's hope the result of his last medical board was through – and favourable – and his period of grounding was over. She sighed, near to tears. Everything going so well – nearly three years of sheer bliss – holding court, entertaining lavishly in their lovely home – money no object – the best servants – the biggest cars – the upper crust wangling and intriguing for invitations. And not once had a single shadow from the past threatened her. She had been accepted – completely and unequivocally – Mrs Hank Dexter, the beautiful English wife of the handsome American commercial pilot. True, the slowness of the Californian divorce and the consequent delay in regularizing her position had been frustrating, but it *would* come through eventually – meantime she had enjoyed every moment of these halcyon days – days in which this stupid war back in Europe had been nothing but a faint rumbling in the distance that had not appreciably disturbed their way of life out here. Old-timers had told her that it had been much the same in the First World War – soldiers, vast numbers of them, had come and gone, and wives and daughters had knitted and sewn and worked in hospitals and raised funds for widows and orphans, but India, the age-old unchanging India, had altered not one whit. It was nearer now, of course, since the entry of the Japanese – Pearl Harbor, quickly followed by the fall of Singapore, Hong Kong, the Philippines, and lastly Burma, had been frightening at first, but now the Army was holding fast on the Assam border, and the Bay of

Bengal, on their doorstep here in Madras, was a comforting mass of warships, British, American, Indian and Australian – and the sky was full of planes – fighters, bombers and lumbering Dakotas. Yes – it was certainly nearer – but still much further in terms of actual mileage than, say, London was from Dunkirk or Calais – and except for a quickly beaten-off token hit-run dash by a couple of Jap planes over Calcutta, they had been spared the terror of air raids. No – there hadn't been much change. More uniforms about, certainly, even among the women now that the Women's Auxiliary Corps (India) – contracted, naturally, to 'the Wack-Eyes' – had been formed. The European and Anglo-Indian women wore smart military bush-jackets and trim skirts and little side-caps, all in khaki cotton drill – while the Indians wore saris of the same material. Lots of the officers' wives and daughters had joined, and there had been much giggling over the necessity for some of them, junior in rank, having to salute husbands and fathers, and, in one case, the reverse happening, when the pretty wife of a lieutenant had been promoted overnight – the uncharitable stressed the 'overnight' – to Captain. Other than that – no great change. Some luxury goods were getting a little harder to come by – scotch had a tendency to disappear under the counter, and there was no wine to be had anywhere, other than some hogwash made in a Goanese monastery. Petrol was short too, and it was soon to be rationed. She'd probably have to forgo the joys of this big Buick that she had learned to drive so well, and fall back on the smaller Morris. Which reminded her – she needed to fill up now.

She swung into a filling station, one of the two they always used, where nothing so vulgar as money was demanded, everything going down on the 'chit' and being presented on a monthly account. The Madrassi attendant was just finishing dealing with a car in front of her. Jane recognized the driver as the wife of a major from the Ordnance Depot, and they exchanged waves after the latter had signed her chit and driven off.

The attendant said, 'How many, Memsahib?'

'As much as she'll take,' Jane told him. 'About ten or eleven, I think.'

The boy squirmed in an agony of embarrassment. 'Memsahib paying cash, please?' he asked, looking at the ground.

'What on earth are you talking about?' she demanded angrily. 'Put it on the chit in the ordinary way.'

'Sorry, Memsahib. Boss give order – all cash money now. No more chit. Wartime, Memsahib.'

She started to see red again, but she screwed down hard on the safety valve and gestured airily as if it were a matter of no importance. 'Sorry, Madhu,' she said. 'I don't carry money – peacetime or wartime. No Memsahib does. I'll sign – like Wilkes Memsahib just did.'

'Boss give order,' the boy muttered. 'I give – I lose job.'

She shrugged and drove out, her face burning with shame. This was it, she thought wearily. She'd heard about it, of course, but had never envisaged the possibility of it ever happening to *her*. The 'kholos hisab' – literally the 'closed account'. If one stall in the bazaar – or shop in cantonments, European, Parsee or Indian, stopped your credit, all others followed suit. The word went round like wildfire.

'Oh, God,' she prayed silently as she drove the last mile home. 'Don't let it be that – Not the kholos hisab, or like the woman in the corner shop in Brixton – "Sorry, love – I know your dad's out of work and all that, but tell your mum I can't put nothing more on the slate until she coughs up a bit off the bill." Let his medical be through by the time I arrive – make them let him fly again – and pay him his money – *our money* – the *bastards*. The report should have been in weeks ago – '

She twisted the rear-vision mirror round and glanced into it. 'I look a fright,' she decided, unjustly. 'And I want a hair-do. I can do other silly bitches', but not my own. I wish to heaven we didn't have this damned thing on tonight. What's the purpose of it? Nobody's going to give him a job. "Keeping the front up" he said. "Got to do that. If the mob thinks you're on the floor, they'll send the leather in. Yes – let's have a party – like the ones we used to give. Show 'em everything's still dandy". Dandy? Oh, God.'

He was standing at the top of the verandah steps when she came in. He said, 'You bring any scotch?'

'Two bottles. All they'd let me have. We'll need that for the party,' she said.

'Fuck the party,' he answered, and went out and rummaged in the back of the car. 'What the hell did you buy all this other goddamn junk for?'

'Whose idea was it?' she screamed at him. 'Do you think I *like* being insulted by counter-jumpers? There's no more credit at the store – or the filling station – or anywhere else. Have you got that? Do you understand? What's the word you American big shots use? Washed up? That's it – we're *washed up*.' She sat down on a cane chair in a storm of weeping.

Quite unmoved he fished the two bottles of whisky up from the bottom of the basket. 'Fine,' he said. 'Well, at least I'm going down singing. You want some of this?'

'No. Hank – please – tell me. Has that report come in yet?' she begged.

'Report? Oh, *that*? Sure – sure – they sent it along from the office an hour ago – just after you went out.'

She stared at him, trying desperately to see through his flippancy a ray of hope – praying that he was teasing her – but reading the truth in the bitterness of his eyes. 'What do they say?' she whispered.

'Say? They say I'm a hell of a nice guy, and that they all love me dearly – but that I ain't flying – *no, sir* – not in this country I ain't. The lily-fingered, yellow-gutted, creep-arsing bunch of Limey bastards. *British doctors* having the gall to ground an American pilot. Can you beat that?'

'Then what are we going to do? Hank – *what are we going to do?*'

'There's only one thing for it. I've got to get up to Calcutta, and go before a *real* assessment board – one that doesn't think that a couple of doses of malaria puts an experienced flier out of the sky for good. An *American* board.' He twisted the foil off the neck of the bottle savagely and poured whisky into a glass and drank it neat – then poured again.

'Will the company have to give you your job back then?' she asked.

'Uh? Oh – sure – sure – ' he said vaguely.

'Then why are they holding up your pay in the meantime? I mean – it wasn't your fault that you fell ill,' she insisted.

'Oh, hell – you wouldn't understand,' he said. 'I sort of ran out of sick time. You're only allowed two months in any one year – then you drop to one-third pay.'

'But we're not even getting *that*.'

'No – well you see, there was this garnishee order they smacked across me back in the States.'

'What's that?'

'That goddamn wife of mine. I'd got a bit behind in the maintenance money I have to give her, and she took out an attachment order on my pay.'

'But surely she can't take it *all*? I mean, they know you've got to live while you're grounded.'

'Yeah, yeah – it's – it's kinder complicated. Leave it.' He poured more whisky.

'But we can't leave it, Hank. Don't you realize? – they've stopped our credit in the bazaar. How are we going to live?'

'Haven't you got *anything* put by? I gave you enough dough to run this place, didn't I?'

'Yes – but as you say, that was to run this place – '

'And a bit over for God's sake. I gave you thousands and thousands. You mean you just blew it?'

'Hank – have you any idea what it costs to run a house like this? – entertaining the way we did? The drink bills alone – '

'Yeah, yeah, yeah – all right. Leave it – like I said. I'll just have to get up to Calcutta. Charlie Oliver is flying up tomorrow. I'll hitch a lift with him – see the medical board at the American air base and get back the next day – or the next – whenever Charlie's returning – '

'Yes – but you'll have to talk to the local office here before you go, and get an advance out of them, Hank. We can't go on like this.'

239

'Sure – I'll do that. Now come on – You better get dolled up before this crowd of free-loading crumbs start arriving.'

They were seeing the last of the guests off across the dew-dampened lawn to where the cars were parked in the drive.

'Good night, Jane darling – *lovely* party – divine eats, as usual. I don't know how you manage it – '

'Absolutely marvellous, old girl. 'Night! And you, Hank you old bugger – '

'Give my love to Calcutta, Hank, I like it better than this damned place – '

But it hadn't been an unqualified success. She had invited forty – and eighteen had turned up. Exigencies of war – extra work – some of the men doing spare-time guard duties – policing – women in the hospitals – and, of course, the new WAC(I). She wondered how many of the excuses were genuine – and how many had got wind of the kholos hisab in the last twenty-four hours. The ones that had turned up, she noticed, were practically all of that dedicated band which found its way to drink parties with the pertinacity and single-mindedness of Saharan camels in search of oases. 'Couldn't stand the feller, meself, nor his bitch of a wife – but they were never mean with the drinks. We used to have some wonderful parties there,' she had heard one zealot reminiscing nostalgically about a departed host.

Hank yawned cavernously as the last tail-light disappeared in the distance.

'Well, that's it,' he said. 'Great bunch – just so's they've got enough free likker aboard. Me for bed – Charlie wants me down at the field at five. He's taking off before first light. I'll doss down in the other bedroom for three-four hours, so I won't disturb you when I go out.'

'But what about that advance?' she asked anxiously.

'Oh – I meant to tell you. That's fixed. I spoke to Chuck Patullo. He'll bring you something down from Bangalore tomorrow or the next day.' He yawned again. 'God, I'm sleepy.'

'Did he say how much?'

'No – he'll have to argue that out with them. Maybe three or even four thousand. Enough to get along on for a week or two until this lot of mine is sorted out.'

'You darling!' she said fervently, and threw her arms around his neck. 'Good luck up there – not that you should need it. *They're* the lucky ones. They've got the best flier in the world coming back to them – and they don't deserve him.'

'Aw – forget it,' he grinned bashfully.

Chuck Patullo bounded round his desk and took both Jane's hands in his. He was a stout little man who perspired freely even in cold weather and she felt as if her hands were being caressed by two small, wet octopuses. He said, 'For God's sake – I haven't seen you for weeks. How's it been?'

'It would be better if I knew when Hank was coming back,' she told him. 'He's been gone a week now – and he didn't think he'd be away more than two or three days at most.'

He looked puzzled. 'Sorry. I'm not with you. Gone where?'

'To Calcutta. He flew up with Charlie Oliver last Tuesday.'

'Sh-h-h!' Patullo put his finger to his lips with exaggerated caution. 'I'm not supposed to know that. We're licensed for freight and mails, not passengers.'

'Surely you wouldn't count Hank as an ordinary passenger?'

'Wartime, honey. Security is tightened up to hell. Even I've got to put myself down on the blood-chit just to fly up to Bangalore to head office once a week. Yes – sure I knew he went up with Charlie. I thought he'd be coming back with him –'

'So Charlie *is* back?'

'Sure – day before yesterday.' He grinned. 'I'm only kidding, honey – but even so I'd rather you didn't mention outside that we've been giving unofficial rides to friends. Let's see what Charlie's got to say.' He reached for the telephone. 'Hello – Charlie there? Put him on. 'Lo, Charlie – when you took Hank up to Cal the other day – what did he say about coming back?' She could hear the buzz of the reply, but could not make out the words. Chuck's expression was changing – the geniality giving place to caginess. 'I see – yeah – yeah – okay.

No – no – it doesn't matter. See you later, Charlie.' He replaced the telephone, and Jane, watching him closely, could see he was considering his words carefully.

He said, 'Hank called Charlie at Dum Dum before he took off on the return flight and said he might be held up for some time, and Charlie wasn't to wait for him.'

She nodded slowly. 'I see. Have you any idea when he might be able to hitch a ride back then? I mean, are you running a regular service up there or not?'

'Not regular, Jane. We're just doing a back-up run there for the RAF now, on an as-required basis. Might be days, might even be weeks before we're called on again.'

She took a deep breath and gathered up her courage. 'Chuck – I'm sorry about this. I hate talking business, but I'm in rather a spot now. Hank told me he'd spoken to you about money before he left, and that you'd said you would arrange an advance against his salary. Is that still all right?'

The caginess in Patullo's face was giving way to something approaching dismay. 'Advance against his salary, Jane?' he said. 'I don't get it.'

'You – or rather the company – can hardly expect one of your pilots to live on nothing a week when he's medically grounded – through no fault of his own.' She could feel her temper rising and was fighting to keep it in check. 'Chuck – do you realize what a humiliating position this puts me in? The wife of one of your senior men having to come and beg – ' She started to cry, and Patullo writhed in an agony of embarrassment.

'Honey – what the hell can I do? What can I *say*? Goddamn it! Hank has been off our payroll for the last three months – '

The tears were still coursing down her cheeks, but her eyes were suddenly hot and dry. She stared at him.

'What? What did you say?' she demanded.

'Just that.' His patience was starting to wear thin. 'He was grounded six months back. We kept him on for the statutory three months, then we had to let him go.'

'A sick man? You *fired* him? Just like that?'

'No, Jane – not just like that. I'm sorry – but if Hank hasn't

242

told you, then I guess I'll have to. He was grounded for being drunk on the New Delhi airfield an hour before take-off.'

'Oh, my God,' she breathed.

'We'd been hoping that they might have eased up a bit – but, you see, Jane – it wasn't the first time. He'd been booked in Ahmedabad and Lahore, and got off with a warning each time. Now, I'm afraid he'll never fly in India again – not as a civilian.' Patullo heaved a sigh of relief and mopped his brow. 'Well, that's off my chest – but I wish the bum had told you himself.'

'But – this trip to Calcutta?' Jane said desperately. 'If the American board passes him – won't you take him back?'

Patullo shook his head. 'Nothing to do with *us*, honey. That board is for the USAAF – *military* fliers. It's the civil authorities here that have busted him.'

'Then why on earth did he go up to see the American board?'

'To get back into the Air Force. He's on the Reserve at present – '

'But would they take him – with that on his record?'

'You're goddamn tooting they would. A drunk on his *civilian* licence wouldn't worry the Air Force. He's in already, honey – I didn't tell you that. He called Charlie a second time and said he'd passed the board and would be flying to England, then back over the Atlantic to the States, but that he'd try and slip down and see you first – There, you've got the lot now.' He opened a drawer in his desk and pulled out a bottle. 'I think you'd better have a shot of this, honey, because now that you're here we've got to get something else cleared up – something I've been ducking. The bungalow, and the two cars – you see, I've been letting Hank hang on to them on the buddy-buddy basis until he got fixed up some place else – but now I'm afraid there's a new guy on his way out, and he'll be needing them. No hurry, of course. Say another week, eh? God, I'm sorry – but what can I do?'

The letter was waiting for her when she got back to the bungalow. The first paragraph consisted entirely of endearments, the second of self-denigration – the message itself was in three short sentences: 'I guess it wouldn't have worked out anyway, because she'll never give me a divorce. Here's a few bucks – sorry it isn't more, but things are a bit tight. I'll see what I can do when I'm back on Uncle Sam's payroll.' Then came more endearments and many thanks. 'The few bucks' was actually two hundred and fifty. She smiled bitterly. Just half of Mandy's pay-off.

She held a fiscal review later that evening, blessing the instinct that had impelled her to build a squirrel store of ten-rupee notes from the not ungenerous housekeeping allowance he had made her. She had three thousand, six hundred and thirty rupees in the coffee tin she kept hidden on the rafters behind the ceiling cloth – nearly three hundred pounds. She cheered up considerably, then opened the carved Kashmiri jewel case she kept locked in her dressing table. But it was no longer locked, and the 'engagement' ring, brooch, ear-rings and several other trinkets of varying value that he had bought her in earlier days had gone.

But at least he had left her George's ring.

The shock had the effect of steadying her, like a bucket of water in the face of incipient hysterics. She realized, perhaps for the first time in her life, that there really was only one person in the whole wide world she could rely upon – one solitary soul in whom she could unreservedly place her trust. Herself. She had managed to extricate herself from worse exigencies than this, time and time again – she, and the 'It' which she could not define. The thing was to get away from this place – unnoticed – because she had been long enough in the country to know that if she made obvious preparations to leave she would be besieged by debt collectors immediately. Yes – she had to get away. But where? Certainly not to Calcutta, Bombay or Gonah – nowhere she had already turned her back on, she decided firmly. Her luck had always lain in new places. Things were different today. They had changed radically in the little over three years since the war began. There were jobs for women now – and not only voluntary service – which meant unpaid chores in hospitals and troops' canteens. Wives and daughters of officers, and also still single left-overs from the immediate pre-war Fishing Fleeters, were coyly admitting to skills they would have indignantly denied in older days. Oh, yes – some of them had even taken secretarial courses in London during Daddy's long leave – 'just for a lark, you know – and because I got so awfully bored – Yes – I actually earned *money*, my dear. An absolute scream – '

But usually one had to be able to type to do that, she reflected, and she couldn't. Of course there were Personal Assistants' jobs, where duties tended to be more amorphous – indeed, there were some, the cynical implied, where looks and a certain broadmindedness were the only requisites. Yes, she'd score there all right, she told herself – but that would be a matter of luck and opportunity – and, although she was, as always, poised ready to seize the latter, she was now far too realistic to rely solely on the former.

Headlights turned in through the gate and advanced up the drive, and she felt her pulse quickening with the nervousness of the insecure, and for a moment she was tempted to slip out through the rear of the bungalow and tell the khitmagar to inform the visitor that Memsahib was at the club, but her ready common sense warned her that that was a slippery path. Once she started to slink it would fast become a habit – one that would be noticed and commented upon. She had so often heard it herself: 'Old Charles seems to be keeping under cover rather lately.' – 'Yes – got the bums on his tail you know – Must be owing thousands now – ' No – that would be fatal.

She went out on to the verandah. A woman climbed from a small and battered car and came forward into the light of the mosquito lamp. It was Bunty Wheeler, and Jane's nervousness was transformed instantly to wariness. This was the champion snapper-up of unconsidered trifles of gossip, unchallenged in her ability to scent incipient disaster anywhere in the cantonment, to stalk and run it down – sift and analyse it – refurbish and embellish it – then present it in all its piquancy with the cocktail snacks at the club. Had she heard a whisper already? Jane wondered. Had that fat, sweaty little bastard Patullo had time to start a hare? But one glance reassured and steadied her. Bunty's face was red and swollen with weeping.

She wailed, 'Jane – Jane, for Christ's sake what do I do? What the *hell* do I do? The swine has left me.'

'Which swine?' Jane asked innocently.

'God Almighty! I'm only married to *one*,' Bunty snuffled.

'Clive – ?'

'Who the hell else? With a spotty-faced cow of a Fishing Fleeter – '

'You mean Audrey Orpington-Knox?'

'You *knew*?' screamed Bunty. 'You mean to say you *knew*, and you hadn't the decency to tell me?'

'Don't talk like a fool,' Jane said with icy contempt. 'It was your description. The poor devil *has* got acne, she was on the last Fishing Fleet to come out – and Clive *has* been pinching her bottom round the swimming pool for some time. Good God, Bunty, you've been out here long enough to know the score, haven't you? She's been doing the same sort of thing with your bloody Clive as you've been trying on with Hank. Only *she* seems to have made it.' She was revelling in a transport of malice, rescued momentarily from her own slough of despond by this heaven-sent coincidence.

'I haven't been trying anything on with Hank,' Bunty protested tearfully. 'What a bitch you are, Jane – just when a woman needs help.'

'How can *I* help?' Jane snapped. 'Where have they skipped to, anyhow?'

'That's the awful part of it. They haven't even had the decency to go to another station. They've got separate rooms at the Panipet Hotel – with a bloody connecting door, I bet. See what they're doing, the cunning bastards? They can screw their ears off, but at the same time keep up an appearance of respectability. By God, they're not going to get away with it though. I'll have him fired out of his rotten company.' Her tears were drying rapidly.

'What good will that do?' Jane asked. 'You'd only be cutting your nose to spite your face.'

'I don't care,' Bunty said viciously. 'I'll tell you something. His contract is up at the end of the year and they're pressing for Indianization – it's an Indian company, you know. They'd

246

only be too happy to have an excuse to empty him out and put in a Johnny-with-a-black-face.'

'Fine,' said Jane dryly. 'You'd have got your revenge then – but if he hasn't got a job you wouldn't get alimony or maintenance.'

'I probably wouldn't anyhow – not for long. Once he loses his job as General Manager at that damned textile mill he is liable to conscription into the Army – and since he's got flat feet and a dicky heart, or says he has, he won't be getting a commission.' She moved into the light, produced a mirror and compact and commenced repairs to her make-up. 'I wouldn't fancy life as a Tommy's wife.'

'Then what the hell are you caterwauling about?'

Bunty turned and looked at her, wide-eyed and smiling. 'I don't know, darling. Natural reaction, I suppose. One doesn't exactly *enjoy* getting the old heave-ho – especially because of a rat-bag like spotty Audrey – but now that I've had my little weep I'm glad – yes, *glad*. I know what I'm going to do now. Good pay, jolly enjoyable social life, and status – in one's own right and not dependent on one's husband's lousy job.'

Jane pricked up her ears. 'Where are you going to find all that?' she asked.

'The Wack-eyes. And I know just exactly how to go about it. I had the tip from Phillipa Russell.'

'There's nothing exclusive about the Wack-eyes.' Jane said. 'Anybody can join. They've had posters up in the club for weeks now.'

'Oh, yes, lovie,' Bunty said wisely. 'You've only got to put your name down at the Secretariat and you're in – as a private – and if you want a commission you've got to earn one by merit et cetera, et cetera, blah, blah, blah. You weren't at the recruiting meeting were you?'

'No – I was away with Hank.'

'Well, that's the way it is – and this end of the country, with the administration trying to woo the wog politicians into supporting the war effort instead of Gandhi, it's the Indian women who are the officers, with the Memsahibs in the ranks, pretending that they prefer it that way. Not for me – not bloody likely.'

'So what are you going to do about it?'

'The sensible thing. Go up to New Delhi. They've got experienced women out from the ATS at Home there. They don't give a damn for local politics – so the PLU are getting the commissions, and the Bhimabhai-Chuddabhais have to take a back seat – and quite right too.'

'What does PLU mean?' Jane asked.

'People Like Us, you idiot. Haven't you heard that one before?'

'I hadn't actually. But surely – you can't just breeze up to New Delhi and say "I want a commission", can you?'

'Not quite. You've got to finesse a bit, Phillipa says. You know – bright-eyed and bushy-tailed – "Yes, ma'am – I'm willing to serve in *any* capacity as long as it will release a man for the front. Anything you say, ma'am – Yes, ma'am, no, ma'am, three bags full, ma'am" – heels together, thumbs in line with the seam of your knicks. Earmarked as officer material right away.'

'But where does all this happen?'

'I told you – New Delhi. There's a Women's Directorate at General Headquarters. Why? Are you interested too?'

'Good heavens, no,' Jane said. 'I was just a bit worried on your account, that's all. I mean, you might be having your leg pulled by Phillipa.'

'That's straight from the horse's mouth,' Bunty assured her. 'Don't forget her husband is head of the Direction of Manpower, or whatever they call it – and that takes in Womenpower as well apparently.'

'Well – best of luck. When will you be off?'

'Oh, I'll be around for a few more days yet. That beauty of mine is not getting off scot-free, I assure you. I'm having a session with Considine, the lawyer, on Friday – and we'll be bearding me laddo together on the following Monday. Incidentally, disregarding your nasty insinuation, how *is* Hank?'

'Oh, fine, fine,' Jane said airily. 'At least, he was the last time I saw him. He's doing a lot of hush-hush flying at present, and he's away far more than he is at home.'

'Give him my love when you see him,' Bunty said wistfully. 'You know, Jane, you're a very lucky girl.'

'I know it,' Jane smiled gently. 'And now let me get you a drink.'

She loaded her suitcases into the boot of the Buick before first light the following morning and drove to Arkonam, up the main line to the north, then, in the seclusion of a private waiting room she scribbled a note to Patullo ' – thank you for everything; I've heard from Hank and now my plans are changed. I am on my way to Bombay, and out of India. Herewith the keys of both cars. You'll find everything in order at the bungalow. I'm afraid I'm leaving a few bills unpaid, but those are Hank's, not mine. Regards, J.'

Then she hired a driver from the local garage to drive the Buick back to Madras, and an hour later she caught the Delhi Mail.

People might wonder at her disappearance from Madras, she reflected, but not for long. This was wartime, and sudden, unannounced moves were the order of the day, and 'Arrivals and Departures', an eagerly read feature of Indian newspapers in peacetime, were no longer allowed to be published.

She sat back and watched the parched landscape glide past. She loved train travel in India. There was always something exciting at the end. Exciting – and, above all, different. She looked at the wedding ring on her finger, then started painfully to drag it off. She weighed it in her palm for a moment or so before opening the window to throw it out, but at the last moment prudence prevailed, and she tucked it away in her purse. Gold fetched a good price in the Chandni Chowk, she had heard.

Chapter Twelve

She stepped down on to the platform at Old Delhi at first light on the third day, and shivered, partly because here, twelve hundred miles north of hot and steaming Madras, there was a fresh spring nip in the air, but more from fear of the unknown. She had been here once before, under vastly different circumstances, when she had flown up with Hank on a three-day visit which had developed into a nonstop party in the American colony. Things had changed greatly since then, she decided. There were soldiers everywhere – British and Indian – although this place was so much further away from the Burma front – and there were armed sentries at the barriers keeping back the flood of luggage coolies which usually engulfed travellers as they alighted, allowing only a favoured few through on to the platform. She summoned one of these and snapped, 'Outside – taxi', when he had asked her destination. This had been the thing that had been worrying her most. She knew only one hotel – Maiden's – and that, she understood, had become fabulously expensive. Still, she had to go somewhere –

She came out through the barrier followed by her coolie carrying her cases and bedding roll, and standing before her were two Army sergeants – male and female – each wearing a white brassard with black letters – RTO – and the girl looked directly at her and said, 'Wack-eye?' inquiringly.

'Yes,' Jane said, confused. 'At least – that is – '

'RTO's office – straight over there.' She pointed across the assembly platform, then turned her attention to a couple of timid Anglo-Indian girls coming through the barrier.

'RTO sahib? – Achcha Miss-sahib – istaraf – this way, Miss-sahib,' said her coolie helpfully, and Jane followed, knowing a great relief.

The office was a temporary structure of corrugated iron and chitthai matting, and there was a notice over it in English, Urdu and Nagri – 'Railway Transport Officer – All Military Personnel Will Report Here'. An elderly Captain stood in the doorway surveying a small but variegated group of young women gathered before him – European, Anglo-Indian and Indian. He grinned cheerfully at them and said, 'Good morning, ladies, there's transport waiting for you outside. Your camp's in New Delhi, about five miles away. You'll be there in ten minutes – and then breakfast, eh what? All right, sergeant – take 'em away.'

Jane started nervously to explain once again, but he had already turned and gone back into the office, and the woman sergeant was behind them, shepherding them briskly through the crowd and out into the station courtyard. A three-ton lorry was waiting with the tailboard down and a rickety ladder in position. They climbed aboard gingerly and helped each other politely with the luggage their coolies passed up to them. Jane was tipping hers a rupee, which happened to be the smallest coin she had, and one of the Anglo-Indian girls murmured reproachfully, 'Oo-ah! That is too much. It spoils them.'

They rumbled out into Queen's Road through the maelstrom of taxis, tongas, lorries and buses – sacred cattle, noticeably thinner and more wary here in this predominantly Moslem area than in the Hindu South, noise, colour, dust and swarming humanity. Right at the Red Fort – the Lahore Gate looking down the Chandni Chowk, the Street of the Silversmiths, with the Jumra Musjid soaring above filthy shacks and festering bazaars – the Golden Mosque on the left, and glimpses of the Jumna running many-channelled through mud and sand-dunes. None of them talked, either too shy, tired or awed, for which Jane was thankful, for once again this sense of déja vu was upon her. Here was another totally different aspect of India – and yet it was so inexplicably familiar.

The lorry turned off the Muttra Road and bumped over an unmade track, bruising tender behinds on the bare wooden seats, and passed a guardroom and went in through gates in a barbed-wire fence, and stopped before a long low building with whitewashed stones laid in the dust before it spelling 'WAC(I)' and a plenitude of fire appliances and brightly polished gongs which were ranged along the verandah with strict military precision. The British driver called out, 'Here you are, Ron lad – another load of split-arse mechanics for you,' and a corporal came out of a doorway and said angrily, 'Watch the language, you stupid bugger, or the Queen Bee'll be having your knackers for doorknobs.' He helped the driver to drop the tailboard and fix the ladder, then he said briskly, 'Right, girls, leave your heavy kit, but for Chri'sake no money or valuables, and follow this orderly. Breakfast first, then MI and documentation after. All right? Good – smack it about, there's good lasses.'

There were drooping zinnias in Benares brass pots in the dining room, and yellow shalloon curtains, and pictures of George the Sixth and Queen Elizabeth, with the elder Princess in overalls and a smudge of grease on her nose expertly stripping down a tank engine, and the tables had bright plastic covers, and other feminine touches were evidence of efforts made to soften the rawness of this induction to an otherwise man's world. But the tempering did not extend to the food. Jane fought down her rising gorge, but had eventually to give best to the two greasy rashers of bacon, greyish fried egg and thick slices of tasteless bread, and settle for a mug of stewed tea that smelt and tasted strongly of onions.

The girl who had chided her over the tip stopped behind her chair and whispered, 'You want to feed with the Indians. Their curry-bhat is not bad,' and she indicated the three serving windows at the end of the room with boards showing their categories, Christian, Hindu, and Moslem. 'Some of us have been in the Depot at Jhansi for over a week,' she explained. 'The European food is even worse there.'

A short, heavily built woman with three stripes came in with a list, and called out, 'Right – pay attention – answer your names – Barker – Chalmers – Cutler – Dalrymple – Harley – ' and on through in alphabetical order, stumbling over the three Indian names, until she had ticked off fourteen of them. 'Anybody not hear their name? she asked.

'I didn't,' Jane said nervously. 'That's because – '

'What is it?' the woman snapped impatiently.

'Jane Curtis, but you see – '

'Curtis, J.,' the woman said, and wrote it down. 'Where from?'

'Madras – but – ' Jane tried desperately to explain.

'Bloody Madras again – always cocking things up.' She scribbled rapidly. 'Right – all of you. You'll be going in front of the Commandant now – that's the same as Major in the men's Army. Her name's Whittaker – and when you speak to her you call her "ma'am" – but you *don't* speak to her until she speaks to *you*, see? Then you speak *up* – she don't like mumblers. She's ATS – out from Home, same as me – just attached to your shower – and by God we like things done proper. Right – outside the lot of you – RCs, Parsees, C of Es and bleeding Tweedle-dees – Come on – *Move!*'

They trailed after the NCO to the administrative block. Some girls, smart in khaki cotton uniforms, were being drilled by an elderly male sergeant on the square – stiff-armed and flexed-kneed, like marionettes, horribly self-conscious but desperate in their earnestness. One or two of the newcomers giggled, and their guide turned and snarled, 'You'd better wipe those grins off your silly mugs. You'll be going through it before long. My bloody oath you will.'

They waited on the verandah, silent and subdued, and were called into the office one by one. Jane was the last. She found herself facing a middle-aged Junoesque woman who said accusingly, 'You weren't attested before you left Madras, I'm told. Why not?'

'Attested?' Jane said uncertainly, then added, 'Ma'am?'

'Enlisted – sworn in – take an oath to serve our Sovereign Lord the King, his heirs and successors and his Generals and such other officers as may be set over you. Surely you know what "attested" means?'

'Oh, no, I wasn't attested – I'm sorry. I thought one had to come up here for that.'

'You couldn't have a railway warrant if you weren't attested.

Did you come up at your own expense?'

'Yes, ma'am.'

'Well that shows willing, anyhow.' The Commandant smiled winterily. 'What were you doing in Madras?'

'Staying with friends.'

'I mean in the way of work?'

'Oh – voluntary work – welfare – that sort of thing, ma'am,' Jane said.

'Well-meaning but totally disorganized, in other words,' the Commandant said disapprovingly. 'Then you saw the light, and decided to take the King's shilling? Better late than never, I suppose. Give me something of your background.'

She had been preparing for this during the long train journey. 'I came out just before the outbreak of war – to be married,' she said looking straight at the older woman.

'And it didn't come off?' the other said.

Jane dropped her eyes, hesitated, then looked up again bravely. 'No. I arrived in Bombay as his regiment was embarking in Karachi. He was killed three months later.'

The other woman softened visibly. 'I see,' she said. 'It's happened to a lot of us. So you stayed on out here?'

'I had no option,' Jane said, with just the right touch of resentment. 'I wanted to go Home to join the ATS, but all non-essential civilian passages had been blocked by this time. I hung on, without committing myself to anything definite, in the hope that I'd be able to wangle a passage – but that doesn't seem possible, so I'd like to join the Wack-eyes – if they'll have me.'

'The W – A – C – brackets I, if you please,' said the Commandant sternly. 'I object to these sloppy contractions. If we wish to be taken seriously by the men we have to be careful when dealing in military terminology. Yes – we'll have you, my dear – if you're a British subject over the age of eighteen and are medically fit. You certainly look the latter. Have you any documents? Birth certificate? Passport?'

'My passport,' Jane said, producing it from her handbag.

'I see – yes – these photos are awful usually, aren't they – but at least this makes you look human. Born 1917 – you don't look twenty-five – lucky you. Now – skills? Do you type?'

'I'm afraid not,' Jane said regretfully.

'Expensive education – like mine, no doubt – and never learned a single useful thing. That right?'

Jane nodded and looked apologetic.

'Drive?'

'Oh, yes,' Jane said eagerly.

'Drive well, I mean, not just trundle a car along the road, bashing into bullock carts and things?'

'I think so, ma'am. I have an Indian licence.'

'Have you? Well, that's something. What sort of car have you been driving out here?'

'A Buick.'

'That so?' The Commandant looked impressed. 'Hm – then a Chevrolet staff car shouldn't worry you unduly.' She picked up the telephone and barked, 'MO' – waited, then said sweetly, 'Oh, doctor dear – I've got a gal here I *do* want pushed through quickly – vital posting – I know you hate queue-jumping but would you – ? If I sent her along immediately – ? You're a darling.' She replaced the telephone. 'I'm not promising anything – but you may be just a little bit heaven-sent. Right – medical – then back here for attestation – then kit issue – then driving check-out – bit of elementary drill, with particular emphasis on saluting – that's *most* important – ' She was scribbling furiously on a pad. 'Local familiarization – map reading. You're going to be a busy little bee if you pass the medicine man – *and* the MT sergeant. Let's see – that's the lot – Oh, yes – local character references. You're supposed to have two. Know anybody on this station?'

Jane shook her head sadly. She had been dreading this one. 'All sorts of people in Madras and Bombay and Gonah,' she said, 'but nobody here.'

'I see. Well, we've no time to waste now. Give the Orderly Room clerk a couple of names I can write to. It's only a matter of form, really – out here anyhow. They've no idea of security. All right! Don't just stand there – along the verandah, gal – last door on the left for your medical – then back here at the double.' Jane disappeared quickly, and the Commandant took up the telephone again.

'Brigade Major,' she said shortly – then, 'Hello, Sholto – I've got a female driver – yes – English – used to driving a Buick. Don't take it for a rockbottom cert – not until your chap has checked her out. Yes – but listen – I'm just a *leetle* bit worried. This one is a looker – my God she is! – absolute pippin – and Benjy is such a randy old sod – I mean – well – you understand – What? – Oh, yes – old enough to look after herself – and she's been out here nearly three years – No, not Fishing Fleet – came out to marry some lad who was killed. All right, I'll give her to you if she passes out well. But, Sholto, dear, I'll want a quid pro quo – Know what I mean? No little tricksie-wicksies in future, like posting gals without my say-so – or cutting down my transport – or sending me riff-raff when I need a man for any particular job. Anything like that and I'll whip her back quick and send you a bloody gorgon. Right? Bye.'

The medical officer, jolted out of his normal professional detachment, patted her over appreciatively and passed her with flying colours; the Commandant handed her a bible and gabbled the oath for her to repeat, and the male quartermaster-sergeant, assisted by his distaff opposite number, was helpful and obliging to a point far beyond the call of duty when fitting her with uniform. Only the MT sergeant was a trifle hesitant, and that in the kindest possible way and entirely in her own interest, after half an hour in the Chevrolet.

He said, 'Oh, yes – I can see that you're used to a big American job – but in a *civvie* sort of way, if you see what I mean. You need more *military* practice – and, of course, I don't know what you're like on night driving. Now, if that bloody old cow will OK it I'll take you on some long runs and have you ticketty-boo-top-of-the-shop in no time at all.'

The elderly drill sergeant, in the manner of his kind, remained stolidly unimpressed when taking her, solo, on saluting drill. He said, 'Jesus wept. The things I do for England. Let's 'ave it again now – *Hup!* One, two, three, four. *Down!*' – and kept it up for two hours before, weak-kneed and wilting, dismissing her the square, with a mordant, 'Best I can do – I've seen worse in Pirbright,' which, from him apparently, was praise indeed.

And so, after a further week on familiarization and reconnaissance, she was finally dispatched with the almost new, sand-camouflaged, lease-lend Chevrolet saloon to Brigade Headquarters on the Ridge to the south of New Delhi, where she reported to the Brigade Major, who raised his eyebrows very slightly, took a deep breath and told her to wait in the car outside until needed. She waited an hour, and then Brigadier W. T. (Benjy) Barnicote, OBE, MC, came out. His reactions were rather less inhibited than the BM's as she opened the car door for him and saluted.

He said, 'I say! The abbess *has* done us well. What's your name, m'dear?'

'Curtis, sir,' Jane said demurely.

'Dammit – I can't call someone like you just plain "Curtis" – no – certainly not plain anyhow. First name?'

'We're not supposed to use them, sir.'

'You're not supposed to disobey an order given by your superior officer, either. What's your first name?'

'Jane, sir.'

'Good. Do you know the Monkey House, Jane?'

'I'm afraid not, sir.'

'The Secretariat?'

'I know that, sir.'

'Same place. All right – take me there please.' He climbed into the back seat. 'That's right,' he said approvingly as she closed the door. 'Firmly but without slamming.'

He sat back and closed his eyes and she was able to study him covertly in the rear vision mirror as she drove. Fifty – fifty-five she decided, with as battered and battle-scarred a face as she had ever seen, puffed and red, with the skin texture of a well-worn tobacco pouch – albeit with a cheerful insouciance about it that she found not entirely unattractive.

She found the pilastered, Italianate building without difficulty, and as he climbed out, grunting with the effort, he called to an Indian military policeman, 'Miss-sahib ke ghari saya mendalo,' and she knew enough Urdu to understand that

257

he was telling the man to find her a shady spot to park, and she appreciated this small courtesy.

He came out after an hour and said, 'Do you know Meerut?'

'I've never been there, sir,' she answered. 'But I know the road out to it – over the Jumna Bridge.'

'It's about forty miles. Good surface, but dusty. Could you do it under the hour, or had I better send for your male counter-part?' He looked at her quizzically.

'I can do it,' she said coldly, and added 'sir' only as a delayed afterthought. She was justifiably proud of her driving, and her hackles rose if anybody impugned it even in fun. She heard him chuckle.

'All right – get going. I'll direct you when we get to canton-ments,' he said, and climbed in.

He did not sleep this time, but immersed himself in a sheaf of papers he took from a dispatch case. The road was clear of traffic and it ran as straight as an arrow flight between a double row of peepul trees and she was able to purr along at something slightly better than sixty the whole way, so she reached the cantonment octroi post in less than fifty minutes. She slowed down and said 'Meerut, sir', as expressionlessly as a bus con-ductor announcing Marble Arch, but he caught her eye in the rea -vision mirror and winked and grinned like an aged school-boy.

'Good girl,' he said. 'I think you and I are going to get on splendidly. I want the regimental HQ of the Royal Scatter-arses. You, being a nicely brought-up girl, would probably know them as the Third Lantshires – TA. Straight ahead up the Mall here – second on the right and you'll see the guard-room ahead of you.'

He looked at his watch when they arrived and said, 'Timed it nicely for a gin-and-nonsense before lunch,' and disappeared into the Mess.

She waited under a tree thinking rather forlornly about her own lunch. She had been warned always to take a haversack ration with her on duty to cope with situations such as this, but the warning hadn't registered with her.

A man in a short white coat and a black bow tie, with three

gold stripes on his arm, found her and said rather sourly, 'Come this way, will you,' and she followed him round the back of the Mess building on to a deep shady verandah. The Mess sergeant pointed to a chair and said, 'Wait there', and a bearer brought her a gin and tonic, and later served her with a solitary lunch on an occasional table. It was an adequate if unimaginative meal of brown Windsor soup, bully beef cutlets, fried brinjal, the eternal caramel custard, cheese and coffee, and it satisfied her healthy young appetite, but she resented what she regarded as below-stairs treatment and it took the edge off her enjoyment. She finished as quickly as possible and returned to the car.

The Brigadier came down the front steps shortly afterwards and went off with a group of officers. She sat in the car and closed her eyes – and didn't open them again until somebody boomed 'Boo!' in her ear. She jumped and stared horrified into the Brigadier's grinning face framed in the front window, and felt herself blushing hotly. 'I'm sorry, sir,' she gasped, and got out and opened the rear door for him.

'No,' he said. 'I'll get in the front with you – in case you go to sleep again.' He turned and saluted, and she saw for the first time a group of officers seeing him off, all standing stiffly to attention with the older ones looking somewhat disapprovingly at this breach of military protocol.

'Bloody popinjays,' he growled as they drove out. 'Did you get any tiffin – or luncheon as these Marks and Spencer's counter-jumpers would call it?'

'Yes thank you, sir,' she said primly. 'On the verandah.'

'British Service,' he said disparagingly. 'If it had been an Indian Army Mess you'd have been asked in properly. We'll have to do something about it. Get you a commission. I'll tap the abbess up sometime. Right-ho – home Jane and don't spare the horses. Wake me up when we get to the Jumna Bridge and I'll get in the back – or some Whitehall bahin chut will be reporting me for making free with the lower orders.'

She dropped him at his quarters late in the evening, and drove back to camp, where, tired though she was now, she went meticulously through the end-of-task routine set down in the manual. Tank topped up – oil checked – water – battery – tyre pressures, not forgetting the spare – and finally log and work-ticket to be filled, initialled and handed in to the MT office. This, she decided, was a job she was going to like. A job with distinct possibilities. It was certainly not one she was going to lose through any shortcomings of her own – or anybody else's if she could help it. Which was why she spoke sharply to the babu in the MT office when he merely glanced at her work-ticket and flicked it into the Pending tray, that repository of Indian clerical procrastination, instead of making an entry in the Stand Down Duty Book, as she herself had been shown the previous day.

The babu stared at her insolently and was about to say something sarcastic about recruits, especially women recruits, but he caught her eye on him, and his own dropped and he murmured 'Yes, miss-sahib', and meekly complied.

'My God! It works,' she said to herself as she went off to the hut that she shared with three others, and there was a new set to her shoulders and a spring in her step. Get you a commission, he had said. Right. She'd be ready for it.

But she met with a setback when she reported to the MT lines after reveille the following morning. 'Sorry, love,' the sergeant said. 'I'll have to send a bloke today. The old bugger's going down to Agra – coupla hundred miles – You'd be away overnight and there's no accommodation for split-ar – er – women ranks.'

'I could sleep in the car,' Jane said hopefully.

'You might wake up and find old age creeping on you,' the sergeant grinned and winked. 'Old Benjy's a tiger for his nuts, they say.'

So she watched the staff car being driven out, heavily handled by a BOR more used to a three-ton truck, and spent the rest of the day checking and listing spare parts in the MT store against a micro-printed horror called The Priced Vocabulary of Ordnance Stores, where a simple bolt could become a 'Bolt – clips retaining – BSC. $\frac{3}{4}'' \times 4''$ – mild. st. (TP)' or a hammer a 'ball-pane – 11in Hick. hd. – Eng.'. But, hot, sticky, dusty and bored though she was, her new-found ambition remained with her, and she stuck the task out with gritted teeth until late afternoon when the Commandant walked round on a casual inspection and asked the sergeant in passing how his latest assistant was shaping – and the sergeant, with the best possible intentions, said enthusiastically, 'First rate, ma'am – absolutely spot-on. First time we've had that bleeding – sorry ma'am – list straight since we've been here.'

'Good,' said the Commandant sweetly. 'This is obviously her métier then. You may keep her, sergeant.'

'Thank you, ma'am,' beamed the sergeant, and almost knuckled his forelock, while Jane, behind a bank of shelves, bit her fist in chagrin.

She spent that night on her hard camp bed in the hot airless hut listening to the snoring of one of her room-mates, the adenoidal snuffling of another and the stifled sobbing of the third, who was suffering from homesickness and a suspected pregnancy, formulating various plans to get out of the MT store, and as quickly abandoning them. No, she decided as the sky began to pale and the mynahs to chatter, she didn't know enough as yet to start wangling. That would come. Meanwhile let her continue to earn the praises of her superiors until such time as she saw another opening – then *bam!* – straight into it. But why had the old bitch changed her mind after practically promising her the damned job? Had the Brigadier turned thumbs down on her? Surely not. She was pretty certain that the silly old fool was starting, even at this early stage, to get ideas – and she had been prepared to exploit the situation to the full – or *almost* to the full – and only when absolutely certain of the end result. She knew her assets now – and their value. Nothing for nothing from now on she avowed. That had always been her mistake in the past. Giving too much, too soon. Then she went to sleep.

She would have slept the earlier, and the easier, had she been privy to a conversation between the Commandant and the Brigade Major over drinks at the club the previous evening.

'I won't have it, Sholto,' the Commandant said angrily. 'The bloody old lecher was riding in the front seat with his arm round the wretched gal – in broad daylight. I had three telephone calls – two of then anonymous – all practically accusing me of being a procuress. Yes – I know – I sent her there – but I realize now that it was an error of judgement on my part.'

'He's making my life a misery,' the BM said glumly. 'When that berk turned up with the staff car this morning he brought the roof down. Look – suppose I dropped him the hint that there has been a bit of station gossip, and suggested that he's a little more discreet – do you think you could reconsider it?'

'No,' said the Commandant firmly. 'Order, counter-order – disorder. He wouldn't reconsider my application for one of those lovely new American jeeps, would he? Front line vehicles – all wanted in Burma, he said. But that bitch of a matron and the head WVS woman each have one I notice.'

'Oh, I could fix that,' the BM said brightly.

'Then why didn't you?'

'I mean I could fix it now, if you play the quid pro quo move you're always talking about. One jeep, one popsie – and everybody will be happy. Come on, Althea,' he wheedled.

'Um – I don't like it,' she said doubtfully. 'I mean – if that old devil ever did get an uncontrollable rush of blood to the fork you never know what might happen to her. You heard about those naval gals and the Vice-Admiral in Trincomalee. All of 'em bundled Home on the first available boat. I don't want to be wearing a tin hat and carrying a torch in darkest Piccadilly for the duration, thank you.'

'Look – I'll have a serious talk to him – ' the BM said earnestly.

'You're his Brigade Major, not his father.'

'But he does listen to me. Please, Althea – '

'I won't promise anything – ' Then she shrugged. 'Get me another gimlet, and I'll think about it,' she said. 'But I want that jeep first.'

Jane turned up with the Chevrolet on the fourth morning, and the Brigadier came bounding down the steps of his office like a spring lamb.

'That's better,' he said from the back seat as they drove out of the compound. 'I thought I'd lost you. I had to lay the law down to old Farting Fanny, that head Amazon of yours, to get you back, by George. She say anything to *you*?'

'No, sir,' said Jane demurely, which wasn't entirely true.

'Seems that some nasty little twerp *did* put in a report of my riding in the front seat – just as I said. Goddamn! The minds of some people!' The Brigadier breathed heavily through his nose and immersed himself in some papers.

They went to Ambala – a hundred-and-fifty-mile run along a road much the same as the one to Meerut – as indeed are all roads in Northern India – except that in this case there were from time to time intriguing glimpses of snow-capped mountains far ahead in the distance – seen for an instant when there was a break in the screening trees and the dust of oncoming traffic.

They arrived in the cantonments before midday, and the Brigadier directed her to Area Headquarters where he was closeted with the GOC for an hour or so. Jane sat in the car and looked at the typed notice freshly pasted on the dashboard: *'The front passenger seat will be occupied by the armed escort (when carried) or the junior rank when more than three passengers are carried. Veh: Regs: 229 1940/41. SO.'* The Commandant had spoken to her – at dawn, just before leaving. She had pointed silently to the notice and said portentously, 'My drivers are like the captains of ships or aircraft, Curtis. In complete command, no matter what the rank of the passengers might be. They will, of course, never be impertinent to a superior, but they will, at the same time, never permit that same superior deliberately to break regulations. Do I make myself clear, Curtis?'

'Perfectly, ma'am,' Jane had said.

'It's purely a matter of personality and strength of character, you see, Curtis. A *nice* gal – a properly brought-up and *educated* gal – would never allow herself to be manoeuvred into a compromising position. The direct look, Curtis. The quietly respectful word in season, if you see what I mean – will always have the required effect. I, myself, have found that to be true time and time again. Right, carry on, Curtis.'

'In a pig's arse, you have,' Jane had said to herself as she saluted and fell out – an unladylike expression she had picked up from Hank. 'Silly old cow.'

But she was still not inclined to take any further risks, and when the Brigadier suggested lunch at a quiet little private hotel she demurred and told him she had a haversack ration and a Thermos flask.

'Bloody nonsense,' the Brigadier snapped. 'Straight up this road and turn right at the church.' And when they arrived he gripped her firmly by the elbow and piloted her into the small European-owned restaurant that had become famous for its food in the days immediately before the war. Being lunch time and in the middle of the week they had the place practically to themselves, and Jane ate a meal that contrasted very favourably indeed with the fare served in the Women Other Ranks Mess. He proved to be a perfect host – attentive, charming and amusing – and on the homeward journey he made no untoward move to the front seat, but even so by the time they reached the Jumna Bridge their relationship had eased and relaxed to a degree of pleasant, natural informality. He had used her Christian name from the moment of their first meeting, and now he said, 'Cut out this eternal "sir", my dear. Out of barracks, anyhow. I'm usually known as Benjy to my friends.'

She learnt that he was married. 'I'd like to be able to excuse my occasional mild peccadillo with the usual plaint of my wife not understanding me,' he said, 'but it just wouldn't be true. She does understand me – only too well – and we're very happy – when we're together. She's at Home now – trapped after our last leave, when they stopped all non-priority passages back.'

'Children?' Jane inquired.

'One girl, eighteen – in the ATS now, of course. How old are you?'

'Twenty-two,' Jane told him, instinctively clipping the statutory permissible three years.

'You don't look it,' the Brigadier said. 'I sigh for my mis-spent youth.'

They ranged far and wide during the next month, to stations within a radius of between one to two hundred miles, and her driving skills increased to a point where she was adjudged competent to undertake her own maintenance and carry out simple running repairs – and the Army Educational Warrant Officer passed her out at map reading – and so she became a Driver-Mechanic, First Class, or in Army parlance, a D/M1, entitled to wear proudly a little worsted steering wheel on her right sleeve, as evidence of her proficiency.

But there was no further word of her commission, and this was beginning to fret her. She dropped an oblique hint to Benjy, as she was now calling him, when on a long run to Jhansi, but he failed to rise to it, so she switched to a more direct approach.

'I'm getting very fed up with this nonsense,' she told him rather acidly. 'Yes, yes, yes, I know – one goes where one is sent – does what one is told   it's all for the war effort and all that – but I don't see why I should have to pig it with Indians and half-chats just to show my patriotism. If you could see some of the wet weeks they *are* commissioning – not even white, a lot of them – !'

'I know, my dear,' he soothed. 'But this arrangement is not bad at the moment, is it? I mean we are able to make these trips, which are very pleasant and I do enjoy your company – '

She bit back, 'And what the hell do *I* get out of it?' and substituted, 'I quite agree, Benjy dear, but it's not an awful lot of fun being treated like a skivvy when we are visiting British Service units, and this business of your riding in the back and having to carry on conversations over my shoulder is giving me a crick in the neck.'

'All right,' he said glumly. 'I suppose I'd better be honest. I did take it up with the bloody abbess – and she said you were just the type they were looking for. You'd be commissioned on the spot – but – ' He trailed off.

'But what?'

'The moment you become an officer I lose you. You'd be too senior to drive a mere Brigadier, and I don't rate a PA yet.' He grinned wickedly. 'As a matter of fact she has tried to whip you away from me several times. I've only been able to hang on to you by threatening to take her jeep back off her if she does. She couldn't stand that – not while the other chief bints have theirs.'

'I see,' said Jane thoughtfully.

'So, if you wouldn't mind hanging on like this for the moment, until I make Major-General and you become my PA – '

'When will that be?'

Benjy shrugged. 'Lap of the gods. All depends on this reorganization and expansion of GHQ they're talking about back in Whitehall. Three months? – six months? – a year? Your guess is as good as mine. Just be patient a little longer, poppet.'

Jane nodded slowly, then smiled sweetly into the rear-vision mirror. 'Of course,' she said softly. 'Anything you say, Benjy dear.'

The Commandant looked at Jane uneasily. 'I don't altogether like it, Curtis,' she said. 'Yes, I know, you're used to long runs – you're a D/M One and all that – but Simla is three hundred miles away. You couldn't make it in a day. It would involve an overnight stop – with no approved women's accommodation laid on.'

'I can look after myself,' Jane said steadily. 'Just as you told me, ma'am – the direct look – the quietly respectful word in season. Remember?'

'Um,' mused the Commandant doubtfully. 'All right when you're within screaming distance of help – but out in the jungle miles from anywhere – ' she pursed her lips and shook her head slowly. 'No – I really think I ought to pass this one on to the male Company.'

'Oh, ma'am,' said Jane, stricken. 'What a climb-down that would be. After what you yourself have said to us so often – that we must show them that we're as good, if not better, than they are. How can we ever gain their respect if we pass difficult jobs to them and keep the easy ones ourselves? They'll laugh at us, ma'am.'

'It's not a case of just *difficulty*, Curtis,' the Commandant said unhappily. 'I mean – well – I stand in loco parentis to you gals

– and I know what brutes men can be at times. I'd hate to expose one of you – er – more *sheltered* gals – I mean – someone from Home, not used to that sort of thing, to – well – you know – '

'Ma'am,' Jane said, looking her superior officer straight in the eye. 'I think I know what you mean, but with respect, we, the girls, are here to do a job – a *man's* job – and we won't do it by dodging danger – particularly danger which might not even exist. Don't call on a male driver – *please*, ma'am. I'd feel I'd failed. I'm proud of our Corps, ma'am. I want it to be proud of me.'

The Commandant had a little difficulty in answering for a moment. She swallowed hard, then nodded and said, 'The Corps is what *you*, and girls like you, make it – what's your first name? – oh, yes – Jane – and it *is* proud of you. You're doing a splendid job, Jane. A *big* job – and I feel that in the not very distant future you may well be called upon to undertake an even bigger job. Very good. Carry on, Cor – er – Jane.'

'Lovely road,' said Benjy, comfortably asprawl in the back seat. 'You know it as far as Ambala. We go on from there to Kalka, at the foot of the hills, and climb six thousand feet in the first twenty-five miles – then drop four, and climb again to seven. The road twists, turns and hairpins horribly. You'll have to let me ride in front with you then.'

'I can manage, thank you,' Jane told him. 'I've driven down south in the Nilgiris. You stay where you are, you wicked old man.'

'Not so much of the "old", you cheeky bitch,' Benjy growled. 'I'll need to ride in front for my own sake. I get as sick as a pig in the back seat on hill sections. You've never been to Simla, have you?'

'Never.'

'You'll love it. Like an English village set down in the middle of the Swiss Alps. Ever been to Switzerland?'

'Only when I was tiny, and Daddy used to take us skiing.'

'There are English shops in Simla – run by English people. The only ones in India. Dammit, there used to be a butcher feller in the Mall, wearing a blue striped apron and a straw hat – and, of course, wonderful women's shops, where English wenches – or as near English as makes no difference – call the Memsahibs "moddom". Marvellous. Got any money, by the way?'

'A few rupees. Why?'

There was a slight rustle of paper in the back. 'You'd better have this, then,' Benjy said, reaching over her shoulder.

'What is it?'

'A couple of hundred rupees. Buy yourself something pretty while I'm seeing His Nibs.'

'No thank you,' she said firmly.

'Eh?' he said, startled. 'What the devil – ? You're not snubbing me, are you?'

'Of course not – but I still don't think it would be right.'

'Oh! For God's sake,' Benjy said, embarrassed and exasperated at one time. 'Don't be damned silly, poppet. Here – take it.'

'I'd rather not,' Jane said.

'As you wish,' Benjy said stiffly, and there was a strained silence between them until they reached Kalka, and he said, 'Are you going to have lunch with me in the railway refreshment room – or would that constitute an attempt upon your virginity?'

'No – I rate that higher than a stale ham sandwich and a Bath bun,' Jane said – then laughter came to their aid – belly-deep and wholesome, and they lunched royally on chicken vindaloo and a noble pilau, washed down with iced Pilsener, and the unfortunate little incident was forgotten.

They arrived in Simla as dusk was falling, and here there was no embarrassment because a room had been booked for Jane in a modest hotel, while Benjy went off to what was to prove a marathon conference which lasted until dawn. It broke up briefly, then reassembled again at mid-morning – so it was late afternoon before they got under way on the return journey, with Benjy heavy-eyed and yawning.

And then the first deluge of the south-east monsoon caught them just below Kasauli. It came on them without warning on a particularly steep section – a solid downpour which turned the narrow road into a swirling torrent in the first few minutes. She felt a loss of steerage control and she slammed on her brakes but there was no reduction in their speed.

Benjy yelled over the drumming on the roof, 'I'd better take over!'

'Stay where you are,' she told him through gritted teeth, but he was already clambering over the back of her seat. He shoved her to one side and grabbed the wheel, and the car swung obliquely across the road and slid with all four wheels locked into the rock face which rose sheerly on their near side, and there was a grinding of crumbled metal as the front mudguard collapsed under the impact.

'You bloody fool,' she screamed. 'See what you've done?'

'My arms are stronger than yours, poppet,' he answered good-humouredly. 'And you mustn't swear at Pappa. Take it easy – I think the Shevgaon dak bungalow is a few miles ahead.'

And it was – and he made it with great skill and coolness, and they drove into the streaming compound, wrenched the door open and made a dash for the verandah.

The place was in total darkness and the front door was locked, but Benjy pounded on it with a noise fit to raise the dead, and a drenched chowkidar came round from the rear quarters and let them in. It was a tiny place – just one room sparsely furnished with a couple of string charpoys, a table and two chairs – meant purely as the most temporary of resting places for subordinate Government officials on tour.

'Probably crawling with bugs,' Benjy grunted, peering round in the light of a hurricane lamp. 'But better than crashing about half drowned in *this* blasted weather.' He shivered. 'Bloody cold, too – up at this height. Kuch khana milsakta?' he asked the chowkidar, and the man shrugged a negative. 'No grub,' Benjy translated to her. 'Good job I've got a bottle of scotch in the car. I'll hop out and get it. Jesus! What a to-do.'

He came back with the whisky, and the chowkidar produced a grimy tumbler and a cracked cup. 'Better not risk the water,' Benjy advised as he poured two generous shots. 'Take it neat.'

But whisky happened to be the one form of alcohol she never had been able to take without feeling sick, so she declined the glass he held out to her. 'Come on,' he urged. 'You'll get fever – flu – all sorts of things – if you don't.'

'I'm sorry – I just can't stand whisky,' she said.

'Dammit! I insist,' Benjy blustered.

'Insist all you like,' she said coldly. '*I don't drink whisky.*'

'Have it your own way,' he said resignedly, and drank both. 'What the devil's the matter with you? You've gone up-stage on me all of a sudden. Anything I've said?'

'You shouldn't have taken the car over,' she told him. 'Particularly when we were moving. It was a very dangerous thing to do.'

'Now look here, my girl,' he said quietly. 'Have your moods and tantrums if you like – that's a privilege of your sex – but don't start trying to teach Grandpa to suck eggs – or I'll tan your shapely little arse for you. Understand?' His taut grin softened the reprimand, but only marginally, and even in the dim lamplight he could see her cheeks redden. He relented. 'Sorry,' he said. 'I know you're tired – and that skid was frightening. Don't worry about the bump. I'll take the responsibility for that when we get back.' He poured more whisky. 'Are you absolutely sure you won't have some of this?'

'Absolutely,' she confirmed.

'All right.' He took it in one and poured some more. 'Well, it's certainly not wise to go any further until this rain eases off. We'd better try and get some rest.' He indicated the two beds. 'Any preference? No bedclothes, I'm afraid. You've always got to supply your own in these dak bungalows.'

'All the same to me,' she said.

'If we had any sense we'd double up on one for warmth,' he suggested jocularly, watching her closely for a reaction.

'No thank you,' she said very firmly indeed.

'I thought you'd say that,' he said regretfully. 'Oh, well – thank God for the demon drink.' He poured yet another and drank it, then stretched out on the charpoy nearest to the door. He yawned cavernously. 'Lordy me – I'm tired,' he muttered, and seemed within a minute to be deep in sleep and snoring noisily. She sat on one of the chairs for a long time, thinking – then she got up and tiptoed out on to the verandah. It was still raining, but not quite so heavily. She crossed quickly to the car, got in, and locked the doors. Then she settled down on the front seat and catnapped uncomfortably until dawn.

Benjy came out on to the verandah, gummy and bleary. He peered at the day and didn't appear to like what he saw. He came across to the car and tried the doors without success, so he pounded on the side. Jane woke and unlocked.

'What the hell are you doing out here?' he demanded.

'I didn't like the bungalow,' she said.

'Neither did I – but at least one could stretch out there.' He winced and put a hand on his aching head. 'Christ, I've got a hangover. I just about saw that three-quarter bottle off on my own. All right then, if you're fit we'd better scoot, unless you want to powder your nose and wee-wee first?'

'No thank you,' she said primly.

'We'll get some breakfast at Kalka,' he said as he climbed in. 'What's the matter with you? Still sulking over something?'

'No,' she said as she started up. 'But would you mind not talking for a while? The road looks slippery and I want to concentrate on my driving.'

'Bloody women,' he snorted. 'You're all the same. If every damned little thing doesn't go exactly your way you get a grudge against the universe. All right then – clam up if you want to.' He settled himself in the corner of the back seat and went to sleep again. And Jane smiled a secret little smile.

The Commandant's pointing finger trembled and her voice was vibrant with icy contempt. ' – good family,' she was saying. 'Niece of a General – sheltered home – product of a good school – motivated only by a desire to do her duty in whatever capacity she is directed to – and without question. Earmarked for a commission – And to be treated like *that*, by someone from whom she had every right to expect protection and respect – ' The '*that*' shot out like a whiplash, and Benjy jumped, quivered and cowered slightly.

'For Christ's sake, Althea,' he quavered. 'Tell me what the

hell the bloody girl is accusing me of.'

The Commandant ennumerated on her fingers. 'You suggested that she slept with you – and you offered her money – '

'Hey! Wait a minute – '

'Allow me to continue, please. You tried to force whisky on her – and when she refused it you threatened her with physical violence – '

'I jokingly said I'd slap her behind or something if she didn't drink it, as I believed she needed it. She was wet through and – '

'Am I to finish, or does the whole matter go before the Deputy Adjutant General?' the Commandant demanded.

'Go on,' Benjy said glumly.

'You drank nearly a whole bottle of whisky, interfered with her driving and caused an accident which could easily have been fatal – and finally she had to lock herself in the car while you slept off your debauch in a wayside shack – '

'Althea, listen – for God's sake listen,' Benjy pleaded almost tearfully. 'I don't know what her object is, but I can assure you – '

'She has no object. She is not even complaining. She merely paraded before me and asked to be taken off driving duty. I could see she was upset, so I questioned her – and it was only with the greatest difficulty that I managed to get the facts from her. My first impulse was to go straight to the DAG.'

'For Christ's sake don't go on and on – ' Benjy moaned. 'Come to the point. What does she want? What do *you* want?'

'I want nothing, other than to let you know that I will not have my gals regarded as camp followers for the amusement of senior officers. She will, of course, not be coming back to you – '

'Thank God for that,' Benjy said fervently, mopping his streaming brow. 'I'll settle for a male driver.'

'I think it would be better,' the Commandant agreed, tight-lipped. 'But it is only fair to warn you that I am keeping this on the Confidential File, just *in case* we have another such incident, in which contingency, of course, I should reserve the right to bring this matter forward again.'

'No need for that,' Benjy rumbled. 'No more of 'em round *this* patch.'

The Commandant saluted punctiliously, turned, and marched to the door – then halted and delved into her shoulder bag. She produced a slip of buff paper.

'Oh, since I'm here,' she said coldly. 'I think this might be attended to. Someone on your HQ has called in my jeep. I thought it was a permanent issue, but of course if you want it back I shall raise no objection, although I consider I have an operational justification – '

'Keep it by all means,' Benjy said graciously, taking the slip and tearing it in halves. 'Somebody in the office getting his priorities wrong.' He bowed her out and closed the door softly behind her, then made an obscene gesture, sighed gustily with relief, and sought the bottle of scotch he kept for emergencies in the Top Secret cabinet.

Jane left for the Officer Cadet Training Unit (Women) on the night express.

Chapter Thirteen

She spent twelve interesting and instructive weeks at OCTU, spared a great deal of the more tedious aspects of the course by the fact that the Commandant had hair the colour and texture of an ageing Airedale terrier's, far beyond the ability of the timid little Anglo-Indian girl who managed 'Marie – Coiffure' in the bazaar to make even reasonably presentable, and she was quick to notice that Jane's hair was invariably immaculate – and the latter explained, when questioned by the Adjutant, that she had undergone professional training before embarking for India, solely to be able to attend to her own hair and make-up, but that she would be happy to lend her modest skill, such as it was, to any of the lady officers who so desired. Thereafter she was in great demand on cocktail party days, and since there were, on an average, six a week in that particular station, she was kept very busy indeed. She passed out fourth in a class of twenty-seven, being pipped only by the niece of a former Viceroy, a Maharanee, and the daughter of a serving General, and was posted with glowing encomiums to the administrative section of a large convalescent depot in Jaigaon.

Jaigaon was a pleasantly elevated hill station that formed one corner of a twenty-mile equilateral triangle with Kasauli and Simla. It remained relatively cool even in mid-summer, and was snowbound one winter in three. Its only link with the outside world, unless one counted a hair-raising bridle-track up to Jutogh and thence to Simla, was a serpentine road that took off from the main Kalka/Simla highway and clung vertiginously to the khudside for the forty miles it made out of the twenty the crow flew between Jaigaon and Kasauli. It had consisted in peacetime of five barrack blocks built in the mock-Gothic so beloved by Victorian architects when designing railway stations, prisons, public lavatories and homes-from-home for our troops, plus a scattering of married officers' quarters dotting the hillsides, a ruined Gurkha fort, a small bazaar and, after Darjeeling, it commanded the most breathtakingly magnificent view of the snowcapped Upper Himalayas in all Asia. For this last reason, if for no other, it was loathed by Tommy Atkins in his characteristic perversity, with a deep and abiding bitterness. Hurriedly enlarged by the addition of chitthai huts on every patch level enough to hold one, it was now serving as a convalescent station for the wounded and the far more numerous malaria and dysentery patients from the Burma front, giving them a brief respite before dispatching them, still gaunt and jaundiced, back to the jungles of Assam and the Arrakan.

Jane, arriving by duty truck from Kalka, found herself in complete agreement with the male driver's summation of 'half the size of Colaba cemetery, and twice as bloody dead', although she answered only with a cold stare that had him immediately mumbling apologies and addressing her as Ma'am. The knack was coming to her quickly and naturally. It didn't need words, she had discovered in the few short days since she had acquired her subaltern's pip. Just that look – icy and disdainful, and decidedly off-putting for the grinner, smirker and potential taker of liberties. The 'Memsahib's look' she called it to herself as she practised it before her mirror.

She was disappointed with this, her first posting, although it had been sold to her as a plum. It was not that she was totally unappreciative of scenic beauty, but she had been hoping for something nearer to one or other of the larger stations – Delhi, Lahore or Rawalpindi – places she had heard discussed nostalgically by the cognoscenti as the social Arcadias of Northern India. But this was a worthwhile job, she had been told – the administration and welfare of upwards of three thousand front-line invalids – men, many miles from home, who had been through varying degrees of hell and who were pathetically grateful for the sympathetic word, the soothing touch and the comforting presence of an Englishwoman. 'No doubt,' she had thought to herself when handed her posting orders shortly after the commissioning parade. 'But why couldn't it be an *officers'* convalescent depot?' But she saluted smartly and said modestly, 'Yes, ma'am – I'll do my best. Just as long as it releases a man for the front.'

She reported to the Adjutant's office, and a plain but cheerful girl with ginger hair glanced at her posting order and slit open the sealed envelope marked 'CO – Personal' which contained her Confidential Report, and read it with some interest.

'Huh,' she grunted. 'Another "Average – unlikely to go to the highest rank". The last one went preggers and got slung. Preggers to an *Other Rank*!' She clucked disapprovingly, then grinned disarmingly, and went on, 'OK, Curtis – welcome to the nunnery. You're to be my assistant, God help you. *I'm* the Adjutant's assistant.' She put the report into a fresh envelope and resealed it. 'Address this to the CO – Personal – will you. She knows my writing. Give it to her yourself when you go in front of her. Had breakfast?'

'No,' Jane said shortly, put out at the cavalier treatment of her report, which she'd paid the orderly room babu at OCTU ten rupees to see before she left, and knew to be extremely laudatory.

'Better push off to the mess then – straight across there in the next building. Your room is one of the chitthais on a shelf above the parade ground. Heavenly view but as cold as buggery in the mornings.' She banged a bell and a girl corporal entered. 'Take this officer to the mess, Gates, will you – then organize a coolie to get her kit up to Number Seventeen, Annex B. Her servant will be Ayah Noola. Be seeing you, Curtis – about an hour. Right? My name's Fenton, by the way.'

She quickly fell into the routine of the place. The men were there to rest and recuperate, so there were no parades or irksome inspections, but, by the very nature of things they were miserably bored, so female personnel, which totalled a Commandant and six more junior WAC(I) officers, plus thirty Other Ranks, a Matron, ten nurses and three physiotherapists, were expected to take a full part in the rehabilitation programme. Dances, picnics and sports were organized by an indefatigable

Recreations Officer of limitless stamina who had once been a Physical Training mistress at Roedean. Fifty women did not stretch far among a shifting population of three thousand woman-hungry troops, but they did their best.

'That's all I will ever accept, Jane,' the Commandant told her at her first interview. 'My officers' and girls' best. The work is hard and demanding – the dear boys do not always appear grateful – and after all, why should they be? It is *we* who should be grateful to *them* – so, however tired we may be after a day's hard slog at our official job – we must always be ready to join in whatever activities have been laid on in the evenings and the weekends. *But* – ' the Commandant paused portentously and raised an admonitory finger – 'we must constantly be on our guard against what I call "PI" – *personal involvement*, Jane. It can happen very easily. It *has* happened – more than once – a woman *officer* having to resign her commission and leave under a cloud because of a shabby little clandestine affair with a *soldier*. *They* are Other Ranks, Jane. *We* are Officers, and never the twain should meet – unchaperoned after dark. Oh yes – some of the men no doubt come from good families, but for some reason or other have not been commissioned – we've actually had an Honourable and a Baronet through our hands – both privates – but even that doesn't alter the status quo. Fullest co-operation, Jane – whole-hearted participation – selfless service – but no PI. Do I make myself clear?'

'Perfectly, ma'am,' Jane murmured.

Actually she found the avocation more arduous than her official duties. 'Legs together and eschew the PI,' grinned Fenton when she reported to the office for duty. 'My God! Wouldn't old Frenetic Fenella welcome an improper suggestion or two from a lovely big sweaty hunk of lance-corporal. She hasn't had a nibble since the Relief of Mafeking, but never gives up hope. Right, here's your main job. The Reforsec Display – simple enough, but it calls for care or some poor devil of a Tommy could easily find himself back in the line when he's really been put down for evacuation – '

The office was lined from floor to ceiling with display boards with grooved metal channels into which slips of white card bearing the soldier's number, name, rank and unit were inserted on his arrival. 'Each chap is reviewed weekly,' Fenton explained, 'and a nominal roll comes down from Medical from time to time showing changes in their categories. "C" means "remain" – the tag goes on the hook here beside his name – see? "B" means they're almost fit again. They stay on that for another week – then, all things being equal, they go up to "A" – normal diet, two hours' light drill and PT each day. They hate that, poor lambs. Then, finally, "FFP" – that's this green tag here. That means "Fit for Posting". When they get that you take them out of the general frame and put them in this one – that's the Drafting Pool. Drafts of fifty-plus go out twice a week – daybreak on Tuesdays and Thursdays. I try to miss it.'

'Why?' Jane asked.

Fenton shrugged. 'Wait until you've seen a few go back – especially when there's a big attack planned and the Reinforcement people are yelling for men – and more men. Some of them look as if they should be going to Blighty on stretchers, poor little devils. Yellow with fever and mepacrin, all eyes, teeth and ribs. Down to railhead at Kalka – shipped out to Nirsa like cattle – then flown in. They're back in action within twenty-four hours of leaving here. No, I don't watch them go if I can help it.'

She found her interest waning after the second week. The Adjutant was a grumbler, Fenton, her immediate superior, was unpredictable and moody, the work was dull and monotonous, and, hardest to bear, there was a total lack of socially acceptable male company. This was a convalescent depot, not a hospital, and the medical staff consisted only of the CO, one Lieutenant-Colonel O'Riordan of the Royal Army Medical Corps, middle-aged and married, with his wife *in situ*, two very elderly Majors recalled from retirement, and an Indian assistant surgeon.

' "Water, water everywhere, nor any drop to drink",' Fenton quoted with a wry grin. 'That is, of course, unless you go in for a bit of Fenella's anathema – the old PI. A hell of a lot *do*.'

'I'm afraid that fraternizing with Other Ranks doesn't appeal to me,' Jane said coldly. 'I've got nothing against the

278

men personally – but, well – I just wasn't brought up to that sort of thing.'

'Balls,' snapped Fenton. 'Don't talk like a bloody stuffed camisole. Neither was I brought up to it – if by "that sort of thing" you mean snogging with the lower orders. But I try not to be a prig about it. Wait until you've been up here a few months before you start judging other people.'

The frequent dances were, however, some slight surcease from the daily monotony. In the floating population there was usually enough talent from which to form a band, the recreation hall was cheerfully decorated, and the nights were always cool, and there was the inevitable proportion of superb dancers to leaven the heavy-footed – and others were interesting conversationalists, and, indeed, some were both. As Fenton put it, 'With the odds forty-five to one against us, Curtis, they can't *all* have two left feet and cleft palates. One does meet the occasional dish.'

Then things took a decided turn for the better when one of the elderly Majors was posted. He had a delightful Kathiawar hill pony on which he used to enjoy morning canters along the bridle track, and he was unable to take it with him to his new station, so, after vainly trying to sell it to one or other of his more sedentary colleagues, he gave it to Jane. Mornings became a time of sheer ecstasy after that. She had a natural seat and balance, and good hands – and she had not forgotten the little that Ian had taught her. Clad in jodhpurs and chukkha boots, she used to be out an hour before sun-up when the whole world was hers alone, and she would ride some six winding miles down to Simla Bridge in the bottom of the valley before turning for home – or, to vary it, she would go in the opposite direction towards Dagshai, where the Americans, with their own particular genius for getting things done quickly even in India, were converting a large rambling ruin of a Maharajah's summer palace into a convalescent depot for their sick and wounded fliers. It was, of course, a much smaller project than Jaigaon, and it was for officers only. She looked at it enviously, and sighed.

*

It was on her fourth or fifth such ride that she met Dan.

She was on her way back along the Simla path and he dropped down from the bank in front of her and held up his hand, and the startled pony shied. He caught the bridle and smiled up at her.

'I'm sorry,' he said. 'I had to be certain. I've seen you go out each morning and I was pretty sure it was you, but you were too far away. I followed you.'

'Dan!' she gasped. 'Where on earth have you been?'

'All over the place – '

'I've searched everywhere – made inquiries – oh, Dan – '
She slid down from the saddle and fumbled for her handkerchief, then smiled at him uncertainly. He was thinner than when she had last seen him, deeply tanned but with a pallor beneath it, and there were lines in his face that she didn't remember seeing before.

'I was pretty static for a time.' He grinned ruefully. 'For a hundred and twelve days, actually – in Trimulgherry Military clink. They busted me all the way down to private and took my trade rating away. That was the bit that hurt. When I came out I got posted as a General Duties man – you know, ward orderly – slinging bedpans and bottles. I went to Braganza Mansions to try and find out where you'd gone, but Maudie Furtado wasn't giving anything away. As soon as war was declared I was sent overseas – Middle East first of all – then back to Burma to a Casualty Clearing Station – then I got sick – amoebic dysentery and malaria – and finally wound up here, three weeks ago.' He smiled again. 'I heard all about you, of course. The blokes hardly talk about anything else but the smashing Wack-eye officer – but I haven't been able to get along to any of the dances because I only came off the restricted list yesterday. That's all,' he ended simply. 'I've never stopped thinking about you, Jane.' And only then did she realize that there was neither animus nor accusation in his eyes.

'Oh, Dan,' she said again. 'I *did* try to contact you – I tried so hard, but I couldn't find out a thing. I didn't even know your address.'

'Didn't Chalky give you any of my messages?'

'No – only that you were in trouble – oh, and of course, your letter with the hundred rupees in it. I left that with Mrs Furtado – in a letter to you, when Chalky didn't come back. Didn't you get it?'

He smiled and shook his head. 'Old Maudie would have smelt it if there was money in it. No – I bet it went into her cracked teapot. But that doesn't matter – '

'It *does* matter,' she said firmly. 'It was a terribly generous and sweet thought, although actually I didn't need it because Daddy's money came through then. I'll give it to you when we get back to camp – Oh, Danny, it *is* good to see you again. I've been terribly worried about you. *And* I've missed you.'

He looked at her intently. 'You have?' he said. 'You really mean that?'

'Of course I mean it. Why shouldn't I?'

'Well – you see – you being an officer and all that – I don't want you to think I'm shoving my frame in, if you see what I mean – '

'You idiot!' she laughed. 'As if that made any difference to *us* – ' And then she was in his arms and he was muttering brokenly and incoherently, and the pony broke away and started to trot down the path. He yelled and ran after it and led it back. He said, 'Christ! Make an officer walk home! That'd be another courtmartial offence. But tell me – what happened to *you*?'

'Nothing. My passage was booked and Daddy's money had arrived – but I still couldn't get on to a ship. Civilian passages were just frozen – so I joined the Wack-eyes, and I've served in various places – and eventually I was posted here.'

'But I suppose I won't be able to see you – away from the hops and bun-fights, I mean,' he said wistfully.

'Of course you will,' she told him. 'But, Danny dear – we'll have to be terribly, *terribly* careful. As far as I'm concerned I'd shout it from the housetops, but this old devil of a Commandant of ours is an absolute terror. If she suspects that there's anything going on between one of her wretched officers and an Other Rank, the girl is posted to the far end of India within twenty-four hours. We'll just have to be discreet, that's all.

This war can't last forever. When it's over we can do what we like without having to ask anybody's permission. We'll be able to meet after dark – while you're here, of course. Incidentally, I must check your category when I get back. That's a board we have with – '

'You don't have to,' he told her. 'I know my category. "C" – remain – and I'm staying that way. Colonel O'Riordan is seeing to that.'

'How do you know?' She was still smiling, but she felt a little flutter of dismay.

'The old boy cheered his head off when I arrived. He was my OC in Colaba. He did his damnedest for me when I was spun up – but it was an open-and-shut case, and I pleaded guilty to save a lot of explanations. He wants to get me my trade rating back – he's pretty certain he can – and then, as I've had a clean sheet since, it won't be any time until I'm made up to sergeant again, or even *staff*-sergeant – and I'll serve on in this place. They've only got a wog pill-roller here at the moment, and he's terrible I believe.' He took a deep breath and smiled beatifically. 'God – isn't this wonderful? The two of us – on the same station again. Pity I haven't got the old mo-bike. Will this nag of yours carry two?'

'Hardly.' She looked at her watch. 'Danny dear – I'll have to gallop all the way. I'm on duty in less than half an hour.' She reached up and kissed him on the cheek hurriedly. 'The dance tomorrow night – I'll see you there, and we can discuss things and make a plan of some sort – ' She gathered up the reins and climbed into the saddle. 'Good-bye for now.' She waved and put her heels in and cantered off down the path.

Her feelings were mixed. Quite apart from the fact that she had been genuinely grateful to him for his strength and support at the time of her greatest need, she had undeniably found him attractive – more so, probably, than any other man she had ever met, with the exception of Robert Powell. She was glad to see him again. Of course she was, she told herself. But she would have been happier if his stay on the station had not been indefinite. He had been very sweet on this first meeting – and he was aware of, and fully appreciated, her delicate position in relation to himself – But suppose – just suppose – he became demanding? Suppose he talked – ? She knew only too well how gossip grew and spread in this small isolated world of theirs. Fenella's warning had not been an empty one. Her predecessor had been 'busted' and removed. Admittedly hers was an extreme case – she had been pregnant – but Jane had heard of others who had not ventured nearly so far along the primrose path being dealt with very severely indeed. 'Lack of Moral Fibre' on one's Confidential Report was the ultimate damnation, and Fenella, apparently, scattered LMFs with no niggardly hand, given the slightest cause.

She would have to tread warily. It would not be wise to avoid him completely. Sick and wounded men could be as neurotic and unpredictable as fulminate of mercury, she remembered hearing in a lecture. No – that might only serve to trigger things off. Better to see him, if only occasionally, under cover of darkness. That in itself wouldn't be unpleasant, she reflected, provided he was sensible. The manoeuvre wasn't difficult. Several of her sister officers were 'pee-eyeing by moonlight' as it was called. Fenton was positively shameless about it, and made no secret of her nightly assignations with the Special Diet Cook – a beetle-browed, hirsute monster of a man who, when he wasn't boiling fish and making calves-foot jelly, used to stand in the doorway of the cookhouse in grimy blue-checked trousers, sweat-soaked vest and high chef's cap, ogling everything female that passed, white, black or halfway. Jane shuddered fastidiously. Dan's profession was, at least, a gentlemanly one, no matter how lowly his present military rank.

He managed to reach her through the maelstrom of a Paul Jones, feet, knees and elbows thrusting aside the politer, weaker and more timorous, and he muttered, 'Out of the side entrance – past the camp cinema and on to the path the other end. I'll be waiting,' before surrendering her as the music stopped.

He chuckled as she joined him ten minutes later, and said, 'I've been doing a night recce. Not as easy as you'd think. There are blokes and bints all over the khudside. This way.'

It was a perfect hill night – the air soft, cool and scented with pine, eucalyptus, mimosa and frangipani. He led the way to a crag that jutted out over a steep-sided valley to which there was no way other than the narrow path by which they came. Far in the distance, floating in ink-blue space, Simla's scant apology for a blackout glowed and pulsated like a resting hatch of fireflies. Below them an owl hooted sporadically, and unseen water splashed on rocks.

'Jesus Christ,' he breathed. 'Did you ever see anything lovelier than this?' She rested her head on his shoulder and squeezed his arm, but didn't answer. 'If I had to serve the rest of my life in India I'd want to do it right here,' he went on. 'It would be bloody marvellous, wouldn't it, if we managed to hang on here for the duration. How would you like that?'

'There's a war on, Danny,' she said, gently chidingly. 'We can't just hide away in comfortable stations.'

'I can,' he said gruffly. 'I've had four damned hard years up at the sharp end. Fighting – yes, bloody fighting a lot of the time. The Nips don't give a monkey's for the Red Cross, Geneva Convention or anything like that, so even the medics have got stuck in when there's a breakthrough. We used to take ammo up the line on stretchers and bring wounded back. No – this place will do me down to the ground until the shit stops flying. Sorry, love – I know you don't like dirty language. I do want to stay here though – especially since you're here too.'

'I'll be staying for quite a time,' she assured him. 'That's if neither of us does anything silly and I get posted,' she added hastily.

'I'll watch it,' he assured her. 'I saw old Paddy O'Riordan again today. The damn fool of a Major had just prodded and poked me over, and marked me "B" – and I was coming out of the MI Room feeling really down in the mouth when old Paddy came in. He took my form from under my arm and looked at it, then he winked and went inside with it – and came out a few minutes later and said, "Right ho, sergeant. Carry on – and always bring this chunk of bumph to *me* after these other medical marvels have had a look at you." And I was down to "C" again. "*Sergeant*" – that was the bit that

284

counted. He was giving me the tip that things were going through all right. He's a bloody wonder, that old Irish bugger. Best bleeding quack in the Army. If they were all like him I'd stay in after the war. Nothing wrong with the pay nowadays, you know. Not for a first class tradesman, anyhow. And it's getting better – and married quarters are really posh in most stations at Home.' He sighed. 'But they *aren't* all like Paddy – so I'm getting out as soon as it's over – that's if it's all right with you. In business on our own. How would you like that?'

'What sort of business?' she asked.

'Pharmacy, naturally. That's what I've been trained for. I didn't tell you, did I, that my old man had died?'

'No.'

'Yes – poor old boy. Dropped dead on his way to work – A coronary. Anyhow, he left me seven hundred and fifty quid. Well, now – I don't know what they'll be lashing out in the way of gratuities when it's all over, but I should think it ought to be a couple of hundred at least. OK – so that makes a thousand or thereabouts. I could raise another thousand on a pound-for-pound basis from any of the big drug firms, and put a down payment on a nice little chemist's shop in one of the suburbs – comfortable flat over it. That's how old Morton started, you know. On a couple of hundred pounds after the last war – and he finished up with three shops. One in Streatham, where I was, one in Brixton, *your* home patch, and another in Wandsworth.' He turned towards her impulsively and threw his arms round her. 'Oh, Jesus! Jane, lovie – can't you see it? *A place of our own.* Somewhere you can shut the front door and give the outside world the two-finger salute. No more standing to attention – Yessir, No sir, Three bloody bags full, sir – A *home*, darling – '

'Yes,' she said faintly. 'Lovely – No, Danny! – you mustn't – *No!* – Oh, look – I've got to be so careful – *Danny!* – '

'Don't worry,' he told her. 'What the hell do you think I'm a chemist for? That's what we'll be founding the family fortune on – selling these things.'

They started meeting three times a week – with perfect safety,

Jane thought, until one morning her confidence was shaken by Fenton saying languidly, 'I say, Curtis, do tell that hefty boy friend of yours to be careful where he puts his feet, will you? He damn nearly trod on the small of my chap's back last night.'

'I don't know what on earth you're talking about,' Jane said, reddening furiously.

'I'm talking about the path of dalliance out to Monkey Point that you've been assiduously wearing down lately,' Fenton told her, grinning maliciously. 'Of course, we all know you haven't been brought up to this sort of thing, and all that – but that's no excuse for sheer clumsiness. And don't forget my chap outranks yours. He's a lance-corporal-cook. You don't want your boy friend to finish up in the soup, do you?'

Badly frightened, she cut the next two dance nights, but he intercepted her as she was returning from her ride a few mornings later, and he was hurt and bewildered.

'I couldn't get a message to you, Danny,' she explained. 'This wretched woman is obviously watching us now – and she's a talker. You don't want me to be posted, do you?'

'Hell, no,' he said gloomily. 'But it's been lousy turning up two nights running and not seeing you. You know – a bloke gets to thinking all sorts of things – like you changing your mind about me – and going off with officers and all that – '

'Oh, Danny,' she chided gravely. 'That *is* stupid. You know – or *should* know – perfectly well that you can trust me.'

'I'm sorry,' he said, deeply penitent. 'But it's a bloody horrible position to be in. So near and yet so far – hearing fellows in the barrack-room talking about you – '

'What on earth could they possibly say about me?' she demanded indignantly.

'Oh, nothing bad. I don't mean that – but, well you know what blokes are like when they haven't had anything to do with girls for a long time. They get randy and talk about things they'd like to do if they got half a chance. I don't mind when they're talking about Rita Hayworth or Ginger Rogers or somebody – but when it's you – Christ – I could kill them.'

286

He was clenching and unclenching his fists convulsively, and his face was drawn and taut – and suddenly she was afraid. She leaned down out of the saddle and smoothed his hair with her string-gloved hand.

'Danny, Danny, Danny,' she soothed. 'Now stop it. Don't be a silly boy. As if anything like that mattered. You mustn't take any notice of them. I'll meet you tonight – no, not at the dance – on the Figure-of-Eight – at half-past nine. I'm Orderly Officer, but I'll slip away for an hour. All right?'

'Yes – but I don't want you to get into trouble – '

'I'll be careful – and you must be too. It can't be much longer now, dear, before we're free to do what the devil we want, without looking over our shoulders all the time. I must fly now, Danny. See you tonight – ' She turned and waved as she cantered round the next bend. He was standing in the middle of the path – a lonely figure. He returned her wave, and suddenly her eyes were misting and she found herself biting her lower lip.

The Figure-of-Eight was a mile-long path that started and finished at the Gurkha Fort, winding round the summits of two adjacent hills and crossing itself in the valley between, thus giving it its name. It was a favourite walk in daylight hours, but it was usually deserted after dark, although the preternaturally nightsighted could often discern glowing cigarettes in pairs among the fireflies glittering in the dense undergrowth that bordered the path throughout its length. It had been an alternative rendezvous of theirs, less favoured by Jane than Monkey Point because she found the overhanging, intertwined babul trees claustrophobic. But Fenton had specifically mentioned the latter, so wild horses would not have dragged her back there.

He came out of the darkness as she reached the shadow of the fort wall, and she could sense his tenseness as he took her roughly in his arms. 'Go easy,' she joked. 'I'm in uniform. I've got to close the Women's Mess and the bar in an hour and I don't want to look as if I've been pulled through a haystack, you brute.'

She could usually jolly him out of the black moods that were assailing him more frequently as their association progressed, but tonight there was no responsive chuckle and he smelt strongly of the local rum the troops called panther piss, which was sold illicitly in the bazaar.

He said, 'Bugger the uniform. Listen, Jane – do you know a bint called Stewart? Lieutenant or subaltern or whatever you call two pips in your mob?'

'Yes – I've heard of her but I've never met her.' She knew what was coming now. 'She's over in Kasauli. She's got married. Why?'

'She married a staff-sergeant, that's why,' Dan said. 'No trouble. She wasn't in the family way or anything. She just told them she wanted to get married, and resigned her commission – just like that. They're living in married quarters over there.'

'How do you know all this?'

'I heard the penpushers talking about it when I was collecting the mail in the Orderly Room. They can't do anything about it if a girl wants to get married. If the bloke's an officer they can both soldier on, but if he's an Other Rank they've just got to let her go.'

'Yes, I knew that,' she told him.

'You never said anything to *me* about it,' he said accusingly.

'I wasn't sufficiently interested – and I didn't think you would be either.'

He stared at her through the darkness. 'Not interested? For Christ's sake, don't you see what it means – to *us*? You can leave at any time you like – We can be married – '

She shook her head. 'Not quite, Danny,' she said softly. 'The circumstances are totally different. The Stewart girl is Anglo-Indian. Her home is in Kasauli – so is that of her husband. He's a laboratory technician – also Anglo-Indian.'

'And I'm a pharmacist – and I'll be getting my stripes back shortly. Where the hell's the difference?'

'Anglo-Indian. I just told you. Listen to me, Danny – I know what I'm talking about – '

'Don't *I*? I didn't join the bloody Army the day before

yesterday, you know.'

'Of course you know, Danny dear – about the men's side of things. I'm talking about the *women's*. I know what would happen if I told the Commandant that I wanted to marry a private on this station. I would be posted within twenty-four hours.'

'But they couldn't stop you leaving the Army, that's the point. You could come back here then – '

'From the time I put my letter of resignation in to the time I was actually released – that is always at least a month – I would be serving in a station a long way from here, Danny dear. I *know*. And as far as you're concerned you'd probably be posted somewhere too – away from Colonel O'Riordan, where he wouldn't be able to help you. They just don't like it, and they have ways of making their wishes felt, without breaking regulations. Just bending them a little. Oh, Danny – you know that as well as I do. Better. Things are going our way. Don't ruin our chances by doing anything stupid – '

'That's twice you've called me stuipid today,' he said bitterly. 'That's really what you think, isn't it? I'm stupid. A boneheaded, beetle-crushing, bloody private who's had the nerve to take up with an officer – and has got to be put in his place – '

She was crying. 'Danny, that's not true – you know it's not true – and I didn't call you stupid – I only said it would ruin things if *we* were stupid enough to make a move too quickly. Please, Danny – listen to me – '

'Oh, Christ, I'm sorry,' he said, stricken. 'Don't cry, darling – All right – don't worry – I won't be doing anything silly – just as long as I can see you – It's being separated and not getting a word from you – '

'I'll see you, Danny – of course I'll see you,' she murmured. 'As often as it's safe. Just leave it to me. It won't be long now – I promise you – '

And she did continue to see him – but the magic had gone from it now, certainly on her side. She was edgy and nervous, hearing in every night sound from the surrounding jungle the stealthy footsteps of a peeping Tom or Thomasina, and their unions, when they occurred at all, were hurried and joyless, and she had taken to volunteering for extraneous duties which she knew would appear in Orders, purely to be able to show them to him as reasons for not seeing him more often. And her disenchantment was becoming daily more apparent to him – and he was drinking vast quantities of bazaar rotgut as a result.

She led the pony out of the stable before dawn and stole away down a side path that joined the Dagshai bridle track by a roundabout route which avoided the necessity of crossing the parade ground which he could see from his barrack room. He used to watch her going out, and would then follow along the path and intercept her on her way back. With luck she would avoid him today. Last night had been more difficult than usual. She had taken his hundred rupees back to him and he had refused them, seeing in this a subtle attempt on her part to break the tenuous link that remained between them. She had tried to force them on him, and he had finally torn the notes up and thrown them away in the darkness, and he had shouted and raved in his fury and she was completely certain that unseen ears had been listening. She had to have time to think this intolerable problem out alone. It was her weekly day off duty and she intended to go further than usual and stay away from the stifling confines of the camp for as long as possible, so she went almost the whole way to the new American hospital.

She heard the tortured scream of the over-revving engine as she climbed the last sharp incline to the small plateau on which the hospital stood, and she wondered how any vehicle had managed to come round this side, because the motor road lay a good mile and a half away to the south. But obviously some brave or utterly foolhardy soul had attempted it, and was now trying to reverse and turn in order to go back. Interested, she broke a cardinal rule and spurred the pony up the slope, and then gasped in horror.

The car was a magnificent Cadillac, and its overlong luggage trunk and half the circumference of its back wheels were hanging in space over a sheer thousand-foot drop. A turbaned Sikh driver was making a highly perilous position impossibly worse by keeping his foot hard down on the accelerator – frozen in his helplessness – and although in neutral gear the vibration was threatening to tip the delicate balance and send several tons of highly expensive metal-work hurtling over the edge. The driver appeared to be aware of this because the noise faded somewhat as Jane dismounted and hurried forward. Then she saw the passenger – a woman – in the rear seat – like the driver, frozen. But the driver had one chance left, and he was taking it. The ground was solid on his side and he was preparing to bail out, and let the devil take the hindermost. The passenger was in a not so happy position. The edge of the drop outside the rear door was already crumbling and, unless she was very nimble indeed, to open the door and attempt to spring forward to safety looked impossible. It was, as it happened, one of the classic contretemps presented to Driver-Mechanics First Class by the MT Examining Board, but with whitewashed lines on safe and level ground doing duty for thousand-foot drops. The technique was the same though. 'Just like kissing a duck's arse without getting a mouthful of feathers,' the MT sergeant had told her. 'You got to be quick. And always keep the door open so you can make a jump sideways if it don't come off right. Plenty of weight in front to keep the balance. In gear, clutch out – rev up like bloody hell – handbrake off – and shoot forward, doesn't matter what's in front of you. A busted radiator is better than a Government Issue tombstone.'

She had approximately a hundred and fifty words of basic Urdu, of which a hundred were Memsahibs' peremptories and the remainder extremely filthy terms of soldiers' abuse which she didn't understand but pronounced perfectly, parrotwise. A combination of the two had the effect of holding the driver in his seat. Then she made him slide gently sideways into the passenger seat while she slid behind the wheel herself. The engine was still purring softly. She made a quick check on the position of the handbrake – pushed the clutch out – slipped into first gear – took a deep breath – pressed down hard on the gas – released the handbrake and let the clutch in with a rush – and within seconds she was not only on the path, but she had missed the rockface on the inner side. The manoeuvre looked as simple as driving into a suburban garage. It was, of course, a supreme example of grossly over-estimated expertise boosting self-confidence to a point where fear, for the moment at least, did not exist. For the moment. The moment passed, and she felt sick and she knew her knees would not carry her for some more moments, so she turned and smiled wanly at the woman. Fear *did* exist for *her*. Her face was ashen and her mouth was opening and shutting without any sound emitting, and she was trembling in every limb.

Just to break an awkward silence, Jane said, 'That must have been rather upsetting for you.' And the woman laughed. She was still laughing five minutes later, while a worried Jane was carrying out the OCTU-taught drill of dealing with hysterical women Other Ranks – Officers, of course, being deemed immune to this plebian manifestation. She gently chided her at first and progressed through an ascending scale of severity to shaking and face slapping. The woman gradually subsided, and the driver partially redeemed himself by bringing an icebox from the trunk stuffed with White Rock Seltzer and Coca-Cola. A tumblerful of the former finally brought her down and she pointed a trembling finger at the driver and hissed, 'Get that black son-of-a-bitch out of this car before I kill the bastard.'

'Don't you want him to drive you to wherever you're going?' Jane ventured.

'That's Simla. *No thank you*. I'll walk first.'

'But it's twenty or thirty miles from here.'

'I'll still walk – at least to the nearest phone. Do you know where it is, honey?'

'Dagshai – the American hospital they're building there. They're on our military exchange but I'm sure they can get through to the civil one.'

'That's fine,' the woman said. She put out her hand. 'My dear, I don't know how I'll ever be able to thank you for what you've done. To go out on a limb like that – literally – for me – a total stranger – '

'Oh, please,' Jane said, charmingly embarrassed. 'It was nothing – '

'Nothing? Well, I suppose not, in a way.' The woman

292

smiled and patted Jane's hand. 'Maybe a lot of politicians in Washington would agree with that, and a lot more would want to ride you out of town on a rail for saving my neck – but *I'm* grateful. I'm Adelina Palgrave by the way.'

'How do you do. My name is Curtis – Jane Curtis.'

'Mrs or Miss?'

'Usually just plain Curtis nowadays. I'm in the Army.'

'Anything but *plain*. Lootenant?'

'Subaltern – the same thing. But what on earth are you doing out in the wilds like this – in this gorgeous great car?' Jane asked.

'Having a look at the American hospital you just mentioned. I'd been taking pictures – and we were on our way back when I found I'd left my camera behind. I told this guy to turn round, and he does just that – on the narrowest bit of the road he could find.' She fanned herself with her wide-brimmed sun hat. 'God! I died a thousand deaths in five minutes. He lost his head and wouldn't stop and let me out.'

'They do panic easily,' Jane said. 'He should be all right now I've put him back on the road.'

'He doesn't touch that wheel again,' Mrs Palgrave said emphatically. 'It's General Lumitz's own auto, and he loves it dearly. I wouldn't be able to face him if anything happened to it. No – I'll just walk back to the telephone as soon as my legs will hold me again and tell the General to send one of his marines down to ferry me back to Simla.'

'I could do that,' Jane said eagerly. 'Either ride to the hospital to phone, or drive you round if you don't feel up to it yourself.'

'*Me* drive on these crazy mountain roads?' Mrs Palgrave said, and shuddered. 'No way. I feel ashamed of myself chickening out, but I just couldn't. I'd be very grateful if you took me back. But what about your horse?'

'The driver can lead him along after us,' Jane said. She had had time to study the other woman now. She was darkly beautiful, magnolia skin accentuating raven hair and velvet eyes, with that ageless quality of which so many American women above a certain fiscal standard are the fortunate possessors. She could have been anything between thirty and forty-five, Jane decided. Attractive voice – faintly but unmistakably American, with what Jane, with her movie-attuned ear, had come to recognize as a slight Southern drawl.

Jane drove round the main road to the hospital after first handing over the reins of her pony to the downcast driver. Mrs Palgrave said, 'He's not going to lose his job. Tell him that, will you, my dear? – Look, what do I call you? Miss Curtis or Lootenant?'

'Jane, if you like.'

'I'd be delighted to. How I love the sweet old-fashioned names. I got stuck with Adelina because of a great-great-grandmother who was a god-daughter of a Russian Grand Duchess by that name, and it crops up in every generation like one of those awful hereditary diseases you hear of in some families. Say – you handle this car beautifully.'

'Who wouldn't?' Jane said. 'I adore big American cars.'

'So do I – just so as they're on big American roads. These mountain tracks scare the pants off me. How come you're so expert? I thought you British preferred smaller cars.'

'I owned a Buick before the war,' Jane told her. 'Then I drove a Chevrolet staff car for one of our Generals. I know the Simla–Kalka route quite well.'

Adelina sighed enviously. 'Do you now? I wish you were in *our* Army. I've got another three hill sanatorium places for our boys that I've got to look at before flying back to the States, and a lot of places on the plains. These Indian drivers may be all right, but they aren't exactly the most interesting of travelling companions on a long trip. I like to be able to talk – to discuss things – to *learn* something of the country. I hope I didn't hurt that boy's feelings back there. I don't usually swear like a teamster, but I remember calling him a son-of-a-bitch and a bastard. That was inexcusable, but I was terrified.'

'He wouldn't have understood,' Jane assured her. 'Very few of them speak English.'

'Maybe, but I'll still have to give him something just to ease my conscience. I notice *you* speak Indian very fluently.'

'Urdu? Not terribly well I'm afraid. We all have to be able

to make ourselves understood, of course. Are you a doctor, Mrs Palgrave?'

'Adelina, if I'm to call you Jane. No, not a doctor, honey. I just happen to be doing a world inspection tour of welfare facilities for our boys.'

'That sounds a big job,' Jane said, impressed.

'It is – but I feel very inadequate. I should spend so much longer in each country – but I can't. I'm tied to tight service schedules. Fly in – run round – fly out again when they tell you your plane is ready. A month to do the whole of India, camps, airfields and hospitals. What the hell – ' She shrugged hopelessly.

They arrived in front of the hospital. Hordes of coolies were working under the supervision of Anglo-Indian foremen and a sense of urgency was very evident.

'But it's still behind planning time,' Adelina complained. 'The first twelve convalescents should be arriving up from Calcutta in less than a week. It doesn't look as if they're going to be very comfortable, poor boys. And we've got staffing problems. We should have six nurses to start with – a colonel, a major, a captain and three lootenants. We're actually going to get a major and a lootenant. Same with the medical staff – shortages, shortages, shortages. I won't be a minute, honey.' She ran up the steps and disappeared into the cool depths of the building, to reappear a few minutes later grimacing with frustration. 'Jane dear,' she called. 'Can you help me with this dingus? It's one of these things you've got to turn a handle on, like Bell did when he invented the durned thing.'

Jane went in and joined her and juggled with the intricacies of the field telephone, Mark III(a) and got through to the military exchange at Kasauli. She turned to Adelina. 'Who shall I ask for?'

'General Lumitz – G.1, Welfare,' Adelina told her.

'Sorry please,' the Indian operator answered when she asked for Simla. 'Simla line out – delay maybe one hour. Keep call in hand, or you ring again later?'

'Cancel,' said Jane resignedly, and hung up. 'The line is out from Kasauli, I'm afraid,' she told Adelina. 'It's always

295

happening. We usually use radio for anything urgent, but of course you wouldn't have it here yet, would you?' Then as the American shook her head angrily, an idea came to Jane. 'I'll see if I can get through to our place and get them to relay the message.'

This time she was more successful, and she asked to be put through to the Adjutant.

'I'm trying to assist an American – Mrs Palgrave – who I found in difficulties with transport near the new American hospital at Dagshai,' she said crisply and professionally. 'The Simla telephone link through Kasauli is out at the moment. Could you please relay a message to – ' She looked at Adelina inquiringly, then read from a slip on which the other had written, ' – General Merril G. Lumitz, US Army – G.1 Welfare – Simla 391, extension 285. Message begins: Senator Adelina Palgrave – ' Jane blinked as she read the words, 'requests that another driver be sent to collect her and car from American Officers' Sanatorium, Dagshai – ' then, as pure inspiration came to her, she winked at Adelina and went on, 'or that services of the British driver who has been helping should be borrowed from her unit, Jaigaon Convalescent Depot. Message ends.'

'What are you trying to wangle, Curtis?' the Adjutant said suspiciously.

'I'm relaying a message, ma'am,' Jane said with dignity. 'Would you prefer to speak with Senator Palgrave yourself?'

'Wait,' said the Adjutant curtly, and rang off.

They waited twenty minutes, nibbling chicken sandwiches and drinking Coca-Cola from the icebox, then the field set tinkled tinnily, and the Adjutant said, even more curtly, 'Speak to the Commandant, Curtis.'

'Jane, dear,' said Fenella. 'I've just been talking to General Lumitz – yes, do that, will you, dear – drive the Senator on to Simla, and continue to render any further assistance she may need. I *do* like my officers to use their initiative like this. So splendid for inter-Allied relations. Jolly good show, my dear. Carry on. The General will see you safely delivered back here afterwards.'

'Yes, ma'am – Thank you, ma'am,' Jane murmured modestly.

Adelina was ecstatic. 'You know, that was in my mean, sneaky little mind all the time,' she said, 'but I hadn't the gall to suggest it. Honey, you're all wool and a yard wide. This will be wonderful.'

She made arrangements with the chief foreman to have a coolie lead the pony back to Jaigaon, then they set out up the road to Simla, in reverse order to that of her previous journey over this same route, for now she, an officer, and her passenger, a Senator of the United States, were in front, with the sorrowing Sikh driver behind.

Lunch in the small but very comfortable Officers' Club of the American Liaison Headquarters was the best and most lavish meal she had eaten since the halcyon days of Hank at his most prodigal – and she was cossetted and courted and made much of, and a coterie of very senior officers led by the General took her round the PX and loaded her with things she thought had vanished forever – cosmetics, scent, candy, nylons – a flood of gifts which her shy protests did nothing to stem. They pressed her to stay overnight, but, conscious of her by now somewhat damp and dusty riding clothes, she resolutely set her face against this, so they reluctantly saw her off from the lower car park just before the barrier closed the route at nightfall.

Adelina said, 'I wouldn't do anything you didn't want, honey – but I'd certainly like you to come round with me to the other places I've got to see at Naini Tal and Dalhousie – up in the hills like this. How'd it be if I tried to arrange it? It'd only take you away from your duties for a month.'

'I'd love to,' Jane said, her voice trembling with sincerity. 'So splendid for inter-Allied relations.'

Chapter Fourteen

It was handled with polished diplomatic dexterity, and Fenella, far from reacting in the manner of a commanding officer having one of her staff filched by higher authority, beamed upon Jane when the request was received.

'This is an honour for the Corps, Jane dear,' she said. 'One in which we can all share. The Americans have had the *sweetest* things to say about you, and GHQ are enormously pleased. There has been the teeniest bit of friction from time to time between their higher echelons and ours, so this sort of thing can't do anything but good. Away you go. I know you'll do everything that is expected of you in a manner which will continue to make us all proud of the Service we belong to. You're seconded to them for a month.'

Fenton said, rather more succinctly, 'Lucky bitch. Bring us a couple of cartons of Camel cigarettes when you come back. These Victory V horseshit things are burning the tonsils out of me.'

The only cloud upon the horizon had been Dan's behaviour. That had really frightened her, because, when she had broken the news to him of her impending departure, he had raved and screamed and rushed off into the darkness, leaving her in the middle of the Figure-of-Eight, and the following morning she had received a scrawled, disjointed note from him begging to see her immediately – in broad daylight, which of course was impossible. She worried greatly in the staff car which took her over to Simla – for the first twenty minutes, then sensibly put it out of her mind for the time being. Many things could come about in a month, she decided.

They came down to Kalka and then swung north through Kathgodam to Naini Tal – to Rawalpindi – Lahore – Jaipur,

298

and on to her old stamping ground of New Delhi – the whole tour being one triumphant procession, with American and British officials, both military and civil, receiving them with little short of royal protocol. They picked up a smart young Marine sergeant at one of the earlier camps and Jane ceased to be the driver, and became the personal assistant, ADC, and Lady-in-Waiting – someone whom, if deemed fit by the gods of Simla to accompany the representative of FDR himself, was surely a person to be deferred to in her own right. And she very wisely did not let it go to her head. If the adulation became a shade too perfervid, or if the younger members of the various messes and Officers' Clubs crowded over-closely round her, she smiled gently and modestly and slipped into the background, a fact that was noted and appreciated by this adept of Washington tactics.

'I don't know what I'd have done if it had not been for this little girl of yours,' Jane heard her say to a senior British officer on more than one occasion. 'She started off by saving my life and since then she's become a daughter to me. I didn't think they bred them like this any longer – anywhere.'

She was a woman, and a politician, who above all else adored a good listener – and Jane was that to perfection and so, in the long hours they drove between stations, she heard the story of the older woman's life – her girlhood in Alabama – Bryn Mawr days – early interest in politics – her husband, now dead – her beautiful home in Maryland and, above all, her son, Stewart, now piloting a fighter somewhere in the Pacific theatre. It was some days before Adelina mentioned him, but once she had, the floodgates were opened.

'Kick me in the ankle, honey,' she said, 'when you feel you can take no more about him. I try, I really do try, to keep him out of day-to-day routine because I know how fond mammas can bore the pants off people about their kids – but, oh God, how I pray for the end of this thing – and for him to have come through it unharmed – or not harmed much – or even to be wounded in combat, but not seriously – just enough to get him out of it till the whole damn thing is over. Yes, I'm chicken enough to wish that – when other mothers have more than one son in it – and husbands, and have lost them. I find myself praying for special consideration – "Spare him, God, and I'll promise you anything you want – and *keep* the promise. Take some other woman's son – but don't take mine." I wait for that cable – or telephone call – that – ' She would often choke on her words, and Jane was wise enough not to offer either sympathy or reassurance. She would merely take the other woman's hand and hold it, and that simple action in itself was usually enough to strengthen her again.

Adelina once said, 'How selfish and unbalanced one can get. I go on and on about my woes, my hopes and my fears – and never once have I asked you about *your* problems. Your family, honey – what about them? Are they in a safe area? I mean, they're not being bombed or anything like that – ?'

Jane had not answered immediately. She sat looking out of the car window for a long time until Adelina, concerned, said, 'Say! I haven't said anything out of line, have I?'

Jane shook her head and smiled sadly. 'No – nothing, Adelina dear – it's just that – well, my mother – I don't even remember her. She died when I was a small child, and I have been brought up almost entirely by nannies and governesses.'

'Oh, for God's sake!' said the distressed Adelina. 'What about your father – ?'

'I think he was always rather disappointed that I wasn't a boy. You see, in our old English families it's so important to have a son to take over the estate. *I* certainly never saw much of my father. He travelled a lot – big game hunting and all that sort of thing.'

'All right,' said Adelina indignantly. 'So the jerk – er – sorry – your father didn't have a son – but he had one hell of a nice daughter to take over his goddamn estate. Didn't *that* mean anything to him?'

'Oh, I'm sure it did. He was never unkind or wilfully neglectful of me – '

'That was big of him.'

'But it didn't make any difference one way or the other in the end. He was ruined by the war – then he died.' She shrugged and smiled bravely. 'There's no more estate – and in a way I'm very glad. It would have been a huge responsibility – and I want to be free – free!'

'You mean he didn't leave you *anything*?'

'Oh – a small amount of money – and various heirlooms. Nothing very much. The title was in another branch of the family, anyway.'

'I don't think it's right,' Adelina averred. 'I don't want to criticize your country, my dear, which, after all, gave *my* country the law – but this system of your aristocracy almost deifying the eldest son to the disadvantage of all the others – particularly the girls – Pah! It makes me wild. You should stand up more for yourselves – fight for your rights – '

'Perhaps we should – but really it doesn't worry me. I just don't think about it – and I certainly never *talk* about it.'

The older woman put an arm round Jane's shoulders. 'I guess that's wise at that,' she said. 'But let me tell you one thing. Your father might have been sore because he didn't have a son. I think the sorrow of *my* life is that I never had a daughter. Oh, make no mistake – I don't mean in place of a son. I mean as well as. You know – there are things one can only discuss with another woman – a woman who is really close to one. So honey, if you ever feel you want to adopt a family in place of the one you never really had – well, here's one waiting for you. Ready made. Will you remember that? Promise?'

'I promise,' Jane said in a small voice, then fumbled for her handkerchief.

They came at last to the big American airbase at Nirsa, whence flew the bombers that were softening up the defences of Rangoon before the air-and-seaborne invasion that was now planned by the Fourteenth Army, and also the supply planes taking food and ammunition over the Hump to Chiang Kai-shek's forces in Chungking. This was their biggest reception yet, and there was a *Life* camera and reporter team waiting to record it, and Jane was photographed again and again, with Adelina, and solo, and with half a hundred keen, clean-run, crew-cut, bronzed young American fliers.

And then the cable arrived.

They were three days ahead of schedule and it had been following them around and was correspondingly delayed. It stated, 'Lieutenant Stewart Jerome Palgrave shot down off Akyab Stop Recovered British coastal forces Stop Condition serious not critical repeat not critical Stop Location Milhosp Calcutta Stop Casevac-cal.'

Adelina took it remarkably calmly, her face a frozen mask, and within twenty minutes they were being flown down to Dum Dum, in the Commanding General's personal aircraft, and there was a staff car waiting for them on the tarmac.

'Fighter cover to the bombers round-the-clocking Rangoon,' the Marine colonel who met them explained. 'He was carrier-based in Bay of Bengal, South. Hadn't been with us long. Hard luck. He's a good boy, Senator. You've got reason to be proud of him.'

'The hell with that,' she snapped. 'How is he?'

'Fine – just fine. Compound fractures both legs, but we have some mighty fine surgeons and orthopedes here and he's being attended to right at this moment,' the colonel told her. 'One or two other little things that they'll tell you about when we get to the hospital – but he's fine – just fine.'

They had in fact been attending to the fractures and the other little things when they arrived, and he was still under heavy anaesthesis, and Adelina, tightly holding Jane's hand, was showing magnificent courage and admirable restraint in face of the colonel's non-stop 'fine – just fine' – but the restraint cracked when an aide handed her a cable and begged her to read it urgently. She verged on lewdness then and snatched the opened form from the aide's hand. It took a minute or so to register, with the close little knot of people round them looking worried.

'President Franklin Delano Roosevelt passed away this a.m. April twelve nineteen-forty-five,' she read aloud slowly. 'That means Truman takes over,' she went on, and Jane marvelled at her complete lack of emotion. 'Jane dear – the one thing that could take me away from here at this moment has happened – '

'We can get you out by Liberator, Senator, in an hour. All long distance flights close down after that owing to operational necessity. That is what I've been trying to tell you,' the aide explained.

'Sorry,' Adelina said. 'Forgive me – I was a little pre-occupied, I guess. I want five minutes with this young woman, then I'm at your disposal. I would also like to speak to the General again.'

To Jane she said, 'Stay with him, my dear. Stay with him for the rest of the month you have been assigned to me – and report to me, *truthfully*, not just comfortingly, every day until he's out of danger. You heard that damned fool of a colonel, with his "fine – just fine". I don't trust any of them. If you think at the end of the month you ought to stay longer, let the General know – I'll tell you the channels, and it will be arranged. Will you do that for me, Jane?'

'I'll do that,' Jane told her earnestly.

But she didn't need to ask for an extension of her secondment, because Stewart had recovered sufficiently by the end of the month to make his removal to the cool hills both advisable and practical.

'Dagshai will undoubtedly be the best place,' the American surgeon said. 'They've got a skin unit in Kasauli near by, and the poor guy has got prickly heat under his plaster cast.' And although Jane would have preferred somewhere further away from Jaigaon and Dan, she had no feasible grounds for such a request.

They travelled up to Kalka in an air-conditioned ambulance coach attached to the Delhi Mail, and thence in specially requisitioned motor ambulances – nor was it all shameless nepotism, because there were twenty other stretcher cases travelling with them, not to mention the *Life* camera team who saw in this an even bigger feature than they had envisaged originally.

Stewart held her hand when she took her leave of him before returning to Jaigaon. 'You'll come back? You'll come back every day?' he begged.

'Of course I will,' she promised softly. 'I told your mother I would.'

'It wasn't for Mom's sake I was asking,' he grinned. Very little of the grin could be seen at this stage, because his head, after extensive skull surgery – just another of the 'one or two other little things' – was still heavily bandaged, and only a small portion of his face was uncovered – and that was still, after five weeks, heavily pigmented with the yellow picric acid the first aid team had applied to the torn and burnt flesh at the time of his rescue. In fact he was only now beginning to emerge as a personality as the tubes were removed from his throat and he was able to whisper hoarsely.

She was received back into the fold right royally by Fenella, the more so because the *Life* team followed her across in order to obtain more background shots of the establishment that could produce English roses of this quality in the foothills of the Himalayas. That was what they called her. 'The English Rose of the Himalayas. The Beautiful Girl who had Chosen to Serve Her Country on the Slopes of Mount Everest Itself Who, in her Compassion, Differentiated in No Way Between British and American Wounded. Their Need was Her Inspiration.' The pictures were magnificent – the one on the cover showing her kneeling beside a stretcher holding a mug of water to the lips of a wounded GI. Inside she was shown against American aircraft, with and without the Senator, at the wheel of a staff car and, the one she preferred to all others, on her pony at the end of 'the punishing ride she took every day through danger-ous jungle' – no, not exactly Jap infested, but there were panthers and bears around, weren't there? – between her own station at Jaigaon and the one at Dagshai with which she so generously shared her services – and then there were others of her beside the bed of Lieutenant Stewart J. Palgrave, the gallant young Marine flyer who happened, quite incidentally, to be the son of Senator Adelina Palgrave.

That was the one that Dan seized upon with the greatest fury when he intercepted her the day the much thumbed copy of *Life* came into his hands.

'If you see the bastard again, I'll kill him,' he told her, and she knew with absolute certainty that he was speaking no more than the plain, cold truth.

'Very well, dear,' she said resignedly. 'I think you're being silly, but if you insist, I won't go over again – except to tell them that I have to give up helping out.'

A series of minor circumstances played right into her hands, as it happened. There was a cocktail party in the medical mess that night, and Colonel O'Riordan, with a Dublin man's eye for a pretty girl, made much of her, and invited her to accompany him to Simla the following day as he had to go there for a three-day conference, but she had, of course, regretfully to decline on the score of duty. Fenton, with the task she hated more than any other having been completed that afternoon – the making up of a supplementary and immediate reinforcement draft – drank far more than was good for her, so it was an easy matter for Jane to slip into the Adjutant's office and whip Dan's card out of the 'C' Remain frame and slip it into the 'FFP' drafting pool – and he was rudely awakened at dawn the following day by the Draft Conducting NCO who wanted to know why the bloody hell he wasn't out on the parade ground with the rest of the blokes – and to get his shrimshanking, leadswinging bleeding carcase out there with his kit ek dum, jaldi, jaldi. Dan, with the habit of obedience firmly inculcated after eight years' service – and in too great a state of shock even to think of questioning the order – went – and was put on a charge by the Garrison Sergeant-Major for being late on parade and unshaven to boot – and was, in fact, still on the Defaulters' List five days later, when he was killed in company with seven others by a Jap mortar bomb which landed on the Advanced Casualty Clearing Post outside Mandalay, in the last set battle of the Burma campaign.

Colonel O'Riordan was very angry and Fenton was severely reprimanded for carelessness. Jane was very sad.

And so the war ended in Europe on the eighth of May, and that in the Far East with the blotting out of Hiroshima on the fifth of August, and now the shouting and the tumult were dying and the captains and the kings were departing in the Gotterdammerung of the Indian Empire – and Jane had written to Adelina – ' – of course I love him, but I know how close you two are, and after all, you know so little of me, so I have not said yes – not until I hear from you and know you approve. If you don't, then that is the end of it, but I shall always be happy to know that I was able to help a little at a very worrying time – ' and quite a lot more in the same vein. The answer had come by cable via American Headquarters in New Delhi. 'Bless you my children Stop Happier than I can say in this durn cable Stop Would dearly love wedding to take place here but won't stand in way if you can't wait Stop All my heart with you both Stop Love Stop Adelina Ends.'

Stewart said '*Now*', but Jane said, 'Darling, it's little enough that she's asking. Don't let us spoil it for her.'

'Have you ever seen a Washington wedding?' Stewart asked. 'No? Well I have – plenty – and I'd rather we did it here, quietly, with our chaplain in the driving seat.'

'We owe her too much,' Jane said wisely, and very firmly. 'Don't let us be selfish. We've got all the happiness in the world between us. Can't we share a little of it with someone who loves us so dearly?'

'Mom has been living my life for me, making my decisions and steering me gently and lovingly along the paths *she* has chosen for me for as long as I can remember,' Stewart said bitterly. 'I had been hoping that I could start thinking for myself.'

'You can, darling,' Jane said softly. 'You will make *all* the decisions. I'm an old-fashioned gal – I don't want to interfere in the really important things. But in this – I do so much want to start off properly with your mother – I don't want to put a foot wrong. Let us wait until we arrive in Washington and you've had your last operation, so we won't have that looming over us.' And he agreed, albeit reluctantly, and two days later all the Dagshai patients were evacuated to Kalka and thence by various means to America – Stewart by air from New Delhi to London and on to Washington. He had moved heaven and earth to get Jane a passage with him, but with the Casualty Evacuation Service jammed to beyond capacity with wounded and sick plus debilitated prisoners of war, released in their thousands from the Japanese cages, every seat counted, so Jane, a fit person, was excluded. He flatly refused to go without her, but the war was over now, and heroes were already becoming just a little dated, and Adelina couldn't be contacted in time, so his stretcher was picked up peremptorily and he was loaded into an ambulance.

'Don't worry, darling, I won't be far behind,' Jane called after him, and then set about obtaining an early discharge and a passage to America through British channels – and here she ran head on to an unsurmountable obstacle. There was only one route to America for the happy but impatient band that had become known overnight as the GI Brides, and that was by a special steamer that sailed every two months from Southampton. It was that way or not at all she was told in very definite terms. So she sent a letter to Stewart, and another to Adelina, and started on the long road Home – down from the hills to Kalka – and on to New Delhi, where she found nobody of any use to her in her search for a priority air passage, so she cut her losses and settled for Deolali and the Demobilization Depot (Women), and then a sea passage on a hastily commandeered veteran of the Mecca–Medina pilgrim trade, which compared most unfavourably with her passage out, but she was buoyed up now by excited anticipation. A door had closed behind her, but another had opened, breathtaking in its potentiality.

The ship was full of dispirited Memsahibs heading back to suburban anonymity in grey, war-emasculated, ration-ridden Britain, while she was going on to brighter things. They looked at her enviously, these grandes dames of so recent a yesterday, because copies of the edition of *Life* that she had graced were still in circulation and it was not long before her presence was bruited throughout the ship. She was, by a process of natural selection, on the Captain's Table; the crummy little cabin she had been allocated together with a major's wife, a nursing sister and some minor official's elderly widow, was quickly changed by a hopeful and concupiscent purser, who was foredoomed to disappointment, for a single berther on the promenade deck. The ship, like all dreary Ministry of Transport controlled vessels, was dry, but she and a select coterie of very senior people were invited every day to luncheon and to pre-dinner drinks in the Captain's day-room – and a deckchair was permanently set for her on the bridge deck high above the shockingly overcrowded common herd. But in spite of it all she remained sweet, kind and gracious, and she was always ready to look after a child while the harassed mother washed and ironed clothes on this ill-found and laundryless ship, and she helped greatly with a series of concerts that were organized to raise funds for some soldiers' widows and orphans who were being repatriated. 'I hate bloody Memsahibs,' the Chief Steward, who could be counted an authority after twenty-five years in the Indian trade, was heard to say, 'but that one is all right. A lady – a pukkha lady. You can tell 'em – the real ones.'

So, all in all, it was not an entirely unenjoyable journey, and the coping-stone was placed upon it when they docked in Liverpool – for there, on Prince's Landing Stage, was Adelina and what looked like half the staff of the American Embassy – not to mention the ubiquitous *Life* camera team, complete with lighting men – and since, as the Welsh say, where there's a crow, there'll come a crow – photographers from the British Press had gathered also.

Yes, it was a royal homecoming for the Rose of the Himalayas, and Adelina, who had made it all possible, was in transports of delight – as was her PR man.

Adelina shouted in her ear over the uproar, 'Stewart sends his love, honey. He went into hospital for the final operation a week ago – and he's fine – just fine, as that damfool colonel in Calcutta would say. He'll be up by the time we get there in two weeks – Wedding early next month – Episcopal cathedral – God's sake let's get out of this ruckus – no, no more pictures, boys, please – can't you see my daughter-in-law-to-be is just about all in – ?'

Limousines whisked them up to Lime Street station after Jane's scanty luggage had been waved through diplomatic channels, and Adelina explained that she had been nominated as the United States delegate to the International Refugees' Council presently meeting in Paris, but was playing hookey, as she called it, for two days to see Jane installed in her suite at the Savoy until she returned at the end of the week.

'No good taking you over there with me, honey. We're going round the most God awful camps all the time, and you'd be dumped in the hotel all day on your own, because the Paris Embassy isn't properly opened yet. Things are tough in this country, but not nearly as tough as on the Continent. The Savoy is all right though – so you just get your feet up and rest until I come back on Saturday. We sail Wednesday on the *Queen Mary* – '

And the Savoy, thought Jane, was very much all right. The Senator's suite consisted of a huge drawing room, two bedrooms, and two bathrooms. In Jane's bedroom were several intriguing parcels, and there were dresses hanging in the wardrobe together with a very good fur coat.

'A bit of shopping I did for you the other side, honey,' Adelina explained. 'I think I managed to guess your size fairly accurately. I knew you'd need warmer stuff than you'd have after nearly six years out there in India. You don't have to wear it, or even like it – but it will tide you over until you can do some real shopping in New York. The alley-cat mink there is an old one of mine – maybe motheaten, but cosy. Now you have a rest, then a leisurely bath and change into something simple – that little blue number there'd suit you fine. We've got a few people dropping in for drinks before dinner this evening. You say thanks just once again and I'll bean you. You don't thank *family*, you mut.'

'No?' said Jane. 'But is there any rule against having a wonderful, warm, coming-home sort of feeling inside – and wanting to cry even though you're happy?'

'No rule against that, honey,' Adelina said, her own eyes filling.

The evening papers had come out while she slept, and Adelina had placed them on the coverlet of her bed. She viewed them with some misgiving at first, particularly the *Evening Standard*, which had reproduced the cover picture from *Life*, over three columns of the front page, together with pictures taken that morning in Liverpool. Was it wise? she wondered, then put her fears aside impatiently. How could she have stopped it? She looked into her mirror. No, that face was vastly different from that of Maxine Wilmott. *She* used to pluck her eyebrows to a thin hairline, until she learned that it was considered vulgar. Now they were natural, and the more beautiful for it – and the difference it made to her face was unbelievable. Her hair was so different too – again a reversion to the natural. Six years ago she would have felt half naked had she not used a curling iron on it each day. Now it fell in its own soft waves – and, tell it not in Garth, she used a rinse in her unregenerate days and the colour had been considerably lighter. Now it was its proper lovely chestnut. And she wore her clothes differently – and carried herself well – and had learned to eat wisely, and had lost a lot of puppy fat as a result. No – nobody would equate Miss Jane Curtis from India, and bound for Washington, with Maxine Wilmott, from Brixton, and bound for Newcastle-on-Tyne when last heard of six years and more ago.

'The English Rose of the Himalayas' – what a lovely phrase, she thought. 'Soon to marry Stewart Palgrave, the American air ace – son of that redoubtable Anglophile Senator Adelina Palgrave, and a millionaire in his own right by virtue of huge legacies from his father and two childless uncles.' Her eyes widened. Nobody had ever mentioned *that* before –

The few people dropping in for drinks turned out to be a dozen of the 'Feed my Lambs' Movement, one of the many well-intentioned but woolly factions proliferating in advance of official Marshall Aid that were currently paying assiduous court to Adelina and similar cornucopias from across the Atlantic. Their leader, a lean and earnest missionary, was putting forward the claims of India as distinct from the war areas further east.

'They weren't invaded west of Assam and the Arrakan,' he was saying. 'Yes – we know that – but they *are* starving,

Senator. They are starving in Bengal, in Orissa, Bihar and the Central Provinces. God knows I would not divert one grain of rice from the war-afflicted, but we must not lose sight of those out of the front-line limelight.'

'I know, I know,' Adelina agreed sympathetically. 'I promise you something is going to be done for those areas – for all India, Reverend.' She put her arm round Jane's shoulders. 'This little girl – my daughter-in-law soon to be – she doesn't know it yet, but she is to be my personal representative out there. She knows India – better than all the officials I met there during the whole of my visit. She took me round – showed me the real India – and I saw the dumb suffering in the children's eyes. She speaks the language – she has the trust of the people. She is going back there, with my son, after they are married, to do our work.'

'Splendid!' the missionary cried enthusiastically. 'They trust women more readily than men. They still garland the statue of Queen Victoria out there, you know. "The Bara Memsahib" they call her – that means "The Great Lady" – and not in any way ironically. Oh, *what* a good idea! Our new Bara Memsahib – so young, and yet I'm sure, so capable.'

'Can I quote that, Senator?' the PR man asked. 'I saw a couple of the Press boys down below.'

'Leave it until I clear it with the Committee in Paris in the next two or three days,' the Senator said. 'I'll want to tell the Secretary of State too. Come to that I ought to clear it with the Bara Memsahib herself. She hasn't even been asked if she'll take it on yet.' She turned and smiled fondly at Jane. 'What about it, honey? Are you going to help me in this? I tell you, it's one heck of a woman-sized job.'

'Oh, Adelina dear, just give me the opportunity,' Jane breathed. 'If you asked me now if there was anything – *anything* in this wide world I'd rather do – Oh, Adelina – ' Words failed her.

'Atta girl,' said Adelina, and turned back to the assemblage. 'Well, there you are, folks – that's settled. And now – '

The telephone was ringing softly in the background, but Adelina was in full spate and did not hear it. The PR man answered, then glanced across at Jane. 'For you,' he whispered.

Jane took the telephone and said, 'Hello – Jane Curtis speaking.'

'There are three people asking for you, Miss Curtis,' the reception clerk said. 'A Mr and Mrs Wilmott and Captain Sprunt. Shall I send them up?'

Chapter Fifteen

Winter 1946

She lay in bed, listening to the faint distant hum of the sparse London traffic. She hadn't managed badly, she thought. Six years of watching and learning had come to her aid, and she had ridden the punch like a boxer and, although damaged and almost out on her feet, she had still been able to say coldly, 'I don't know anybody of those names – you will *not* send them up, and please don't put any more calls through to this room.' But she hadn't been able to control the draining of blood from her face, and Adelina, glancing across the room, saw that she was white and trembling, and she rushed to her side.

'For God's sake, honey,' she said, deeply concerned. 'You're bushed. You're completely tired after that durned ship, and here we are loading more on to your shoulders.'

'I'm all right, Adelina – I really am,' Jane had tried to assure her, but the Senator would have none of it.

'Off to bed with you,' she insisted, 'and you'll stay there all day tomorrow if I have to hogtie you. Come on – say good night to these good people, and away you go.'

And she had been glad to go, although it had meant tossing sleeplessly until early morning, her thoughts, fears and wholly irrational hopes chasing each other in succession through her fevered brain. Would her denial of them have put them off for good? Were they certain of her identity – or, struck by the resemblance in those horrible Press photos, were they just drawing a bow at a venture? – just checking? Damn! Damn! Damn! If only she had had the sense to wear dark sunglasses, like Greta Garbo. But who would have thought of the Press waiting for her here – in England? But perhaps she'd scared them. They wouldn't come back. Two of them had convictions for blackmail. They couldn't risk too much. Might that be a good idea? Take the fight to them? Get a taxi and go out to Brixton while Adelina was away, and face them? Offer them money? No – fatal. They'd know she was frightened then, and they'd never leave her alone thereafter, even in America. All right then – no money – just say, 'Lay off or I'll have the police in' – 'Miss X' them. Suppose they called her bluff? What if they said, 'Go ahead. We haven't asked you for anything. We just recognized your pictures in the paper and came to verify. Natural thing to do, isn't it? Blood's thicker than water. We just wanted to see you – to know that you were all right. We don't want anything from you. We wouldn't take it if you offered it. Go ahead – call the police.' But they wouldn't – or would they? That old swine Uncle Bill, he'd do anything for money. Oh God! Oh God! Oh God! – If only she'd gone straight to America – if only Adelina hadn't been here to meet her with those *bloody* reporters and cameramen – And so on, until Adelina tiptoed in before dawn to say *au revoir* before leaving for her special plane at Croydon.

'Stay right here, honey,' she had said. 'You want two days' solid rest. I'll call from Paris as often as I can – just so as these terrible phones are working properly – to check on you, and I'll take a hickory to you if I find you're out of this bed. Promise?'

'I'll promise,' Jane smiled. 'Thank you so much, Adelina. You're so good to me.'

'Nuts,' said Adelina tersely. 'The boot's on the other foot. Now go to sleep again. I'll tell them not to disturb you till you ring for something. Bye, honey. I'll try and be back by the weekend, but I may be held over until Monday or Tuesday. I'll be calling you though, all the time. Now you rest – you've got a big job ahead of you.' And she tiptoed out again.

She was glad to obey because she discovered that she really was tired. She had a light breakfast, then sat in her dressing gown until midmorning, reading and browsing through the pile of books and magazines that filled a large canterbury in the drawing-room, then she bathed and spent much time trying on the clothes that Adelina had provided. She lunched in the suite, then read some more, and was surprised at the speed with which the day had passed, because she had not found one minute hanging heavily on her hands. The telephone rang late in the afternoon and Reception said apologetically, 'Senator Palgrave gave orders that you were not to be disturbed, madam, so no calls have been put through to you, but now Paris is calling. Do you wish to take it?'

'Oh, yes please,' Jane said, and then Adelina was on the line.

'Are you obeying orders?' she asked.

'Yes indeed,' Jane told her brightly. 'I haven't been out all day.'

'Good girl. All right – but don't get bored. Tell them down at the desk to get you some theatre tickets – anything you think you'd like – and I've told them at the Embassy to send you an overseas visitor's permit so you won't have to use those coupon dinguses they give you people to buy clothes with. You should get it tomorrow morning – then you can do some shopping. I've got charge accounts at Harrods, Liberty's and Fortnum and Mason. Get what you want – but *don't overtire yourself.* I'm afraid I'm not going to make it back before Tuesday. OK, honey – I'll call you again tomorrow.'

She slept better that night, because the terror had receded. Just hang on here in the citadel, she told herself, where no danger could reach her. Hang on until Tuesday – and then they'd be away to Southampton – and the *Queen Mary* – and the wide ocean would be between her and this awful thing that had crawled out of the pit of the past. She shuddered, then shrugged impatiently and rang down for a double martini and the dinner menu.

'I thought you'd like the Sunday papers, miss,' the floor waiter said, 'so I've brought them all. The pictures are very good in some of them.' He put the breakfast tray down on the bedside table and went out.

The top one – by accident or design – was *Attention*, a tabloid of fairly recent vintage that dealt in the 'Butler to

Lord and Lady Scantlebury Tells All' type of story. The *Life* cover picture, which had now apparently been syndicated, took up one half of the front page, under the banner headline of 'MYSTERY OF THE HIMALAYAN ROSE SOLVED!' and the by-lines, 'Brixton Girl Makes Good in India', and 'Echoes of Famous Blackmail Trial'. There were pictures of Mum and Dad and Uncle Bill together with one of herself hurrying away from the Old Bailey with Mr Sinclair and a bewigged barrister – and much more recent ones of Adelina meeting her at Liverpool. The name Maxine Wilmott leapt out of the paper at her – and Jane Curtis – and the words Deed Poll – Attempted Blackmail – Acquitted – Mr X – Father and Uncle Sentenced – 'Mother says "No bitterness – It is *her* life" – "Proud of her and wonderful work she has done in India for Our Boys and Yanks", says Father – "We have paid our debt to society".'

Then she was falling into a bottomless pit of blackness.

The letter, delivered by Embassy courier, stated tersely that Senator Adelina Palgrave was returning to America direct from Paris and that there would be no further communication from her, but that Miss Curtis was at liberty to remain in the Savoy suite until 12.30 p.m. that day. The effects the Senator had left there could be regarded by Miss Curtis as her property.

The telephone rang two hours later, and Uncle Bill said, more in sorrow than in anger, 'We wouldn't have pulled the bung on you like that, lovie, if only you hadn't given us the bum's rush out of that posh pub of yours. That hurt, Max. Your own flesh and blood, lovie. We'd even forgiven you for the fifty quid. Remember that, Max? I sent you a note from the Bailey after your dad and me had been done. In a cigarette tin, I told you. Under the floorboards in the bathroom. Get hold of it, I said, and let your ma have a couple of quid a week until your dad gets out again. Don't give it to her all at once because she wouldn't know how to handle it proper, I said. Remember, Max? You went and got it, didn't you? And you hung on to it. That was a bit naughty, lovie. But we don't bear no hard feelings. Like your dad said to the newspaper blokes, we're *proud* of you, Max. And now we've *all* paid our debt to society. Good-bye, dear.'

Without a word she replaced the telephone, then sat for a long time looking out of the window towards the river, over the bare and dripping trees along the Embankment. There was a dank grey mist over the water. So this was it, she thought dully. The end. And she had almost made it. Within a hair's breadth of being *there* – home and dried.

So what now? Just sit here until they sent the hall porter to dump her, bag and baggage, out into the Strand? No – she wouldn't wait for that final indignity. She'd have to make a move. But where? Where in the name of God did one go in post-war England, in the lousy winter? Certainly not to another London hotel. Not a posh one, anyhow. The pack had smelled blood now. They'd pick up her scent and be after her. That little pub in Richmond where George had put her after the trial? She shuddered. No, thank you. No retracing of steps. Whenever she had made a break from cover in previous crises she had always gone for fresh woods and pastures new – and she had finished right end up every time. And she would again, by God. No – this wasn't the end, she swore through set teeth.

She rose from her chair and took her bank passbook from her dressing-case. She had had little occasion to spend money over the last six months, and her accumulated back-pay plus her gratuity, when added to the nest-egg she had always kept intact since those terrible early days in Bombay, made quite an impressive total. Just over two thousand pounds. A girl with her head screwed on the right way could go far on that. No – she wasn't finished. Not yet.

She had better get on with her packing, she decided, and went through to the bedroom.

The papers were still strewn on and around the bed, the crass headlines and her own damned silly Mona Lisa smirk, as she now saw it, mocking her from a dozen different angles. Furiously she started to bundle them and stuff them into the wastepaper basket.

And then she saw it.

Robert gazing at her steadfastly from the gossip columns of one of the soberer weeklies.

She stared at the picture in blank disbelief, the text of the accompanying paragraph not at first registering with her –

– another career soldier sees the warning light? Colonel Robert Maldwyn Powell, an old Etonian with a most distinguished war record, stated that with the coming of Independence he could see a diminishing role for British officers in the Indian Army, 'and rightly so,' he added. At the same time, Colonel Powell went on, we will undoubtedly be required there in business for many years to come, which was his reason for leaving the Service and accepting a seat on the board of the Hollins-Bland Tea Company, with Headquarters in Assam. A keen sportsman – he was the pre-War Number Three for the All-India polo side – and a bachelor, he was once tipped as military secretary to Earl Mountbatten, who might well be the last Viceroy to be appointed, but it is said that he declined the post because –

The Deputy Assistant Manager tapped softly once again and then, receiving no reply, signed to the floor waiter to use his pass-key. He stood in the doorway and coughed discreetly.

'We don't wish to hurry you, madam,' he said apologetically, 'but I'm afraid this suite is booked for new arrivals at 12.30. If you *could* allow the chambermaid – '

Jane looked up from the neo-Chippendale escritoire. 'I am writing a letter,' she said icily. 'When I have finished it I shall ring down to you and you will then call me a taxi. In the meantime, hut jao, bhagao – I'm sorry – I mean, you may go.'

The young man bowed and withdrew, and a wan sun came briefly from behind the clouds, and an errant ray shone through the double-glazing and struck an answering gleam from the belly of the little brass Lakshmi on the dressing table.